Kyana was too stunned to move.

She knew all the gods had fangs but they were never seen. Never used.

The slight tug of Ryker's lips caressed her neck as he took a single, long pull. It had been eons since anyone had tasted her blood. Not even the night of her Turning had the magnetic draw to surrender been this overwhelming.

She told herself she didn't like it.

She was lying.

Another, more forceful tug reminded her who was in control, and it wasn't Kyana.

Kyana tried to raise her dagger, but his hand tightened around her wrist, shaking it painfully until her grip loosened. Her dagger made a pathetic thud against the wooden planks of the ferry.

He leveled himself off her, straddled her waist, and stared into her eyes. The red glow of his glare drilled into her.

He licked her blood from the corner of his mouth. Feeding was against the rules. The Order would punish him for the assault against her. To hell with that. She would punish him herself. She gripped his arms, determined to push him aside, but his fingers bit into her shoulders, holding her hostage.

"I don't want to hurt you, Kyana." His voice dripped with warning. "But I will."

By Sable Grace

ASCENSION

ASCENSION

A DARK BREED NOVEL

SABLE GRACE

AVON

An Imprint of HarperCollinsPublishers

AVON BOOKS
An Imprint of HarperCollins*Publishers*
10 East 53rd Street
New York, New York 10022-5299

Copyright © 2011 by Heather Waters and Laura Barone
ISBN 978-0-06-196440-4
www.avonromance.com

First Avon Books mass market printing: May 2011

Avon Trademark Reg. U.S. Pat. Off. and in Other Countries, Marca Registrada, Hecho en U.S.A.
HarperCollins® is a registered trademark of HarperCollins Publishers.

Printed in the U.S.A.

10 9 8 7 6 5 4 3 2 1

To Kyle, for never once saying I couldn't,
and for believing when I can't.
And to Mom. If dreaming is healing,
I wish for you a million dreams.
—Heather

To Carmine, for always believing in me,
for being proud of me, and for giving me
the freedom to chase my dreams. But mostly,
thank you for showing me what a true hero is.
I love you.
—Laura

Acknowledgments

HEATHER: I would like to first and foremost thank the most supportive family in the world. Writing a book is much like running a marathon. Sometimes, there's no one there when you cross the finish line to throw confetti and set off fireworks, but without the support of loved ones, you'd never get to finish at all. Who else is going to be there at the side of the road, passing you water and encouraging you when you think you're out of steam? So while my family passed me those refreshments and waved their pompoms while I staggered by, writing with a partner this time means I had someone at the finish line to finally feel what I feel, and Laura, bravo. I'm proud of you.

LAURA: First, a special thank you to my family for cooking their own dinners, and doing all the laundry, and for entertaining the four-under-four, and most of all for telling everyone you know that mom just sold a book, and yes, you're going to get a copy for your birthday. Your support means the world to me and I can't tell you with words how truly special each and every sacrifice you've made—even those with complaints—is to me. To the Plot Queens for helping me learn the craft of writing and giving me the skills I needed to see this dream come true. And to the SG Cheerleaders—Tag-team sisters Cheryl and Deb (don't worry,

Deb, you're still Captain of the squad as promised!), Jess, and Krysta, thank you for picking up your pom-poms and glowing words of praise for each and every milestone we cross.

Sable Grace would like to take this opportunity to apologize for destroying the world, most especially the beautiful city of St. Augustine. Rest assured, you will be rebuilt! It takes a lot of people and a lot of work to rebuild from devastation, and so we'd like to thank the men and women who rise to the challenge every day to rebuild what nature and mankind have destroyed—those who get their hands dirty and spend their days saving lives and hunting the true monsters of this world. Military and civilian, you have our whole-hearted thanks and love.

We would like to thank our amazing agent, Roberta Brown, for believing in a new idea that could have been an enormous pain in her ass. We'd also like to thank the amazing team at Avon Books, most especially Erika Tsang, our fantastic editor, who wasn't afraid to make us work and believed we could . . . over and over! Amanda Bergeron, thank you for the final thoughts, and the art department and sales team that made us so excited for our debut, we've been impossible to be around. We'd also like to thank Detective C.C. Aiple of the St. Augustine Police Department for agreeing to answer any questions we might have while writing this series and for doing the job you do. One last special thanks goes to Hunter Waters for naming Kyana. We hope one day, when you're old enough to read this stuff, that she does you proud.

Chapter One

D espite the chaos of war around her, she couldn't help but hum Queen's "We Are the Champions" in her head. Of course, *we* had become *I* as she'd twisted it to fit her mood for the night. She had an irresistible urge to flex her muscles, or strut, or . . . something equally tacky.

It had been a long night, but a successful one. Most of the Chosen were safely tucked Below. The one her minions, Farrel and Crag, now carried was the last of the living on her list. The rest would be found . . . and buried . . . at daybreak. But what had her feeling as smug as a pig in dog shit was not the number she'd managed to find and save, but the *who*.

Jordan Faye. One of the most crucial finds on the Ancients' list of Chosen.

Kyana slipped her daggers back into the sheaths at her back and boot and reached for the flare gun tucked in its holster on her hip. Behind her, Farrel and Crag grunted and whined about the burden they carried. Every Vamp within the Order of Ancients had minions to assist with the grunt work. Sadly, Farrel and Crag were hers. One look would shut them up, but she was in too much of a hurry to bother.

When they neared what had been the Castillo de San Marcos's pay station only a week ago, she fired the flare gun and waited for the fiery burst to explode overhead and dissolve into a flurry of white dust that would alert the sentinels manning the gate. Like tiny puffs of smoke, the name Kyana slowly formed in the night sky, and the newly working drawbridge lowered in recognition.

The Castillo was the oldest piece of stonework in North America. That it had held up against so many attacks over the years had made it the best choice for the Order to set up headquarters in the southeastern United States the moment the war between Hell and Earth had begun seven days ago. Sentinels walked the bastions, ready to fight to the death at any sign of trouble, and in the old storerooms beneath the sentinels' patrol, Mystics had opened a portal to Below where the Chosen were taken for safety.

The night Tartarus opened and unleashed masses of Dark Breeds onto Earth, the residents of St. Augustine and neighboring cities had flocked to the old fort. Most of the Order argued to save as many as possible, but Kyana saw the folly in such emotionally driven suicide. Sure, she didn't want the world wiped clean of innocents any more than the gods of Olympus did, but there was no way they could all be saved. Wiser to focus on the Chosen first, make sure *they* had a safe place to lay their heads. Then the Order could see to the everyday, average Joes and Janes.

Behind Kyana, wails and shrieks, both human and non, had become the city's soundtrack. There were Dark Breeds nearby. She could smell the scent of urine emitting off the demons, feel the blighted Vamps, and taste the sulfuric, restless souls that had been uprooted from their earthly graves to become what humans called Zombies and the Order referred to as Leeches. Kyana's body itched to return to the streets and hunt, but she couldn't. Not until she'd safely placed her catch inside the fort.

"Take her in," she said, waiting impatiently for Farrel and Crag to adjust the weight of the woman they carried and shuffle up the walk toward the gate. Her gaze didn't waver from the unconscious body they toted. Other tracers had declared Jordan's trail cold days ago, but Kyana had been too stubborn to admit defeat. There was a reason she was the best at her job. She had something other tracers lacked—the ability to hold on to a scent for days without it losing its potency. Jordan hadn't been home in days, her trail *had* grown cold . . . for the others. But Kyana didn't rely on tracking perfumes and other unstable, common odors. She clung to a particular pheromone and could follow it to Hell and back, no problem. One tiny trace of leftover fear in Jordan's bed had led Kyana all around St. Augustine, and finally to the damned garbage bin behind St. George Street that had smelled so foul it had *nearly* tripped Kyana up.

Though there was no tangible reward for doing their duty, competition among the tracers to find those at the top of the lists was high. Only one other tracer had ever come close to besting Kyana. But not tonight. She couldn't wait to see Geoffrey's face when he learned she'd been the one to find and rescue Jordan Faye.

As though summoned by her smug anticipation, Geoff stepped into Kyana's path at the gate and cast a glance at the body in Farrel's and Crag's arms. "Another wee Mystic, I'm guessing?"

The spotlights bordering the walls of the fort cast him in an eerie glow. His small fangs glinted like freshly sharpened daggers and his dark blue eyes danced in the moonlight. At well over six feet, and broad enough to strain the threads of his black T-shirt, Geoffrey oozed danger. Her hormones kicked into overdrive. He reminded her of those exotic dancers at an all-male revue she'd stumbled across once while on the hunt—hot and ready to deliver on a girl's fantasies. As usual, Kyana was torn between strangling him and shoving him against the wall to see if he was just as thrilling naked as he was clothed. But sadly, Vamp-on-Vamp action was forbidden by the Order.

Geoff might be off-limits for her sexually, but taunting him was its own form of entertainment.

"Actually, it's Jordan Faye," she said, keeping her gaze on him to watch his reaction.

His pale face strained with shock.

Kyana smiled, offered him a sarcastic salute, and followed her quarry down the stone steps and into a hollow room. Jordan's new quarters looked more like an ancient jail cell sans the bars, but the cauldron of glowing blue ointment glittering in the corner smelled bad enough to make any prison piss pot proud. Farrel and Crag clumsily placed Jordan's limp body atop a dusty blanket spread out on the floor. She was a pretty thing, with an elegant, long pale neck that brought a hollow ache to Kyana's belly. Eighty years since she'd fed on fresh blood, yet the desire was no less than it had ever been.

When Farrel and Crag left the room, Kyana addressed the Mystic kneeling at Jordan's side. "Looks like she's been shot. Tend that wound first."

Too many of the Chosen they'd found had been shot by the very police they'd hoped would save them. Cops had been ordered to kill on sight, not taking the time to make certain those they targeted weren't human.

Kyana forced her gaze away from Jordan's throat and settled it upon something far more interesting. At first, Kyana thought it merely a shadow falling on the white breasts hidden beneath Jordan's lacy black bra, but as she stepped in for a closer look, her night's victory took on a whole new level of triumph.

"I'll be damned." She knelt and pushed down the bra to get a better look. Because Jordan had been at the top of Kyana's list, Kyana had known the human was important. But now that she'd seen this specific mark, Kyana suspected Jordan was far more valuable than any of the other Chosen she'd brought back this week.

"Please don't disrespect my patient." With a slight shove of her hip, the Mystic scooted Kyana away from Jordan.

Kyana growled. Rather than cower, the Mystic glowered right back. Slightly impressed by the lack of fear, Kyana readjusted Jordan's bra and stood. "Someone stays with her at all times, understood? I'll be back shortly."

In long, determined strides, she made her way around the plaza courtyard to a larger room where war memorabilia from colonial times were stored for peppy little tourists to examine. Two sentinels stood on either side of yet another hole cut into the coquina walls, but rather than lead to another cell, this one was hollow. Should someone try to enter without permission, he would spend eternity spiraling through a black void.

"Let me through," Kyana said, staring up at the towering men. They stubbornly blocked her passage.

"Hands, please," the sentinel on the right said, holding out his own hairy fingers in her direction.

She grumbled and placed her right hand in his, offering her left to his partner. "I'm in the bloody fort. How could I be in the bloody fort if I'm not already cleared?"

"It's the law, Dark Breed."

She gritted her teeth. Yes, technically, she was a Dark Breed. But her decades of loyalty to the Order should have earned her the respect not to be addressed so degradingly.

Kyana snatched her hands away from the sentinels and sneered. "Are you done? You smell like cow shit."

The sentinel's cheeks grew as pink as his bald head. "It's a poultice for my stomach pains."

"Whatever. Am I clear or not?"

The one on the left stepped aside. "Go. I hope you linger on the other side, Dark Breed. The lot of you should never have been brought into our circle."

She jerked her head toward him and flicked her

tongue over her fangs. She leaned toward him, flaring her nostrils as she breathed in the scent of him. "*You* don't smell like cow shit. *You* smell like dinner."

He stumbled backward and clasped his hands over his thick neck. "It's forbidden by our laws!"

Kyana smiled and straightened. "Lucky for you I'm not in the mood to break the laws. Who knows how I'll feel when I return, hmm?"

She fanned her fingers in a silent farewell and stepped through the portal.

Below wasn't technically below anything. More like sideways or parallel to the other two realms—Above, where the humans resided, and Beyond, a.k.a. Olympus. But Below was where nonhuman creatures did their daily business. Though some, like Kyana, preferred to live Above, smack in the middle of the action, most lived here. This was where magical herbs were tended, where lesser gods and demigods resided, where the Order's Vamps hid from daylight. It served as a mirror to the Earth, so to speak, where the sun burned hot and bright, but was merely an illusion, just as were the sea, the moon, and the stars. In other words, Vamps could sunbathe Below without becoming a spectacular fireworks event.

The portals leading from Above to Below had become revolving doors for Order members since the breakout, but right now, in the predawn hours, the alcove and streets around it were blessedly quiet. Moonlight bounced off the white marble buildings, disorienting Kyana. She squinted and made her way past the small marketplace that, come morning, would be busy with the hustling herbalists peddling their wares to Mystics and Witches.

A little farther down the narrow street, a butcher shop was ablaze with lights, busy in its late-night workday for Vamps who came in for sustenance before sleeping the day away in their chosen shelters. As Kyana passed the building, she closed her eyes and breathed in the sweet aroma of fresh blood. Not nearly as rich and decadent as human blood, but still quite addictive.

She turned away from the intoxicating scent and pressed on.

Along the cobbled streets, tiny alcoves carved out of alabaster led to different locations within the human world Above, as well as a very potent, magically guarded portal alcove to Olympus where gods could come and go to do their duties. But the one Kyana sought, however, led directly to the River Styx.

She headed to the end of the street, enjoying the stillness of the city. Soon, other night dwellers would be wandering the curving roads, loud and bawdy as they boasted of their latest feats and accomplishments, but for now, the quiet was the first bit of peacefulness Kyana had experienced in a week. She entered the cave nestled between large marble boulders, her keen eyes having no trouble finding the path in the dark. Down. Down. Down. The carved steps spiraled like a snail's shell, and soon she was able to hear the faint whisper of water lapping at sand.

The darkness shifted, giving way to a faintly glowing gold light a short distance away. As her foot made contact with the soft sand, she breathed in the scent of death that always came with entering the River Styx, and made her way to Charon, the ferryman. Flipping two coins at the haggard old spirit, Kyana stepped onto the long, flat boat and braced her feet for balance.

She loathed the River Styx. She hated the smell of death and the low wails coming from Tartarus below that chilled even her icy Vampyric blood, reminding her of her fate should true death ever find her. While some of the spirits waiting for eternal placement roamed visibly along the banks of the river, some remained unseen, and those she hated most of all. It was as though they passed through her, each of them pleading quiet demands to her soul as she tapped her foot impatiently at the torturously slow ferry.

"Can't you make this thing go faster?"

Charon didn't acknowledge her request. He stood at the helm of his little ferry, not needing to do anything more than stare in the direction of their destination to make his vessel obey.

If threatening, intimidating, or shoving him off his damned ferry would get her there faster, she would have done it. But Charon didn't scare easily. In fact, she wasn't sure he felt anything . . . ever. He was just a cold, transparent, expressionless being that almost . . . *almost* . . . evoked her pity.

Having no other choice but to bear the slow journey, she focused on the distant cave and turned her thoughts toward Jordan Faye and the strange mark on her breast. There were thousands of Chosen, but only three were branded with that mark. Two others were still out there. Perhaps safely Below. Perhaps discarded like all the other meaningless humans littering the mortal roads. Only time would tell.

When the boat docked, she snarled at the ferryman before stepping onto the rocky beach. Dark water
licked her boots, but no tide touched the path leading to
the stone chamber in front of her.

Kyana heard the faint sobbing before she made out
the shadowed silhouettes of the three women huddled
at the end of the cave. Their forms hunched over a
smoking cauldron, the scent of which stirred within
her a fresh hunger. She'd never learned what, exactly,
the contents of that cauldron were. The scent seemed to
change depending on the person smelling it, becoming
intoxicating, reminding them of something they desperately wanted but usually couldn't name.

For Kyana, the longing made her woozy and slightly
sad. For what, she didn't know. Desperately trying to
place the desire kept her occupied as she made her way
down the passage, but she couldn't remember a time,
living or undead, when she'd been as melancholy as the
nostalgic sensation that aroma evoked in her now.

As she approached the women, they stepped away
from the cauldron and lifted their hoods in greeting.
The middle woman wiped a tear from her cheek, her
shaky smile not quite genuine.

"Kyana," she whispered. "You've come unannounced."

Much lovelier than Shakespeare's interpretation of
them as the Wyrd Sisters, the Moerae, also known as
the three Fates, peered at Kyana with youthful eyes.
Their entire beings glimmered with golden dust,
though that dust was nowhere near as bright as it had
once been.

Kyana nodded in greeting. The beacon she refused
to wear burned in her pocket. She was being sum-

moned by an Ancient. More than likely, Artemis. But the Goddess of the Hunt would have to wait. Kyana wanted answers before she went anywhere. "I'll only need a minute."

Clotho adjusted her long golden braid over her shoulder and fixed Kyana with a cold stare. Vamps were still considered outsiders, even those who'd proven their allegiance over and over as Kyana had. She prided herself on her ability to stare others down, to intimidate them with the quickest of glances, but Clotho's penetrating blue eyes forced Kyana to avert her gaze.

"Speak quickly, Kyana," Clotho said. "It takes us far longer to tend our souls these days."

"I would think your tending wouldn't be so tiresome, given the lack of human life Above. So many are dead."

Tears welled in the Fate's eyes. "We don't need a Vampyre to remind us of our failures. We are faced with them every day."

At least she hadn't called Kyana Dark Breed.

Uncomfortable with the tears, Kyana blurted out, "I found Jordan Faye."

"We know." Atropos, the eldest of the three sisters and by far the most menacing, tossed something green into the cauldron and gave it a quick stir.

For a blessed moment, that taunting, mysterious scent vanished and all Kyana could smell were the rotting waters of the River Styx.

"Of course you do." If Jordan had died, Atropos would have known before anyone else. She was, after all, in charge of death, and guided those newly deceased to the river where they'd await their eternal fate.

"I want to know about the mark on her breast. Is she what I think she is?"

Scowling, Atropos raised a black brow. "You demand answers from *us*?"

"Not demanding. Asking." Kyana softened her tone. "Is she one of you?"

The sisters looked to one another. The middle sister, Lachesis, began weeping again. Atropos and Clotho wrapped their arms around the beautiful redhead in quiet comfort. Again, the scent rose from the cauldron and twisted Kyana's belly. What the hell *was* it?

"You think we enjoy knowing we are to be replaced?" Atropos hissed. "That we are to hand over the duties we've been charged with for ten thousand years?"

The very walls shook with their combined anger. Kyana held her ground and remained silent. No one wanted to be replaced, but the Fates couldn't deny that their time had come. For more than two centuries now, Oracles had been professing that the power of the gods would soon wane. Since then, the Fates had been marking Chosen, making certain strong bodies were born on Earth, capable of absorbing the enormous powers of the gods when the time came to transfer them into newer souls.

That demons and other Dark Breeds now walked the earth was proof that the power of the Fates *and* the gods no longer held the strength it once had. Their era of reigning was over, and hope rested on the shoulders of their replacements.

Time stood still as the Sisters whispered comforts to each other. Kyana strained to hear the hushed conversation but her head was full of the powerful scent, the unknown ache, the wanting. The heat of the beacon seared her thigh, pulling her mind back from the hypnotic effects of the cauldron's aroma. Artemis's impatience over Kyana not arriving at the god's temple Below was burning a hole in her leather.

"Are answers the only thing you came for, Kyana?"

She flinched. Her skin itched. She needed to get out of here. Needed to clear her head. "Yes. No. I want to protect her if my suspicions are right."

The Fates studied her, then one another, as though sharing a conversation she could not hear.

Lachesis, the weaver of destiny and the keeper of truths, dried her eyes with a lock of her fiery hair and addressed her sisters. "She is honest. Though I suspect her offer is not completely unselfish, she means no harm."

To Kyana, she said, "You are correct. Jordan Faye is one of us. When the time is right, she will take my place. With her and the others like her, the Order will have a chance of winning the war you fight Above. But not until the time is right."

Kyana shook her head. "And when will that be? The Order is outnumbered. We're getting—"

Clotho fingered her golden braid. "She must learn her way. Learn of who she is. Of *what* she is."

"Who will teach her?"

"That is not your concern."

"Then what *is* my concern? To follow orders? To fight battles we can't win? To save those you deem important, then sit on my hands and do nothing?"

Atropos's black gaze silenced her. "You will do your

duty, Dark Breed." A twisted smile contorted her face. "No, not Dark Breed. You're even more vile, are you not, Kyana? You're a foul Half-Breed who forgets her place."

"Enough!" Clotho pressed a hand to her sister's chest, lightly pushing Atropos backward, out of Kyana's reach.

"It's all right, Clotho. I know your sister disdains my kind." Kyana narrowed her gaze on Atropos. "*Both* of my kinds. Yes, Half-Breed suits me well, but it is both breeds within me that make me Artemis's best tracer. Without my Lychen half, I would be forced to wait until dusk to hunt like all your other Vamps. I go where they can't, *when* they can't, faster than they can. So we play nice with each other, don't we, Atropos? Whether we like one another or not, because we're *both* vital to saving your beloved humans."

Atropos swung her gaze away, but her pinched face was proof that Kyana had struck a nerve. Even more than Atropos hated Vamps, she loathed Lychen. She thought the werewolves lacked the ability to control their animalistic instincts, and if there was one thing Atropos couldn't stand it was the lack of self-control. And since Kyana was both, the two of them would never get along. Kyana was the last Half-Breed of her particular kind, and the Order couldn't afford to lose her. That gave Atropos even more reason to hate Kyana. Aside from breaking a major Order commandment, there was nothing Kyana could do that would allow Atropos to get rid of her.

Checkmate.

Looking to the more reasonable, less bigoted sisters, Kyana pulled the conversation back to the task at hand. "What will become of Jordan Faye?"

Clotho sighed, weariness etched in the pocketed shadows of her eyes. "She and the others on our lists will be protected at all costs."

"They should have been brought in when they were born," Kyana grumbled. "We could have kept them safe until the time of the exchange."

Atropos narrowed her dark gaze, the shadows of the cave making her look momentarily haggard and worn. "If they have not lived amongst humans and learned the importance of humanity, then they would never become fair and just to those who worship them. Humanity. Humility. They are foreign concepts to you, Kyana. I do not expect you to understand, but I do expect that you do not question our ways."

Thinking very little about either concept, Kyana rolled her eyes. "I want Jordan Faye's guardianship."

"We have another task for you," Lachesis said, digging noisily through a golden chest behind her as Kyana turned a murderous stare to the other sisters.

"No way. I found the one that everyone else had given up on. It's my right to be her guardian."

"Because you think such a post will give you power?"

"No. Because she is my responsibility."

"Liar," Atropos hissed. "You're as power hungry now as you were when you first came to the Order."

Lachesis turned back to the group. In her hands, she held a golden chain with a flat, square hunk of obsidian the size of Kyana's hand dangling from the end of it. Lachesis turned the block of glossy ebony so that Kyana could see a roughly cut pentagram-shaped hole in the center.

"Sisters, I think the choice belongs to our tracer." Lachesis held out the stone pendant, her lips curving into a sly smile. "You found our Chosen, and you may guard her if you wish."

Satisfied, Kyana started to nod in acceptance, but the gleam in Lachesis's eyes stopped her. "What's the catch?"

Lachesis looked to her sisters before turning back to Kyana. "You may play guardian to Jordan Faye or you may take up a more important job."

Her curiosity piqued, Kyana reached out and touched the sharp edges of the cut stone. "What job?"

Lachesis slipped the chain around Kyana's neck. The thing weighed as much as a small hippo.

"A simple task, Kyana." A smile lit Lachesis's tearstained cheeks. "We want you to save the world."

Chapter Two

The enormous chunk of obsidian dangling from Kyana's neck felt like a glacier. Frozen solid. Its icy burn wove through the thin threads of her tank top and bit into her rib cage. The overpowering odor of sulfur nearly choked her.

"As you can see, the stone isn't whole." Lachesis stepped away from her sisters and circled the altar between the Fates and Kyana.

Kyana ripped the chain from her neck and thrust it back into Lachesis's hands.

"It is painful, I know," Lachesis said, reaching out a long, nimble finger to touch the grooves in the stone as a mother might caress her child's face. "I was hoping it wouldn't be so noticeably cold to one like you."

Cold-blooded, she'd meant. Of course, it wouldn't occur to anyone without Vampyric blood that what was cold to someone with hot blood running through her body would be torturously worse for one without the body heat to at least make it bearable.

"What the hell is that thing?" More importantly, what did it have to do with saving the world?

"I told you she wasn't strong enough to carry it," Atropos said.

Kyana glared at the dark-haired Fate and snatched the stone back from Lachesis. "The hell I'm not. But if you slip an ice cube down someone's shirt, they're going to flinch. A little warning would have been nice."

"Or is it nothing more than an excuse because you find yourself lacking?" Atropos continued.

Lachesis turned away from Kyana and pointed at Atropos. "It was you who suggested Kyana for this task. You called her the most skilled of Artemis's puppies, or have you forgotten?"

Atropos looked positively horrified by the accusation, and Kyana was certain her face had gone even paler in shock. A compliment from Atropos? The world was *definitely* coming to an end.

"It's all right," Kyana said, juggling the cold brick from hand to hand to protect her fingers from frostbite. "I'll pretend I didn't hear that so you can hang on to your pride."

Atropos sat ladylike on the bench behind the cauldron of mysterious brew, the eerie green glow of the contents making her look more alien than immortal. "Regardless of my feelings toward your race—or races, rather—you *are* capable of tracking things others cannot. Jordan Faye is proof of that. We don't believe saving the world is enough in itself to lure you into doing the job, but rather, the glory and power of it that appeals to you. Are we wrong?"

Kyana opened her mouth to deny the unflattering accusation, but instead sighed and nodded. No point in lying to the Fates, most especially to Clotho, who chose the souls for each body, and Lachesis, who guided those souls until the time came for Atropos to cut their life threads. They could smell lies faster than Vampyre could sense the approaching dawn.

"Does it matter why I'm interested?" she asked instead. Her fingers were cramping now, and it was all Kyana could do not to toss the stone to the ground.

"It doesn't," Atropos said. "You know of Cronos, I hope?"

"A bit of the lore, yes. He was father to Zeus, Hades, and Poseidon, along with a few others. Cast out for trying to kill his sons because Oracles told him they'd grow up and overthrow his reign as supreme god."

"I'm impressed." Atropos's dark brows rose to meet her widow's peak before falling back to give her a very teacherly expression. Sensing this was going to be too long a conversation to continue pretending the painful cold didn't bother her, Kyana discreetly slid the rock onto the altar.

"Long before we gave numbers to years, Cronos was rendered powerless and exiled to a penal isle located between realms. Our actions that day divided up Olympus amongst Cronos's children. But he took something with him that we were all unaware existed until Tartarus broke out seven nights ago."

"Which was?"

Atropos's gaze fell to the obsidian on the altar. "The key to that lock you can't bear to touch. We'd heard rumors, but with no one in contact with Cronos, it was impossible to verify. Besides, if the key was in exile with him when he died, why worry—"

"Stop." Kyana held up her hand. "Key to *what* exactly?"

"Tartarus, of course. That stone is the very lock that holds the Dark Breeds in Tartarus."

Kyana tried to keep her jaw from hitting the floor, but failed miserably. "There's a *key* to *Hell*?"

"Apparently, yes. But Cronos died with it, secluded and alone. And given that no one suspected until recently that the legend might be real, no one was worried."

"But Dark Breeds broke out, so someone had to have unlocked the gates," Clotho added.

Understanding hit Kyana like a wrecking ball. "Which means all the demons we've been killing this week get sent back to Tartarus only to crawl back out again until the key is found and the gate's locked."

"An endless, *pointless* cycle. One we must correct if we ever hope to give Earth back to the humans."

How many tracers had died to capture these Dark Breeds? How many more would lose their lives? All because the gods hadn't believed in the key?

Kyana's pocket pulsed continuously as the beacon inside came alive with more urgency this time. The pain nearly made her ask the Fates if they could continue this conversation after she talked with Artemis. However, the need to know all the details caused her to push aside the burn.

"No one believes in you anymore, and the lot of you hate that you've been reduced to characters in children's stories. Yet you had a 'myth' all these millennia about a key to Hell and you couldn't believe in it long enough to send someone out just in case it was true?"

"Of course we did," Atropos snapped. "Just a few decades after Cronos's exile. No one found anything more than a weak, pathetic Cronos."

"Someone is obviously better at playing lost-and-found than your guys. Hell is open, which means someone went out there and did what you failed to do. They found the key." Kyana touched the obsidian, even more hesitant now to hold it, knowing the darkness within it. "If Cronos had the key all this time, wouldn't the gate have been opened when he took it?"

"No. It was locked, much like you can lock a house and stick the key in your purse. It remains locked until the key is placed back inside and turned to *un*lock it. Someone's found the key and left our house unlocked, Kyana. And until we get it back, it's going to be Hell on Earth. Literally."

"And you want me to find the key."

"And whoever managed to find it in the first place."

Excitement warmed Kyana's blood for a blessed moment. A real challenge. A *real* hunt. If she was the type to do so, she might have burst into song. "No problemo." But before the ants in her pants could party, she froze. "Wait. I thought only Hades and Hermes could get into the Underworld. No one else has the means to get down there."

"Precisely why we're so baffled," Clotho said. "*We* can't even descend to Tartarus or the Underworld encasing it. When we wish an audience with Hades, we send a missive through Hermes."

"And no one's questioned Hermes? Gods *have* been known to go bad."

Atropos's face resumed its normal pinched expression. "He is the one who delivered that lock to us upon Hades's request. Lachesis read him. He is still pure."

"Do you think you can find whoever's responsible and retrieve that key, Kyana?" Clotho asked, her voice as muted as her colorless face.

"If she can't, I can."

Kyana turned to find herself staring into a face she'd hoped never to see again.

"Ryker," she breathed.

Just the sight of him made her stomach flip and her heart stutter even though there was nothing about him that should have appealed to her.

Her cheeks burned just as they had the last time she'd seen him. Embarrassment, humiliation. Both flung her off the high horse of her glorious meeting with the Fates and slammed her ass right back into reality.

Artemis appeared behind him and glided into the cave, followed by her three enormous mutts. Kyana could barely spare the goddess a glance, her attention locked on the man who'd rejected her so blatantly ten years ago.

"Hello, Kyana."

A spontaneous eruption of butterflies took flight in her stomach at the mere whisper of her name from his lips. Lips she'd once craved more than blood. Zeus, she hated her body's betrayal. This guy had pheromones that made avoiding naughty thoughts impossible.

Ryker looked more like a surfer than a member of the Order. Wavy blond hair, short in the back, messy and long on top. His bronze skin declared he spent as much time beneath the sun as Vamps did beneath the moon. She sneered at his loose jeans, faded and tattered yet strangely flattering. He wore sandals and a partially buttoned white shirt, revealing a broad, smooth chest and a white conch shell necklace. The fact that underneath the surfer boy façade lay a deadly warrior was what drew her. Dressing so casually caused others to underestimate what Kyana knew Ryker was capable of. It gave him an immediate advantage against whatever Dark Breed he'd been sent to retrieve.

"What are you doing here?"

Before Ryker could answer, Artemis stepped between them. "You didn't answer my call, Kyana," she said, dropping her leashes to the ground and moving to stand behind the cauldron with the Fates.

"I was getting to it." Kyana tried to keep the bite out of her voice, but with Ryker so close, she was having trouble holding her temper.

Atropos's sharp cry pulled all attention to her. The Fate stood, her golden glow accentuating the paleness as all color drained from her face. No one spoke as she lowered the stinking cauldron to the ground below the altar and replaced it with one filled with golden liquid. Several threads lay draped over the lip of the large pot. "Forgive me," she said, gently cradling them in her palm. "These . . . must be tended."

Kyana inched away from Ryker and struggled to keep her gaze straight ahead. Artemis loomed behind the sisters, watching with fascination as Atropos placed two of the threads inside the mouth of a deadly pair of golden scissors and snipped.

"Olivia Stanton. Nadine Kline."

It took Kyana a moment to realize that her summoning and the discussion with the Fates had been cut short by unexpected deaths that Atropos needed to tend immediately. Kyana was watching death unfold right before her eyes, a ceremony she was pretty certain very few others had ever witnessed.

"Beautiful, isn't it?"

Ryker's breath brushed her cheek. She jerked her head around, horrified by the tightness of her stomach, the weakness in her legs, that his nearness conjured. "Beautiful? You're sick. It's death."

"Death isn't ugly if there's someone to tend your soul. Someone who cares about the life you led. Someone who cares about your crossing." Ryker pointed to the Fates. "They've never met these humans, yet their lives are honored and cherished. They will be mourned."

"And you think that makes it all right that so many have died? Just because Atropos is sorrowful doesn't erase that they died in vain."

Ryker frowned. "In vain? Every death, human or non, is avenged. This is war. People will die, but it is never in vain."

Kyana wanted to laugh at his delusional statement. Was he so protected, so safe here Below, that he had no clue what was happening Above? She might have bought into his beautiful declaration if these people had lived full lives instead of being mowed down like needless trash.

"Is that something Daddy taught you?"

Ryker stiffened and stepped away from the alluring scent of Kyana's hair. His momentary pleasure over seeing her again died right along with the next thread Atropos snipped.

"Nice to see you haven't lost your ability to cut straight to someone's sore spot," he muttered.

"Mm, sorry." Kyana stared straight ahead, her profile like chiseled, soft stone in the dim light of the cave. "Must be terribly hard having Ares as a father. What with his being able to give you your every heart's desire and all."

Ryker clenched his teeth so hard his jaw ached. Artemis stabbed them both with a glare that forced him to hold his tongue, when all he'd wanted to do was throw Kyana's own heritage back in her face. She, of all people, should know that being born from a powerful, wealthy father didn't guarantee unconditional love. He was pretty sure if he brought up *her* dear daddy, blood would be spilled.

"Amanda Gray." Atropos cradled another dingy, yellow thread in her hand, glanced sorrowfully up at her sisters, and dropped it into the cauldron that now fumed with black smoke.

Ryker quieted his anger and focused on the miracle he was witnessing. This was a ceremony he'd rarely been allowed to watch, and the thought of those clipped souls finding their way to their eternal rest always filled him with awe. As Ares's son, he'd grown into the position of general in the God of War's army of sentinels. He brought death, delivered unto his enemies as easily as he breathed. Knowing that they'd be well taken care of once his job was done had made it easier to do. The good deserved eternal bliss. The bad . . . they deserved the eternal damnation awaiting them.

"Jonathan Tidwell." Another dirty thread slipped into the pot.

Clotho sniffed.

Lachesis wailed. "So sad. So, so sad."

Atropos cleared her throat and eased her old, yet beautiful body onto the stone bench behind her. "We've no time to mourn. We must find new replacements for Asclepius and Dione. Their power is all but faded now, and Asclepius would be a large boon to our war efforts."

"These were their Chosen?" Ryker asked, scratching his jaw. That wasn't good. Asclepius was a huge benefit, with her overseeing healing and medicine. Who would take charge over the Mystic and Witch Healers now? And Dione . . . shit. She was Aphrodite's mother and quite the diva. When she found out her Chosen had died . . . there was going to be hell to pay.

"Yes, as well as others'. All of them were Chosen."

"I was meant to train Nadine," Clotho said. "We must find a replacement for her before the others. We must have three strong Moerae again. It is priority!"

"You think you hold more priority than the gods?" Artemis's voice caused the cauldron to bubble over.

Atropos glared at Artemis over the cauldron, her black hair blending in with the black smoke. "If your replacement dies, who is going to create a new one? No one, save for us. There will be no more Goddess of the Hunt." She turned her loving gaze onto Clotho. "We cannot randomly grab someone and make them one of us," she said softly. "Their blood must be special. You know this better than any."

Lachesis looked to Clotho. "We know every soul ever born. We'll find two more capable of taking our places and stop our entire world from crumbling around our ears."

"You should worry about foreseeing more deaths, not about saving your own collective asses," Kyana said.

Ryker glared at her. Her lack of respect for the gods and Fates in general pissed him off. Even as much as he loathed Ares, Ryker showed him respect. He knew their worth, knew what the world would be without each and every god to oversee it.

"It's time the three of you accepted the facts," Kyana continued. "You are no longer all-knowing."

Ryker snapped his attention to Artemis. "Maybe we should take our meeting elsewhere and allow the Moerae peace while they see to their task."

Kyana stepped back and dug her heel into his sandaled foot. Ryker grunted but didn't step away, letting her have her fun while she still could. The minute she found out why Artemis had summoned her, her day was going to turn very, very bad.

Atropos leveled her black eyes on Kyana. Kyana kept her head high, her gaze on the Fate.

"She doesn't bother us," Atropos said. "She is easily forgotten."

If only. Ryker had been trying to forget Kyana for ten years and had failed miserably. She was like a permanent imprint in his mind, a ghostly loop that played over and over again, unwilling to go into the light.

As though silently saying that Atropos was just as easily dismissed, Kyana ignored her and spoke to the one goddess Ryker had ever heard her address in a respectful tone.

"Why did you call for me, Artemis?"

Artemis's gaze drifted between Ryker and Kyana. This was about to get very good for Ryker, and very upsetting for Kyana. He wished he had popcorn for the show.

"We need to talk about the key you've been sent after."

"The Fates told me what I was after. I'll find it."

Ryker almost chuckled at the certainty in her voice. Sure, Kyana was known for her ability to find people others had given up on, but the object she was being sent after possessed no pheromones. She'd never find it alone.

The goddess lifted a satchel from her shoulder and dug through it. She pulled out a wooden box and opened it, the old hinges creaking like a century-old coffin. Inside, on a bed of royal purple velvet, lay a golden pentagram she'd already shown Ryker.

"Does this look familiar?" Artemis asked Kyana, trailing a slender finger over the etched center of the gold.

Ryker watched to see Kyana's reaction. As he expected, disappointment darkened her brown eyes to almost black. Proof, as if he'd needed it, that his warning to Artemis was true—that Kyana was after glory, which made her very dangerous on this mission.

The only thing that kept Ryker from making the ultimatum that he'd work with a different tracer or Artemis could find someone else to do his job was the fact that it would rub Kyana raw knowing she had no choice but to work with him. He'd like to see her try to avoid him now.

"Is that the key?"

Artemis smiled. "It's the sister key." She carefully set the box on the altar. "This is the first time Zeus has allowed it to leave his possession, but given our dire need, I convinced him you would benefit from seeing it. Wise to know exactly what you're looking for before looking."

Kyana visibly perked up and stepped closer to the altar. "What does this one open?"

"Olympus. It's how we've kept it locked to outsiders all these years."

"If everyone knew there was a key to Beyond, why didn't anyone look for one Below?"

As Kyana bent to examine the key, Ryker tried not to allow his gaze to fall to the nicely shaped ass smoothed out with black leather, but his eyes were defiant. Kyana's pale arms hung at her side, and he knew if he reached out and touched them, they'd be like ice beneath his fingers. Once, he'd offered her his warmth, and she'd taken it eagerly. But it hadn't been enough for her. She'd taken his refusal to have sex with her personally, and the battle lines between them had been clearly drawn.

He wasn't stupid. He knew why the pull to her was so strong. She was half Lychen, and that half of her needed to mate for life. He'd gravitated to that need immediately, felt right away that *he* was meant to be that mate for her. But Kyana was also half Vampyre, and that half kept him at a distance. While Lychen mated for life, Vampyre were ridiculously polyamorous. He knew which half Kyana had embraced, but if he'd taken her as she'd wanted him to, he would never have found satisfaction again with another.

Shaking himself out of his stupor, he squeezed his eyes shut and exhaled. This was never going to work. Ares should find someone else to work the sentinel post alongside Kyana. If Ryker remained on the job, he'd be insane before it was over.

Kyana leaned against the far wall of the cave, trying to take in everything Artemis was saying, but so much of what was being told was pissing her off. How could these gods and goddesses, who hated being thought of as fictional myths, ever allow themselves to disbelieve *anything*? Especially when it might involve unleashing Hell on Earth? If they'd taken any of the legends about the key seriously, the world wouldn't be in such a chaotic state right now.

"We see now how foolish we were not to have assumed Cronos would have made a similar key for the Underworld," Artemis said. "Even Hades was never told. The lock wasn't found until after the key had been turned. Our only blessing is that Cronos didn't have time to snatch this one as well when he was exiled."

Which brought up a damned fine point. Unless Cronos had known his exile was coming, how had he known to grab the key in the first place? Kyana glanced at the Sisters, then back to Artemis, going out of her way to completely ignore Ryker looming beside her.

Artemis raised an eyebrow. "You have questions you're afraid to ask in front of them?"

This time she looked at Ryker before focusing on Artemis again. "Perhaps *we* should have this meeting in private."

"What is said between us will not leave this cave."

"All right, then. Are you sure Cronos took the key with him?"

"What are you suggesting?"

She didn't know which sister had asked the question, and didn't take her gaze off Artemis to find out.

Artemis raised her hand for silence. "Let her talk. At this point, it's safe to say we can't rule out anything."

"Or anyone," Kyana mumbled.

How the hell did she find a key no one knew existed, who took it, or who might have it now? She hunted *people*, or at least beings with scents. She was not a freaking metal detector. She paced the cave, allowing her mind to run through several possible scenarios. First option, Cronos took the key, he died, someone found it and used it. Didn't really make sense to her since no one knew of the bloody thing.

Second option, Cronos made a friend, told him about the key before he died, and the new friend used it. Didn't fit either. Even the need for revenge wasn't enough to make a lunatic think opening Tartarus was a good idea. Kyana rolled her neck, letting the bones crack and ease the tension. Third option made her skin itch.

"Where was Cronos sent? Was anyone ever seen with him? Inhabitants of the island maybe?"

Artemis shook her head. "Informants were sent to check on him at intervals until his death was reported. They never spoke of seeing anyone else."

"What are you thinking?" Ryker's voice flitted over Kyana's ear and made her head pound. Why the hell was he here anyway? She shot him a glare and rolled the possible scenarios over and over in her mind.

The itch beneath her skin intensified. Someone had warned Cronos of his pending exile, allowing him time to seize the key to Tartarus. That meant Cronos had loyal followers at the time. Followers who could have passed down the truth about that key to later generations.

But why open Tartarus? What did anyone hope to gain by unleashing a mass of Dark Breeds on the humans? The conversation between the Fates rang in Kyana's mind. The Chosen were being assassinated.

She looked to Clotho. "Three states in America were untouched by the demons that broke out," she continued. "Nebraska, New Mexico, and Rhode Island. Why?"

Clotho's wide eyes looked ready to pop from her head. "Because—"

"Because there were no Chosen on your list in those areas." Satisfied that her accusation was finally being taken seriously, Kyana smiled. "Someone is trying to stop us from replacing all of you. Opening Tartarus was just a distraction. People are dying, yes, but your Chosen are being picked off with precision that can't be coincidental. The breakout and the murders are tied together. I'm positive."

Ryker cleared his throat. "The only way that's possible is if the person who opened Hell also came here and saw the names of the Chosen."

Even though she was pleased someone seemed to understand her, she was slightly irritated that it had been Ryker.

"No one can get into this cave without our knowledge," Clotho said.

"No. No one *could* get into your cave. Since your powers have begun to wane, it's not entirely impossible anymore."

"They have to be wrong," Atropos insisted. "Artemis, tell them they're wrong."

Kyana would have called the old Fate a fool, but waited to see what Artemis would do. Much to Kyana's relief, Artemis nodded in agreement. "She's right. We must find out where the key is, and which of our trusted Order members took it."

Artemis looked from Kyana to Ryker and back again. "And you two are going to have to work together to find both."

Chapter Three

O h hell no. No no no no no. Kyana wouldn't work
with Ryker. He was arrogant, stuffy, and prone to
giving orders she wasn't prone to taking.

The already tiny cave suddenly felt smothering.
"Give me any details you have. I'll keep you posted on
my progress, but I'm not working with him."

"I chose you for this task, Kyana." Artemis narrowed
her authoritative gaze. "Don't make me regret it. This
is not merely a task for a tracer." Artemis picked up
her leashes. "Alone, you both fail. Together, the world
stands a chance at survival. You'll find the key, and
he'll apprehend our traitor."

So Artemis had already suspected a traitor. Why else
would she have already summoned the aid of a sentinel
general like Ryker? They were afraid that Kyana would
find the key and stash it inside the head of the person
responsible. Ryker, on the other hand, would remain as
collected as ever and bring him in for questioning.

Nice to know my reputation is intact.

"Find me just after sunset and I'll make certain you

have everything you need to get to the penal isle where Cronos was exiled," Artemis said as she prepared to leave. "I want you on your way as soon as possible, and I think you'll agree your search should begin there."

As she watched Artemis walk away, anger warmed Kyana's normally icy skin. She didn't know what pissed her off more—that Artie didn't trust her to do the job alone, or that she believed Ryker was the best choice for a partner.

"I can go alone! I won't go off half-cocked!" she shouted at Artemis's back. The goddess didn't even turn around, certain she'd be obeyed without question.

With more bite in her voice than she'd intended, Kyana snapped her gaze back to the Fates. "No more lists. Whatever replacements you choose, find another way to give the names to the tracers. We can't chance having more of their identities discovered before we can bring them in."

Clotho scowled. "We must create the lists. We mark the names for their positions. It is magic, Kyana. Without scribing their names on that parchment and marking them appropriately, there *are* no Chosen." She pointed at the familiar mark beside Jordan Faye's name on their current list. "That mark you saw on Jordan's breast is this mark. The moment I branded the parchment, her body became branded as well. Do you see?"

Yeah, she saw all right. She saw more opportunities for their traitor to get his or her hands on more names. Saw more blood spilled. More threads clipped. Even Artemis's tracers had never seen that list before. Each tracer was given four or five names for each night of hunting, and that was it. No one but the Fates knew the list in its entirety. Well, no one except the Fates and the traitor, that was.

"Then I suggest this time you don't let the damned list out of your sight for a second. Stick it up your ass if you have to, but our traitor only has the names on that first list. Unless you screw it up, the new Chosen should remain safe until we can find them."

Kyana marched to the exit, banging shoulders with Ryker in an effort to pass him. She shoved harder than necessary. "I'm not working with you."

"Hey, I'm not exactly jumping for joy right now. We don't have a choice."

As Kyana stomped down the tunnel that led back to the river, Ryker met her stride for stride. "Tell them no. At least, tell them to put someone else on the job."

Great. The ferry was gone. She'd have to wait for it to return from toting Artemis out of the cave system. More time with Ryker. Yippee.

"How 'bout *you* tell them to find a new tracer?"

"Because I'm the best."

"Ditto." Ryker grabbed her arm and spun her around to face him. "The faster we get this job done, the faster you can run and hide from me again. You should try to be a little more cooperative."

"And you should try cyanide." She glared daggers at him, wishing they were real and at this moment making him bleed. "I never hid from you. I hide from *no one*."

She'd left because her assignment in the Everglades had been complete. Leaving Ryker behind had only been a bonus. Sure, she hadn't gone out of her way to run into him since she'd thrown herself at him like a bitch in heat. But that wasn't the point.

"And," she said, the need to ooze out the venom inside her nearly crippling her, "for the record, you're *not* the best. You're just a product of nepotism. If your daddy wasn't the God of War, you wouldn't even be here—"

"Enough." He straightened, suddenly looking too tall and broad for her comfort. Kyana found herself fascinated with the swirling silver in his eyes and the way the gray gave way to blood red. Ryker hissed. "Don't underestimate me, Kyana."

"Back atcha, *Ryker.*"

Charon's ferry putt-putted over the black, glassy river, coming to a bouncy stop at the dock.

Without touching Kyana, Ryker managed to swoop around her and board the ferry. "Come or don't come, Kyana. But I have a job to do, and I'm not waiting for you to get your head out of your ass long enough to do it with me."

Zeus, she wanted to push him into the river and let the restless souls beneath the water have their way with him. However, if she kept lashing out at him, he'd know how much his presence bothered her. She'd be damned if she'd let him know how much baggage she still carried where he was concerned.

Kyana stepped on the ferry, but she wasn't about to let this go. "Go to Ares. When he realizes I'm the tracer assigned to work with you, he'll pull you off duty, no questions asked."

Ares hated her kind, or maybe her in particular. She

didn't know for sure and didn't care enough to ask. Normally, his contempt irritated her. Now, it might work in her favor.

"It was *Ares* who assigned me to this duty when he found out who the tracer would be. He doesn't trust you, remember? So I'm your babysitter, ready and willing to make sure you get what you're after and leave the bad guys to me so we can figure out who all is involved in this mess." Ryker raised his eyebrows. "Tell you what, you go to him and explain why you're unwilling to work with me and maybe he'll take pity on me and pull *you* from the job. While you're at it, tell him *why* you find the idea of working with me so repulsive. He'd get a kick out of that."

"You want me to go to Daddy and tell him that I was desperate for a fuck and you weren't game? It must be such a disappointment for Ares to know his son doesn't follow in his womanizing shoes."

His jaw clenched. His eyes flashed red. Bingo. She'd found the nerve she'd been prodding for. Kyana put her hand on her hip, not so much because she wanted to look sassy, but because it put her fingers that much closer to the dagger hilt protruding from the back of her pants. Zeus, she wanted to hurt him. Badly. If he gave her just one reason, she'd have him flat on the ground and her dagger at his throat.

"Just a fuck, huh? Didn't feel like that to me when you were begging me to—"

She wasn't quite sure how her dagger ended up in her fist or how her dagger-wielding fist ended up at Ryker's throat, but suddenly, she was pressed to him, nose to nose, her hand shaking with the need to slit his throat and dance in victory. But before she could so much as make another move, his eyes turned red again, and he had her pinned to the floor, his teeth buried in the tender flesh of her neck.

She was screwed.

Chapter Four

Kyana was too stunned to move. She knew all the gods had fangs but they were never seen. Never used. The slight tug of Ryker's lips caressed her neck as he took a single, long pull. It had been eons since anyone had tasted her blood. Not even the night of her Turning had the magnetic draw to surrender been this overwhelming.

She told herself she didn't like it.

She was lying.

Another, more forceful tug reminded her who was in control, and it wasn't Kyana.

Kyana tried to raise her dagger, but his hand tightened around her wrist, shaking it painfully until her grip loosened. Her dagger made a pathetic thud against the wooden planks of the ferry.

He leveled himself off her, straddled her waist, and stared into her eyes. The red glow of his glare drilled into her.

He licked her blood from the corner of his mouth. Feeding was against the rules. The Order would punish him for the assault against her. To hell with that. She would punish him herself. She gripped his arms, determined to push him aside, but his fingers bit into her shoulders, holding her hostage.

"I don't want to hurt you, Kyana." His voice dripped with warning. "But I will."

Kyana struggled to buck him off her. She growled, her fingers biting into his forearms.

Ryker didn't flinch . . . or move. The corner of his mouth curved into a grin, though the swirl of red in his eyes held no humor as he pushed to his feet. "You can't beat me, Kyana."

No one got the upper hand on her and walked away to brag about it.

Kyana stood. Her neck throbbed. Weakness and fatigue threatened to buckle her knees. The river swam before her eyes and she reached out to steady herself, but other than the solemn, unfazed-looking Charon, there was nothing there to offer balance.

She struggled to stay on her feet. Gently, she touched the marks on her throat. Her fingers came away bloody.

"Stop the flow." If he didn't close the wound, she would die.

Really die.

"You're not going to die."

His reading her thoughts had nothing to do with spells, but rather the temporary mingling of her blood with his. A shiver raced through her. When she'd been a feeding Vamp, she'd always taken a bit of her victims' memories with her after a meal. She knew things about them, felt what they'd felt. Was Ryker doing that with *her* blood now? The idea was too horrifying to contemplate, much less ask about.

Until she could regain her strength, he had the power and control. But she wouldn't give him the submission his now silver eyes said he wanted. Kyana watched him move slowly toward her.

"Truce?"

Not a chance. Rage poured through her veins, increasing the flow of blood down her neck. She didn't bow to anyone. Not even when she'd joined the Order had she submitted. She stood her ground. "The gods don't use their fangs. What the hell's wrong with you?"

With a growl, he grabbed her head and forced it to the side. The bones in her neck crackled in protest. His lips covered the punctures and when his tongue caressed the bite marks, sealing the wounds, Kyana barely managed not to moan in pleasure.

"I'm a demigod not a god." Ryker released her but didn't move away. "I do whatever needs to be done."

Her hand moved to her neck. Instead of blood, her fingers brushed the tiny, throbbing scabs of his attack.

"Cover them completely," Kyana demanded.

Ryker shook his head. His eyes swirled. "It will do you good to have my mark on you—a reminder, so to speak since we'll be working together so . . . intimately."

He'd left his mark on her ten years ago. He just couldn't see it.

Injured pride had Kyana reaching for where her dagger should've been. It still lay at her feet. She picked it up. Fisted it in her hand. Weighed the rush of her anger against her weakened state, then sheathed her weapon. She needed to gather her wits now, feed, and figure out the first step in finding the key to Hell. Kicking Ryker's ass would have to come later.

The ferry squeezed through the exiting tunnel that would eventually take them back to shore. Kyana might not have had the strength to take him down right then, but what little strength she'd held on to wouldn't be wasted.

She held out her hand. "Truce."

Self-satisfied smugness washed over Ryker's face as he slid his hand into hers. "Good girl."

Kyana let herself enjoy the warmth of his fingers for a split second, then jerked him toward her, lifted her leg, and shoved her boot right in his belly. Ryker went overboard with an ear-splitting curse and Kyana waved at the rippling water as the ferry took its time making its escape. The tunnel was too narrow for Ryker to climb back on board. He'd be swimming his way out of here.

Served him right.

As his blond head surfaced and bobbed on the water, he treaded in place, sputtering the foul-smelling water as he tried to talk. "What the hell . . . did you do that for?"

He was a strong swimmer. He nearly made it to the back end of the ferry before it turned the next corner. Ghostly hands were pawing at him, however, hindering his progress.

"I do what needs to be done too, Ryker. And you were in desperate need of cooling off your overblown ego. Enjoy your swim while I have my dinner."

As she watched his bobbing body become smaller

and smaller as distance separated them, her feeling of victory was washed away by the rage and self-loathing warring inside her.

She hated Ryker, but at the moment, she hated herself more. Ryker had always been stoic, quiet, and stuck-up, and yet she'd been drawn to him anyway. Now, she saw him in a new light, and that attraction had become full-blown desire. His one show of violence aimed at her would have saturated her panties if she'd been wearing any. The fact that she was so hot and bothered by the strength and power he'd exuded disgusted her. She needed to cool off as badly as he had, if only to remind herself that she found Ryker obnoxious—not so damned sexy it made her breasts tingle.

Chapter Five

Kyana stood outside the butcher shop watching other Vampyre exit with their daily fortification. As the scent of blood filled her nostrils, her mouth watered. Her body craved fresh blood. But tonight, she needed something stronger. *A lot* stronger, since she knew Ryker would catch up at any moment and very likely want to start round two.

Turning away from the tantalizing aroma, Kyana made her way down the winding, cobblestone streets to the *kafenion* where the bartender, Marcus, would have a bottle of raki handy. Unlike eating solid food, which was indigestible, she *could* drink. Human liquor like Crete's raki was more than palatable. It was a pity she could no longer get drunk. Especially after a long day like this one. But still, the licorice-tasting drink would help thin her blood and therefore clear her head.

Fatigue weighed down each step. She took several deep breaths. By definition, her kind didn't require air, but the oxygen penetrating her bloodstream usually acted as an energy booster. Thankfully, that little trick was still within her power. As if coming alive, her skin tingled and her senses sharpened.

Grateful for the reprieve, Kyana continue through Below to Spirits. The ancient tavern sat crammed between a Turkish bath and an herb shop, lending it the appeal of rich aromatic herbs on one side and a scent not unlike that of the Above's chlorinated pool water on the other. A sense of cleanliness entered the *kafenion* with you, but when you left, you stunk of hookah smoke and overcooked lamb. Occasionally, if Marcus liked them, they could get their raki served fifty/fifty with fresh lamb blood, and when she decided to eat tonight, that would likely be her request.

Kyana pushed through the semicircular door of Spirits and let it close behind her. Her entrance would have been silent if not for the sound of her boots on the freshly polished marble floor. Several heads at the bar turned to stare at her, then, deciding she deserved no further attention, returned to their drinking, eating, and smoking. Glass hookah pipes decorated every table, occupied and empty. Purple. Green. Red. The slinky tubes coiled around the bottles like bracelets, waiting to be lightly puffed upon.

"Fifty/fifty?"

Kyana looked up and caught Marcus watching her as he wiped down his shiny countertop. His chest-length, bushy black beard rubbed the front of his denim shirt, making him look more like a rough lumberjack than the retired Mystic he was, but his dark eyes held no menace. Vamps of the Order were welcome at Spirits, so long as they remained on their best behavior and didn't have his customers for dinner.

"Straight raki tonight." She pointed toward a secluded booth in the back. Nothing in Spirits was dark enough to fit her mood, but it was the darkest corner she could find to hide in. She needed to focus on the task ahead.

How did even a skilled tracer go about finding a damned key that could be virtually anywhere? It wouldn't be overflowing with pheromones to track or a pulse to follow. And on top of that, the damned thing was a pentagram. In her world, the pentagram was as common as a cross to Christians.

Whatever. She'd figure out a way. She always did.

She leaned her head against the wall, half lost in thought, half watching the door in anticipation of seeing Ryker again. Marcus appeared and slid a tumbler of what looked like murky water in front of her.

"Bad night?" he asked.

Usually, he didn't talk to Kyana much. She must have looked pretty pathetic for him to think she needed a friend.

"Nothing unusual," she lied.

His attention traveled to the blood staining her T-shirt. His gaze returned to hers, waiting for her to satisfy his curiosity. She'd come in beaten and bloody before. She hadn't explained then, and she wouldn't do so now.

"Hope you got a good prize for your efforts." With that, he turned to leave Kyana to her sought-after solitude.

"Wait."

Marcus had been with the Order his entire adult life. Only recently had he retired his Mystic ways to open

Spirits. And from what Kyana remembered, he'd been a pretty big mover and shaker within the Order's ranks . . . at least as far as Mystics went.

"Yes?"

"What do you know of Cronos?" she asked, choosing her words carefully.

His eyes widened, then narrowed in suspicion. "What everyone else does. Bad god. Exiled. Dead."

"What about rumors? Anything about him survive all these years?" Kyana sipped her drink, trying to keep her voice casual. The last thing she wanted to do was raise interest in her mission, but she needed some clue to the god if she hoped to discover what happened to that key.

Marcus rubbed his beard thoughtfully for several seconds. "Nothing really. Why the interest?"

"Just curious."

The barkeep watched Kyana intently, as if trying to read her intentions. His fingers stroked the large angry scar visible between the open buttons of his work shirt. Mystics were human born, and it looked as though Marcus had undergone open heart surgery recently.

"I don't know what you're fishing for, but you'll have to find it in another pool. Cronos is a legend. A dead one. If there's anything to know about anything there, I can't help you."

Disappointed, Kyana sagged against the back of her booth and sighed. From the bar, Marcus kept a close watch on her. She doubted she'd just endeared herself with him and hoped it didn't mean he'd stop serving her fifty/fifty.

"Well now. Looks like you've had a good tumble."

Geoffrey's rich, Irish lilt washed over Kyana's shoulder. "Did it at least include a lot of sweating and panting?"

She twisted in her seat, letting her gaze linger over the well-sculpted chest straining against his black T-shirt a moment before raising her eyes to his face. "Have you always been this nosy?"

"Best way to find out stuff." Geoff lifted her hair from her shoulder to get a better look at the marks on her throat. "Hmm," he mumbled, running his fingers lightly over the still-throbbing scabs. "What attacked you?"

Kyana shoved his hand away. "Nothing."

"You weren't marked when I saw you tonight." Geoff sat across from her, took her drink, and downed half the glass. "Those punctures are too large to be Vampyre. Too small for demon. So that leaves . . ."

She shrugged. She wouldn't tell Geoff whom she had a tumble with. No way would she spend eternity with him teasing her over Surfer Boy getting the best of her. "I told you. It was nothing."

His dark blue eyes held hers. "All right, then. Why are we talking about Cronos?"

"You really are a nosy ass."

Kyana caught Marcus as he moved to tend a pair of Witches at the bar. "Bring a whole bottle instead. Otherwise Geoff will leave me with nada."

A moment later, he brought a full bottle of raki and an extra glass of ice, sliding it in front of Geoffrey before slipping away again.

Geoffrey leaned forward. "I hear you've been assigned something big." He ignored his glass, opened the bottle, and drank deeply.

She eyed him, wondering how much he knew or if he was full of shit. Neither would surprise her. Geoff had ways of knowing things that left Kyana feeling more than slightly uneasy.

"Don't know what you're talking about."

His eyes lit up with humor as he reached behind his head to pull loose the black queue of hair at his nape. It fell about his face like a lion's silky mane, and Kyana's girl parts purred. Anyone looking at Geoff could see the danger there. It was blatantly sexy, but the quiet danger lurking within Ryker made Geoff's blatant sexuality a bit of a letdown.

But after her run-in with Ryker, she was still hot and bothered. There was no doubt that if she offered it, Geoff would make her howl at the moon.

Sometimes she really hated the laws of the Order.

Damn Ryker. She should be furious that he'd gotten the best of her. Instead, she was just confused by his lack of interest. Between her Vampyric allure and Lychen pheromones, how did he remain immune to her charms? Okay, so shoving him into the River Styx hadn't been her most charming moment, but she'd been on her best behavior when she'd met him and had still failed miserably at seducing him.

"So you're really going to play dumb about the key, lass?" Geoff refilled Kyana's tumbler and slid it closer to her.

Kyana froze. How did *he* know? It wasn't likely that the gods would want this tidbit of lore to get out.

The door opened, pulling everyone's attention. Everyone's except Kyana's. She knew by the slack-jawed stares who had entered. The sound of wet footsteps smacked against the marble floor, growing louder with each angry stride.

"Looks like someone else had an altercation tonight too. And, love, he looks like he's going to wring your pretty little neck for it."

Kyana took her drink and sipped, trying to appear unfazed. Ryker leaned over the table toward her so their noses were only inches apart. For the first time since she'd met him, he didn't smell like sunshine and vanilla.

With a grimace, she sat back and stared up at him. She smiled. "I'd offer you a drink, but maybe you should skip this round and go grab a shower."

Without much effort, he shoved her down her narrow booth and slid in beside her. "So, what're we talking about?"

That was it? No scene?

Of course not. Never a scene for cool, calm, collected Ryker.

Kyana sighed. She was pretty certain he wasn't going to let the issue of his lovely swim drop, but he wouldn't be unprofessional and bring it up now. His saturated jeans pooled water onto their vinyl booth, drenching the backside of her leather pants. She tried to scoot away, but only dragged the water with her.

"Kyana was just about to tell me about the key," Geoffrey said.

Kyana shot Geoffrey a look that begged him to die a painful death for that lie, but surprisingly, Ryker didn't seem to care whether Geoff knew anything.

"Oh? Know anything about it?" was all Ryker said.

"He doesn't know anything," Kyana snapped. "And

whatever he thinks he knows, we're not talking about it."

Ignoring her still-empty stomach, she downed the rest of her drink and tried to nudge Ryker out of her way so she could stand. He didn't budge.

"As a matter of fact," Geoffrey said, leaning across the table, "I *do* know something. Turns out I know quite a bit about many things. Want to hear some of it?"

"What do you know?"

Kyana looked at Ryker, waiting for the punch line. Apparently, there wasn't one. Ryker actually bought into the bull Geoffrey was selling.

"You don't know jack, Geoff."

But the serious looks on both men's faces had her skin tingling. Geoffrey *did* have an appalling ability to know things he shouldn't. Why should this time be any different?

Geoffrey's grin spread from ear to ear. "Simple. You want to find the key only Cronos knew about, you find his followers."

Kyana rolled her eyes. "Gee, why didn't I think of that? Why don't we just ask for a show of hands right now? Anyone want to give themselves up for being a traitor? Yeah, we should do that."

"Let him finish." Ryker reached across Kyana and pulled a wad of napkins from the dispenser and used them to dry his arms and face. "I'm guessing he has some idea how to find these followers or he wouldn't be here."

That raised her hackles. What the hell was going on? Ryker and Geoff didn't exactly like each other. Before now, she'd never heard them do more than grunt at each other. Usually they just glared in passing. Why would Ryker have faith in Geoff all of a sudden?

"Okay," Kyana said. "I'm listening."

Geoffrey rested his elbows on the table. "Someone nicked that key from Tartarus when Cronos was exiled. Maybe Cronos himself. Maybe not. Even if it was Cronos, he had to have passed it off to someone for it to be used now, right?"

"What's your point?" Kyana took a long pull from the bottle of raki. She'd already covered that much with Artemis and they'd already determined that the key was used as a diversion to kill the Chosen.

"My point is," Geoffrey continued, his blue eyes twinkling, "Cronos's name has been muttered more lately than I can ever remember. Weeks before Tartarus even broke loose. I don't think much of our population was as surprised as you'd expect when Tartarus opened."

"You're trying to say we have a lot more Cronos supporters than we thought. So what? Sad as it may be, it's not a crime to be a Cronos lover."

"Supporters who weren't shocked when Tartarus opened? It doesn't bother you that they might have known it was going to happen? I think that *is* a crime."

Great. So instead of one asshole, they were dealing with several?

"It shouldn't be hard to start rounding them up. Eventually you catch the right bastard."

"Mmm. A concentration camp for Cronos followers. I don't much care to become a Nazi, thanks." Kyana pushed her drink away and folded her arms across her chest. "And even if that *wasn't* a disgusting thought, you make it sound like these people are walking around with scarlet A's on their chests."

The heat of Ryker's sudden stare pulled her attention. He looked utterly flummoxed. "What?" she asked. "I can read, you know."

He shrugged. "I just pegged you for more of a Stephen King fan than a Nathaniel Hawthorne."

Kyana rolled her eyes and directed her attention back where it belonged. On Geoffrey. "Okay, smart guy. What would you suggest we do?"

"Get a list of Cronos's worshippers, obviously. Start from there."

"Right," Ryker said. "Because that would be simple without those scarlet A's to tip us off."

Kyana smiled. A thought began to take root. "Geoff's right. It's a place to start. Only . . . we don't look for the scarlet A's that exist today. We look for the ones that existed when Cronos reigned."

"What will that get us?"

Kyana fiddled with her napkin. "If we trace their friends and family forward we can get a list of those who might be following in the paths of their ancestors. Catholics tend to breed Catholics. Pagans breed pagans. I'd bet money that some of Cronos's followers passed down their beliefs to their descendants."

"For thousands of generations?"

Kyana and Geoffrey both looked at Ryker in exasperation.

"Hell yes," Geoffrey said. "Good on you, lass." To Ryker, he continued, "There's a reason most wars are started over religion. People hold tight to those beliefs even when they seem ludicrous."

"Add fanatics to the bunch, and you have loyal worshippers today that can be traced back for thousands of years," Kyana added. "You're on it, Geoff. You wouldn't have come here if you hadn't been looking for a taste of this mission, so here you have it. Get me a list of those who loved Cronos back in the day and trace every descendant, every close friend they ever had."

"Over ten thousand years? That shouldn't take longer than another few thousand." Geoffrey stretched.

"You're telling me you can't do it?"

He stood and glared down at her. "Of course not. I'm telling you that you should let me bend over so you can kiss my sexy arse for being well connected. I'll have your names for you, but you owe me something in return."

Kyana shrugged. "What?"

He leaned across the table, over Ryker, and came nose to nose with Kyana. "Let's put it this way . . . you'll be sweating and grunting like mad."

"You want a lay?" Kyana asked, her cheeks burning hot. Not because of Geoffrey's request, but because Ryker had heard it.

"'Course not, lass. That'd be against the laws." He straightened and smirked. "I want you to clean my pad. Top to bottom till it shines."

Chapter Six

Kyana lay sprawled on her sofa, her eyes drooping closed. She hadn't slept in days. Her kind didn't need more than a few winks a week, but it had been longer than that since she'd done more than close her eyes. The world around her small, two-story house had grown cold and quiet. Perfect for sleeping. But even though she'd spent the afternoon trying to rest before her journey, sleep had not come. Too much was on her mind, and the restlessness of sitting at home, waiting for the sun to set so she could find passage to a mysterious island and begin her hunt for the key, wouldn't let her find peace.

She pried open one eye and glanced at the clock above the television. An hour till sunset. She could survive that. By the time she finished packing, she could be on her way. She'd just close her eyes for a minute first.

The minute she did, Ryker's face popped into her head again. She groaned and flopped onto her belly. At least he had agreed to go pack his own bags without following her home, though it did irk her that he seemed confident she wouldn't make her escape without him. He certainly was a cocky sonofabitch.

She rubbed her eyes, wishing she could scratch the imprint of him from her mind. But he was as stubborn in her brain as he was in person. Permanent. Rooted. If she could just go back to that evening they'd met, she would have done so many things differently. Found someone else to turn to in her moment of grief after watching a dozen fellow tracers get slaughtered. Found someone else to leach warmth from. A willing person . . . not someone who'd rejected her and made her feel dirty for her wants. But she'd chosen Ryker because that particular night, she'd needed more than someone who would roll off her and walk away. She'd needed someone to hold her through the night and make the nightmarish images vanish, and Ryker's arms had been the only ones she'd wanted around her.

Her pull to him had been instant and more powerful than any spark she'd ever had with Geoffrey or even her most recent lover, Silas. She'd wanted more than to just have Ryker inside her. She'd wanted to fully know him. And that had scared the hell out of her.

She wasn't sure she'd survive this job if he was tagging along—

Something clicked in the doorway. Kyana's eyes snapped open, her body instantly coming alive with adrenaline, all thoughts of Ryker forgotten. Her body quivered as her gaze moved to the doorknob. It clicked left, turned right. She was on her feet in a fraction of a second, her back pressed to the wall behind the door. Perched on the balls of her feet, ready to pounce at the first sign of danger, she reached for the knob, turned it, and thrust the front door open, lunging at the intruder on the other side.

"Kyana, stop!"

The sound of her name shouted in a familiar voice stopped Kyana in her tracks, sending her off balance and slamming into the doorjamb. A genuine smile eased the ache in her shoulder.

"Zeus, Haven! I almost killed you."

The blond Witch tossed her tan arms around Kyana's neck. "The world has gone crazy!"

"No shit." Kyana hugged Haven back and, though she couldn't see it, felt her friend's reprimanding stare. Haven was always chastising Kyana for her foul mouth. She probably had a point, but Kyana was far too old to change her ways now.

As a Witch, she inhabited a world that was so unlike Kyana's. Haven's polar opposite in every possible way, Kyana had instantly hated the other woman. Haven dealt with life and light, and her pretty-girl persona was enough to drive Kyana to do physical harm. That was until they'd been forced to defend themselves against a rogue band of Dark Breeds terrorizing the Everglades ten years ago—the same fight where Kyana had first met Ryker. Instead of shrinking away and hiding until the battle was over, Haven had fought by Kyana's side as skillfully and brutally as Geoffrey might have. They'd become family and roommates, and Kyana protected that bond above all else.

"Where have you been?" Kyana asked, easing out of her friend's choke hold. "I haven't heard from you since Tartarus broke loose." She gestured to the momentarily calm streets that undoubtedly would be overcome with chaos again soon enough.

"Panama City." Haven gathered her abundant hair in a manicured hand and slid the loose ponytail to dangle over her breast. She pointed at a long, angry cut that marked her from ear to jaw. "Drake and I were ring shopping when the Lychen attacked."

"Have you seen a Mystic?"

Kyana wasn't worried about her friend being changed by her encounter with the werewolf. That, like coffins, lack of reflections, and garlic for Vamps, was only urban legend. She was, however, worried about infection. Lychen had vile bacteria in their teeth and claws that, when injected into a non-Lychen's bloodstream, could be lethal.

Haven crossed her arms and glared. "You know I can heal myself."

"I know." Kyana smiled and stepped out of the way so Haven could come in. "I've been worried about you."

"Hey, I was trapped in a mall for a week. It was heaven. " She rolled her eyes. "Okay, the occasional demonic attack put a damper on things, but still, good times were had by all."

Kyana grinned, knowing Haven was only half teasing. As she closed the front door, Kyana recalled her friend's earlier words and allowed herself a quick glance at Haven's left hand. "Ring shopping?"

"We were interrupted, obviously. But soon."

Marriage? Between Haven and Drake? A Witch and a Mystic? That would be the strangest union in history. Mystics were almost monklike. They didn't typically engage in romance, even when they retired from service as Drake had. Okay, so Mystics and Witches were pretty similar in their abilities, but Witches were born and Mystics chose their path. That led to a lot of conflict between the two groups, the Mystics jealous of the Witches' birthrights, and a lot of prejudice from the Witches toward the lowly Mystics. Did Haven have any idea how much flak she was going to get from her family when she brought a *Mystic* home?

Distaste coated Kyana's mouth. Why Drake of all beings?

It wasn't just that she couldn't stand Drake's pompous ass that brought resentment to Kyana's heart. It was the knowledge that, once the vows were said, her already scarce time with Haven would become even more sporadic. Drake didn't like Haven socializing with the Order. Since he'd left the Order himself to make his money Above, he'd done everything he could to snatch Haven out, as well.

They'd had this discussion at least a hundred times over the past few months and it hadn't made a difference, but she felt she had to try once more. "Haven—"

"Don't." Her sharp blue eyes bored into Kyana, silencing her. "It doesn't matter if you like Drake. You like *me*. That means you'll come to the wedding and stand by my side the way Hope would have if she was still alive."

"Damn it, Haven. Don't play the dead twin card. It's not fair."

Haven lowered her gaze, and Kyana nearly apologized. "Please keep my news secret. I'd really prefer to announce our engagement when all of this has passed." She turned and made her way to the kitchen.

When all of this passed? Kyana's head reeled. Did Haven think this was some minor spat between Zeus and Hades? Did she think this was going to be resolved soon? Haven had her ditzy moments, but she wasn't stupid or naïve. At least, Kyana had never thought so before.

Not sure what else to do, Kyana followed Haven. Hoping to ease the strain between them, Kyana smiled. "Glad you're home."

Haven smiled and tossed her pink duffel bag on the floor before opening the fridge. "Thanks. I can't wait to sleep in my own bed. Will be way more comfortable than Dillard's cold floor." She narrowed her eyes at Kyana. "Why are you home, anyway? Shouldn't you be out kicking demon booty?"

Kyana studied her, wondering how much she should tell Haven. Neither Artie nor the Fates had forbidden Kyana to discuss her mission. And she knew Haven would protect the Order with her life if necessary. Besides, talking it out might help her form a more detailed plan of action. All she had to go on now was whatever Cronos's island gave her. Kyana wasn't quite sure what to expect once she got there, but she certainly didn't expect to find the key. Maybe just a hint as to where it had gone.

"I've been pulled off tracer duty for something more important."

Haven paused in her task of tossing salad greens into a large bowl. "More important than sending Dark Breeds back to Hell? Details. Now."

Kyana turned toward her room, motioning for Haven

to follow. "It seems the Fates have discovered how the Dark Breeds escaped Tartarus."

"Well, it's about time." Haven entered Kyana's room and flopped on the bed, catapulting a piece of lettuce onto Kyana's satin comforter. She picked it up and popped it into her mouth. "So how did they escape?"

Kyana opened her closet and pulled out a backpack. "Someone stole the key."

Laughter filled the room. Deep, you-gotta-be-kidding, belly laughter. When Haven pulled herself together, she sat cross-legged and stared at Kyana. "The key? To Hell?"

Kyana turned from the closet and held Haven's gaze. If the subject weren't so serious, Kyana would've laughed about it too. But it *was* serious. Until the key was found, the Dark Breeds would continue to wreak havoc on Earth. And until they discovered who unlocked Tartarus in the first place, the Chosen would continue to die.

"You're not kidding."

"No." Kyana turned back to her closet. "I'm not kidding."

She stuffed clothes into the bag, then tossed it on the bed. As she dug through the chest of amulets Haven had made for her, Kyana continued, "My mission is to find the key and close Hell and give Above back to the humans."

"Sounds dangerous. Should be fun for you." Haven nodded to the bag. "Where are you going?"

Kyana tossed a handful of Illusion Charms into the bag and sat at the foot of the bed. "To the last known place the creator of the key was. If Cronos took it with him when he was exiled, maybe I'll find some clue as to who took it from the island when he died."

"Cronos? Good gravy. Why don't you look more excited?" Haven scooted to the end of the bed and rested her hand on Kyana's knee. "You're after something big. You should be on cloud nine."

"I'm not exactly a beach bunny, and who knows if I'll be able to find shelter from the sun there," Kyana said. "If I can't, I'll have to spend most of my time as a Lychen."

Kyana didn't have to explain to Haven why this was an issue. Though Kyana could fight in Lychen form, she was nowhere near as strong as she was in her Vampyric body. The wolf in her was an amazing tracer, but the Vampyre in her was what kept her fast and deadly. If she ran into trouble on that island, she would have to pray for sunset in order to remain confident in her abilities.

Haven dug into the Greek salad she'd whipped up for dinner. The stench of feta cheese and black olives stank up Kyana's bedroom. If it lingered on her Egyptian cotton sheets, she was going to rip Haven a new one.

"So I'll come with you, keep you juiced up on potions to sustain your energy while you're a pup."

Kyana considered the option but just as quickly discarded it. She didn't know what she would find on that island. Most likely nothing at all, but she didn't want Haven in danger if she was wrong. However, Haven did have a good point. Kyana hated the thought of anyone walking blind into a potentially bad situation, but better a trained Healer than her best friend.

Haven didn't give Kyana a chance to verbally refuse before changing the subject.

"Did you hear that Dallas just made its last evacuation? Sending another plane of refugee humans to D.C."

"What are they going to do there?" Kyana asked. "Last I heard, D.C. was infested worse than anywhere." So many had fled to the three safe zones that the human military had closed the states, refusing to let anyone or anything in. She accepted that the humans needed to get out of the danger zones, but they should at least make sure the relocation zones were safe.

"They seem to think they can control their capital." Haven scooted off the bed and left the room. Kyana followed, interested in any tidbit of news.

Haven grabbed the remote and clicked on the large television to one of the few working news channels. Pain seared through Kyana's head. Technology didn't agree with her mix of breeds. The radio waves bouncing through the room had her ears ringing and her head pounding. The need for news made her push aside the pain, though she did move farther out of the living room to sit on the stairs.

The images flashing on the screen were of wide-eyed, sleep-deprived news anchors yapping in front of monitors showing a massive explosion in the downtown Dallas area.

"Nice to know even demons running rampant on the streets can't bring down FOX News."

Pointing the remote at the screen, Haven glanced over her shoulder at Kyana. "The military set off bombs to act as a diversion. It worked long enough to get about three hundred humans boarded on planes. D.C., apparently, has opened up all major buildings for shelter."

A Latino boy screamed on the television, his arms outstretched as a soldier lifted him out of his father's arms and onto the airplane. "They're not taking any men yet," Haven continued. "Looks like they might end up with a matriarchal society if we don't pick up the pace."

Kyana looked at Haven, who chewed daintily on an olive. "And what would be wrong with that?"

Haven grinned. "I like men, thank you very much. Don't want to see the entire species wiped off the face of the Earth."

"Humans have a sinking ship mentality, women and children first," Kyana said. "They need to save those who matter. Those who can put the world back in order when we complete our task."

But given that the human government didn't exactly have a roster of the Chosen to work from, or know anything about them really, Kyana wasn't sure how they were supposed to do that. And sadly, while bits of the Order were spread out across the world, there weren't enough of them to work as hard and fast as the mission required.

Haven glanced at the screen. "I don't know why they're sending everyone to D.C., though. It's on the verge of being overrun as it is. Once the Dark Breeds realize they've put all their hens in one little henhouse, it'll be a slaughter."

Kyana tried to care. Really, she did. But humans, in her experience, weren't the innocent beings of light that the gods and goddesses seemed to think they were.

They were just as murderous, just as power hungry as most Dark Breeds. Yes, she cared about the world in general, but the human race? They were no better than any other breed Kyana had come across in her lifetime.

Still, no race deserved to be wiped out completely. Maybe Leeches, but they were brainless, useless fuckers.

Kyana pulled herself to her feet and made her way back to her room, calling out over her shoulder, "Let's hope that we can get a couple of our people in D.C. to help sway the human powers-that-be into being more sensible."

"We already have people there, but even with everything going on, it's difficult for humans to believe we truly want to help them."

Which was why so many had died, and were still dying.

"I'm off." Kyana snapped her satchel closed, slung it over her shoulder, and grabbed her leather jacket from the back of her door. "Be a good friend and shut off that TV so I can come through without my head exploding."

There was a click and then blessed silence as Kyana shut her door and headed back toward the living room.

"You're going to wear that?" Haven asked, eyeing Kyana like a mother.

Kyana glanced down at her leather pants and boots. "Yeah?"

Haven knelt and rested her arms on the back of the sofa. "Those pants have been mended more times than I can count. Not sure I can save them if you shift in them again."

Right. She loved these pants. They'd been tattered

so many times by Kyana's shifting, they'd become remarkably comfy. But Haven was right. They were on their last legs. "Fine. I'll change."

With a sigh of regret, she stomped back to her room, threw open her closet, and pulled out a similar pair that still had the price tag attached. She lovingly placed her battered pair on the bed and slipped the new ones on, loathing the thought of ruining these too. The Illusion Charms Haven created for her didn't stop her from ruining clothes during a shift. All they did was fool people into believing she wasn't running around naked. She'd fought bare-assed more times than she could count, but luckily, no one else could see that. She needed a cheaper clothing habit, for sure. Maybe take up denim, but denim didn't become a part of her body as leather did, and it didn't offer much in the way of protection. But the Order didn't exactly pay their employees, and Kyana's stash of old money wouldn't last forever. Especially now with the human world so out of whack, all of her investments were kaput.

She sighed, zipped up the pants, and headed back to the living room. "Better?"

Haven looked her over. "Yep. I can save those if you don't screw them up too badly. Just bring me the pieces." She straightened and cocked her head. "So I'm guessing this means you're refusing my offer to keep you drowning in potions?"

"Haven, if I knew what I was facing, you'd be the first person I'd want with me. You know that. But I have no idea where I'm heading or what might be there waiting. I can't be my best if I'm worried about you."

"Okay."

Okay? Just like that? Kyana didn't trust the innocent look on Haven's face. "I mean it, Haven."

"I know. Go. Be safe. I'm going to go shower."

She disappeared down the hall, humming, and left Kyana to watch suspiciously as her blond head bounced away.

There was no time to pursue Haven, however. She had to meet Artemis and Ryker. She wasn't sure she'd find anything useful on the island, but the thought of walking around such a legendary place and seeing for herself where a bastard like Cronos had died amped her up.

As she opened the front door and headed out into dusk, Kyana picked up speed. She wasn't willing to sap any of her energy by using her Vampyric sprint. It would only last a minute and she'd be worn out for an hour. She was already in dire need of a nap and couldn't risk outright exhaustion. And no way in hell was she shifting already. She'd lose her bag and her clothes, and she sure as shit wasn't strutting naked around the island—even if she was the only one who *knew* she wasn't clothed. But she kept her strides long as she wound her way down the back roads separating her little restored bed-and-breakfast home and the Castillo de San Marcos.

Once she entered Below, Kyana stopped long enough to grab some warm supper to go from the butcher near Spirits before making her way to the gods' temple on a large hill overlooking this part of the realm. Ryker and Artemis stood waiting already, and though Kyana wasn't late, she wished she'd been the one to arrive first.

So much for hoping that after his rancid swim he'd plead for reassignment.

"You're really going to make him go with me?"

Ryker smirked. "You expected me not to show up?"

"I was hopeful." She doubted it would do any good, but she had to try one last time to get Artemis to change her mind about the two of them working together. "You said his job was to find the persons responsible for using the key. This trip is a scouting expedition for clues. I doubt we'll find people there. There's no need for you to make him go with me to help search the island."

"That's not why I'm going."

"Then why bother?"

"Have you ever used a port before?" Artemis asked.

Now where had that question come from? "Uh, I'm here, aren't I?"

"Not a portal. A port. You'll be taking one today."

She frowned at the goddess. "What's the difference?"

"A port isn't like stepping through the gate between Above and Below. It's not an easy passage. It's bright, loud, and very dangerous, especially when more than one person is being ported."

"Then why do I have to use one of these port things?"

"Because it's not only the quickest way to reach Cronos's island, it's the only way."

Just lovely. Kyana wanted to ask exactly what to expect, but a part of her really didn't want to know.

"It's not all about the skill of the porter, but directly involves the willingness of the portee—you—to do what's required to make the jump complete."

"Have you ever— Wait, port*er*? As in, thing that ports?"

Dread settled in Kyana's gut as her suspicions raised

the hairs on her arms. She swung her gaze to Ryker, whose smug smile confirmed her fears.

Shit.

"A porter isn't a thing, Ky. It's a person." Ryker gripped her shoulders as though he thought she might bolt. "And in this case, I'm going to be your personal airline service."

Chapter Seven

You're going to be my what?" Kyana picked up her jaw from the proverbial floor and stepped away from Ryker.

"Your porter. It's a rare gift. From my father's side." He knelt in front of her and bowed his head. "You'll have to hold on to me and shut up because if I break my concentration on the location I'm trying to send us to, we could end up somewhere on shit's creek and out of luck for a while." He rotated his neck, flexed his shoulders. He looked more like he was preparing for a workout than for a magic session. "Once I port us, I can't summon that power again for twenty-four hours. Understand? We don't have time to get thrown off course."

Twenty-four hours? *A full day?* She'd known there was a probable chance of being out on that island for a sunrise, but now she was going to have to deal with a full day of Ryker. On a deserted island. How was she supposed to survive that? Artemis had one sick sense of humor, but Kyana wasn't laughing.

"Couldn't *you* just do this?" she asked Artemis. "The two of us alone? We're going to kill each other."

"No, I cannot. And you'll not be alone." Artemis waved at someone near the door. "I've arranged for a Healer to accompany you."

Kyana twisted to find Haven smiling like a pig in dog shit. "I *knew* you were up to something. Gave in way too easy. How did you beat me here?"

"Swiftness Potion." Haven grinned. "Tastes like strawberries."

"Figures." Turning her gaze to Ryker, whose head was still bowed, she asked, "What do we have to do?"

"Each of you take a shoulder. When I begin the chant, I'll need complete and absolute silence. If you release your hold on me at any point, you'll be left behind. Well, some of you will be. Can't guarantee at least a bit of you won't come with me."

Kyana chuckled. He was kidding. But there was no humor in his eyes. He . . . *wasn't* kidding. His mouth started moving, quiet words fluttering past Kyana's ears as she watched his long fingers draw a circle in the dirt around him.

"Stand inside," he said.

And when Kyana and Haven obeyed, he threw back his head, spewing a blinding light from his eyes like someone had shoved a flashlight in his sockets. Words of another language flew from his mouth and Kyana frantically shoved her hand on his shoulder and held on to his shirt for dear life.

She bit her tongue, fighting the array of curses desperate to be spoken, terrified of muttering even one lest they end up in the middle of the damned ocean. She searched Haven's eyes, saw the fear within the blue depths, and relaxed the smallest bit. If Haven sensed Kyana's fear, Haven would lose control and throw them all off course.

Ryker's body spasmed. His head fell forward, and Kyana suddenly felt as though she'd been turned inside out. She squeezed her eyes shut against the nausea, and when she opened them again, she was inside a golden tunnel so blinding, tears poured down her cheeks. She was pretty sure her hair caught on fire as she spiraled through what looked to be a light worm, the stench of burning hair clogging her throat. Her cheeks and neck burned. She ached to snatch her hand away and shield herself from danger. Had he taken her to the fucking sun? She needed to shift, needed to turn Lychen and save herself from exploding into dust right here and now.

But she held on to Ryker, desperate to keep all her body parts if she was going to die anyway.

The blinding light burst like fireworks behind her closed eyes, and when she next opened them, she was cast in utter blackness. Not even her superior Vampyric sight could penetrate the dark. She was thrown forward, her fingers desperately clawing at Ryker's shirt to keep her grip, and in the next instant, she was flat on her back, her mouth full of grit, her throat and nose closed with tiny particles of . . . sand?

She reached out her free hand, felt around in the darkness. Cool, grainy sand slid between her fingers and dusted her pants. She coughed, spitting the beach back into its rightful place. Her eyes were open, but it was still black.

"Ryker?" she called out. "Haven?"

"We're here. We're fine." Ryker's voice was only inches away.

She rolled over, felt for his face, then lifted her hand and slapped the shit out of him. "You bastard! I'm blind! What the hell did you do to me?"

"Damn it, Ky!"

She felt him scoot away and she reached after him like a desperate peddler after his goods. She rose onto her knees, following his sounds. Her hands fell into water, splashing the burning, salty liquid into her mouth. The ocean. Yippee.

"Libero!"

Ryker's shout jerked Kyana to her feet. It took a moment to realize that he'd just ordered someone's freedom, and another moment to realize it had been hers. She tentatively opened one eye, and it burned from the salt water. But she could see. She stood in front of the bluest waters she'd ever seen. Sand the color of snow piled beneath her boots, offset by small rocks so black they looked like tiny oil spills.

"This the place?" she breathed, her panic calming as the sight of the gray sky filled her focus. It was twilight here too. She hadn't been sure it would be. She didn't have to worry about shifting . . . yet.

"Hope so." Ryker was bending over the water, splashing it onto his face.

"Yeah, sorry 'bout the slap. I . . ."

"Panicked. I know."

She frowned at him and turned around to make sure Haven wasn't missing her nose or something from their little adventure. She looked pretty intact, though out of breath as she lay flat on her back, her arm flung over her face as her chest rose and fell in a heavy, steady rhythm.

"You okay?" Kyana asked, falling onto the sand beside her friend.

"I'm. Going. To. Puke." Haven rolled onto her side and groaned.

Glad to know it wasn't just her own weak stomach flopping around, Kyana smiled. It would be interesting to see who tossed her cookies first.

"We have all night to prowl the island," Ryker said. "Take a few to recover and zap yourself some potion to settle your stomach. We'll rest for an hour, then we're off."

He was right, but Kyana didn't like him issuing orders. "Thirty minutes. We'll need time to look for shelter from the sun as well since we're stuck here until tomorrow night."

"Fine. Thirty minutes." He dried his face on his shirt and strode to Haven's side. He reached into her satchel and pulled out a bottle of water, tucking it inside her folded arms. "Drink."

Kyana blinked up at him, unable to stop the warmth of satisfaction she felt at seeing the welts of her palm print on his cheek. "I shouldn't have slapped you."

His hard glare rested on her. "No. You shouldn't have."

"I should have punched you instead."

They probably could have used the hour, but at exactly thirty minutes, according to Ryker's watch, Kyana insisted rest time was over. Ryker had to bite his lip to keep from putting her in her place. True, this was technically *her* mission. But he outranked her by a mile. He was used to giving orders, not taking them.

He watched her help Haven to her feet, watched the pair of them move together in the shadows as he gathered his belongings and stuffed them back into his bag. They were quite a pair—the blond Witch and the dark Vamp Half-Breed. Normally, he would have been all over Haven's sort of beauty. Perky, good-humored, optimistic. He liked all her qualities, and Zeus knew, she was damned beautiful. But his gaze never lingered on her long. It always found its way right back to where it shouldn't be—on Kyana.

Your own mother couldn't find it in her heart to love you, Ryker. She all but threw you in my arms when I came to claim you as my son. My, but you are a masochist, aren't you? You choose to give your heart to a bloodthirsty Half-Breed who will never want more from you than your cock. You're strong, son. But you are a king of fools.

Ares's words rang in Ryker's ears as he slung his bag over his shoulder and followed the women off the beach and into the surrounding jungle. He'd made the mistake of allowing his father to overhear his prayers for peace. That Ares knew of Ryker's feelings for Kyana had only strengthened their mutual disdain for each other. Another bone of contention between them, because as Ryker envisioned Kyana's hair spread out upon his pillow, her whispered words of love in his ear, Ares had seen only the Half-Breed in Kyana, a threat to steal his son's attentions away from his duties. And since Ares wanted nothing more than for Ryker to take his place as the God of War, any distraction from that post had been immediately stomped to death. Most especially women, which Ares considered the most inconsequential beings on the planet.

Ryker didn't want or need his father's approval. Hell, he hadn't even acknowledged Ares as his father to anyone but himself. He just loathed hearing Ares belittle the connection he knew he had with Kyana. He hated that *she* belittled it too. He didn't want just her body. He wanted all of her. All the time.

A branch smacked him in the chest, pulling him out of the thoughts that were conjuring his temper like a tempest. Kyana led the way through an overgrown trail Ryker had found while she and Haven had rested. Still, the path toward the center of the island was anything but a walk in the park. He felt like he should be in front, knocking the brush from their path to make it easier on Kyana and Haven, but he was pretty sure if he tried to act so gallantly, Kyana would push him off a cliff. Or another damned ferry. His small home Below still stank like death thanks to her little stunt at the river. But that was only one of the many things he liked so much about her. She was the only nongoddess female that he'd ever failed to intimidate.

As he slashed through an overhanging tree that dusted his hair with moss, he forced himself to focus on the trek ahead. He still wasn't a hundred percent sure they were even on the right island. Having never been here before, all he'd had to go on was the coordinates Artemis had given him, and it seemed the very vegetation was out to prevent them from finding even the smallest hint that those numbers had been accurate.

Branches slapped their faces. Hidden roots reached out with gnarled fingers to trip them. Walls of vines and brambles blocked their path, forcing them to use their daggers to slice a way through.

By the time they'd pushed through the last barrier and stumbled into a small clearing, the moon had risen high in the sky. A rock-ringed campfire lay cold and unused. By its lack of odor, and the grass that had woven its way between the rocks, threatening to overtake the pit, Ryker guessed it hadn't been used in ages.

Haven dropped her backpack. "I'm going to explore."

"Don't go far," Kyana and Ryker said together.

"Yes, Mommies." Haven rolled her eyes. "I'm here to provide puppy power because I *don't* need a babysitter."

As Haven walked to the edge of the clearing, Ryker shook his head. "That kind of attitude gets people hurt."

"Or worse," Kyana mumbled.

"Don't worry, I'll be careful."

Satisfied that Haven wouldn't let her guard down, Ryker turned back to the fire pit. "You think this is it?"

"How am I supposed to know? You were the one who drove this crazy train." Kyana pulled a clump of grass and held it in her hand as if it might speak up and answer the question. "It's obvious someone had been on this island. And if they'd taken the time to ring their campfire, they were probably here for a long time. But there's no telling *who* lit the fire."

"Well, I really don't know," Ryker said. "I don't usually have such technical details like coordinates when I do this, so I'm hoping they were accurate. Either way, we have a whole day to explore the place and figure it out."

"I hope for your sake that this is the right destination."

"My sake?" Ryker glared. "Are you back to threatening me?"

"It's not a threat. If I have to go through that swirly, blinding, turn-your-insides-out light again, I really will punch you in the face."

Ryker grinned. He'd never seen the mighty, unstoppable Kyana rattled. He rather liked it. "I still have to get us home."

"Yeah, don't remind me."

"I think you guys might want to check this out." Haven pushed her way through some vines to wave at them.

Ryker trailed after Kyana and Haven down what, at one time, might have been a path. They'd gone about a hundred feet when they entered another, smaller clearing. This one, however, housed a cave entrance instead of a campfire.

Ryker nodded toward the entrance. "What's in there?"

"How would I know? No way was I going into a dark, deserted, most likely rat- and/or bat-infested cave alone without a flashlight. Some of us don't have Spidey senses." She crossed her arms and glared. "You know bat poo in confined places can kill those of us required to breathe."

"Would you like to wait here while we check it out?" Ryker asked.

Kyana glared at him. There really was no pleasing

her. He wanted to make sure her friend was safe, and all he got for the effort was attitude.

"I'm not staying out here by myself. I watch scary movies. I know what happens to the blond girl in the woods."

"In that case, I'll lead the way," Kyana said.

Haven jabbed a finger into Ryker's chest. "I don't mind being mauled by Dark Breeds. It's the little things with tails, wings, or too many legs that I don't deal with. So if you see one, you stomp it to death, got it?"

Ryker wasn't certain but he thought he saw a spark of jealousy in Kyana's eyes as she watched them. He smiled and threw his arm blatantly over Haven's shoulders. "You got it, Goldie."

Kyana's scowl deepened. Oh yeah. She was jealous, all right.

"You two ready, or would you rather wait here and chitchat while I check this out?"

"Lead on. Just take it slow," Ryker instructed.

As Kyana entered the cave, she blocked out the image of Ryker's arm draped over her best friend's shoulders and forced herself to keep her pace slow, even though a small piece of her wouldn't have minded if Haven tripped a little. Then again, Ryker apparently liked his damsels in distress, and she didn't want to give them even more reason to cozy up. Though why she should care was beyond her. Getting Haven away from Drake would be a plus.

But the thought of the diversion coming in the form of Ryker made Kyana's stomach twist.

Silently cursing her girly moment of jealousy, Kyana scanned the dark crevices and ceiling for anything that might be a threat. When she neared the back of the cave, she paused long enough to hold up her hand to silently instruct Ryker to keep Haven still before moving to the distant corner. She knelt among the scattered remains of animals and various clay and metal utensils.

"Ow!"

Kyana jumped at the sound of Haven's holler and spun to find her friend bracing herself against the wall.

"You let go of me and—oh my God. That is way grosser than bat poo!"

She was backing away, her gaze locked on the corner by her feet. Kyana followed Haven's attention and saw a skeleton wrapped in a thick layer of dust resting precariously against the rough stone wall.

Kyana moved closer to the body. She rested her hands on her knees and scanned the time-whitened bones. When Ryker knelt beside her, she gently lifted the bony right hand in hers, cradling her left under it to keep it intact.

"I'll be damned," he muttered.

"What is it?" Haven fumbled in the darkness, and Ryker produced a small penlight and clicked it on to guide her to their side. "Don't touch it, Kyana! That's freaking disgusting."

"It can't hurt you, and if it does come alive, we'll feed Ryker to it while we make our escape."

"I'm not sure even *I* know how to take out bones," Ryker mumbled.

Kyana didn't either. They'd probably need Haven's witchery for that.

"So who's the bony guy?" Haven asked, keeping her distance.

Ryker turned the tiny beam to Kyana's hand. Not even time had stolen the luster of the large, golden ring still on the right hand of the skeleton. On the ruby red stone in the center, an engraved sickle.

The mark of Cronos.

"Definitely the right island." Kyana moved to slide the ring off the fleshless finger when Ryker's hand stopped her.

"Don't."

She shook free of Ryker's warm touch. "Why not? We should take it. Maybe seeing it will bring some of his followers out of hiding."

Ryker shook his head, his blond hair falling over his eyes as he stared down at the corpse. "It's his conduit. The equivalent of Zeus's staff, Hades's amulet—"

"Oh, it's one of those!" Haven's sudden excitement had her apparently forgetting her disgust long enough to kneel and examine the ring herself. "Do you have *any* idea the kind of spells I could manage with that thing? Oh, Kyana! Astral projection! I could finally get it right."

She reached for it, but just as he had with Kyana, Ryker pushed Haven's hand away. "Only the gods possess the ability to hold the Eyes of Power. If either of you touch it, it will kill you."

Kyana stood, suddenly unwilling to even breathe on the ring, just in case Ryker's threat was true. "So we should leave it here? Risk it being taken by someone else?"

"It's probably safer here," Ryker said. "Only two of us can even port here anymore."

"And yet, the key might have vanished from here, Ryker. Are you so confident that you'd risk it?"

"Why would they take the key and leave the ring?" Haven asked. "Wait—never mind. Death to whoever touches it. Got it."

Kyana didn't acknowledge Haven's comment. Her staring match with Ryker was so heavy with tension, it filled the small cave like fog. Finally, Ryker closed his eyes and muttered, "Shit," before reaching for the ring. "It shouldn't affect me."

Kyana grabbed his hand. "You're only half god. *Shouldn't* doesn't sit too well with me."

"It's all we've got. Either I hold on to it, or it stays. Make the call, boss lady."

Kyana stared at the ring, debating their options. If they left it, then the chance of someone else getting her hands on it would gnaw at her. However, touching it could kill Ryker.

If they left it, it might remain somewhat safe. After all, it had been here, untouched, for thousands of years. But she couldn't bring herself to risk leaving it behind. She didn't know what kind of power a conduit might hold, but it was enough to worry Ryker, and that was reason enough in her book to make sure it returned with them.

"We take it." She squeezed Ryker's arm. "But don't be macho. If it starts to affect you, get rid of it. I don't care where you lose it, just don't die on me."

"Ah." Ryker smiled and squeezed her hand. "You're worried about me."

Warmth spread up her arm. She snatched her hand away. "Without you, we spend the rest of our lives on this island. And I have a very long life expectancy, so don't do anything stupid."

They held their collective breaths as Ryker reached for the ring, slid it slowly off the bones, and tucked it into his front pants pocket. When his leg didn't fall off and he didn't start screaming in pain, everyone exhaled. Poor Haven looked as though she was going to pass out.

Kyana felt as if she already had.

"Let's get out of here," Ryker said, not looking too good himself.

"You're okay, then?"

He nodded, though Kyana noticed a small bead of perspiration forming at his hairline. "I will be once I get some air."

Kyana watched both Ryker and Haven climb safely out of the cave before leaning heavily against the rocky wall. She took a moment to collect herself, unwilling to delve into the reason her heart was still racing.

"He isn't yours to lose," she whispered to the now lonely cave entrance. But even knowing that Ryker didn't belong to her, she couldn't help but feel weak in the knees at the thought of his death—and it had nothing to do with being trapped on this island.

Chapter Eight

They'd been on the isle for close to twelve hours and Ryker hadn't seen, heard, or smelled anything. Not even a bird had chirped. It was kind of eerie in a peaceful way.

Still, they had several more hours to kill before he could use his porting abilities again. Kyana wanted to explore the island further in hopes of finding a hint that someone else had been here. She had her mind so set on finding the key's trail that he hadn't been able to make her listen to reason. The chances of finding anything more than they had were slim. They would have picked up something by now.

As they plowed their way through even more brush, daybreak was fast approaching. Kyana had refused to break even though Ryker had made the suggestion several times, worried that the human-born Witch wasn't up to so much vigorous hiking. She'd impressed him, though. Hadn't complained once, with the exception of the moment she'd walked through a spiderweb and had shrieked loud enough to wake Cronos from his permanent nap.

Haven sat on a fallen log and pulled a bottle of water from her bag. "The sun's going to be up in ten. We need to get you ready, I'm trying a new potion." She stirred the pinkish brew with her finger. "It's full of adaptogen herbs and Reishi mushrooms, and those little blue bits are Labradorite crystal flakes. You shouldn't taste them, though. I put enough persimmons in this sucker to hide the metallic taste."

Curious, Ryker took a step closer, sniffed the now pink water. It didn't smell like persimmons. In fact, skunk ass might be a closer description. "What's that for?"

"This should keep her strength up longer *and* keep her from being so drained tonight."

He was about to ask why she needed a potion for any of that, but Kyana took the bottle, toasted Haven with it, and downed the contents. "Nope, not enough persimmons," she gasped, setting the bottle at her feet. "Why don't I get any of the strawberry potions?"

"Those are mine." Haven grinned. "Besides, strawberry isn't strong enough to hide the bitterness of those herbs. I was hoping persimmons would be."

"What about licorice?" When they both turned to stare at Ryker, he added, "Ky likes raki. Anise has a strong licorice taste. It could hide the taste of just about anything, I'd think."

Though Kyana didn't look like she much appreciated his butting in, Haven offered a soft smile. "I'll try that for her next time."

Kyana grabbed her bag and slung it over her shoulder. "I'm going to change." She walked toward the thick brush surrounding their clearing and offered one last glare from over her shoulder. "I'd tell you not to look, but I'm sure that wouldn't be a problem anyway."

He sighed. She still thought he wasn't interested. Probably better that way, but irritating as hell with all her snide comments.

He watched her make her way to a short bush that was only tall enough to hide her rear end. Great. He should really turn away, but as she pulled off her jacket and tank top, he couldn't muster the strength to look away. Her pale white back glistened with the day's perspiration, making her glow like an iridescent goddess. Slender, well-toned muscles rippled down her arms and back, her waist diving inward just where it was meant to, giving her an hourglass shape that had him growing hard in an instant.

If she offered herself to him now as she had so long ago, would he be strong enough to refuse? Not likely. Not with the itch consuming his fingers as they begged to trace the path from her neck to the small of her back where the rise of her ass peeked out from the top of her hiding spot.

"Want a napkin for your drool?"

At the sound of Haven's voice, Ryker jumped like a thirteen-year-old caught with a *Playboy* magazine and turned away. "Just guarding her back."

"Her back*side* more like." Haven's smile made Ryker's cheeks burn. "You like her, but I won't tell. Whatever it is about the two of you that makes you think you have to keep hating each other is hard to watch, though. You should just fornicate and get it out of your systems."

"Fornicate?" Ryker snorted. "No one's used that word since Lincoln was president." The sound of the bushes rustling caught his attention again, but he refused to look. "Besides, it's not like that with us. She's Vampyre. I'm . . . not."

"When was your last relationship, Ryker?"

The question caught him so off-guard he answered without worrying about how personal it was. "Five years ago."

Simone had been lovely, patient, kind. But sadly, he hadn't thought about her in years.

"And how long did it last?"

He shrugged. "Nearly two years."

Haven nodded. "I thought so."

"Thought what?"

"You're probably some sort of serial monogamist. That's why you turned Kyana down. You know she's not."

He raked his hand through his hair and narrowed his gaze on the spot Kyana had been standing moments ago. She was gone. "No, she certainly isn't. She likes to play."

"Playing can be fun. You should consider trying it. Oh, here she comes." Haven pointed at the bushes, which were twitching like they were having a seizure. "Try not to stare, okay? And remember, she's not a big dog, she's a wolf. Treat her like one."

Haven offered him a bright smile before heading toward Kyana. "I'm going to grab her clothes. Be right back."

He saw Kyana's muzzle first. The long ebony snout peeked out of the brush, nostrils flaring as she breathed in the scents around her. As she eased into the open, Ryker sucked in his breath. She was beautiful. Glossy fur; clear, sharp eyes. Her legs moved in determined strides, flesh stretching over toned muscles, full of nothing but grace. He'd seen Lychen before and had never given them much thought. But Kyana . . . was stunning.

"You're staring," Haven said, carrying a folded bundle of clothes and tucking them inside Kyana's satchel.

He cleared his throat and shifted his gaze so that he could watch her from the corner of his eye. Kyana sat on her haunches beside Haven. When Haven absentmindedly reached out to scratch behind Kyana's ear, Kyana bared her teeth. "See. Wolf, not dog. Sorry, Kyana. Just give her a minute. Her eyes have to adjust."

Ryker nodded and tried to watch without staring. He couldn't help but be curious, couldn't help but wonder if it was painful for her to shift so drastically from one form to another. She wouldn't appreciate his concern. He pulled a bottle of water from his bag and started for the woods. "I'll give her a bit of space."

"She thanks you."

"You can understand her in this form?"

Haven laughed. "Not even a little, but I speak woman no matter what form they're in. She'd appreciate the privacy, I'm sure."

He moved toward the thicket they'd cut their way through earlier. "Ten minutes good?"

Haven nodded.

He felt Kyana's stare and turned to see her eyeing his tattered bag. Would she dare? Judging by the way she watched him, yeah, she would. He went back into the clearing and slung the bag over his shoulder. "Just in case."

"Just in case what?" Haven called out.

"Just in case she decides to express her dislike of me by relieving herself on my belongings."

Haven's laughter followed him into the trees.

For several hours, Kyana led the way through more overgrown trails. Ryker offered no suggestions this time, knowing she was in her element. This was what made her the best tracer the Order had. The Lychen in her would find it if there was anything to be found.

He could tell by her intermittent pauses and huffs that she would have preferred to do this hunt alone. They were slowing her down, as she could maneuver over and under the branches Ryker and Haven had to either duck or climb. If he hadn't needed to make sure Haven didn't fall behind, Ryker could have kept up with no problem, but as it was, he was forced to maintain a human pace.

So far, they hadn't found a single thing useful in telling them who might have taken the key or where it might be now. Hell, they hadn't found *anything* since finding Cronos's bones. Not an animal or a human seemed to exist on this island any longer. The Order had stopped using this as a penal isle centuries ago, but still it made no sense. It wouldn't matter what realm they were in, animals should have existed here.

Once they caught up to Kyana again, she set off to explore the next area just outside their view. She bounded over a fallen log and skidded to a stop. She turned in a slow circle, taking in her surroundings. Not exactly a clearing, but the grass had been crushed, small trees uprooted, and bones obscured the dirt.

Ryker watched as Kyana nosed the bones closest to her, trying to keep hold of whatever scent had caught her attention.

Haven's eyes widened as she gripped Ryker's shoulder. "I am *not* walking in there."

Moving back to the felled tree, Kyana nipped Haven's hand. Haven jerked back and stuffed her hands into her pockets. "Forget it, Kyana. You either find me a way around or I'll wait here."

"I'm going to check and see how far the bones are scattered." Ryker jumped over the log. "Then I'll come back to get you."

He followed Kyana through the mass grave, examining bones as he went. "What is her deal with bones? She said she could hold her own but freaks every time there's a body of some sort lying around."

Kyana growled low in her throat.

"Yeah, I know you can't talk to me, but . . ." He picked up a skull and examined it closely. It looked like a gorilla skull, or the skull of some other really large primate. "You should see if one of the Ancients has a spell that will allow you to talk in Lychen form. It would make things a lot easier. Ever watch Scooby Doo? You kind of remind me of Scrappy."

This time her growl was much deeper, like she'd take great pleasure in biting him.

"Okay, I'll stop." Ryker chuckled. "Looks like we know why there are no animals around." He held the skull beneath her snout. "It's been bleached clean, so it's been months maybe since these were left here. Can you catch a scent of what might have devoured it?"

Kyana hesitated, then sniffed the skull from every angle. When she was done, she huffed and sat down. He took that to mean she'd found nothing. "Was afraid it might be too clean." He dropped the bone, stood, and brushed his hands on his jeans. "Let's see how far this goes."

Together, they moved through the thicket a couple dozen feet. As quickly as it had started, the debris ended. There was something seriously wrong on this island. He couldn't put his finger on what the danger was, but he only had to look around at the scattered bones to know something lurked in the shadows.

"I'd feel better if we all stuck together. Wait here, I'll go get Haven."

Once Ryker lifted Haven into his arms to carry her over the bones, Kyana pushed through a narrow opening in the underbrush and entered another clearing. Ryker and Haven followed, pleased to see this opening was much larger than the one they'd found last night. Structures that looked on the verge of collapse littered the clearing. Kyana lifted her head and inhaled.

Ryker didn't need any Lychen blood to smell what she'd picked up on. Death. Worse, even, than the foul stench of the River Styx. She released a low howl, bringing Haven and Ryker to her side as she turned in a slow circle, following the gust of wind.

"What is that smell?" Haven cupped her hand over her nose, her eyes locked on Kyana.

Kyana pressed her nose deeper into the soil, apparently inhaling enough dirt to make her shoot off half a dozen doggie sneezes like miniature gunshots.

"Is it coming from under us?" he asked her, not sure how to read her if she bothered to answer.

She growled though, and it sounded to him like an affirmation. When she started digging furiously, he knelt to help her.

Together they dug through inches of grass and gnarled roots beneath. The more they dug, the stronger the scent became. When they hit concrete, Kyana sat down on her haunches and howled in victory.

"We've got something," he said, glancing over his shoulder to beckon Haven closer. He leaned back so the Witch could see the rusted hinge they'd revealed. It was attached to a trap door smack in the center of the clearing. It took Ryker a few attempts to open it, but while the hinges and latch were rusted, there was no squeak when it finally popped open. It had been used frequently and recently. A gush of warm air whooshed out of the deep hole and he staggered backward.

"Dear God. The stink is even worse down there." Haven cupped her hand over her mouth and nose again. He couldn't blame her. His own eyes were burning and watering like he'd just been Maced.

It smelled like a thousand freshly mutilated carcasses coated in rotting meat and vegetation.

"That," Ryker said, a racking cough bending him over his knees, "is the smell of death."

He'd smelled some foul things in his life, but this topped even the burning pyres set up around St. Augustine to dispose of the bodies that littered the streets. Beside him, Kyana whined. He could only imagine how her acute sense of smell was reacting to such vileness.

Ryker picked up a rock and tossed it down the hole, counting as it fell, and fell . . . and fell. Finally, there was a faint splash and thud. It had landed.

On his hands and knees again, his nose tucked in the collar of his shirt, Ryker felt around the ledge of the hole, backed up, and brushed off his hands. "No ladder. There's no way down other than jumping." He looked at Haven. "You'll have to stay here."

"Oh, I don't think so. I've seen *Lost.* There's no way I'm going to wait around for the mysterious polar bear to come out of hiding and eat me."

Ryker pushed himself to his feet. "I don't know the math for how fast a stone falls is equal to so many feet, but I do know it sums up to that being one deep-ass hole. The fall would break your kneecaps, or your neck. Depending on how graceful a faller you are." He turned to Kyana. "I know you could make that jump without problem in your normal state, but how 'bout in Lychen?"

She gave a low bark.

"Good." Without giving Haven time to prepare, he scooped her into his arms. "Hold on tight. We're going down."

He pushed off the ground and leaped into the dark, unknown cesspool.

Chapter Nine

When she hit the bottom of the hole, Kyana landed just behind Ryker, sending dirty, foul-smelling water in every direction, drenching her coat. She shook her neck to make sure the Illusion Charm still hung around it. When it thudded against her chest, she shifted. Disgusted by the rank water on her bare flesh, she stood naked and shivering behind Ryker and Haven and gave the charm a moment to work its magic so, to them, she'd appear to have on clothes.

"I can't believe you did that!" Haven smacked Ryker's shoulder. "Don't you put me down. I'm not walking in this filth."

Ryker set her on her feet anyway. "You said you weren't staying behind."

Haven buried her face in her shirt. "Yeah, which meant one of you should have stayed up there with me."

That never would have worked. Kyana wouldn't sit by while Ryker explored the hole. And he wouldn't let her go alone. Stalemate. Ignoring the tirade, Kyana scanned the area. The water barely reached her knees.

Bones floated on the murky surface, much like the ones they'd stumbled across above. However, these were accompanied by carcasses—fresh and large, bloated and decomposing. She moved slowly forward, trying not to disturb the filthy water any more than necessary.

Her breathing as shallow as possible, Kyana scanned the walls. It took her brain a second to realize that she was looking at dirt and tree roots. Through the darkness, she could see a fork ahead, and paths leading north and south. It looked like some sort of crude tunnel system.

Ryker stopped beside her, his mouth and nose hidden beneath the collar of his shirt. His gaze raked over her. Up and down, a slow smile stretching his mouth wide. Kyana looked down. Though she was naked, she could see leather and cotton covering her body. What was he staring at?

Kyana continued on to the fork, and stopped at the intersection. No light or sound drifted from either opening. With the rankness surrounding them, Kyana had no hope of picking up the scent of anything else.

Only one way to find answers. Kyana turned to the left. "You two check out the right fork. If you find something, yell." She'd barely moved a foot when Ryker's hand bit into her arm, stopping her progress.

With a hiss, she faced him.

His silver eyes swirled. "We're not going in there."

Like hell she wasn't. She shook off his grasp. "This tunnel could hold the secret to what happened to the key." It didn't matter if she had to go it alone, she wasn't turning back until she'd at least checked it out.

"Don't fight me on this, please," he said, his voice

barely above a whisper. "Whatever lurks in here is pure evil."

How the hell do you know? she wanted to scream at him. But she didn't need to. Now that she was still, and wasn't thinking about what she might find, she could feel it too. It settled around her, pressing in on her like a physical being. The hair at her nape stood on end. Whatever was down here, it was unnatural. More unnatural even than Kyana's screwed-up genetics.

Still, she couldn't leave this island without some hint as to where that key might have gone. This was the only thing they'd found that had given her any hope. She turned back to face Ryker, intent on telling him to take Haven and go back—that she'd go it alone. But the look on his face froze her in place. His normally tanned skin had grown so pale, he practically glowed in the stark black tunnel. He leaned against the muddied wall, clutching his chest, his features twisted and distorted. He looked like he was having a heart attack.

Forgetting everything other than the fact that Ryker looked ready to croak, Kyana rushed to his side. She gripped his shoulder, shaking him, trying to get him to snap out of whatever had taken hold of him.

His eyes fluttered open.

"Are you okay? What's happening?"

He panted, and when she took his arm, the trembling muscle beneath his skin sent a tremor of fear through her.

"Talk to me."

"Don't know." He bowed his head, sank lower against the wall. "Can't breathe."

Worry had her reaching for his pocket. "Is it the ring? Get rid of the damned conduit."

He shook his head and grabbed her hand, a drop of perspiration slipping onto his nose. "Not the ring. It's . . . this place, I think."

She tugged his arm, pulling him back a few feet to stand beneath the opening above. The minute he stepped into the ventilated area, he gulped in a huge amount of air, and color slowly painted his cheeks. Kyana backed up, not willing to chance a stray ray of sun poking through the opening, but kept her eyes on him.

"I'm okay," Ryker said. He released his death grip on his shirt, flexed his fingers, and bent over his knees. With his head that close to the water, she was afraid he'd suffocate again.

"Look at me, Ryker."

He lifted his head. His eyes had gone red. They were doing that cloudy, swirly thing again. "I'm all right, Kyana."

Pointing to the tunnels behind her, he shook his head. "I can't go down there. I don't know what it is, but something . . . There's something in there that's evil, Ky. And not Dark Breed evil. Evil enough that the mere nearness of them was about to kill me."

"I don't get it. Dark Breeds *are* evil, but you fight them, no problem."

"We have to get off this island."

"Go. I'll be up in a few minutes—"

"You're not going in there either!"

He hadn't yelled the demand. More like roared it. Kyana jerked, surprised by how important this seemed to him. "It didn't affect me, Ryker. You can't expect me to leave this place empty-handed."

"We're not empty-handed. We have the ring."

"Kyana, maybe you should listen to him," Haven insisted, trying to pull Kyana to the opening. "I really want us out of here."

Kyana pushed Haven at Ryker. "She doesn't need to be down here either. Take her with you." The red of his eyes deepened to near maroon as he glared at her. "I'm leaving. I'm taking Haven and we're gone. If you want a port out of here, you'll come now."

She narrowed her eyes. "You'd leave me here?"

"In a heartbeat."

She bit her tongue, ready to give him a piece of her mind regarding his ultimatum. But there wasn't time for another argument. "One hour. Take Haven, get back to camp, and if I'm not back in one hour, start your circle without me."

"Ky, don't!"

But his words echoed behind her, and she strode into the shadows.

She didn't look back until she reached the fork. The emotions on Ryker's face filtered from rage to concern. Finally, he nodded. "I can't go in there. It will kill me. That means I can't go in there to stop you either. Or to save you, Ky. One hour. Don't make me leave you here." With that, he wrapped Haven in his arms, knelt, and shoved off with his feet. As Haven screamed for Kyana to come with them, Ryker's body clung to the sides of the vertical tunnel like Spider-Man and he leaped from side to side until he'd pulled them through the opening.

"Get your butt up here right now! No, we're not leaving her down there. Kyana!"

Haven's voice faded. Kyana guessed Ryker had dragged her away from the opening. Haven would be safe. Ryker would protect her. With a sour feeling in her stomach, Kyana turned back to the fork, checking both tunnels. North or South? South had always been good for her.

Her senses on overload, she moved slowly. Most of the forks she'd come to were caving in or completely blocked. She stayed on the main branch, checking the dirt, water, and darkness for any signs of life. There weren't even any spiders in this hellhole. No beetles mucking around in the mud. No worms to be seen anywhere.

She'd been in some pretty nasty places before. Crypts and tombs, graveyards and mausoleums. Never had she been creeped out the way she was now. Her instincts told her to turn back and follow Ryker out of here. But she'd yet to fail at a job, and returning to Artemis empty-handed felt exactly like failure.

Pushing forward, she came to a wide chamber flanked on either side by narrow hallways that looked impassable for anyone over four feet tall. In the center, a mound of dirt and debris formed a tiny island in the pool of murky, stagnant water. Kyana lowered herself closer to the ground in preparation to defend herself, then climbed onto the island. Fresh air wafted in from somewhere. She didn't know if it was imagined because she was no longer walking in shit or if there was another entrance nearby.

She dug through the debris highest on the mound.

Clay pottery. Cooking utensils. A crude comb. Had whatever lurked in the shadows killed the inhabitants? Something was still here. She could hear it breathing.

The scent of danger clogged whatever fresh air she'd imagined, and her skin tingled as if a million eyes watched her from every direction.

Okay, time to bail. She wasn't taking on whatever this was alone on their turf. Her gaze surfed the dripping ceiling, searching for the source of her unease and finding nothing. She wanted to back slowly from the room, but not knowing which direction the danger was coming from, she wasn't sure which way to face.

As if sensing her pending retreat, the shadows moved. Kyana charged off in the direction from which she'd come. This time, she didn't take it slow. She summoned her Vampyric strength to push her way through the water, leaping and bounding toward the exit.

When she stood beneath the opening, she skidded to a halt. She strained her neck, trying to see the sun. Eerie, skin-crawling grunts were closing in, accompanied by countless slaps of water splashing in her direction. She'd have to risk it.

Unlike Ryker, she didn't need to climb her way out of the hole. Pressing herself as low to the ground as possible, she jumped and made the vertical ascension gracefully, landing just outside the opening before falling to her knees. Dusk and exhaustion greeted her. She didn't have time to rejoice over not being deep-fried. The creatures below were close enough now that she could smell them. The stench of shit hadn't come from actual fecal matter. It had come from whatever was hunting her.

She swung around, frantically grabbing for the hatch, desperate to lock whatever was chasing her inside. She slammed the lid closed, but before the lock could catch, the hatch exploded off its hinges. It soared overhead, clattering into the trees, removing all hopes of locking the beasts inside. She caught the faintest glimpse of a white hand protruding from the opening before she was on her feet again and running back toward the clearing. She leaped over fallen logs, forced her way through crude paths. Vines and branches whipped at her face, her arms, her legs. Thorns ripped at her breasts and sliced at her thighs. Illusion Charm or no, sheer determination not to die bare-ass naked kept her moving.

"Ryker!" She hoped her voice would carry on the wind.

Only the snarls of her pursuers answered.

Kyana risked a quick glance over her shoulder. There had to be dozens behind her, but they were moving in a blur, making it impossible to get a good look at them. They moved through the trees, trying to surround her. They were strong. And fast. And blindingly white.

It had been too long since she'd last potioned up. She didn't have the strength to call on her Vamp power again and sprint. Shifting had drained her resources. She'd have to outrun them the old-fashioned way.

"Ryker!" She had to be close. It felt like she'd been running for hours. How far had they traveled?

"Ky?" Her name was barely more than a whisper.

Relief made her stumble. She managed to keep her feet. "Get us the hell out of here!"

"He's starting his incantation," Haven shouted, her voice louder. She was close. "Hurry!"

Using the last of her energies, she sprinted through a thicket and into the clearing. "Go go go," Kyana gasped.

"Keep them off me," Ryker said. "I'm going as fast as I can."

"What is it?" Haven pressed a vial into Kyana's hand.

Kyana downed the potion, then grabbed Haven's arm and moved her closer to Ryker.

"You're about to see for yourself." The words were no sooner out of her mouth when the creatures broke into the clearing, a swarm of white blurs spilling out of the trees and onto the beach. "If they get by me, keep them off Ryker so he can finish his spell. I want out of here."

Haven handed Kyana one of her daggers and gripped the other in her fist. "You and me both."

Kyana charged into the middle of the clearing, drawing attention to her. Bodies flew at her in every direction, still too fast to get a good glimpse at what they were. Hands pulled at her arms, her legs, her hair, threatening to overpower her before Haven's potion had unleashed its potency. Without the protection of her real leather attire, she was far more vulnerable than she cared to be. Every inch of her skin was exposed to their attacks. She lost count of the bodies she sliced at. It seemed for each one that fell, two more took its place.

"Hurry up!" Kyana yelled at Ryker, retreating to keep from being completely surrounded.

"Two minutes."

His voice sounded so weak, it drew Kyana's attention. He knelt on the sand, one hand gripping his chest.

All color had drained from his face, and his breaths were so shallow she could barely see his chest move. The spasms that shook his body hindered his attempts to draw his circle. Was he going to be able to pull off his mojo with these things so close to him?

A fist connected with her jaw, pulling her back into the fight. The force of the blow nearly brought her to her knees. She staggered backward, tumbled to the ground, and rolled back onto her feet.

"We don't have two bloody minutes!"

Kyana felt something at her back. She spun, dagger raised. Haven held up her hand. "I've got your back. Together we can buy him a little time."

It was good in theory, but Kyana doubted the two of them could buy Ryker more than a few seconds. They were outnumbered and overpowered. She'd never fought anything so fast or strong before. What the hell were these things?

She didn't have the time to ponder the question before the next wave rushed them. She sliced and stabbed and punched, but still they came. She risked a glance at Ryker, silently pleading with him to hurry. His gaze caught hers. His lips moved in a blur as he spoke his spell.

Haven's scream of pain pulled Kyana's attention back to the fight. "You piece of garbage," Haven shouted, slicing the throat of the demon who'd had the nerve to strike her.

Kyana tried to move them closer to Ryker, but the circle was closing in.

"Let's go. Let's go. Let's go," Haven pleaded.

As Kyana retreated, something grabbed her hair and yanked her back a few feet toward the trees. Thick, rubbery wings cocooned her chest, creeping up her throat to squeeze with enough force to snap her neck. She kicked out, struggling against the pressure, but it was like being trapped in a spider's web. She was being lowered to the ground. If she didn't act fast, she was going to become dinner.

She thrust her dagger between the webbing covering her eyes and sliced through the latexlike flesh. The thing howled and released her, splattering Kyana with black blood and sending her stumbling into Haven.

"It's done. Run to me and hold on tight!"

Kyana grabbed Haven's arm, took three running steps, and dove at Ryker. One of the winged things grabbed Kyana's ankle. She wrapped her arms around Ryker's waist and held on for dear life. In a flash of blinding light and ancient words, they left the island behind.

She squeezed her eyes tight and prayed the rush wouldn't affect his targeting. She wanted to be back in the familiar and wanted to get there in one piece.

They landed with a thud. Every bone in her body groaned in protest at the impact of butt on stone. Kyana hung on to Ryker, waiting for him to say the words to free her from the blindness he'd cast to protect them during porting.

"*Libero*," Ryker mumbled, releasing them and letting his hands fall to his sides. His voice was strained, and Kyana reached out and pressed her hand to his back. He was shaking, trembling, his breath no smoother than it had been when they'd been surrounded on the island. "Gods, what *were* those things?"

A low growl spurred Kyana's eyes to snap open. The face that stared back at her wasn't Ryker's or Haven's. It was inhuman and milky white and drooling down her imaginary tank top.

Chapter Ten

S omething between fascination and sheer terror
held Kyana captive. She'd never seen a creature
like the one kneeling over her now, and was certainly glad she hadn't gotten a good look when she'd
been fighting them. She wasn't sure she would have
been as quick on her feet. Pure evil glistened in the
creature's near-white eyes. It wasn't until she heard
Ryker's gasp for breath, felt his body seize, that she
reacted. Drawing back her fist, she punched the thing
in the face. It slumped over unconscious, pinning her
to the ground.

She kicked her legs free of its weight, grabbed Ryker
by the arm, and dragged him to the other side of what
appeared to be a cave. Ryker must have been in agony
during the port, because they'd obviously gone off-
course. This wasn't the Fates' cave or any other place
Below that she recognized.

She grabbed Haven's hand, pulling her to her feet
and over to Ryker's side. Kyana knelt beside him. The

color was coming back to his face and his breathing had eased.

Relief flooded her.

He sat up, resting against the wall. "What happened?"

Kyana sat next to him and eyed their guest. "We made a friend."

"Friend?"

Haven pointed to where the creature lay. "What is that thing?"

Hell if Kyana knew.

"Evil," Ryker finally answered.

Leathery skin clung to its body, wrapping around what looked like nothing more than a deformed skeleton, and at the same time barely seemed to cover its vitals. Rubbery wings, much like a bat's, jutted from its back. She swallowed the bile that rose in her throat at the sight of those wings, remembering the putrid smell of them wrapped around her face.

"Yeah, well that doesn't tell us *what* it is," Haven pointed out, her gaze shifting to take in their surroundings. "Or where we are."

"We're Below. I think."

"You think?" Kyana shoved her hair out of her face. "We have a fourth member of our party that I don't particularly want to travel with any longer. We need more than an *I think*."

"Considering the circumstances we were in, be glad I got you here with all your fingers." His gaze fell to her chest. "And all your other body parts."

"That's the least of our concerns," Haven said, putting an end to the brewing fight. "We're stuck in a cave with that thing, with no way to restrain it for twenty-four hours."

"I can fix that." Kyana stood and searched for her dagger, cursing when she couldn't locate it. She'd been using it when they'd ported. With a sigh of irritation, she asked Haven, "You still have my other dagger?"

Haven still gripped the borrowed weapon. Kyana took it and walked cautiously to the creature's side. "Don't look. This could get gross."

She raised her dagger, pressed her foot to the beast's belly, and bent forward to sever its head.

"No!" Ryker's shout threw Kyana off-balance. Her weight shifted forward and she found herself nose to, well, hole-in-the-face with the foul-smelling creature.

"No?" She rolled off the creature, but didn't move too far away. "No *what*?"

"Don't kill it. We'll find a way to keep it submissive and away from me, but alive. It might be the only link we have to what happened on that island and where that key might have gone."

Oh. Right. She supposed this was what Artie had meant when she'd been afraid Kyana might go off half-cocked. Disappointment curdled in her belly as she walked away, trying to scrub any stench from her face that might have rubbed off on her.

"Oh no. I vote for killing it!" Haven said, her eyes dancing with something resembling lunacy. "Seriously."

Her shrill voice had chills slithering down Kyana's spine. In an effort to calm Haven, Kyana smiled. "Don't worry about it. Beating it senseless every time it moves will keep me entertained until we can get out of here. And look on the bright side—"

"There's a bright side?"

Kyana grinned. "Not really. Just wanted to make you feel better."

"Very funny. How can you joke when we don't even know where the heck we are?"

Ryker rested his hand on Haven's shoulder. "We're Below."

His reassuring tone didn't have its usual effect. "How can you possibly know that?"

He tried to smile, but to Kyana it looked more like a pain-filled grimace. "I can sense we're home. As soon as I can function I'll get us out of here."

"And what about that?" Kyana jabbed her thumb toward the unconscious psychopath.

Ryker looked at Kyana. "I can't be near that thing. I'll have to lead from a distance."

Great. Kyana grinned at Haven. "Looks like it's up to the two of us to haul its nasty, smelly ass out of here."

They'd barely managed to tote their captive the length of a football field through the dark tunnel system when Ryker stopped and held up his hand. Kyana didn't need an explanation. She could also hear what had stopped their progress. Footsteps. A lot of them.

The low moans and cries that had accompanied them seemed to stop long enough to listen, as well. She didn't know where they were, but those cries sounded very much like those of the lost souls beneath the River Styx. She dropped the creature she'd privately nick-named Icky and joined Ryker, peering over his shoulder to stare down the long hall, watching and waiting to see whom the footsteps belonged to.

"Who is it?" Haven asked, stretching onto her toes to peer over Kyana's shoulder.

As the familiar scent of ambrosia and ginger curled around Kyana's nose, she smiled. "Artie. Damn, she's good."

Sure enough, a moment later, a trio of women came into view, led by Artemis and her three enormous hounds, Dumb, Dumber, and Dumbest.

"What happened, Kyana?" Artie called out, gliding down the hall with her quiver strapped to her back, sword tethered to her hip. She made no noise, unlike the sorry Nymphs beside her whose footsteps were far too bold for their dainty stature.

"Ryker threw us off-course!" Haven volunteered, looking far more chipper than she had for the last hour.

Kyana shot her friend a glare. "He was in a lot of pain."

Artemis scowled. Her gaze traveled over Kyana and disapproval marred her beautiful face. "The Oracles saw his death. I was a second away from making Ares port me to you when he sensed your return." At the doorway now, Artie eyed Ryker. "Are you injured?"

"Not injured." He was still pale, still not breathing normally, but at least he didn't look like he was having a stroke anymore. "Just . . . I don't know."

Artemis followed his gaze and landed it squarely on their sleeping, gurgling captive behind them. When she moved closer to inspect Icky, she seized her throat and stumbled backward, clutching at the wall.

"Abomination," she gasped, backing from the room.

When Kyana turned and found the goddess on her knees, panic set in. She'd *never* seen Artemis show an ounce of fear before. Whatever their captive was, it was evil enough to bring a goddess to her knees. *That* was why it had affected Ryker and not Haven or Kyana. He was half god.

What kind of unholy hell were they dealing with?

She helped Artemis to her feet, suddenly wishing she hadn't listened to Ryker and had murdered the blasted thing. "It came back with us. A slew of them attacked when we were trying to get off the island."

"And you let it live?" She shot a glance at Ryker. "Get out here, you fool. You will die if you remain close to it."

She lightly nudged Haven out of Ryker's way so he could safely step farther down the hall. They had to find a way to get the creature somewhere else, someplace they could question it or . . . do nasty little experiments to it. Maybe impregnate it or probe it or whatever aliens did to humans.

"We didn't kill Icky because we thought he might be useful in figuring out what happened to the key," she said.

"Icky?" Haven asked.

Kyana pointed to the nasty creature. "Have to call him *something.*"

"Does it speak?" Artemis asked.

"No, but it gurgles. A lot. And makes this horrible little squealing noise like a pig."

Artemis's amber eyes narrowed. "And yet, you wish to question it."

"Hey." Haven unwisely pointed a finger at the goddess. "When I wanted to join the Order, Lachesis performed that Jedi mind trick thing on me to see if I was honest, to read my intentions. Why can't she do that?"

A confused look contorted Artie's face. "Jedi mind trick?"

"Don't ask," Kyana said. "But Haven's right. I've seen Lachesis question people without actual questions. Couldn't she do the same here?"

"When Lachesis reads people, she is reading the souls placed in those bodies. Not their minds or hearts. She knows those souls because she's been nurturing them since Clotho found them homes."

"Okay, then, let her read this fuc—this thing's soul."

A dark brown eyebrow rose in a comical fashion as Artemis gave Kyana her first glimpse of a goddess eye roll. "Kyana, that thing doesn't *have* a soul. It's what makes it impossible for me to be near it."

"Evil. Like I said." Ryker turned to look at the white beast and shuddered. Kyana couldn't help but do the same.

"Come," Artemis said, turning and gesturing for her Nymphs to fall into line. "Let's get him safely put away before he harms another of us. And Kyana . . ." Artemis turned and once again, her gaze scanned Kyana's frame. "Put on some clothes."

Kyana felt her chin hit the floor. "But . . . how can you—"

"I'm a goddess. I can see through most Illusion Charms." She nodded at Haven. "Nice work, by the way."

Haven grinned. Kyana's ears began to ring as her eyes fell to Ryker. "Wh-what about demigods?"

Artemis shrugged. "I'm not one. You'd have to ask him." She jutted her chin toward Ryker, and Kyana's chest squeezed painfully as his face lit up and a wicked grin painted his too-happy lips.

"I hate you," she said, and made a mad dash for her bag and the clothes inside.

Chapter Eleven

With a torturous amount of whining and complaining from Haven, they managed to tote Icky to a magically charged prison cell Below. Kyana could have called for Farrel and Crag, but they would have taken too long to arrive. Besides, she enjoyed watching Haven squirm. If she'd listened and stayed home as Kyana had asked, she wouldn't have had to tote nasty little Icky through Below.

A sentinel had been sent to retrieve the Fates in hopes that they could read the beast's mind to see if it knew anything about the key, but once the Sisters had been told what had been brought back from the island, they'd refused to come. Now Kyana and Haven, along with Artie and Ryker, watched from outside the cell as Icky rushed the magically charged gate only to be sent back across the small quarters each time the electricity pulsed through its bony body.

"What do we do now?" Kyana asked, quickly bored with the show.

"Since it doesn't speak, our options are limited," Artemis said from her spot closest to the exit.

"Can't you force the Fates to obey orders so Lachesis can read him?"

Ryker frowned. "You can't force people to do things your way. If they don't believe they can assist, then they have a right to refuse. It's called free will."

"*Free will* is overrated," Kyana mumbled. She looked at Haven. "Do you know of a spell that can make the mute speak?"

"No, and it wouldn't work even if I did. I don't think that thing's been taught a language. And there's no spell to do that either, so don't ask."

Kyana studied the creature. There had to be a way to read into its mind. To see its past. To discover if it knew where the key was or who had taken it.

"What about an Oracle?"

"What about them?" all three asked in unison.

"Couldn't they somehow read Icky's past?"

"Oracles see the future, Ky."

She huffed. "Well, they're not too good at that either. They should think about expanding their horizons and learning a new skill."

"Disrespecting them isn't going to get us a solution," Artemis said.

Kyana paced the small confines of the antechamber. There had to be a way, she just needed to find it. She froze mid-step. There *was* one option left to consider, but the very thought turned her stomach.

Kyana faced Ryker. "You have fangs. If you ingested a little of its blood—"

"I'm not a Vamp, Ky, and besides, it would kill me."

Oh yeah. Couldn't have that. "What if I went in and got you some blood?"

"It would kill me quicker." He sighed. "Kyana, when I bit you, I was in your head for that moment. I couldn't see your history the way Vampyre can. All I'd see from that thing is its fury for this instant in time. *I'm* not the one you're looking for."

Ryker's gaze locked with hers. He didn't voice his knowledge that she was the perfect candidate to attempt such a task, but she could read it in his eyes. She could also see his compassion. He wouldn't draw attention to her Vampyric skills, which gave her the ability to drink in a person's memories when she fed, but he was sure as hell hinting about them.

"But you could do it, Kyana." Haven said what Ryker wouldn't. "Your skills will let you pull in Icky's memories. Then you can relay what you see to us."

Kyana grimaced, mentally impaling her friend's heart with her glare. "I don't want to be the one who bites the damned thing." With a heavy sigh, Kyana nodded to the sentinel closest to her. "Release the gate."

He did as Kyana ordered and quickly backed away. Artie and Ryker stepped back also, but Haven ducked inside. "Just in case it tries to eat you."

Kyana handed Haven a dagger. "Thanks."

Icky's stench nearly gagged her, but if Haven could tolerate it, Kyana wouldn't complain. The minute she moved closer to it, Icky scampered across the cell, bared its fangs, and hissed like a deflating balloon. Kyana leaped straight up and over the creature's head, squeezing between Icky and the rock wall. Before it could turn on her, she wrapped her arm around its throat and pressed its back to her chest, locking it in place. Her fangs sank into Icky's jugular, and it howled for mercy as the first drops of sulfuric blood spilled onto Kyana's tongue.

Her brain turned to a curtain of fog and she could no longer see the inside of Icky's cell. The high of feeding made her moan, made her forget the foul taste and drink until the fog lifted and the images inside Icky's head became clear. The island. A tall, handsome man with ebony hair that reached his slender waist. A coven of other creatures who looked just like Icky, bowing to a group who looked like the human Vampyre Kyana had come to know.

She searched in Icky's mind for its breed's name, but found nothing. Only the hollow, haunting whisper that declared *it* was a *she* and her kind *had* no name, created when Vampyre bred with Vampyre, then left to die when their usefulness expired. *This* was why Vampyre weren't meant to breed with each other.

Darkness. Humidity. The dank caves Kyana had traveled within. Pain seared through Kyana's brain as she watched the long-haired man feed from Icky's children. He raped them, bred from them more children to fill his stocks. The grotesquely horrific scene nearly forced Kyana to pull away. But she held on, dug her teeth in deeper.

Flashes of Vampyre feeding off the exiled prisoners, breeding with them, creating more like Icky and her family. These monstrous creatures were the first Vampyre. Kyana's origin. In a sick sense, her family. She gagged as the thick blood coated her throat. It rushed so quickly, she couldn't swallow fast enough to drink it all in. The image of the long-haired man dying, whispering promises to the beasts he'd created.

Then, Kyana herself. Creeping into Icky's family lair. Snooping where she didn't belong. The last image Kyana saw was of herself seizing hold of Ryker's shoulder, and then the blinding light of Ryker's port consumed her. Icky fell limp in her arms. She was dead.

"What did you see?" Ryker's soothing voice filled the chamber. He looked as though he wanted to enter the cell, but wouldn't chance it. Even dead, Icky might have posed a threat to the gods.

Haven took Kyana's hand, helped her step over Icky's body, and guided her from the cell. Kyana pushed out of Haven's grasp, raced to the corner, and expelled the near-black blood from her belly.

When she collected herself, she quietly told them of Icky's past, of how she'd come to be. "Cronos did this."

She knew in her soul that the long-haired man had been Cronos.

"Did you see the key?"

Kyana shook her head. "No, just Cronos's determination not to die. His disregard for the children he created. I'm not sure why, but I'm certain the key was never there." She looked at Ryker. "He promised to return to them . . . when he was dying, he promised to come back. How can he come back?"

"He can't." Artemis pressed her hand to Kyana's shoulder. "There are none left powerful enough to work that kind of magic."

Though the goddess sounded confident, the doubt in her eyes did nothing to alleviate the fear that had filled the room.

Artemis had better be right. If Cronos came back, it would take more than a tracer and a few worn-out gods to save this world.

"Well, that was scary." Haven sat on one of the stones leading away from the prison and back to Below.

Kyana sat behind Haven and Ryker, leaning her head against the exterior wall of the prison. She was still woozy and her stomach wouldn't stop churning, though she was pretty certain it wasn't the taste of Icky's blood that caused her nausea. She and Icky were separated by only a few branches on the Vampyric family tree. If Kyana ever had children—

She shuddered. It was near to impossible for Vampyre to become pregnant, but the possibility was still there. The Order was right to have the no Vamp-on-Vamp law. The idea of birthing a creature like Icky was too horrid to contemplate.

"Don't worry about it. Even if there was somebody powerful enough to bring Cronos back, he'd still be trapped on that island." Ryker sat next to Haven. "He couldn't get off it then, he wouldn't be able to now."

"Dead bones are one thing, but walking bones . . ." Haven shivered, her gaze drifted to Kyana. "At least we learned a little history."

"History I could have done without." Kyana tried to ignore their uncomfortable stares. All the things she'd loved about her race were now tainted, ugly. She could have gone another lifetime without ever knowing the truth.

Salt spray washed over them, pulling Kyana from her troubled thoughts. If possible, the mist intensified the odor of Icky and the shit hole and who knew what else that had covered them in the past day. She wrinkled her nose.

She turned to look at Ryker. His face was tan again, his eyes alert. Did whatever part of Kyana that resembled Icky cause him pain? Was that why he kept his distance from her? She doubted he'd ever look at her again without seeing what really lived inside her. "You okay?"

He nodded, his gaze drifting toward the moonlit sea. "I've never felt like that before."

Kyana gingerly placed a hand on his shoulder. He didn't flinch or brush her off. She was pleased. She was also pleased that being around him right now wasn't renewing a decade's worth of bitterness. "I wish Icky had shown me something about the key."

"Yeah. Instead all we got was a scary promise of Cronos's return." Haven rubbed at a stain on her torn jeans. "What are you going to do with that ring, anyway?"

Ryker gave a halfhearted smile. "Give it someone who can keep it safe."

"Who?"

"The less people who know, the better."

Kyana didn't care enough at the moment to press him to answer Haven more thoroughly. She was exhausted and a tiny bit freaked out by everything Icky had shown her. Besides, the ring wasn't important. The key was. And they were no closer to finding it now than they'd been before.

"Think Geoffrey has that list of Cronos followers yet?" she asked, standing on tired legs.

"Who knows." A strong gust of wind blew, and Haven wrinkled her nose. "I'll go track him down for you after I shower. You two should do the same. We smell like butt."

Haven was right. Kyana needed a shower. She was pretty sure if she'd been drawn as a cartoon, there would be little puffs of yellow stink clouding her character. "Go on. I'm heading home shortly. I'll meet you there."

"Okay, then. I'm off. See you in a bit."

Kyana would have walked with Haven, but she wanted to make sure Ryker was all right before heading off for the night. A part of her felt responsible for what he'd gone through on that island. He'd begged her to go and she'd insisted on staying. She'd almost gotten him killed.

She stretched, wondering how to approach the topic of what had happened to him on that island. "You okay?"

"I'll be fine once I shower and eat. You really should do the same. You look like hell."

"Thanks." She took his offered hand of assistance and let him pull her to her feet. Her chest bounced lightly off his, and her gut clenched. He didn't stink. He didn't smell like sunshine at the moment, but he'd somehow managed to not get ucky like she had.

Still, the dark shadows beneath his eyes worried her. "I know we're not friends, but—?"

"I'm fine, Ky. Drop it."

He shook his hand from hers and walked away. Kyana stood, staring after him for a long while before following. She was still harboring a lot of resentment toward him, so why did it bother her that he hadn't confided in her? Did he have someone he could turn to? She didn't want to know. But more than that, she didn't want to examine why the possibility caused her heart to sit heavy in her chest.

She walked the streets, listening to Below come alive. Vamps pushed past her as she shouldered her way into Spirits to order a meal to go. She ignored the grimaces and stares of the other patrons and slid onto a bar stool.

The barkeep didn't move toward her, but turned from the Mystics he was serving to glare. "Butcher shop's down the street."

Kyana tapped the shiny bar with a less than clean hand. "I'll take a bottle of fifty/fifty. To go."

"Only Marcus does that. He's not here."

"Great, then I'll wait for him." Several patrons stood, gave Kyana dirty looks, then left the café. If stinking repelled others, maybe she'd give up bathing altogether. She was due some alone time. "When's he due back?"

"You're costing me customers," the man grumbled, fixing Kyana's dinner and sliding it toward her. "Just take it and go."

"Hey, I don't smell or look this bad because I want to. I was out *doing* something about the mess we're all in. How 'bout you?"

The barkeep's face softened, and feeling his intent to apologize, she pulled out the little cash she had. He shook his head. "It's on me. Just go."

With a nod of thanks, Kyana grabbed her bottle and turned to leave, but stopped as her gaze fell upon Ryker striding by the window. Something in his stride was determined, not like a man on a mission to bathe, but maybe to confront. Hell. What was he doing? She waited a minute, giving him time to walk ahead, but watched from inside the tavern as he slipped through the portal and disappeared.

She should let him go. Whatever trouble he was looking to find, he could handle on his own.

She sighed, and followed the path he'd taken. She wasn't going to stick her nose where it didn't belong, but she owed it to him to at least make sure he wasn't killed.

Ryker stalked down St. George Street, no calmer now than he'd been when he'd left Ky. The concern on her face was burned into his brain. Anger, self-loathing, and sheer frustration hummed beneath his skin, making him antsy. He sure as hell wasn't going to beat himself up, but he'd find something to take his anger out on before he rested for the night.

It wasn't just the helplessness he'd experienced on that island that had him so eager to crack a head or two, though, granted, that was a huge portion of the adrenaline rushing through him now. He'd wanted to take part in that fight so badly, keeping his distance had almost hurt more than the physical pain the Vampyre had caused. But while the anger over not being able to fight for the first time in his life was still palpable, it was Kyana that had his blood pumping more.

He had to have her. Soon. But how did he take what he wanted from her and still keep true to his beliefs?

Ryker jogged around a corner, passing a ransacked ice cream parlor, and kept on. With so many abandoned businesses, it was the perfect spot to look for trouble.

Sunrise was a good half hour away. If he was lucky, he'd find a band of Dark Breeds looking for a place to sleep away the day. He'd take out his frustration on them with pleasure.

The smell of the urine hit his nose minutes before he spotted the small band of Dark Breeds breaking into a popular bar and grill. Grinning, Ryker crouched and softened his steps, quietly closing in on the demons as they threw themselves through a window.

It wouldn't have taken any effort on his part to pick them off one at a time, but he wanted a fight. A long, dirty, someone-had-to-bleed kind of fight to release the pent-up emotions he'd held to so tightly since they'd entered that damned hellhole on Cronos's island. Since Kyana had shifted back to Vampyre and had given him way more than a teasing glimpse of her body. He twitched, his pulsing blood making it difficult to push that image from his mind. By the time he finally managed, he'd given the demons just enough time to move away from the window. He entered behind them and blocked their escape.

Four sets of black eyes turned to face him.

The first thing he taught his men was to never take on even one lone Dark Breed on their own. They were too unpredictable; their powers never quite clear if you weren't certain what breeds they consisted of. Better to come back with friends than have a search party sent to retrieve your body. Since he never asked his men to do something he himself wouldn't do, he'd never broken that rule. Today would be an exception. "Looks like you picked the wrong building to break into."

The biggest of the group let out a throaty growl.

Feeling cocky, Ryker beckoned the big guy forward.

The boss grunted to his minions. With a lethal-looking grin, he tilted his head back and revealed his retracted fangs. Sharp claws stretched from beneath the demon's black-blue hands and its naked body shivered in delight as a set of nasty, thin wings broke loose on its back. It had gone from resembling a human to looking almost like Icky.

A Hatchling. Ryker studied it, unable to help his fascination. He hadn't seen one of these since the turn of the century. The children of the dragons of Tartarus had almost become nothing more than legend.

When it looked at Ryker again, its black eyes had gone stark white. Feeding time.

Ryker could have fended off the demon with just a look, but he let it run until it was within arm's reach. No weapons. No god powers. Just brute force.

He easily dodged the slow swings, taunting the demon before drawing back his fist. The sound of breaking bone brought only a moment of relief. He looked from the unconscious beast on the floor to his buddies, slightly disappointed that it had gone down so easily. "Is that the best you got?"

With growls of outrage, the second and third rushed him at once. The fourth stretched out its wings and flew straight over Ryker's head to land behind him. Ryker pivoted, thrust his fist through the flyer's face, pulling back bits of sinew and bone. The beast crumpled to the ground before the other two could even reach him. These, he would take down more slowly. Would make the fight last until he was too exhausted to think about weakness or women.

Ryker lost track of how long the fight raged on. The Hatchlings seemed to sense that Ryker was playing with them, seemed to know they should be dead by now. And knowing this seemed to intensify their fear. He could smell it on them as strongly as he could smell their urine stench. They watched him, waiting to see what his next move would be. He flexed his fingers, giving them time to decide if they wanted to continue the fight or run. Not that he was going to let them run, but still, it would be sweeter to kill them if they thought they might slip away.

One of the two left attempted to take flight. As it passed overhead, Ryker reached up and caught it around the neck. With a roar, he twisted. The sound of neck bones shattering filled the now silent restaurant. He dropped the body to the ground. Turning slowly, he faced the lone survivor.

"What the hell are you doing?"

Kyana's voice spun Ryker around. She loomed in the broken window, her gaze darting from one fallen Hatchling to the next. The survivor took Ryker's distraction as its chance to escape, and made a mad dash toward another window. The moment the glass shattered, Ryker sighed and sent it a searing glare. His telekinetic power sent the Hatchling flying back into the bar.

"You almost cost me a kill," he said, stalking to the bar and leaning over the wannabe escapee. "Get out of here, Ky."

"The hell I will." She leaped through the window, knocking loose glass onto the floor.

Saddened that this kill would have to be a quick one,

Ryker grabbed the beast's head in both of his hands and gave it one hard twist. Another broken neck. Not nearly the satisfaction he'd wanted. He shoved the body from the bar, then vaulted over the stools and counter. A moment later, he turned back to Kyana, holding a near-empty bottle of Jack Daniel's and a shot glass. He wasn't a drinker. Looked like tonight was full of exceptions. Pouring most of the booze over his busted knuckles, he filled the shot glass with what remained.

"Are you still pissy that Icky affected you like he did?" Kyana stepped over body number two and eased onto a bar stool. Ryker glanced out the window to see the still-gray sky. No immediate threat of sunrise to spur her home. Damn his bad luck. She had a good twenty or thirty minutes before she'd *have* to leave him in peace.

Or shift.

Zeus, he didn't want to go there again. If she shifted to Lychen, she'd eventually have to shift back. And when she shifted back . . . she'd be bare-ass naked to him again. Blood rushed to fill his loose jeans, and suddenly, they weren't so loose anymore.

Ryker stayed behind the bar for cover.

"Looks like a mess of testosterone exploded in here," Kyana said.

He shrugged. "I handled it." He rubbed his knuckles and tried not to stare at the way her white tank top hugged her breasts. Even sweaty and dirty, he wanted her. "Thought you were going home."

"Thought you were too." She pointed to his bottle of booze. "Gods can't drink. What are you doing?"

Her gaze fixated on his hands as he slowly turned

the shot of Jack. "Half human, remember? Besides, gods can drink. They just . . . don't."

"Right." She scanned the bar. Her gaze rested briefly on the demon's body before returning to him. "Looks like I missed all the fun."

That was the problem. She was way too concerned with *fun* all the time. He didn't want to be anyone's fun. He wasn't built that way. He eased back over the bar and nudged her thighs apart so he could stand between them. Maybe he *wasn't* built to be anyone's fun, but why couldn't she be his? Just for one night? Tomorrow, he could kick his own ass, but tonight, he needed release and she was here, looking so tempting.

"You want fun. Let's have fun."

Not giving himself time to think, or her time to react, he gripped her shoulders and claimed her mouth. Her gasp of surprise gave him the entrance he sought to deepen the kiss. He ground his mouth over hers, giving her what she'd always said she wanted—rough, hot, and fast.

It took him a minute to realize her hands were pushing him away, not pulling him closer. He lifted his head and caught her eyes. "What? You don't want this now?"

He leaned toward her. She turned her face away. "This isn't you."

"But it's what you want. What you've been begging for since the night I met you." He gripped her hips, lifting her from the bar stool to the bar, and pinned her in his arms. "I think I finally understand how it works now. No emotions. Just sex. And then we walk away. Right?"

"Please," she whispered. "Don't."

It wasn't the pleading in her voice that brought him to his senses, but the fear in her eyes.

Stepping away from her, Ryker grabbed the shot of Jack and downed it before smashing the glass against the wall.

Kyana jumped, but remained where he'd left her. Ryker had been born fighting. Even before he'd known what he was, who his father was, he'd developed a reputation for himself. It was why Ares had claimed him instead of ignoring his existence the way he'd ignored his other bastards and Ryker's mother when he'd raped her and left her pregnant and alone. But tonight, he'd broken all his rules when it came to engaging the enemy. He'd been stupid. Stupid for going out and looking for a fight. Stupid for facing down the demons alone. Stupid for letting his emotions rule his actions. He prided himself on his ability to control his anger, on not being anything like his father. Ryker saw the fear, the wariness still in Kyana's eyes. Maybe it was true what they said about the apple not falling far from the tree.

"Go home, Ky."

"Don't tell me what to do." The calmness in her voice was forced. She was shaken. Regret tore at him.

She reached around the bar, grabbed a bottle of whiskey, and ignoring the tray of shot glasses in front of her, drank deeply.

"The sun'll be up soon. Go."

Kyana's heart was pounding so loud, there was no way he couldn't hear it. Whatever had gotten into him was scary. Not because he kissed her, but because he looked like he'd been possessed, like another person entirely. That wasn't who she'd wanted to kiss. She liked it rough and hot, sure, but not forceful. She'd had her share of that, thank you very much.

She struggled to appear unfazed by Ryker's sudden show of force and looked out the window. Faint rays of pink would soon sprinkle the clouds to the east. She couldn't linger long, but there was still no need to panic. Besides, if worse came to worst, she could always shift and make her way home in Lychen form. Right now, she wanted answers from Ryker, but she didn't think he was going to be compliant.

Her lips still tingled from his violent kiss. And as much as she'd liked it, the look in his eyes had scared the hell out of her. In her past life as a human, she'd thought she'd loved her sultan husband. But she'd been a young, naïve fifteen-year-old girl who hadn't suspected he might turn that love into something ugly and violent. He'd used her that night, left her heartbroken and bloody. And the look she'd seen in Ryker's eyes tonight had been very similar. His need to use her to take the edge off whatever he was feeling had turned her right back into that fifteen-year-old girl.

The difference between Ryker and Mehmet, however, was that Ryker had stopped. He wouldn't hurt her, and even though she'd practically begged him to make love to her once, he wouldn't assume she still wanted it when she said no.

For that reason alone, she stayed now, needing to make certain he was all right before she could leave him.

Ryker swayed on his feet. His eyes had a glazed sheen to them that hadn't been there a second ago.

"Are you . . . drunk?"

"Maybe."

She frowned. "You were sober five seconds ago."

He smiled, his grin lopsided and devilishly cute. A far cry from the angry, hostile Ryker who'd kissed her senseless. "Had a full one of these." He shoved a shot glass in her direction.

"Wow. Impressive." One shot and he was loaded. "Think I just found out why gods don't drink."

He gave new meaning to the phrase *cheap date*. Her gaze flittered toward the window. "Sun's coming soon, Surfer Boy. I can't sit here and babysit you, and if I have to shift, I'll be out of commission for longer than we can spare."

He didn't seem to hear her. He leaned toward her and looked like he might topple off the stool. She caught him and held him upright.

"So?" He slurred the word, giving it far too many syllables. "Go."

She had to go, but she couldn't, wouldn't just leave him here. He was too vulnerable and there were still Dark Breeds around. "Okay, cowboy. Let's go. I'm taking you home."

"How can I be a surfer *and* a cowboy?" He slid off the stool, allowing Kyana to slip her arm under his shoulder. He didn't protest when she guided him around the tables to the door. "Make up your mind."

"Walk faster."

If her senses hadn't been thrown off by the stench of booze emitting from Ryker's pores, she still had plenty of time to make it before sunrise. But she didn't want to take the chance of slowing down and becoming bacon.

They passed the small cemetery that rested barely a block from her place, and saw the interesting interlocked tree that had called to her since she'd moved here. She wasn't sure what types of trees made up the glorious oddity, but one species of tree grew inside the other, two separate beings had formed into one, becoming stronger together than either would have been apart.

A lot like Kyana.

She ushered Ryker past the tree and back onto the sidewalk. "See that big yellow two-story on the corner?" she said. "That's where we're headed. I need you to concentrate and move those big-ass feet a little faster, okay?"

"I can walk by myself," he muttered.

She caught him before he smashed his pretty face into a light post.

"Sure you can."

When they were about ten feet away from Kyana's house, he stopped beside a swaying palm tree. "I shouldn't have kissed you back then."

"Hey, you were on a high after the bar fight. It happens."

"No. Not just now. Back *then*. When you came to me. I shouldn't . . . have kissed you then."

She should have left him in the bar. "That was ten years ago, Ryker, and you made your feelings on that pretty clear."

His face contorted as though he was in pain. Kyana leaned him against the side of her house and took the stairs two at a time, opened the door, then returned to Ryker's side. He wouldn't budge.

"I mean it. Big mistake. You . . . make me crazy. Always have."

What the hell was that supposed to mean?

The wind picked up, slamming the door closed again. "Damn it. Stay put."

She leaned him against the wall again, opened the door, and turned back to find they weren't alone. Leeches. Seven of them.

They were surrounding Ryker before Kyana could so much as warn him.

Chapter Twelve

Leeches were mindless killing machines who usually worked under the control of someone else. But they always had their sights set on the aura of the gods. And given the way all seven Leeches were now moving slowly toward Ryker and ignoring Kyana completely, his aura must have called to them immediately.

A wide band of pink lightened the sky to the east. This was going to get interesting. The sun was going to rise soon, and unfortunately, Leeches didn't share her need to hide from it. Tick tock.

She glanced at Ryker. He was spinning in a circle, obviously using his telekinetic abilities to try to hold them back, but the booze was muddling the process because each Leech staggered backward only a few steps before stalking toward him again and again.

Kyana jumped from the entryway of her house and placed herself in front of Ryker. She used their lack of focus on her to get the advantage. Never taking her gaze off the approaching attack, she slowly eased her dagger from her belt and sliced the throat of the Leech closest to her.

Its shriek of pain was brief before it crumpled to the ground. The other six halted, no longer intent on Ryker. Kyana grabbed Ryker by the front of his shirt and shoved him out of the way. The first rays of sun would soon stab their way through the treetops. She attempted to back them toward her house, trying to move the fight indoors, but as stupid as they might be, the Leeches seemed to understand her intent and stayed put.

"Get inside, Ky."

She ignored Ryker. If she locked herself indoors, the Leeches would break through the windows once they'd seen where she'd gone. She couldn't have her home so exposed. The shutters were all that kept the sun at bay as it was. There were too many windows . . . she'd have too few places to hide.

"Don't move!" She rushed the Leech closest to her, kicking off the wall so she could smash in its face with the heel of her boot. Its nose crumbled inside its head like papier-mâché.

One jumped on her back and Kyana thrust backward, crushing it between herself and the wall. Its bones sounded like splintered wood as the stink of its foul blood oozed from its nose. She turned and kicked it away before turning back to its five friends.

"You wanted a fight, you should have waited twenty damned minutes!" she called to Ryker.

Sadly, he took her frustration to mean she needed help and leaped into the fray. Even in his drunken state, he handled two of them with little problem. Using only his mind, he seemed to break through his drunken barrier and tossed one of the Leeches into the air, impaling it on a branch with nothing more than a hand motion and a glare.

As Kyana ducked an attack from the two in front of her, she caught sight of Ryker chasing after his remaining victim, and turned her focus back to the two vile beasts in her face.

Her fangs tingled in preparation for attack as she summoned more energy. The sun was closer. Already the coolness of the morning was giving way to slight heat. The Leeches came at her as one. One on her back, one on her front. She dipped to her knees, causing them to collide with each other before she rolled onto her back and leaped to her feet. A flick of her wrist, and she flung her dagger straight into one's open mouth. It gurgled and sputtered, its jaw hanging open at a grotesque angle as it fought to pull the knife from its throat.

"Come and get me, big guy." While one Leech was indisposed, she pulled the other's attention to her, leaping onto the small brick wall bordering the sidewalk. She swung around the lamppost, kicking out and catching the Leech between her calves. She twisted her legs, listened with satisfaction as the sound of its neck breaking drowned out the Leech's scream of agony.

As the dead creature slumped to the ground, the final Leech finally managed to rip the blade from its throat and toss it to the ground. The clank of silver on stone screamed of anger, and the beast raced at her with a viciousness its brothers had lacked.

Kyana pushed off of the wall, but the beast caught her ankle and jerked her to the ground, sending her skidding across rough concrete. Her chin smacked against the base of her steps and it took her a second to gain her bearings before rolling onto her back and swinging herself to her feet. As she stood to full height, the weight of the Leech crushed her into the banister and slid her body up until her head cracked against her shuttered window. She tried to crush it between her thighs, but already, the approaching sun was weakening her. The pink rays were frighteningly close.

All she could do was inch her way inside the house and pray she could finish it off before it could expose her to sunlight.

The Leech seemed to read her intentions like it actually possessed a brain. It seized her foot and threw her once again to the ground, then dragged her all the way back to the corner where the fight had begun. She thrust her free foot into its shin, sending the thing to its knees. One deadly ray of sun broke free of the trees and seared her cheek. Kyana screamed and broke free of the Leech's hold, shoving past it back in the direction of her house. It caught her before she could take the steps and pinned her to the ground.

She was too weak to fight any longer. The sun was coming to claim her power, and the only thing that would save her was to use the last remnants of her strength to shift and save herself from the sunlight. Her shift came painfully, but as her Lychen half took form, she was able to slither her body out from under the Leech's hold. It looked stunned by her transformation, and she used its disorientation to head for the steps once again.

Pain tore through her thick coat and seared her ribs and breast, causing her to howl. She slumped over. Her attacker snarled. She fought to maintain form. Her body ached to return to Vamp, but the sidewalk was dusted with dots of sun, and they would turn her into a pincushion in two seconds flat.

Pain like nothing she'd ever felt gripped her body. Forcing her head up, she caught a glimpse of her own dagger protruding from her side. She'd never known Leeches to use physical weapons before. Now was a fine time for them to learn.

She struggled to maintain the only shield she possessed from the sun, but the pain stole her focus. Her injuries were extensive. Blood soaked her fur and pooled beneath her body, creating a tiny river in the sidewalk crack beside her. Blinded by the mind-numbing ache in her belly, she lost her tenuous grip on her Lychen form. She quickly shifted from wolf to Vamp and back to wolf several times, making the world around her flicker like Christmas lights before she lost the struggle and her Vampyric form won out.

Immediately, her exposed skin warmed and blistered. Kyana bit her lip to keep from crying out. Behind her, she could hear Ryker's muffled voice calling her name, felt the Leech being thrown off her, heard the Leech's sudden scream and just as sudden quiet. Ryker was hovering over her in the next minute, jostling her. But she couldn't respond. She was slowly being burned alive.

She squeezed her eyes shut, waiting for the last bit of shade protecting her naked body to fade. The stench of burning flesh clogged her nose and seared her throat. Strong, gentle hands lifted her, and then she was floating, drifting, desperately clinging to consciousness.

Something warm and soft covered her. She risked opening her eyes enough to see Ryker's shirt resting over her naked body. He was trying to shield as much of her from the sun as possible.

He tightened his grip and raced up the steps, stumbled, but quickly regained his balance. The rays scorched her back, her arms, her legs. Her cry of pain and Ryker's roar of frustration rang in her ears.

He shouldered the door open and kicked it closed behind them. Gently, he carried her down the hall and into the bathroom, setting her naked body into the large tub. The sudden coolness of water soaking her caused her to quake and threatened to rip the skin from her body.

She flailed, splashing bloody water all over Ryker and the bathroom floor, but Kyana couldn't stop the trembling. The hilt of the dagger hit the side of the tub, vibrating against her ribs like a tuning fork. Kyana roared, slamming her skull into the porcelain.

Ryker knelt at her side. "I've got to get that out."

Kyana blinked to clear the stars from her vision. The dagger wound wouldn't kill her, but it sure as hell hurt. It was her scorched skin that was going to do her in. Already, the poison of the sun seeped through her pores and into her bloodstream. Soon, it would attack her heart and stop it completely. She'd rather not be in so much pain when that happened, so she struggled to stay still and bit her lip in preparation for Ryker's drunken ministrations.

He gripped the hilt in his fist, then tilted her chin, forcing her to look at him. The look of devastation on his face made her close her eyes. He quickly pulled the knife from her body. A long, slow hiss found its way from between her clenched teeth.

"Shit. Kyana, I'm sorry." He reached for a washcloth and pressed it to her wound to stanch the flow of blood. With the poison working its way through her body, she could barely cover his hand with hers.

The water eased the burning, but at the same time, intensified the pain. She glimpsed her arms. The skin was charred black. Any second, it would slide off the bone.

Ryker snatched a large towel from the rack and covered her with it, then lifted her from the tub. He carried her to her bed and set her in the center. She felt him kneel beside her. Felt him watching her. Kyana refused to meet his gaze. The last thing she needed was to see his pity as he stuffed the towel against the knife wound. He whipped off his belt and fastened it around her waist to keep the towel in place. She wanted to tell him to stop, that it didn't matter how much she bled. The wound wouldn't kill her. It was the rest of her that needed tending, and yet, there was no tending that could be done.

"You should have let them have me." He gripped her chin, turning her head toward him. She could see his struggle to focus and was willing to bet that, after this, he'd never touch booze again. "May the gods find mercy for us both." He raised his arm and tore open his wrist with his fang. Not giving her a chance to refuse, he held his wrist to her mouth. His warm, rich blood coated her tongue.

Kyana tried to move, tried to make him stop. This wasn't the same as feeding off Icky. Icky had been a soulless beast, with no essence to feed her. Ryker definitely had a soul, definitely had a powerful essence that could drive her into insanity.

She couldn't feed. Couldn't become the Dark Breed she'd been. It had taken years of agony to control the thirst, the agonizing addiction for living blood. She'd rather die than go through that again.

"Drink, damn it." He flexed his fist to make the blood flow faster. "It's the only way."

Blood filled her mouth and spilled down her throat. She coughed against the burning taste of alcohol as her throat closed around the thick drink. She fought against him like a drowning victim fighting the waves for air. Years of suppressed need flooded her. Kyana gave in. She gripped his wrist in both hands and drank deeply.

She didn't know how long she fed with her gaze locked on his, his body swaying with each suckle. Her mind struggled to untangle his jumbled thoughts from her own. Between the pain and the thirst and the infusion of the booze he'd consumed making her head spin, she couldn't make sense of anything she heard or felt. She gave up trying and simply let his blood begin healing her wounds.

When she'd satisfied her need, she eased her grip. "Sleep," he mumbled, to himself or to her, Kyana didn't know. He covered them with the satin bedspread, lay beside her, and rested his arm over her waist. "Sleep."

For the first time in her Vampyric life, Kyana did as she was told without argument.

The loving gaze staring back at Kyana in her dreams wasn't that of a lover. It belonged to a father not born of blood, but of heart. As Kyana slept, Ryker's blood soared through her veins, easing both her external wounds and the agonies she'd carried with her for centuries. The dream took her back to Istanbul and to her human body where Henry, her Sire, knelt beside Kyana's canopied bed and fed her from his wrist. His black eyes locked on hers, screaming a silent apology for what he was about to do, as her broken, raped body lay exposed before him. He'd tried to cover her with his jacket, but the bitter winds had still ripped through her shutters and torn at her abused, twenty-year-old flesh.

It hadn't been the first night the sultan had raped her. No, he'd taken that liberty on their wedding night—Kyana's fifteenth birthday. But this night, the rape had extended into the wee hours of morning and had left her all but dead. Henry had found Kyana in the stairwell outside Mehmet's private chambers and had carried her so tenderly to her own that even now, while she slept, the tears of gratitude were just as real. Her own father had never been so kind, so tender. From that second, Henry became Kyana's family, her heart. She would have thrown herself from her window had he asked it of her.

Her dream filled with tension as the taste of Henry's blood then mingled with the taste of Ryker's now. The Lychen in her came alive. The Vampyre in her soul screamed out to feed. She'd fed and found revenge in one evening, leaving behind a carnage in Mehmet's palace that had Turks everywhere speaking her name in fear for decades to come. She'd gone from a naïve human child to the bogeyman that had prompted children to sleep. The cautionary warning for young ones not to enter forbidden woods. The monster in their closets.

"They know nothing of what you will be, my Kyana," Henry had said. *"I'm not merely Vampyre, Kyana. I am rare in my blend of bloods. That same blending now lives in you. Half Vampyre. Half Lychen. The beast in you will one day be tamed and they will still never see you for more than a monster. I will go to my grave sorry for what I have done to you."*

"What you have done? You have given me life. True life. Where I will never be at the mercy of another. Henry . . . Father . . . you have given me freedom."

Henry's long brown hair fell over his face as his worried gaze watched Kyana feed. "There is no freedom in what you have become. You will search until death has truly found you, Kyana, and unless you are far luckier than I have been, that search will prove fruitless and painful."

Kyana had smiled, had thought him to be foolish. "I am Vampyre. I will want for nothing."

"We are also Lychen. The restlessness of that half will never be content until you find the one meant for you. You will forever be prisoner to it. Do not delude yourself that you are free."

But Kyana hadn't listened. Lychen or not, she'd never again become the property of another man. Not in the name of law, and most certainly not in the name of love. She took one last look into Henry's eyes and reached for him, needing to hold him, to remember a father's touch. But as her fingers drifted through his ghostly form, she bolted awake and stared wide-eyed at her bedroom ceiling.

On trembling legs, she made her way to the bathroom, casting a glance over her shoulder to make certain she hadn't wakened Ryker. He still slept peacefully, his rhythmic snores the only sound in the house. She locked the bathroom door, dropped her towel, and draped herself in her long, red robe before collapsing onto the edge of the tub. Her body convulsed as she realized what had awakened her.

Fear.

The expectation, the waiting, the dread of what was to come, kept her from leaving the room.

What have we done?

That dream had reminded her of the pain that had come with Turning, the agony of learning not to feed in order to tame the beast Henry had created that night. She was healed. She'd fed from Ryker, and by doing so, she had to have released the monster within her that had lain dormant for eighty years.

She tried to focus on the horrible paisley wallpaper she hadn't yet replaced, but the harder she stared, the more the walls threatened to close in on her.

An image of Icky struck her like a fist to the gut. Deformed. Demonic. The most inhuman, unhuman thing she'd ever seen. *That* was what lived inside her. Diluted but there.

Moving to the mirror, she checked her reflection. Her small canines still hadn't elongated into sharp, piercing daggers. Her eyes hadn't dilated to all black. She held up her hands. Her carefully trimmed nails hadn't stretched and grown into long, deadly weapons. She looked exactly as she had for the last eight decades.

It made no sense.

She'd fed from human, Vampyre, Witch, even a demon or two in her one hundred plus years as a Dark Breed before joining the Order. Each time she'd taken blood, the change had been immediate. Each time she'd become stronger, faster . . . deadlier.

She closed her eyes, remembering the last time she'd tasted warm, fresh blood. It had been three weeks after Henry's death. The Van Helsing wannabe who'd taken Henry's life had begged for his own. His request, much like the pleadings of her Sire's, had fallen on deaf ears. She'd been left alone then, orphaned. So she'd joined the Order of Ancients and tried to make a new family within it.

Working for the Order, even with its rules and dislike for her kind, gave her that peace she'd searched for when she'd gone after her Sire's murderer.

She'd made her vow to the Order not to feed again. She'd gone through months of the most painful withdrawal imaginable. It had taken charms and potions and a full year to tame the instinct to feed, and she'd sworn she'd never put herself through that again.

Now that she had, what the hell was taking so long?

Maybe it was the alcohol in Ryker's blood. Vampyre couldn't get drunk, but maybe they shared the effects when consuming blood from someone who was. Her head swam and her belly swirled and her mouth still tasted the strong booze he'd drunk before she'd found him. Maybe it slowed the change.

Sitting back down on the edge of the tub, she wrapped her arms around her belly. Waiting. Dreading. Fearing.

Hoping.

Maybe it wasn't the booze at all. Maybe it was just *Ryker*. He was a demigod, and she'd never fed off anything like him before. Maybe she was as immune to him as she'd been to Icky.

Strange pinpricks danced across her skin. She rushed back to the mirror.

Nothing.

The pinpricks traveled up her legs and arms, making the hair on her nape stand on end. Ryker. She was feeling *him*. Sensing *him*.

Kyana stared at the closed door. He'd awakened and was worrying about her.

She rubbed her eyes, trying to block out his thoughts and emotions. So the connection of feeding off him was there. Why this when none of the other changes had happened?

His soft rap on the bathroom door made her jump. She didn't move. Didn't bid him entrance.

He opened the door, knelt in front of her, and rested his hands on his knee. "You okay?"

She forced a smile. "I will be."

"You're not going to change, Ky. Come back to bed."

He sounded so sure, she couldn't help but believe him. Relief made her knees tremble. "Thank you. For what you did, I mean."

He pulled her into his arms and guided her out of the bathroom and back onto the plush carpet of her bedroom. "I wouldn't have had to do anything if I hadn't put you in danger in the first place."

"I can take care of myself."

He placed her gently on the bed and watched until she lay down. Once she was situated, he lifted the sheets and tucked them under her arms before collapsing beside her. He yanked her to his body, forcing her onto her side so he could scoop her backside against his hips.

"What time is it?" She yawned, suddenly exhausted now that her worry had passed.

"Probably around noon." His breath washed over her hair and neck. "Rest until sunset."

"We really don't have time—"

"Feeling up to shifting to escape the sun already, then?"

The sensitive skin of Kyana's tender toes brushed Ryker's bare foot. "Maybe not."

His hand rested lightly on her waist as though it belonged there, as though they really did *like* each other.

"I do like you, Kyana."

Kyana scowled. "Get out of my head."

"Go to sleep, Dark Breed," he said, his voice drugged with sleepiness, his insult soothed by the faint grin she felt pressed to the back of her neck.

Ryker waited until Kyana drifted to sleep before he allowed himself to close his eyes. Instinctively, he tightened his hold around her waist and pulled her to him. Her dream had been as vivid in his mind as it had been in hers. The connection between them would fade soon, but he hadn't just bitten her this time. This time, he'd fed *her*. By mingling their blood, he'd been given a taste of her past that made him ache to protect her as only one other being ever had.

He'd felt Kyana's Sire's love for her. Had felt the fatherly affection. Had suffered Kyana's painful thoughts regarding a true father who had terrorized her childhood until he'd sold her to the sultan to become wife number seventeen. The painful memory of the sultan's acts of violence and the cruelty toward Kyana doled out by the other wives and the sultan's mother.

How had she lived through all of that and still managed to remain the strong, independent woman she'd become?

The restlessness of that half will never be content until you find the one meant for you.

Her Sire's words were stuck on replay in Ryker's head. He knew exactly what Henry had meant by that. Kyana's Lychen half would never be at peace until it found its life mate, and from the moment he'd met Kyana, Ryker had felt that connection to her. It scared the shit out of him. His instinct was to run like hell and never look back. But running would accomplish nothing. He was bound to be with Kyana or die alone.

The Fates had dealt him a sour hand.

Chapter Thirteen

The soft snore woke Kyana from a deep, fitful sleep. She pried open her eyes and stared into the darkness of . . . her bedroom. A moment of panic seized her as she tried to remember how she'd gotten there, in her bed, draped in her red robe and satin sheets. The snore sounding beside her brought a rush of memories that forced her eyes closed once again.

Ryker. The sun. Ryker's protection. The pain. Ryker's blood.

She jerked upright, eagerly searching her hands for claws, her tongue flicking over her fangs.

Still nothing.

She was safe. Ryker hadn't lied. The change was not coming.

"Praise Zeus," she whispered, unable to fight the grin creeping onto her face.

Ryker had managed to save her by feeding her . . . without Turning her again. Halle-freakin'-lujah.

She tested her toes, her fingers, her arms. No pain. She was whole again. Strong again.

She rolled over and placed herself nose-to-nose with Ryker and found his silver eyes staring back at her.

"Hi," she whispered, focusing on the thick, black lashes lining his eyes.

"Is it sunset already?" He yawned and twisted to look out her window, but their shuttered darkness offered him no answer. There wasn't a single clock in the room. The only way to determine the time was to push open the shutters and peek outside, or walk downstairs to find the clock. She was too cozy to do either; too afraid the slightest movement would send Ryker skittering back into hands-off mode.

Instead, she reached out with her Vampyric senses, attempting to read the path of the sun. "Soon, but not yet, I think."

Ryker flopped onto his back and folded his arms beneath his head, studying the ceiling. "Nice place. Not at all what I expected."

The sudden absence of his hand on her hip and his breath on her face made her cold.

"Expecting a graveyard?" she only half teased.

She studied him, the cleft in his chin, his dimpled cheeks. "Maybe."

She tucked deeper beneath the blanket and tried to see her home through his eyes. She'd chosen the old bed-and-breakfast as her home because of the history she'd seen within it. It had reminded her of the eighteen hundreds when she'd been living it up as a hunting Vamp. She'd picked out the navy blue shutters that blocked the sun from every single window on the two-story structure as the charm of the house had given way to necessity. She adored the little home she shared with Haven.

She smiled and raised herself up on one arm. "If it makes you feel better, it was a funeral home more than a hundred years ago. They used to stand up open coffins downstairs and place them in the windows so passersby could see the work they'd done on corpses."

He glanced at her from the corner of his eye, his brow raised. "Morbid."

Shrugging, Kyana lay back down. "Maybe, but it's eccentric. Suits me fine."

He slipped his fingers beneath her arm and lifted it so they could both see. The flesh was pink like raw chicken, but the charred black scales that had covered it at daybreak were gone.

"How do you feel?"

As though it contained a mind separate from her own, she watched her hand lift and her finger trace the bridge of his nose. The gesture was so human, so normal, it was as though she hovered outside her body, watching herself do something so daring as to touch him so gently.

"Pretty fantastic, actually . . . Ryker?"

"Hmm?"

Rather than brush off her touch as she'd expected him to, he closed his eyes. His dark lashes fanned out atop his skin, feathery and beautiful. Would they tickle the tip of her finger if she continued her daring ministrations?

"What did you mean about me making you crazy?" She'd known the question was on the tip of her tongue. Known she was drowsy enough to voice it. Sadly, her confidence died the moment it flitted out of her mouth and drifted through the air toward his ears.

He slowly opened his eyes to stare at her. The pewter shimmered as her question hung in the air between them.

Darkness flickered in his eyes. "Go back to sleep, Ky."

She sat up and twisted to glare down at him. "Go back to . . . I just saved your life. The least you can do is answer my question."

"No." He eased himself up against the headboard to watch her. After several seconds of intense scrutiny, he continued, "And I saved your life too." He brushed a stray strand of her hair from her cheek. "But thank you. You risked yourself to save me and I owe you way more than a drink from my blood."

"Just not an answer to my question?"

Ryker forced himself to keep his expression neutral as he waited for Kyana's outburst. The moment he'd awakened and found her in her bathroom, he'd remembered every drunken word he'd spoken and could have cut out his own tongue in regret. He was only surprised it had taken her this long to call him on what he'd said. Hell, his words weren't the only thing he remembered. He remembered forcing a kiss on her too. And now that he'd linked with her after sharing his blood with her, he knew enough about her past to know why he'd seen the fear in her eyes.

He was every kind of asshole.

He'd struggled his whole life not to be like the father he'd hated. The father who'd swooped down to Earth to possess a young, faithful worshipper long enough to rape the young woman, who, shortly after, gave birth to Ryker. A mother who'd loathed her son from his first breath to the day his father came to claim him. He'd only forced a kiss on Kyana, but was he capable of doing more? Of being the same entitled prick as his father?

When Kyana's gaze fell to his mouth, his dropped to the crowns of her breasts peeking from beneath her velvet robe. He laced his fingers behind his head to keep from reaching for her. No, he wasn't the same as his father. He knew his limits and would never reach out to take what wasn't his. And as many times as Kyana might offer herself to him, she wasn't his. Not yet.

She flicked her tongue against the peak of her upper lip and his body tightened in response. Ten years was a long time to hold on to an obsession like the one he'd been carrying. If he didn't put distance between himself and Kyana soon, it was going to become a do-her-or-die situation.

"I make you crazy because you *do* want me, don't you?"

"I never said I didn't."

But to take the brief affair she offered would make him no better than the men in her life who had used her for their own pleasure, then walked away . . . it would make him no better than his father.

She stretched. "There aren't many men who'd turn away from what I offered you."

"Sex, you mean." Ryker rolled onto his side to face her, his long fingers tracing a pattern on her shoulder.

"Mm hmm. It would be mind-blowing, you know."

"Believe me, I know." He pressed a soft kiss to her mouth, a tremble seizing his muscles at the taste of her, then lay back on his pillow. "But I'm not a fuck-'em-and-leave-'em guy."

Kyana touched her lips with her fingertips. "I could teach you how to be if that's all that's stopping you."

This moment between them felt almost human. Almost ordinary. Gods, how he longed for ordinary. His chest suddenly tight, Ryker dropped another light kiss to her forehead before easing from the bed. "Get some rest. I'm going to borrow your shower and go find some food. I'll be back to check on you later."

"You already showered."

"Yeah," he muttered, turning back to face her again. "But this one's going to be cold."

The sound of frantic whispers nudged Kyana awake again. She forced her eyes open and started when she saw Farrel and Crag hovering over her.

"Get the hell out of my room!"

She never let them in here! They knew that.

"Back off, darlin'. They're just doing what I asked." Haven's voice drifted in from Kyana's doorway. Kyana sat up on her elbows to glare at her. She nearly asked where Ryker was, but caught her tongue before she could slip and let everyone know he'd been here at all.

"What's going on?"

Haven stepped into the room but remained a good distance from the bed. "The last time I tried to wake you, you nearly crushed my spine. I figured since they were here, they could do it for me."

Groaning, Kyana swung her legs over the side of the bed and pulled her robe tightly closed. "Way to abuse my minions." She glared at Farrel and Crag and pointed to the door. "Out. Now."

"Yes, Mistress," Crag said, fear causing his pocked cheeks to pucker.

His freshly oiled bald head glistened with light sunburn. She was willing to bet he'd spent his time off duty at the beach, as he loved to so often do. Having a mistress of the dark had to suck for a beach bum like Crag.

"You look like poop, Kyana."

"Thanks." She rolled her head and flexed her shoulders. Regardless of what Haven thought about her appearance, Kyana felt fan-freakin'-tastic. "Where've you been?"

Feeling a little guilty over not having even noticed whether Haven had been home, Kyana worked her way to her feet and strode to the closet.

"I went to find Geoffrey, remember? I wanted to see if he had that list of Cronos supporters."

"And?"

"He wants us to meet him Below."

Kyana was irritated that she'd been forced to waste an entire day because of her injuries. Regardless, maybe the day hadn't been a complete waste after all. If Geoff had put together anything useful, they might have a new place to start tonight.

Her steps a little lighter than they'd been in a while, Kyana ripped a pair of leather pants from their hanger and shoved her arms through a leather vest before stepping back out of the closet. Haven watched Kyana pull on her pants and boots, then handed Kyana her holster.

"Found this outside. And this"—Haven reached behind her back and pulled out Kyana's stained dagger—"in your bathroom. The only reason I could think that you might have left your weapon belt outside is if you'd been forced to shift. Run into trouble?"

Kyana eyed her, wondering how little she could get away with telling. "Leeches and sunlight don't mix."

Haven's blue eyes widened and her perfect little mouth formed a dainty O. "Is that why your skin's all pink? Holy goodness, Kyana! You were burned!"

Kyana shrugged. "I'm fine."

"I can see that! What I can't see is how or why. Vamps don't just bounce back after meeting the sun face-to-face."

"This one does, apparently."

"Are you going to tell me what happened or not?"

Kyana preferred *not*, but was pretty sure Haven wouldn't let the subject drop until she got some kind of answer. "I was careless. Got caught outdoors in the middle of a Leech attack. That's it." She purposely left out the bit about saving Ryker's ass, sure he wouldn't appreciate her telling others about his moment of weakness. "The sun is not kind. I don't understand why people all but worship it."

"Even I can tell this is new skin." Haven gingerly touched Kyana's bare shoulder. "I can't stomach the thought of how bad these burns were this morning. Or what you had to do to rid your body of the poison." Haven's face suddenly fell and her concerned eyes turned suspicious. "He fed you to keep you alive. Only someone with gods' blood could heal you this quickly."

She didn't have to say who *he* was. They both knew whom Haven was referring to.

"He did what he had to," was all the information Kyana was willing to give.

Haven smiled. "Good for him."

"Not a word to anyone." Kyana zipped up her boots. "I mean it."

"You know I'd never do that. But I am telling Geoff to come here to meet you. You should rest."

"I've rested enough." Standing, Kyana wrapped her belt around her waist, then tied her hair at her nape with the elastic band sitting on her night table. "In fact, I feel amazing."

"So where'd he go, anyway?"

"Who?"

"Ryker. I hope he didn't just 'do what he had to do' and then leave without making sure you were okay."

"He stayed." Haven didn't need to know that Ryker had stayed in bed with Kyana practically all day. She'd make way more of a big deal out of that tidbit than was necessary.

"Well . . . okay, then. So we're off to see Geoffrey, then? You sure you're up to it?"

Kyana rolled her eyes. "I'm sure."

They should probably find Ryker before meeting Geoff, though. He wouldn't be happy if she started work without him. And despite her desire to work solo in the beginning, she was starting to enjoy having him around. Today had been nice. The most normal day Kyana had had in a long time—if she discounted the Leeches and the near-death thing. But curling up in bed with Ryker all afternoon had stirred up all sorts of warm, cozy feelings she didn't even know she was capable of. Hell, she was practically purring.

Kneeling beside the bed, she pulled out a wooden box and opened the lid. Inside was an array of specially crafted knives, all identical in look and weight. She selected one and tucked it into her boot. After wiping the mixture of Leech and her own blood off the dagger Haven had returned to her, Kyana tucked it into her holster next to her flare gun and started for the door.

Before she could step into the hallway, she ran smack into Ryker. He gripped her shoulder with one hand, the other holding a bottle of raki. She scanned him from head to toe. He'd changed from his surfer boy attire to a black tee and camos tucked into military-issue boots. It was totally hot.

Speaking of hot . . . his gaze heated her blood as it traveled slowly over her freshly healed skin. Her breath hitched. His escaped in a long, slow sigh.

A soft sound from Haven, much like a giggle, reminded them they weren't alone. Kyana looked away.

"You okay to get back to work?" he asked after a tense, awkward moment.

"Yeah, but the next person who asks me that will be walking with a limp. Let's go."

As she brushed past him, he thrust the raki into her hand. "It's fifty/fifty. Please feed."

Pleased that he'd been thinking about her while she'd been asleep, she tore off the cap and swallowed a burning sip. "Thanks," she said, twisting the cap back on.

As they started downstairs with Haven trailing behind them, Ryker's fingers rested on the small of her back. It was such a mindless touch, she doubted he even realized he'd done it. Doubted that he had any idea how it affected her.

But when they hit the first floor, his touch vanished and her skin instantly returned to subzero temperature.

An annoying chirp sounded behind them as they reached the front door, and Haven pulled her cell phone from her hip.

She grinned. "It's Drake! You two go on. Geoffrey said he'd meet you in front of Spirits." She flipped open the phone and spun around. "Drake! Where are you? Are you okay?"

It took all of Kyana's willpower not to snatch the phone from Haven's ear and stomp on it. Zeus, she hated Drake Mallone. "C'mon. Let's go before I vomit listening to their baby talk," she muttered when they'd moved out of Haven's hearing distance.

"What's wrong? It's kind of sweet." Ryker shut the door behind them and they stepped into the gray of dusk. The bodies of the slain Leeches had already been swept up by the cleaning members of the Order, but traces of their blood, and Kyana's, was still splattered on her wall, the sidewalk, and the street, and sprayed the palm trees. She was going to have to hire someone to pressure wash the place when things calmed down.

"Sweet in the sense of watching a Leech devour a newborn. You have to be perverse to enjoy it."

Chapter Fourteen

What the hell took you so long?" Geoff all but shouted the minute Kyana arrived outside Spirits. He'd been talking to Marcus, who excused himself and ducked back inside. "I sent Haven after you nearly an hour ago."

Kyana wasn't the least bit intimidated by Geoff's show of anger. The twinkle in his dark blue eyes said he'd found something good. She could've been a day late and he would've still been waiting.

"Let's go in. You can tell us what has you so excited."

Geoff placed his hand on the door, keeping Kyana from opening it. "Not in there. Follow me."

Geoff led them through Below to a small garden behind the Healing Circle—a sort of hospital for the mystical types. He sat on the lone bench and Kyana sat beside him. Ryker chose to remain on his feet, towering over them both. "Okay, what gives? I haven't seen you this excited about something since that time we went out deliberately looking to be ambushed."

"You wanted to be ambushed?" Ryker leaned against a large oak. "Why would you do that?"

"We were bored," Geoff said, as if that explained everything.

In short, it did. Until the breakout, things were known to get dull from time to time. They'd had to make their own sort of entertainment. Kyana felt Ryker's questioning gaze burning into her face. "What? He's a bad influence. Glare at *him*."

Geoffrey laughed. "Sorry, lass. Not taking the credit for that one. It was all you and your mate, Silas. I just tagged along for kicks."

Pulling the conversation back to the present, Kyana said, "Have you found something that will help us find our traitor?"

"Oh have I." He pulled some crumpled pages from his hip pocket. "Back in the day, Cronos was well loved. According to the stories, even his exile didn't make his followers waver. When he told them that he'd be back, they believed him."

Kyana's gaze found Ryker's. Icky had been told the same thing.

"That kind of magic doesn't exist anymore," Ryker insisted.

"Some apparently believe it still does." Geoff smoothed the pages on his knee. "Stories of Cronos's greatness are still being passed down through the generations. From what I understand, not many follow in the footsteps of their ancestors. But there are a few"— he winked, holding the pages just out of Kyana's reach—"that may even surprise you."

Her fingers itched to reach out and snatch the papers

from him, but she wouldn't play his game. She'd learned a long time ago to let him wear himself down. He'd eventually get tired of being the only one to know his secret and tell her.

Ryker, however, hadn't learned that. When Geoff waved the pages trying to get her to reach for them, Ryker leaned forward and took them.

"Hey, that's taking the fun out of everything."

"We don't have time for *fun*," Ryker growled, handing the paper to Kyana. "What is he, five?" Ryker whispered in Kyana's ear as he leaned in to scan the names with her.

Kyana chuckled. "More like two hundred and five." She leaned in closer to Ryker. "Peter Pan syndrome. He's the poster boy."

Geoff glared, but quickly forgot the insult as Kyana began to read the names on the list. "So these are descendants of original worshippers?"

Geoffrey nodded. "After a little checking, I discovered that at least fifteen are dead, and another fifty were in human lockup when the breakout happened. They could be dead now too but regardless, they weren't free to unlock Hell."

"So many in jail?" Ryker asked.

"Hey, they're not exactly holding to morals down here. Why would they be Above? It's my guess that most of these window lickers have committed their share of crimes."

Kyana looked at the names with the sloppy asterisks next to them. She read each one, but none of them was familiar to her. "There are still a lot who aren't dead or in prison," she muttered.

"About thirty that I found, yeah. But that's a good sixty-five less than you would be searching through."

"And how many more are there that we're unaware of because their families never supported Cronos? There are bound to be new recruits," Ryker said.

"At least as many as those on this list who never supported the beliefs of their ancestors," Kyana said, flipping back to the first page to begin scanning the names to see if she recognized anyone to give her a starting point. "Not everyone with a great-great-great Cronos-supporting granny is going to carry on the tradition."

That meant a lot of these names were going to be useless.

She kept scanning, waiting for a glimpse of the names Geoffrey had thought might surprise her.

"Oh, and there is one other thing."

Not bothering to look up, Kyana nodded. "Sure, what?"

"As payment for gathering that list, there's one person on it that I get to question personally."

"Payment? I thought a clean house was payment."

Geoffrey's eyes hardened. "Let me question him and you're off the hook."

The fine hairs on her nape stood at attention. She shook her head and returned to quickly scanning the list. She spotted him about halfway down the second page. "Are you sure?"

"Yeah, lass, I'm sure."

Ryker leaned over Kyana's shoulder to find the name that had caused the conversation to halt. "Drake Mallone? Isn't that—"

"Yeah," Kyana answered before he could finish asking his question. "Haven's boyfriend."

Kyana was halfway back to the portal alcove before Ryker caught her. He spun her around to face him, gripping her shoulders painfully. "Neither one of you will go anywhere near this man."

"Watch yourself, Surfer Boy. We're working together. I don't take orders from you."

"True, but you do take them from Artemis. If we determine that Drake Mallone is, or has ever been, a Cronos supporter, *I* will question him. Do you understand?"

"His name's right there." Kyana slapped the crumpled pages against his chest. "What more do you need?"

"Proof." Ryker's grip loosened. "You said yourself that most on that list will not be Cronos supporters. Just because his ancestors might have been, doesn't make him a traitor."

"But he could be."

"Maybe. And if he is, he'll need to be questioned. A lot. I won't have either of you bloodsuckers quieting someone who can potentially lead us to a whole herd—and possibly to the key to Tartarus."

Bloodsuckers? Kyana stepped back. She'd thought they were beyond trading insults.

Ryker flinched. "Sorry. I didn't mean—"

"Yeah," she said. "You did. But it's okay. We *bloodsuckers* have thick skin." She turned for the portal once more. "We won't touch him, but we *will* be there for questioning, and I want to make damned sure that Haven isn't around when we do it."

"Kyana, wait." This time, it wasn't Ryker who tried

to stop her. It was Geoffrey. "We can't just pounce on Haven's beau without solid proof first. At least proof that he's a supporter."

He was right, but that knowledge did nothing to soothe Kyana's temper. "And how do we get that?"

Ryker eased between Kyana and the portal and slipped Geoffrey's list from her hand. "I was thinking about that." He shook the papers in his fist. "This isn't the only list that's been created lately. The list of Chosen has also been written and rewritten with each Chosen's death. The deaths of the Chosen means that someone other than the Fates have seen that list."

Kyana propped a hand on her hip. "Yeah, we already know we're dealing with a traitor."

"A traitor with the means to sneak into the *Moerae's* cave?"

Her hand fell to her side as she began to understand what Ryker was getting at. "So that narrows the list down to Mystics and Witches. Someone who could cast a cloaking spell."

"Right," Geoffrey added. "Because even if a Witch or Mystic cast such a spell on someone else, it wouldn't have lasted long enough for our traitor to make it down to the cave and back. It would have had to have been cast again. Good thinking, wanker."

Ryker shot Geoffrey a glare. "Okay, so we start there. We scratch off all non Mystics and Witches."

"If we knew all the names on the list, sure. But we don't know what race each of these names belongs to."

"The Moerae do. We go see them, and our job is cut in half, hopefully."

Without waiting to see if Geoffrey and Kyana would

follow, Ryker stormed off in the direction of the Fates' cave. Since Ryker had the list of names, Kyana chose to follow. He might be on to something. It was worth waiting to lash out about the whole Drake thing later to finally get somewhere now.

To get to the cave that would lead them to the River Styx, they had to pass through a wide street with an open view to the human sanctuary the Order had created on the beaches of Below. As they walked, Kyana's gaze scanned the small white tents packed along the shores. The humans were quiet tonight; a lone bonfire in the distance seemed to have become the gathering point. She watched them, saw a young boy run out from a pack, his arms flailing over his head while his small mouth emitted a horrible siren noise that shattered the peaceful evening.

The child ran up to a smiling woman and poked his finger in her back. "Freeze, lady! You're under arrest!"

The play session ended in a tickle fest on the sand, and Kyana didn't realize she'd stopped walking till Ryker called out to her a fair distance away.

"Coming?" he asked, making his way back to her side.

"Yeah." But still, she didn't move, her mind spinning, her feet frozen to the walk that bordered the beaches. "No. Geoffrey said a lot of our names were in prison. We're talking about a group of morally defunct people. So isn't there a chance that even more of them have been arrested at some point?"

"I guess. Why?"

From over Ryker's shoulder, she watched Geoffrey make his way back. "What's going on?"

"I was just thinking," Kyana continued. "If we're dealing with Cronos supporters, we're not dealing with the good guys, right? We already know a lot of them are criminals. I'm willing to bet even more are. If they support Cronos, then they support his belief of take what you want, to hell with the consequences."

"So?" Ryker studied her, making Kyana shift uncomfortably. "Even if they were busted for something, it's not going to bring us any closer to knowing who's picking off the Chosen."

"Maybe it will."

Geoffrey eased himself between Ryker and Kyana, earning him a stern glare from Ryker. "What did you have in mind?"

"We've already determined that it would take a Witch or a Mystic to cloak themselves and get into the Fates' cave to see that scroll. That makes our traitor human born. This is one time the humans actually have something useful that we don't."

It was Ryker who spoke. "What might that be?"

"A human fingerprint-scanning thingamajig."

When Ryker rolled his eyes, the heat of both embarrassment and irritation crept up Kyana's cheeks. "Why not? Humans and human borns are the only ones who'd leave fingerprints. If they touched that scroll to see the names of the Chosen, they wouldn't have been able to conceal the evidence that they'd been there. There's no spell for that that I know of, and even if there was, no spell is permanent. It had to have worn off by now."

No one looked all that eager to throw Kyana a bone.

"What would it hurt to run it through the thingamajig?" she asked.

"It's not a bad idea," Geoffrey said. "At least it's a place to start."

"You're calling it a thingamajig," Ryker said. "How do you plan on using their computers when you don't even know what it's called?"

Kyana glared at him, peeved that she didn't have an answer. "How hard can it be? Push a few buttons, ba-da-bing, done."

"How 'bout here, lass? Look around. A thousand or more humans right in front of us. There's bound to be at least one who can help us."

"See." Kyana smirked at Ryker. "Ba-da-bing."

Chapter Fifteen

Flanked on either side by Ryker and Geoffrey, Kyana approached the lapping sounds of the ocean and led the way onto the beach. They'd decided to go ahead and look for help dusting for a print before heading to the Moerae's cave. Better to make that trip once, and have their human with them to do the job immediately. Between the Moerae scratching off names that didn't belong to either a Witch or a Mystic, and a possible fingerprint, they might finally figure out who would want the Chosen dead so badly that they would open the gates to Hell.

"I'll take the eastern side of the beach. You and Geoffrey can take the western," she said to Ryker. It wasn't that the thought of strolling the moonlit beach—faux moon or not—with Ryker wasn't appealing. It was. *Too* appealing. She didn't need the distraction.

"I'm not taking Peter Pan. He stays with you."

Geoffrey scowled. "Uncalled for, mate."

Kyana rolled her eyes. "Fine. We'll meet in thirty minutes."

When Ryker stalked off in the opposite direction, Kyana stepped to the end of the jetty and drank in the strangeness before her. She'd known the Order had taken in humans, had heard Geoff say there were thousands, but she'd thought he'd been exaggerating. She hadn't imagined they'd be packed in like sardines. There were tents as far as the eye could see. People huddled together in groups, their weary faces filled with disbelief and fright as they stared into the ocean and the vastness beyond.

Her distaste for them grew exponentially. Spineless. If it had been Kyana's world that had been overrun with Dark Breeds, none of those who called Below home would have rolled over and played dead. Instead of fighting for their homes, these people were leaving it to others to save them. Maybe the world *would* be better off without the human race. When they weren't killing each other, they were cowering in the corner. A flipping shame.

But, that they were here, hiding from the chaos that had overrun them, produced a new problem for Kyana. She ran her tongue over her fangs. These people had seen more than their kind was ever meant to see. They'd never believe anyone with fangs was the good guy.

Moving down the beach, she and Geoff studied the people, searching for someone they could approach. Someone with fight left in them who didn't show fear. It was like trying to find gold in a pile of shit.

Several feet in front of them, the child she'd seen playing earlier shot out from one of the tents. His laughter rang out carefree and joyous as he ran from whoever might be playing with him. When he neared

Kyana and Geoffrey, his steps faltered and he fell backward in surprise.

Geoffrey stooped and helped the boy stand. " 'Ello."

Even a boy, no more than four, knew danger when he saw it. The laughter died. A scream split the air. "Daaa-ddy!"

Two dozen heads poked out of their tents. The people on the beach seemed to turn in unison to stare at the sudden commotion. Kyana could tell they wanted to assist the little boy, to defend him; however, fear kept their feet rooted to the sand.

Kyana sighed and glared at Geoffrey. "Had to talk to the little shi—"

"What's going on?" A mousy woman in coveralls stepped out of the nearest tent to lay a protective hand on the screaming boy's shoulder. Kyana recognized her as the woman the kid had played with before.

No use taking all night to find someone who'd help them. Now that they had everyone's attention, might as well make the most of it. Kyana raised her hands in the air and let out a shrill whistle.

"Yep! We're Vampyre!" she shouted. "Now that we've cleared that up, let me remind you that, more than likely, it was a Vamp who saved your sorry asses and brought you here. Set your distrust aside for five minutes and gather 'round."

When the more than two dozen bodies took their sweet time obeying her, it was all she could do not to scream in complete frustration. She understood their hesitation, but, damn it, she was tired of being looked at like she was the bogeyman. Most of the time, she reveled in that. But now, when she had a job to do, their fear was more annoying than ego-boosting.

She faked a yawn and poked Geoff in the ribs. "Wake me when they stop pissing their pants and get within hearing distance."

Something touched the small of her back and she turned her head to see Ryker standing behind her, his hand playing with the back of her shirt as he stared out at the crowd around them. A wave of delight rippled over her. It disappeared just as quickly when he dropped his hand and stepped forward to address the crowd.

"I'm not Vampyre," Ryker announced. "We're all on your side here, so please, come forward. We need your help so we can start righting the wrongs done to all of you."

Charm oozed out of his voice, out of his pores, hypnotizing the crowd. Kyana rolled her eyes. Mr. Magic Tongue. He could sweet-talk his way into a ninety-year-old man's pants if he wanted to.

"Funny," she muttered. "I thought I just said the same thing."

He looked down at her, his lips curled into a light smile, his blond hair whipping about in the sea breeze. "It's not in the words. It's in the tone. It's called compassion. They can hear it."

"Thanks for the tip."

He seemed to have missed her sarcasm because he nodded and said, "Sure thing."

After what felt like an eternity, they had a nice little circle of meek human stench surrounding them.

"This is Kyana." Ryker grabbed her shoulders and gave them a light shake that made her ache all the way down to her toes. "She'd like to talk to you for a minute, and if you can ignore her fangs and remind yourselves that she's as harmless as a spayed kitten, we can be done here and let you all return to your evening."

Kyana plastered on a fake smile and muttered, "Asshole," between clenched teeth.

To the crowd, she simply said, "We need a cop. An ex-cop, a new cop, an old cop, a bad cop. Whatever. So, who's game?"

If beaches housed crickets, the chirping would have been deafening.

"Oh for the love of Zeus. Don't tell me there's not a single cop here in the middle of a tiny sea of humans? No one wants to be a hero? Seriously?"

Chirp, chirp.

The screaming boy's mother nervously bit her lip, her gaze darting between her tiny tent and Kyana.

"What?" Kyana asked, fighting to keep the biting tones from her voice. "There a cop in there?"

She nodded, her eyes wide and full of fear. "My . . . my husband."

"Jesus, Cynthia!" a voice bellowed from within the flimsy fabric. "I told you not to let them know I was in here!"

"What kind of cop hides from possible danger while his wife and kid are smack in the middle of it?" Kyana demanded.

"The kind who's had a shotgun trained on your ass since you stepped onto our beach," the man said.

Sure enough, the nose of a double-barreled shotgun

showed itself from the flap in the tent. It nudged the flap open, then G.I. Joe himself stepped into the night. Brown hair cut military short, bulging biceps, thick neck. He was the portrait of steroid abuse, and his hard eyes found his wife immediately.

"Get inside."

Distaste for how the man spoke to his wife coated Kyana's tongue. But as Cynthia passed him, the softening of his gaze and the slight movement of his lips sounding a silent *I love you* kept Kyana quiet. He was afraid for his family.

"You're a cop?" she asked him when his family disappeared inside, the sound of soft, childish whimpers weaving through the fabric of their shelter.

"Retired, but yeah, I am."

She stuck out her hand and pushed her fingers into the barrels of his gun. "You can put that away. Even if you had the nerve to use it, it wouldn't do anything but piss me off."

The gun remained trained on her chest.

"Fine. Have it your way." She ripped the gun from his hand, pressed the barrel to her thigh, and fired. The bullet ripped through her pants and tore into her leg. She flinched, more for needlessly ruining another pair of pants than for the prick of pain. Her skin hung open like a slaughtered hunk of meat, and as the crowd let out gasps and cries at the carnage and blood soaking her, they hushed as her skin pulled itself back together and healed in seconds.

"Try silver bullets, big guy. These don't do shit."

Still wouldn't kill her, but it would hurt like a bitch and take a long time to heal. It was why her daggers were made of pure silver without a hint of any other metal on them.

She looked to Ryker. His eyes were silently scolding her. "What?" she asked, dropping the gun onto the sand.

"Could've been silver for all you knew," he said through gritted teeth.

Kyana shrugged. "Wasn't though."

The cop picked the gun back up and trained it on her once again. Stupid man. "What's your name?"

"Detective Walker."

"There are no detectives anymore, Mr. Walker. A real name."

His left eye twitched. His jaw was clenched so tightly she could hear his teeth grinding. "Hank."

"Good then, Hank. It's your lucky night. You get to be a hero! Fun, right?"

He didn't look even slightly amused. Disappointing. "What exactly do you want from me?"

"If we provided you with an object, would you be able to dust it for prints?"

Hank's jaw ticked. He nodded.

"And then run it through the system to see if it's identifiable?"

"Maybe. If the print is salvageable."

"Will you try, Hank?" Ryker asked. When Hank hesitated, Ryker motioned toward the tent. "We're asking a lot of you, and we understand your reluctance to leave your family, but by helping us you'll be keeping them safe."

That seemed to gain his interest, but his wary gaze took in Kyana and Geoff. "How do I know I can trust you?"

"You'll have to take us at our word." Ryker shoved his hands into the pockets of his camos. "If this works, and you can lift a print and find a name to go with it, we might be able to save your world a whole lot faster."

"I know what's out there," Hank said. "I'll have to use the computers at the police station to run your print. That means going back up *there*. You can't ask me to leave my family *at night* to go with you."

"You don't strike me as a coward, Hank," Kyana said.

He looked at her as though she was shit on his shoe. She was getting really sick of that look. "I'm not. But I have a son who needs his father. Especially now. I'll go with you at dawn."

"Hank, come now, and you'll be back by dawn. Nothing up there is going to screw with you while you're with us."

As though sizing up an opponent, Hank raked his gaze over Kyana, then Geoffrey and Ryker. "You don't look like much. Just because you can stand up to a gun doesn't mean you can stand up to what I know is out *there*."

Ah, nothing hurt quite as badly as an insult from a human. Kyana sneered. "I might not be a feeding Vamp, Hank, but I'm still a Vamp. If I spit hard enough, I could blow a hole through your brain. Understand?"

He didn't flinch, but the slow rise and fall of his difficult swallow was victory enough.

"Fine. Let's go." Hank stuck his head inside the tent and said loud enough for them to hear, "If I'm not back by dawn, I'm giving my son permission to hunt you until the day he dies."

"Good times," Kyana said, glad to see the cop they'd nabbed had a bit of grit. Hooray for nonwuss humans. They were a rare breed.

As he rejoined them and the group made their way through the thinning crowd back toward the main streets of Below, Hank shook his head, his face red and blotchy.

"Guess it's better we go at night," he said. "If I'm going to die, I don't want to see it coming."

Kyana stood on the shores of the River Styx and listened to the discussion between Ryker and Hank. Their big, badass cop didn't want to get on Charon's little boat. Hell, it had taken him nearly an hour to enter the cave leading to the river in the first place. Then another half an hour to convince him to finally give up the shotgun he'd brought along. He was like a kid on a big slide, ready to wet his pants at the thought of sliding down, yet unwilling to face his fear to climb back down the ladder either.

Between finding Hank, locating the tools he'd needed, and waiting for him to get a grip on his fear, they'd wasted most of the night.

"Oh, to hell with this." Kyana pushed by Ryker to stand nose to nose with Hank. "Get your coward ass on that boat or we will *put* you on the boat."

He folded his arms over his chest and shook his head. "I'm not going down there."

And you can't make me. Hank didn't say the words, but they were written all over his stance.

Kyana looked at Ryker. "We do this my way."

She flung Hank over her shoulder in a fireman's hold and stepped onto Charon's little boat.

"Don't tell me what you will or won't do," Kyana growled, dumping Hank on his ass.

She looked at Ryker. "Now pay Charon and let's get this over with."

Ryker did as she said, but his glare remained fixed on her. "You can't go around manhandling people. We need him."

"Is this about the free will thing again?" Kyana braced herself and watched the distant shore. The last thing she'd tolerate was a damned human challenging her. "We're trying to save *his* world. He doesn't get to choose whether he wants to help. It's his duty. And ours to make sure he does it."

Ryker frowned. "Is that your answer to everything? To force people to do things your way?"

"Yeah, it works well for me too."

"Well it doesn't work for me. Some of us believe in compromise."

"Compromise?" She lowered her voice. "You lie to get people to do things your way. I intimidate. Same difference except my way produces faster results."

"I lie?"

"You told him he'd be safe with us. That the Dark Breeds wouldn't challenge us. That's a lie. They'll come after us faster because he *is* with us. It'll be a hell of a victory if they can take one of us down."

Ryker stuffed his hands in his pockets. He stared thoughtfully at the approaching shoreline. "So they would succeed?"

"Hell no."

He grinned. "Then I didn't lie."

Chapter Sixteen

There was no doubt that Kyana's request to let Hank handle the list of Chosen hadn't set well with the Fates. Atropos hadn't stopped glaring since Kyana had stepped into the cave, and Clotho was obviously more than put off at the thought of anyone else getting her hands on that scroll. But Lachesis had seemed to think Kyana was on to something.

Kyana suspected this was the only reason Clotho had given in.

With a grace no mortal could possess, Clotho floated to the far side of the Sisters' cave. She pulled a glowing emerald from her neck, then bent and placed the stone securely into a chest the size of a shoe box and opened it. Kyana had to shield her eyes from the intense glow that spilled forth. The scroll was ten times wider and thicker than the chest itself, installed there, of course, by magic.

"I'm telling you there's no evidence of our culprit on this scroll," she said, cradling the treasure to her chest. "The parchment isn't normal. It would tell us if someone other than a Fate had touched it. There would be smudges or . . . oh my goddess."

As she handed the scroll to Lachesis, she too stared at it bug-eyed. "It cannot be! There was no evidence of it being handled when we last saw it."

"I don't understand," Clotho said. "She's right. There was nothing here before . . ."

"Illusion Charm." Kyana reached into her vest and pulled out her own Illusion Charm. "Whoever read this list had an illusion cast and it's worn off. The question is, could it be a mark left by a god who might have touched it prior to the charm's use?"

"No," the Fates and Ryker answered in unison.

Kyana looked at Ryker. "How can you be so certain?"

"Gods don't have fingerprints," Lachesis answered instead, her voice a whisper.

"Oh." Why hadn't she known that? Kyana held out her hand. "May I see the scroll?"

Clotho looked as though Kyana had just asked to feel her up. "You've seen the damage it causes. No one touches this list."

"Yeah, well, no one finds the key to Tartarus with an attitude like that." Kyana thrust her hand closer.

With a look to her sisters, Clotho reluctantly handed over the scroll. Because she could sense the fragility of the wax-coated parchment, Kyana lightly gripped the corners and examined the smudged thumbprint. She raised the scroll to her face, ignoring the smell of dust and Clotho, and focused her attention on the print. She sniffed deeply, pleased to find it held exactly what Kyana had been hoping for. A scent. Something she could finally trace.

Carefully, she set the scroll on the altar before turning to Hank. "Treat that as if your life—all our lives—depends on it. Don't touch it more than you have to." Then remembering the black powder Geoff had had to hunt down, she added, "And try not to make a complete mess."

When Hank reluctantly nodded, she returned her attention to the Sisters. "Let me see the lock again."

No one said anything as Atropos dug through the same chest Clotho had opened and handed Kyana the obsidian lock they'd pulled out of Tartarus. Ignoring the freezing burn on her fingers, she sniffed it. The sulfuric odor on the lock constricted her throat. The odor was the same inhuman one she'd smelled on the island. She forced herself to hold the lock, to breathe in its scent, to search for an underlying smell. This one was different from the one on the scroll. Damn. She'd been hoping to find proof that whoever had seen that scroll had also opened Tartarus. They were dealing with more than one person.

Clinging to the new smell of sulfur and pheromones on the lock, she committed this one, and the one surrounding the print—an odd blend of tea and . . . bad cologne—to memory. Satisfied that she'd remember both, she set the lock beside the scroll. "Dust that too."

Hank grumbled incoherently, not looking up from his task. His oversized hands cradled the wax-coated scroll as he gently copied the dusted print onto some tape, then pressed it to a card and stuck it into the makeshift tool kit Geoff had helped put together. The release of tension was palpable when he handed the scroll back to Clotho and turned his attention to the obsidian lock.

Now that the Sisters had their precious scroll back, Kyana tapped Ryker's chest. "Give me Geoffrey's list."

Ryker's gaze warned her to be respectful, but he placed the crumpled pages in her hand.

"You three know everyone within the Order, right?"

Lachesis nodded. She toyed with her braid. Her intense stare focused on Kyana. "When someone pledges loyalty to the Order, I read their intentions to make sure they're pure. So yes, we know of everyone."

"Can you tell us which names on this list are human-born?"

"Of course," Atropos stated. "Why?"

"Because with any luck, a name on this list could match the owner of that fingerprint. It would help narrow down Hank's search if we knew which names belong to people who actually *have* fingerprints."

Clotho stepped forward. "Ryker, do you and Geoffrey also believe knowing the races of those on your list will assist you in capturing our traitor?"

Kyana bit her lip to keep from flinging a stinging insult at the Fate. She hated that they'd put her in charge of this mission, but didn't trust her now to do the job. Insulting them wouldn't gain their assistance, though, so she gritted her teeth and remained silent, while shooting deadly glares at Ryker and Geoff, daring either one of them to contradict her.

"We do," Ryker answered.

"Very well, then." Clotho held out her hand. "Let me see your list."

Kyana set the pages on the altar. The Sisters leaned over it, conversing softly. Even though she stood only a few feet away, Kyana couldn't make out the words. She looked to Ryker, saw him nodding, and knew he was privileged to their conversation. When she looked at Geoff, she found him watching her.

"How come we can't hear them speaking?" Kyana whispered.

Geoff raised a dark brow. A slow grin teased his mouth. "Who says I can't?"

"You can hear them?"

"I can't," Hank muttered.

Somehow, that the human couldn't hear the Sisters didn't make her feel a damned bit better.

"There are still about thirty names on your list, but more manageable than what you started with." Atropos held the pages out to Kyana. "I also took the liberty of marking off those who have passed beyond your realm of questioning, as well as those who have stood before us recently and we know are still loyal to the Order."

Kyana quickly scanned the list looking for one name. There was a golden mark next to Drake Mallone's name indicating his race, but he had not been crossed off as a known loyal.

"Thank you, Sisters," Ryker said, taking the list from Kyana and stuffing it back in his pocket. "We appreciate your assistance."

"Kiss ass," Kyana and Geoff hissed, earning them glares from the Fates and a chuckle from Hank.

With a grin, she nodded at the lock. "How's it coming? Almost done?"

"Nada. I can salvage the one on the scroll, but there's nothing on this." He dropped the lock back to the altar and rubbed his hands on his jeans. "How can a chunk of rock cause frostbite in Florida . . . well, under Florida, or wherever we are?"

No one bothered to answer the question. They had the print on the scroll and needed to get to work finding its owner. "Let's go," Kyana said, starting for the entrance. "We've lost hours tonight. We only have about three left before sunrise."

"You're welcome." Hank's face was red, his hair sweaty. He looked like a man who'd just defused a bomb with half a second to spare.

"Thank you, Hank," Ryker said, clasping the big man on the back.

"Don't break out your pom-poms yet." Gesturing for everyone to follow her back to the ferry, Kyana tossed a quick glance back at their nervous cop. "He still has to find us a match."

Ryker waited for the others to move past him before following behind. His gaze steadily locked on the back of Hank's head. This time, if he hesitated to get on the ferry, Ryker himself would toss the man on. They really didn't have much time to waste.

Luckily, Hank seemed far less hesitant to step on the ferry this go-round. Heading *out* of death's realm was loads easier than heading *into* it.

"You do know it's not guaranteed that the owner of this print is in the system?" the cop said.

"I know." Kyana stretched her arms over her head.

Ryker pulled a coin from his pocket and tossed it to Charon. The old spirit caught it, and it promptly vanished into thin air.

As Hank collapsed onto his backside and rubbed the back of his neck, he peered up at them, pale-faced.

"You're not going to kill me if I can't trace it, right? You'll know it's not my fault?"

"We're not the bad guys, Hank," Kyana said. "I'd hoped you would have realized that by now."

"Wow," Geoffrey said, grinning. "Not going to take the piss out of him? No obvious enjoyment over the idea of killing him for no reason?"

Ryker had been thinking the same thing, but the way Geoffrey teased Kyana made a gnawing irritation simmer in Ryker's gut. He swallowed it down, reminding himself that Geoffrey and Kyana had known each other for decades longer than he'd known either of them. Jealousy was a useless emotion, but it wasn't easily dismissed.

Kyana shot Geoffrey a glare. "I'm just anxious to get this done so hopefully we'll have somewhere to go from here."

"Like bed?" Ryker said. His gaze fell to the hint of cleavage squishing out of the top of Kyana's vest. Bits of debris dusted her long, black curls and a smudge of dirt stained her otherwise porcelain cheeks. She looked good disheveled. So good, in fact, it must have been written all over his face, because her eyes darkened when his stare locked on hers.

Ryker cleared his throat, aware, suddenly, that Geoffrey and Hank were watching, amused. "To sleep, I mean."

Hank sneezed, jolting Ryker out of his wide-awake wet dream. "Sorry," Hank said, digging a tissue from his back pocket and blowing his nose. "Can't seem to get that smell out of my head."

Kyana's gaze finally pulled away from Ryker's. "What smell?"

"The one in that cave. No idea what it was, but it was driving me crazy. Think it messed with my sinuses."

"I hate that damned cauldron," she muttered. "You guys didn't seem disturbed by it. You smell it when you go there, don't you?"

Geoffrey nodded.

Ryker shrugged. "I didn't use to. Started smelling it a few years ago, though."

"Do you know what it is?"

The ferry jolted to a stop. Kyana obviously wasn't ready for it and nearly toppled over the side. Ryker grabbed her by the arm and kept her on her feet. "I don't know what it is in particular, no. It's different for everyone," he said, helping her from the boat. "But supposedly, it's like liquid contentment."

The entire troupe stopped walking, all eyes on Ryker. Even know-it-all Geoffrey was interested in what Ryker had to say.

"If you can smell it," Ryker continued, "you're lacking the one thing that will make you truly content in this world. Clotho makes it and inserts it with the souls she places into bodies. It gives the soul something to search for while it lives. A mission to complete, so to speak."

A mission he hadn't found until he'd met Kyana ten years ago. Since then, that smell had been just as strong for him as it seemed to be for others. That pull to her Lychen half, that desire that ate up his insides like wildfire, had crept up on him instantly and made him susceptible to what lay in that brew. His life's mission . . . incomplete now that he'd met Kyana.

No way he'd tell her that, though. She was already commitment shy. If he told her he knew they were destined to be life mates, she'd run from him and never look back.

"So if you don't smell it . . ."

Ryker swallowed. "Then whatever it is you were meant to find has found you. You should be content . . . or dead."

Or left to spend eternity completely miserable and alone.

You should be content.

Kyana pondered that statement all the way back through Below. She liked her life. A lot. That was contentment, right? So why could she smell whatever was in that cauldron? It wasn't exactly a subject she considered often, if at all. She lived, hunted, ate, bathed. That pretty much summed up all her desires. Except sex, of course, but that was becoming as scarce these days as human blood in her drinks.

That particular thought sent her gaze roaming over Ryker's backside as he led the way down the street toward the portal alcove that would take them back into St. Augustine. Her blood heated, briefly taking the chill from her skin. Ah, sex. How she missed it.

And what about him, anyway? He'd said he'd only started smelling it a few years ago. What had changed for him? What had cost him his contentment?

They stepped through the portal into the fort where Farrel and Crag waited loyally beside Geoffrey's minions, Larkin and Cahir. Ryker eyeballed them. "What are they doing here?"

"I figured we might need them," Geoff said.

"But how'd you— Never mind." Kyana shrugged. It didn't matter how Geoff had called for the minions. She'd stopped guessing about Geoffrey's mysterious ways a long time ago. It was a handy trait at times— and since this was one of those times, she wasn't about to push the issue.

"We don't need—"

"Yes, we do," Kyana interrupted Ryker. "We'll need more eyes if we want to get to the police station and back without Hank losing vital bits."

Hank's eyes bulged. "I vote for taking them with us."

"How the hell do you do anything with so many bodies around all the time?"

"They're coming," Kyana said, waiting for Hank to regain his composure after having all his energy sapped from the portal. "They're silent, Ryker, and even though they have their idiotic moments, they can be very useful."

"We ready to do this?" Geoff asked, pulling his hands out of his pockets.

Kyana nodded, checking each member of the group to make sure they too were ready. Everyone stared at Hank.

His shoulders were pulled back, his jaw clamped with obvious determination. He might be scared, but he wasn't going to wuss out this time. She watched as he reached beneath his shirt and whipped out a pistol. His beefy hand gripped his gun like his very life depended on it.

They'd managed to take his shotgun from him before entering the Fates' cave. No one had thought to check him for another weapon. Someone should take the useless gun from him before he hurt himself. She could do it, would do it if she had to, but she'd pushed their new friend pretty hard . . . and they hadn't even begun the fun stuff yet.

When no one else seemed inclined to broach the subject of turning over the pistol, she sighed. "Didn't I prove that thing's totally useless for what we're up against?"

Hank nodded.

She held out her hand. "Trust us to keep you safe."

His hand tightened around the weapon. "Forget it. It may not kill you, but I know it slows some of you down. It'll give me a fighting chance if you're not as good as he says you are."

"Oh, I'm that good. You can keep the gun for now if it makes you feel better, but if it becomes a problem I'll take it away and beat you with it."

"I'm really starting to hate you."

"Then I'm doing my job." And maybe, with a little luck from the gods, she'd be able to keep him alive. "Where's the police department?"

"Over on King Street. We can drive there in a couple minutes."

They all shook their heads. A vehicle would draw more attention than their little scouting party could handle. Kyana mapped out the fastest path in her head. They'd have to stick to side streets and backyards. It wouldn't be an easy stroll. "We'll have to hoof it."

Ryker nodded, Hank looked like he was going to

be sick all over his shoes, and Geoffrey was staring at Kyana's neck with more than passing interest. She shifted uncomfortably, wondering what the hell he was looking at. Turning her gaze away, she led the way to the gate, but was forced to let Ryker and Hank move past her when Geoffrey grabbed her arm. His fingers bit into the tender flesh.

"What?" she hissed, easing herself out of his grip.

His jaw clenched. "What the bloody hell happened to your neck? Is that a sun blister?"

She followed slowly behind Ryker and Hank as they wended across the fort's courtyard. "I'm fine, Geoffrey. Look, it's almost gone."

She stretched the collar of her vest down to offer him a better look as he strolled beside her.

He peered down at her throat, his gaze narrowing. "Why didn't a Healer tend you?"

"How do you know one didn't?" Hell, Kyana could barely see the pink of her skin anymore. What Ryker had done for her had been better than anything a Healer could have done.

He leaned toward her and inhaled deeply. "Because if they had, you'd smell like lavender. Not shampoo."

"Since when are you so well versed in herbal remedy?"

"I hooked up with a Mystic a couple years back." Geoff shuddered. "I learned a lot about their potions."

"Oh?" Kyana laughed. "What exactly did you learn?"

"Most importantly is not to piss them off or they will fix things you'd never considered broken."

Just thinking about poor Geoffrey spending an

entire week without one of his constant hard-ons made her chuckle. "Taught you a valuable lesson, did it?"

He nodded. "Damned right. Don't screw around with people who can screw around with your ability to screw around. Thank the gods it was only temporary, but I've sworn off Mystics and Witches."

"Even Haven?"

He grinned. "I wouldn't go that far. If I could just get her to lose that prick Drake, I'd make her purr. Now 'nough dodging me, lass. How'd you heal from the sun?"

Of its own accord, her gaze drifted to Ryker. She snapped it away the instant she realized what she'd done, but it was too late. Geoffrey had seen.

"Ah. Friendlier than I thought, the two of you. Fed you, did he?"

"Geoffrey . . . mind your own business."

Kyana's dismissal seemed to work. Geoffrey grinned and nodded at Ryker, who'd slowed his pace to glare over his shoulder at them. "I think your boy toy is jealous."

"He's not my boy toy."

"But you want him to be."

Kyana elbowed him in the ribs and quickened her steps to avoid his probing gaze. The sentinels acknowledged their group, wished them a successful hunt, then slowly lowered the old drawbridge. She positioned Hank between herself and Geoff, then instructed the two pairs of minions to lag behind slightly. If anything tailed them, they'd know it.

As they made their way toward Castillo Drive, she scanned the shadows and sniffed the air. Most of the bodies had been cleaned off the road, but the lingering stench of death still mingled with the scent of the bay. She glanced over her shoulder. Ryker and Geoff were also scouting the roads ahead. When they'd reached the same conclusion that, for now, they were alone on the streets, Kyana set off at an easy jog.

Adrenaline pumped through her blood, warming her chilled skin. Her senses on high alert, she scanned every shadow and darkened window. Anyone, human or non, was the enemy. They couldn't let their guard down.

She stopped at an intersection and pulled the troupe into the shadows. Squatting, she watched the darkness. Their target was almost within sight. However, the fine hairs on the back of her neck were tingling. She strained her ears, but the only sounds she detected were Hank's labored breaths.

"What is it?" Hank's whisper sounded like a shout in the stillness.

Kyana raised her head, sniffed the air. Rot and decay burned her nose. "Things are about to get interesting."

"I don't see anything," Geoff said, his voice barely a whisper on the wind.

"Me either," Ryker admitted. "Do we risk it?"

"See what?" Hank asked.

"Leeches." Kyana couldn't see them either, but she could sure as hell smell them. She looked at Ryker. "They're looking for something."

His silver eyes swirled. "Or someone."

Stay and fight, or run like hell? If not for Hank, Kyana would have opted for a good fight. She owed them an ass-kicking for the knife wound still itching her ribs. Not to mention the burns. But now wasn't the time for revenge.

"Ryker, if they make it by our minions, keep them off our asses."

Then she sent Farrel and Crag in one direction and Larkin and Cahir in the other.

Satisfied, Kyana fisted her hand in Hank's sleeve. "Stay close, don't make a sound, and you might just live to see your son again."

Chapter Seventeen

Kyana dragged Hank behind her as she took off toward King Street. They made it the last hundred yards to the police station undetected. She scanned the single-story building. Every possible entrance—be it door or window—would bring anyone in hearing distance down on their heads if she broke through them. She motioned to Geoff to guard the human, then swung her body onto the roof and pressed her belly to the shingles.

Not wanting to attract any attention, she slid her way from one end of the building to the other, then flipped over the side to examine the back windows. Just as she'd hoped, one was broken. There was hardly a building left in the city that hadn't been broken into or out of by either terrified humans or hunting Dark Breeds. The police station seemed to be no exception.

She lifted herself through the tiny opening and into a bathroom, where her boots crunched against broken glass. Making her way quickly through the building, she searched for any signs of movement before heading back to the front door and unlocking it from the inside.

As soon as the door popped open, she reached out and grabbed Hank by his shirt, yanking him inside. "What do you need?"

Hank pointed down the long, dark hallway. "The computers are that way."

He shuffled his feet down the dark hall as he was told. When he entered the large room filled with quiet computer banks, he looked at Kyana. "I have to power up the equipment. It's going to create quite a glow."

Just lovely. They'd made it inside undetected, now the light would attract every species of bogeyman roaming the streets. "Find something to cover the windows."

Hank picked his way across the room. "Or we could just close the blinds."

"Not dark enough. Trust me, you don't want them to know we're in here."

Ryker thrust a pile of blankets into Kyana's arms. "I think he gets it."

"Where'd you get these?" Kyana asked.

He pointed over his shoulder, where half a dozen sleeping bags and kerosene lamps lay in a pile.

She pawned the blankets off on Geoffrey, and the three men made short work of turning the room pitch black while Kyana double-checked the closed offices for any signs of survivors or Dark Breeds she might have missed on her first pass.

When she returned to the guys, the room was bathed in total darkness. Though she still didn't like their chances of remaining undetected with the extra light, she had no choice but to give her okay. They clicked on a desk lamp and left the overhead lights off.

Hank rubbed his hands together, then began pushing buttons. Electronic equipment whirred to life. Monitors flickered on. Green lights glowed. Kyana cupped her ears, the intense whistle of radio waves so close to her head making her eyes throb. She backed into the hallway. Zeus, she hated electronics.

After several long minutes, Hank leaned back in his chair. "There ya go."

Breaths held, everyone but Kyana moved forward. She could almost taste roasted traitor on her tongue. "Who does it belong to?"

"I don't know. It's running now."

"What? I thought that thing read the print and ba-da-bing, we have the owner."

Hank shook his head. "Only on television. It takes time to run through all the databases. And then there's still no guarantee we'll know the owner."

"Well, how long does this take?"

Even in the darkened room, Kyana could see the color drain from Hank's face. "It could take hours . . . but more likely days."

The tickle of approaching dawn penetrated the dim room. Kyana could shift if the sun rose. Geoffrey could not. No way was she going to let him get trapped in here until it cycled back to nightfall.

"We don't have hours, and we certainly don't have days. We need this information now so we can get out of here."

"There's nothing more I can do but wait." Hank stood, his knees popping. "I don't know what to tell you."

"Stop the scan," Ryker said, rubbing his eyes.

"What? Why?" Frustration built in Kyana's chest, and she wanted to lash out and smash the glass monitors. "We need to give this a chance."

"Stop the scan," he repeated, directing his gaze at Hank. "Tell us what equipment you need. We're taking it with us."

"Taking it where, exactly?" Geoffrey asked, leaning his hip against the metal desk beside him.

"Below. Marcus has a television, so we know electronic equipment will work in Spirits. Even if we have to use magic to power it up, we know it can work." Ryker rubbed his forehead as though trying to scrub away a headache. "Listen, this thing might have to run for days. We can't leave it here and chance someone, something, shutting it down, or this place getting ransacked. We can't ask Hank to stay here for days and risk his life more than he has already. If we have to leave it running and leave Hank in charge of it, we take both him *and* the equipment to safety."

His dictatorial tone left no room for argument. Since he wasn't discarding the fingerprint idea, Kyana refrained from pointing out that he wasn't in charge.

"How're we going to get it back to the fort?" Geoffrey wore the faint trace of a grin, as though he thought Ryker had lost his mind. "I'm good, but even I don't have a hundred arms to tote all of this and still help protect the human. None of us do."

Ryker made his way to the door. He eased it open, allowing predawn light to filter in through the crack. In a loud whisper, he called for Crag. Kyana could hear nothing but their muffled conversation, and then the door closed and Ryker returned.

"Taken care of," he said, bending to help Hank unplug a computer tower. He looked over his shoulder at Geoffrey. "We'll tote this stuff to the door. I want you on the other side ready to take it to the car."

"What car?" Kyana demanded.

"The car Crag is finding for us. This time, we'll take our chances in exchange for speed. We'll drive the damned thing right up the drawbridge if we have to, but we should be able to outrun whatever might be stupid enough to chase us."

Kyana bit back a groan. Okay, so truthfully, she had discounted a vehicle as the method to get to the police department because it *would* have been loud and noisy. But she'd also discounted it because she really didn't do well with motion sickness. Charon's ferry made her queasy. She'd been inside a car only once, and when the mad, crazy taxi driver finally dropped her off at her destination he'd charged her extra to reupholster his cab. Three plane rides in her entire existence had also proved to be very bad ideas.

This did not brighten her mood.

"Can't we find a wheelbarrow or something?" she asked, only half joking.

Geoffrey watched her, his faint grin now a full-blown smirk. He knew her problem, had been by her side on one of those fateful plane rides. "Just aim out the window, Kyana. These pants are damned hard to clean."

Chapter Eighteen

Kyana choked down the queasiness rolling her near-empty stomach as she watched Hank, Geoffrey, and Ryker carry large pieces of computer equipment out the police station door. She hadn't even gotten into the damned vehicle yet and was already carsick.

"Here." Ryker stood before her holding a small vial and a bottle of water. He poured the powder into the bottle, swirled it, then handed it to Kyana. "Drink this."

Kyana didn't need to take the bottle to know it was something she didn't want to swallow. "It smells like rotten eggs." She lowered her voice. "I'm trying not to embarrass myself here."

"It will settle your stomach."

"That obvious?" Kyana winced. "Where'd you get this?"

"The people I port only turn that putrid shade of green if they suffer from motion sickness." He smiled. "I keep some antinausea potions on me, just in case I get passengers like you."

Would have been nice to know when he'd ported her out to that damned island.

He pushed the bottle into Kyana's hand. "Drink."

Resisting the urge to hold her nose, Kyana downed the liquid. Her throat closed. Her stomach rebelled but she managed to keep it under control. It tasted like she'd swallowed a fart.

Grimacing, she handed the bottle back to him. "Do all potions smell or taste like bodily functions?"

Ryker rubbed her back for several long, soothing moments before answering. "If it'll keep you on your feet, and not with your head tucked between your knees, all of us will thank the gods for this foul-tasting brew."

"We're almost done," Hank said, his voice carrying from one end of the building to the other, silencing her retort. "I don't know if we'll need all this, but I'd rather bring it than have to come back here again."

"If I have to get sick, I'm going to aim for your shoes," Kyana muttered as she pushed past Ryker and made her way to the door. Geoff jumped out of the back of the battered pickup Crag had commandeered and draped his arm around Kyana's shoulders. "You ready for this?"

She glared at him. "If I leave now, I could probably beat you guys back and not have to ride in that stupid invention."

"You'd trust us to keep your cop alive? Look on the bright side, you can hang your head over the side and won't get vomit on anyone's clothes."

"Bite me."

Geoff wiggled his eyebrows. "I'd love to, but you smell pretty bad."

"Damned potions," Kyana mumbled, easing out from under Geoff's arm. She looked at the sky. The blackness of night was giving way to the gray of dawn. "We need to get moving."

"I'm done." Hank set a box in the bed of the truck. "Now what?"

"Drive. Don't stop for any reason. If something gets in your way, run it over," Ryker told him. "We'll fight off anything that gets close."

Geoff bounded into the back of the pickup and held out a hand to assist Kyana. She ignored it, leaped in, and found a place near the cab to stand.

Ryker found his way to her side, his body tense and alert as they waited for the minions to pull themselves over the bed. The foursome settled around the boxes of electronics, then Ryker tapped the hood.

The engine roared to life. "Hang on to something," Hank yelled. The truck banged into gear and shot over the curb and onto the road.

Wind whipped her hair into her face. As she focused on the street, her eyes watered. The breeze carried the stench of danger, and Kyana's keen eyes picked out silhouettes crouched curbside.

"There," she warned.

"Things are about to get fun," Geoff said, moving to stand at her other side.

Groups of Dark Breeds approached from every direction. She gripped the knife at her back in her damp fist. Geoff did the same. She glanced at Ryker and frowned. He had no weapon.

Just lovely. She retrieved her dagger from her boot and passed it to him.

"I don't need that." His eyes darkened.

"You can't mesmerize them all with your swirling eyes." She forced the weapon into his hand.

He stubbornly tucked the dagger into his waistband. Kyana moved closer to the driver's door.

"It's party time." Geoff laughed as the first body flew in their direction.

The Dark Breeds seemed to understand if they took out Hank, they'd be able to take out the vehicle and leave the others open to attack. They came at him in groups of twos and threes. Kyana used her fist and her knife, working through them as quickly as possible, but still, they came.

Bodies dove at them, springing off the roads like they'd been picked up and tossed by funnel clouds. A fist connected with her lower back. Kyana roared with rage. She spun around, twisted the Leech's neck in one quick motion, then shoved its body over the side of the pickup. The sickening sound of bone and muscle giving way under the truck's tires brought great satisfaction to her aching body.

Her joy was short-lived as another barrage of Dark Breeds attacked. Hank fired out the window in rapid succession with one hand, the other frantically trying to keep the truck under control. The gun didn't stop them, but he was right, it did slow them down.

But not for long.

The closer they got to the fort, the faster the demons attacked. When they neared the end of King Street, a row of Dark Breeds blocked their path. Kyana hit the cab with her fist.

"Go through them!" She sliced the throat of the

Lychen trying to make it through the window to Hank. Blood spurted on her face, sprayed her vest. The body collapsed in the bed of the truck, only to be casually tossed out like garbage by Geoffrey.

"Hang on," Hank shouted. He floored the pedal, pushing the old pickup to its limits. Though some Dark Breeds were smart enough to leap from Hank's path, some weren't so quick. One hit the front of the truck with enough force to throw its body into the air and back into the windshield with a loud crash. Hank threw his arm up to shield himself from the imploding glass.

Ryker reached over the cab, grabbed the Dark Breed, and slung it to the street. He might not be skilled with weapons, but he held his own. His face showed evidence of battle. Bloody nose. Busted lip. Gashed cheek. She watched as he sent several Dark Breeds flying with nothing more than a wave of his hand. His telekinetic abilities kept several more Dark Breeds at bay, and those that made it through, he quickly dispensed of with his fist, the borrowed dagger still tucked in the waistband of his camos. It was apparent that he had earned the rank of general in Ares's army and hadn't merely been given the title. She owed him an apology. One he probably wouldn't get, but it was nice to know she could count on him to have her back when things got ugly.

She ignored the blows to her face and back, making those who struck her pay even while her tender flesh screamed for mercy. Geoff's roar ripped Kyana's attention from her duty of protecting the human. She turned to find a demon, his massive arms wrapped around Geoff's throat, attempting to pull him out of the truck as the vehicle swerved onto Castillo Drive and plowed through an overturned horse buggy.

Without moving, Ryker sent the Dark Breed flying out of the vehicle and somehow managed to keep Geoff from going over the side too.

Geoff wiped blood from his nose. "Thanks, mate."

Ryker nodded and returned his attention to the fight.

Kyana squinted against the wind to focus on the fort that was now in full view. However, an army of Dark Breeds stood between the truck and safety. They wouldn't make it without help. Kyana grabbed her flare from her hip and fired twice to alert the sentinels that they were under attack.

Hank ignored the parking area, bounced up the curb, and charged forward to the old pay station. Arrows flew from the bastions, raining fire down around them. Kyana jumped to the ground and ripped open the driver's door.

She hauled Hank out. "Move it," she yelled, half dragging, half carrying him to the nearest sentinel. "Get him inside!" She waited only long enough to make sure her orders were followed, before returning to stand with Ryker and Geoff. Even with the archer's arrows, they were outnumbered.

She looked at Geoff. A huge grin lit up his face. "What about it, lass? Head-on or tails tucked?"

If they retreated, there was no way the sentinels could get the drawbridge raised again before the Dark Breeds followed them into the fort. Ten to one odds weren't good for them, but promised to be interesting.

"Lock 'er down," Kyana yelled at the sentinel still manning his post. He hesitated for half a second.

"Now," she snarled, spurring him into action. She looked at Ryker, then Geoff. "We can't risk them getting inside."

"Which one?"

Kyana had gone on enough hunts—and been outnumbered enough times—to know what Geoffrey's question meant. There was always a leader. The one standing off calling the shots. That was the one they'd go after first.

Kyana pointed to the big beast standing on the low wall next to the bay. The creature spread its wings and cocked its head in Kyana's direction. "The Hatchling."

"Should be fun," Ryker said, his eyes going red.

Turning long enough to give their minions orders to guard Hank's equipment, she faced Ryker again. "Clear a path and we'll kill anything that gets close."

Moving as one, they worked their way into the middle of the fray. Even when Ryker sent a dozen of their pals flying with nothing more than his mind, the Dark Breeds didn't back down. The going was torturously slow. Bodies came at them from every direction, circling them, closing in. Arrows flew all around them. Only a bit of magic and a lot of luck kept them from being burned alive like the Dark Breeds they fought. Cries of pain and the scent of scorched flesh filled the air. Kyana lost count of the number of bodies she sent to the ground. Still they came. And still the trio moved forward.

Geoff's roar caused her to lose her focus. A fist connected with her jaw. "Piece of shit!"

Kyana slit her attacker's throat from ear to ear, then turned to check on Geoff. A group of Dark Breeds had him surrounded, and they were trying to pull him to the ground. If they succeeded, Geoff's chances of getting up again were somewhere between slim and never.

Not giving herself time to think, she rolled over the back of the closest demon, planting her boot in the face of another. In one smooth motion, she pulled Geoff upright, then bracing against him, kicked out, sending another pair stumbling. Several more went flying in every direction like bowling pins. She turned, nodding her thanks to Ryker, then grabbed Geoff's arm, pulling him behind her. It took her tired mind a moment to realize why he was so sluggish. The sun was quickly approaching. The leader of the group of Dark Breeds seemed to notice the same thing. Its small wings quivered. Its grunted order carried on the wind. Those that were still able, retreated.

Ryker moved to give chase, but Kyana grabbed his arm. "We'll get them another day."

Slowly, his eyes shifted from blood red to swirling silver as he scanned her from head to toe. Like him, she was covered in blood and not sure if it was all demons'.

"You and Geoff. Below, now," he said. "Leave the minions here to help. We'll meet you there shortly."

"We're capable of holding our own," Geoff said.

"Yeah, and I'd like to keep you that way." Ryker spoke to Geoff but his gaze stayed on Kyana. He pointed up. "Move it before we're sweeping your ashes off the sidewalk."

Not willing to risk another meeting with the sun until she was sure she could hold her Lychen form, Kyana took Geoff's hand and tugged until he reluctantly led the way over the lowering drawbridge and inside the fort. They quickly located Hank in the courtyard, where a Healer was tending his wounds.

Kyana was in no mood to be social. A low growl rumbled in her throat. She was tired, hungry, and hurt like hell. "Is he all right to go Below, or will the portal be too much for him?"

The woman nodded. "His wounds are minor. Most of the blood on him isn't his." The Healer looked from Kyana to Geoff and back again. "I'm happy to tend to your wounds too, if you're in need."

Kyana nodded in way of thanks . . . and dismissal. She held out her hand and pulled Hank to his feet. "We're fine."

Stepping into the portal alcove, Kyana sent Geoff through first, then Hank. She gave the men a couple of seconds—sure Hank would appreciate the time to gather himself—before she joined them. Both men leaned against the alabaster wall. Their breaths short and ragged. Exhaustion, along with the portal's drain, had taken everything they had left. She moved to stand between them, then slowly slid to the cool floor.

"Is it always like that?" Hank questioned as he sat.

Kyana shrugged. "The attack or the portal?"

Geoff sat with them and closed his eyes. "Not sure it matters. The answer's the same either way. Dark Breeds always fight with everything they have. Not usually in the numbers you saw tonight, though. Whether they're captured or killed, they're returned to Tartarus—Hell—so they literally have nothing to lose."

"And the portal?"

"It's a protective device. It momentarily weakens everyone to keep the gods safe should they come under attack." Kyana found herself smiling. "I'd tell you that you'll get used to it, but all you have to do is look at the two of us to know I'm lying."

"Just don't make me go through again anytime soon. Feels like my insides are being ripped apart, then put back together with Super Glue."

"Deal." Kyana grinned, pushing to her feet. She led them to Spirits. Hank needed to get set up as quickly as possible so he could hurry back to his family and let them know he was alive and well. Odd, but she was regarding him a bit more softly than she had before. He'd done them a service, and after his initial display of wussiness, hadn't cowered like others of his kind likely would have. If for no other reason, he'd earned a bit of her respect.

Chapter Nineteen

"You'd probably be more comfortable if you found a bed."

Kyana jumped at the sound of Haven's voice. Pain slithered down her spine as she stared up at her friend with fatigued eyes. Her throat ached for a drink. Kyana tried to stand, but her legs refused to move. Geoffrey slept beside her, his head resting on her thigh.

They'd been in one of Spirits's spare apartments, waiting for Hank to finish the tedious task of setting up his equipment while the minions brought in load after load of computer parts and Marcus attempted to enchant all of it to work Below. She hadn't meant to doze, but boredom and exhaustion must have taken over.

"Where'd you come from?" Kyana asked.

"I ran into Geoff moving this stuff in about twenty minutes ago." Haven smiled, but a sadness filled her eyes that made Kyana wince. Her mind instantly pulled up the image of Drake's name on their list of possible traitors. Haven needed to skedaddle before Hank started getting close to scanning that particular name. If it turned out he was guilty, Kyana wanted to be the one to tell her. If it turned out he wasn't, Haven would be pissed to all hell that he'd been included in their search at all.

Kyana squeezed her eyes shut to ease their burn and searched for an excuse to get Haven out of here.

"Any progress with those computers?"

Hank looked up from beneath a shaky metal table. "Almost done. Waiting on a couple more pieces and we should be all set."

Marcus slid out from beneath the desk, his face ruddy and drenched in sweat. "I ran as much magic through the cords as I could, but it's going to interfere with the café's television reception. Do what you need to do fast or I'll start charging per lost customer on game days."

"Way to support our mission," Kyana grumbled, watching Ryker pass Marcus fifty human dollars. Where he was planning on spending money now was beyond Kyana, but if he kept serving her fifty/fifty, she wouldn't poke her nose in his business.

Marcus shoved the money in his pocket. "I'll be in the kitchen if you need me. Keep the noise down. I don't want this interfering with the atmosphere downstairs."

As Marcus stalked off, Hank looked out the window. The faux sun was high in the sky. "Do you know how much longer Carol and Frag are going to be?"

"Farrel and Crag," Kyana corrected.

"Oh, right. Sorry. It's hard to keep the four of them straight."

"Mine are the polite, helpful ones." She nodded at Geoffrey. "His are brutes. Did you need something?"

Hank toyed with a computer cable, avoiding Kyana's gaze. "I know you're anxious to get this up and running, but . . ." His Adam's apple bobbed, but he finally lifted his head to meet Kyana's eyes. "If Farrel and Crag are going to be a while, could I go check on my family? I promised my son I'd be back at daybreak. He's watched so many go out into the night and not come back. I need to let him know I'm all right."

Kyana couldn't imagine what the past two weeks must have been like to a small boy. Nor could she understand why her heart felt like a brick in her chest. "Bring them back here. You can keep an eye on them while you work."

"Thank you."

She nodded at the door. "Be back in an hour."

When the door closed behind him, Haven sat across from Kyana and wrapped her arms around her legs, scanning her from head to foot. "You know, when people were complaining about Vamps stinking up the place, I thought they were just being derogatory." Her nose wrinkled. "You guys reek. What is that smell?"

Kyana sniffed her hair and winced. "Dismembered demon."

Haven grinned. "It's not flattering." Her smile faded. "The Healer who tended Hank said it got ugly. Are you okay?"

Only a Mystic could describe what they'd gone through as *ugly*. Did the Healer know words like *mass carnage*? *Bloodbath*?

"I'm fine. We're all fine." Pain burned in her back.

She tapped Geoff's shoulder. Without opening his eyes, he lifted his head, let Kyana reposition herself, then put his head back on her thigh. His even breaths told her the simple movement hadn't pulled him completely out of sleep.

It was obvious Haven wasn't buying what Kyana was selling, but she didn't comment further. "Why don't we head home? I picked up this fabulous bubble bath a couple weeks ago that you have to try." She closed her eyes and sighed. "And Ryker will appreciate you smelling like flowers and not dead demon, believe me."

"I don't *care* what Ryker thinks about my smell."

"Yes you do, lass." This from Geoffrey, who turned over, nestling his face far too close to bits she'd rather he not nestle.

Haven nudged him with her foot. "Come on. Let's find you two some clean clothes and a shower. Then we'll grab lunch. Maybe by then Hank will be ready to start working and Ryker will be back."

Kyana frowned but didn't toss back a verbal assault since Haven provided the way to get her out of here before Drake's name was mentioned.

Without bothering to open his eyes, Geoff grumbled and threw an arm over his face. Kyana smacked him on the head. "Move. My legs are numb."

He sat up, rubbing his head. "Didn't your mum ever teach you manners?"

"I'm sure she tried."

He stood and helped Kyana to her feet. "A complete and utter failure, your mum," Geoffrey teased as they headed downstairs through the restaurant portion of Spirits, waved farewell to Marcus, and stumbled their way outside. As they passed the portal alcove, Farrel and Crag stepped through. Then Larkin and Cahir. Kyana stopped. Watching. Waiting.

Disappointed, she huffed. She hated the idea of wasting an entire day. It didn't matter that they were beaten, bloodied, and bruised. They had a job to do, a key to find, and a traitor to hunt. Sitting on her hands would do nothing to improve her mood.

"Finally awake?"

Ryker's low voice turned her around. Her gaze traveled over him. He'd showered and now wore a horrible Hawaiian print shirt unbuttoned to reveal a white tee over a pair of worn khakis and, of course, sandals. The only evidence remaining of their adventure was a faint bruise on his cheek.

"My God, you're blinding me. Who taught you how to dress?" She covered her eyes in mock horror.

"Very funny." He brushed dirt from her hand. "You look like shit."

"You sure know how to make a girl feel special," she muttered.

He studied her in silence, his silver eyes softening. "Take the night off. I'll help Hank start comparing the print with those names on our list. We can meet back up in the morning."

Kyana hardened her stare. This was her investigation, her hunt, and she intended to be involved every step of the way. "There's nothing wrong with me that a shower won't cure. I sent Hank to get his family. He won't be back for an hour, so if I'm quick, I can squeeze one in."

Ryker smiled. "That was a kind thing for you to do."

Kyana rolled her eyes. "I need him to concentrate

on his job. If having his family near allows him to do that, then I'll suffer through having two more humans stuffed into that little room."

"Still, maybe you're learning to try something besides fear and intimidation to get your way."

"Maybe you're suffering from brain lesions from all the colors you're wearing and reading way more into my actions than exist."

"Come on, lass. We've got showers and a nice big bed calling our names."

Ryker's smile died a quick death. "You're going home with him?"

Ryker forced his features to stay neutral. He knew the rules of the Order kept Kyana and Geoff apart, but he hated that smooth, easy bond they shared. It ate at his insides knowing Geoff knew a part of Kyana that she'd never introduce *him* to.

"I need a shower and his place is more convenient than mine," Kyana finally answered. Her eyes darkened. "Unless you have a better offer?"

Gods, did he. He just wasn't stupid enough to voice it. If he offered her *his* shower, she wouldn't be taking one alone, and that wasn't good for either of them, no matter how much she protested otherwise. Even dirty and bloody, she was still the most beautiful creature he'd ever seen. He wanted her, and had come close to convincing himself he could take Kyana on her terms without losing himself. It didn't matter that now wasn't the time—that their combined missions had to be their main focus. Sex, on his terms or hers, would complicate everything. And another complication was something they didn't need.

Still, as petty as it sounded, he wanted to get her away from Geoffrey.

"We could find a Seer. Maybe get some insight on the names on our list."

"While that's not a bad idea, it's a bit disappointing." She smiled. "Besides, shouldn't we wait until *after* Hank runs the print? He could find a match, and a trip to Seer land won't be needed."

Kyana looked at Haven and Geoff. "You guys go ahead. I'll catch up."

"Fine," Geoff muttered. "But that bloody wanker's just going to put you in a bad mood."

"Who knows, perhaps he's going to take my advice and get it right." Haven's soft laughter hung in the air as she grabbed Geoffrey's arm and pulled him away.

When they were alone, Ryker found Kyana watching him. Though she was still smiling, it no longer reached her eyes. "What now?"

"Haven gave you advice? About me?"

"Yeah, she did." He rubbed his hand along the back of his neck.

"Elaborate?"

Ryker wasn't sure what prompted him to lace his fingers with Kyana's, but it felt right. Tingles of heat spiraled up his arm as her skin absorbed his warmth. "We have about an hour before Hank's going to be back so why don't we just walk on the beach or find someplace to sit quietly for a while and forget about advice and embarrassment."

The image of her curled around his body as waves licked at their skin seared his blood and made him hard. Being good was coming with a very steep price to pay. Maybe the sane and safer thing to do would be to just fuck her and get her out of his system.

Could he do that? With the strong pull to her, could he just walk away and pretend it never happened? As Geoffrey would say, *Not bloody likely.*

She grinned and pulled her hand from his. *Nope, she definitely isn't ready for more than a quick lay.*

"We're on a mission to save the world and you want a stroll on the beach?" She placed a hand to his chest.

"What are you doing?"

She shrugged. "Just checking for breasts."

He stroked his finger along her jaw. "Very funny."

If her gaze fell now, there'd be no hiding his attraction to her. He shifted and turned away, pulling her behind him.

He led her toward the bungalow he lived in on the beach. He wanted to see her hair spilling over his pillows and touch her till the scent of her body covered his sheets. If he offered it, she'd take it. And he'd spend a million nights afterward regretting it.

It might be worth it.

Chapter Twenty

Ryker lay on the sand next to Kyana, her head resting against his shoulder. Surprisingly, she hadn't snatched her hand away this time when he'd laced his fingers with hers as she slept, and now her fingers tightened around his as she fought off whatever demon plagued her dreams. It hadn't taken more than a few minutes for her to doze off beside him, but since they couldn't do anything until Hank was ready to work again, he let her sleep, wishing his connection to her had lingered long enough to witness what had her so disturbed.

Was it Henry again? The sultan? Maybe the father he'd sensed Kyana loathed. Whatever it was caused Kyana to moan and rub her body against him in fitful slumber, forcing him to tighten his hold on her until she calmed.

Lying beside her now didn't make it easy to keep his boundaries from crumbling.

When they'd first arrived on the beach, she'd bathed in the shower he'd built outside his bungalow and toweled off, refusing to dress again until her body completely air-dried. Leather, it seemed, did not slide easily onto a damp body.

It hadn't been the first time Ryker had seen her body, but seeing it covered in the ocean he worshipped had nearly crippled him. She'd lain down to rest, and the minute she'd fallen asleep, he'd covered her body with his shirt and cradled her against his bare chest, her breasts pressed against his skin, killing him a little each time she moved. He was glad she hadn't asked him to go inside his place. He hadn't wanted her in his home. Hadn't wanted to return there later, alone, and have it smell of her. It would have driven him mad.

Now, more than the feel of her naked body, it was the closeness he craved, the bond that was forming between them. She no longer looked at him with loathing in her eyes, recalling his ten-year-old rejection. He couldn't push for more.

Yet.

Careful not to wake her, he shifted enough to watch her. Even in sleep the lines of stress around her eyes didn't ease. Did she ever completely relax? Did she ever allow anyone to take some of the pressures off her shoulders? Did she ever trust anyone?

He knew so little about her. And what he had learned over the years wasn't favorable. Now that he'd worked so closely with her, he knew most of what people feared about Kyana was nothing more than her way of keeping people from getting close. She'd fight to the death to protect her friends or to do her duty to the Order. But despite her claim not to care, he'd never seen her deliberately harm, or allow harm to come to an innocent.

Not even the humans. And if anyone had reason to hate the human race, it was Kyana. He'd seen enough of her dreams to know she was justified in her anger toward them, her mistrust.

And demigod or not, he wasn't sure he had the power to make that hurt go away for her.

"Uh-oh. Looks like someone's thinking."

Kyana's voice ripped through Ryker's musings. "What's wrong with thinking?"

"In your case it usually means the fun's over and the all-too-serious Ryker's back in control." Kyana pressed herself closer to him. Her nipples brushed against his skin, making him hard all over again. "You might as well tell me whatever it is."

As her gaze drifted downward, a small O formed on her lips. "Or maybe I can guess."

He adjusted his pants to hide the evidence of his thoughts. "What do you expect?" His fingers tightened around hers. Forcing several deep breaths into his lungs, he fought for control. "You're naked."

"Glad you finally noticed." Laughter lightened her sleep-husky voice.

Finally? Surely she wasn't that dense.

Ryker rolled slightly so they lay nose to nose. She snuggled against him, her warm breath caressing his neck. For the first time since he'd rejected her advances the night they'd met, she wasn't demanding or trying to goad him into using her body for a few minutes of pleasure. He wanted her, but not like that.

This time, she seemed content to take what he had to offer and not ask for or demand more. When she was like this, it was easy to forget they were so different.

That they wanted opposite things, both out of life and from each other. This, he wanted.

Her body relaxed against him as sleep threatened to take hold of her again. Ryker caressed her back. She purred, lifting her face, silently asking for his kiss. He told himself not to give in to the moment. That nothing lasting would come from the time they shared, but his body refused to listen. Slowly, he closed the distance between them and covered her mouth with his, his heart pounding at the sound of her surprised gasp.

Teasing her lips apart, he lost himself to the taste of her, to the feel of her tongue dancing across his. There was no competition, no struggle for control. He could give himself this much. He could hold on to his control and delight in the feel of her . . .

It didn't take long for the fog of sleep to finish lifting from Kyana's mind. Ryker was kissing her. She hadn't asked for it, hadn't coerced him. *He'd* come to *her.* As hunger and greed for what he offered overtook her, she became the aggressor, nipping Ryker's lip, demanding more.

Not giving herself time to think about what she was doing . . . or why he was suddenly so pliable . . . she opened to him. He slipped his tongue over her fangs, then paused. It took twice more before Kyana caught on to his silent instructions. It had been a lifetime since she'd mated with someone who had fangs. Kyana mimicked his actions. Desire spiraled through her, pooling in her belly. She groaned, rocking her hips against his, cursing the khaki barrier between them.

Ryker ended the kiss and leveled himself up enough

to look into her eyes. His cock throbbed against her belly. "No games, Kyana."

"I don't want games," she mumbled, trying to capture his lips again.

He avoided her caress until frustration forced her to look at him.

"Don't turn this into a power struggle, Ky."

Kyana held his gaze. He knew her far too well for her own comfort. He'd tasted her blood. He'd seen her thoughts. Denying her intentions would have been pointless. But why did it matter that she liked to be in control? They both wanted this. He could deny it, but the evidence not only throbbed hot and hard against her, but darkened his silver eyes to steel.

"Are you afraid of losing?" she asked quietly. "A power struggle, I mean."

His gaze never wavered. "Yes."

That shocked her all the way to her toes. Ryker was afraid of *her*? She almost purred with satisfaction.

She finally understood the reason for his uncertainty now. This was about trust for him. About her finally believing that he was a good guy who wouldn't hurt her. For her to prove to him that she could make this about *them* and not just about herself.

A part of her almost backed off. If she let him believe she wanted more than an orgasm, she could wind up being the one to inflict pain. Sex, in life and death, had always been about control. Wasn't it the same for him? Had he ever found his release without the power struggle to see who dominated?

The softness in Ryker's gaze begged for her decision. She sighed and relaxed her arms, trailing them slowly across his back, and grabbing the waistband of his jeans to give them a firm tug. "I draw the line at being docile."

Ryker smiled. "Active participation would be nice."

Not sure exactly what he wanted from her, or why she wanted so desperately to give it to him if only for a few minutes, she did something she hadn't done willingly in two hundred years. Kyana tilted her head, offering her neck in momentary surrender. If he wanted proof that this wouldn't become a power struggle for her, she could offer him no grander gesture.

Ryker's low rumble echoed with the waves. He cupped her jaw and eased her gaze back to him. "No stupid games," he repeated, then claimed her lips once again.

Kyana lost herself in the gentleness of his caress. She slid her hands slowly up his back, loving the way the muscles rippled in response. The heat of his skin warmed her fingers. Her breath hitched. She pressed him closer, rocked her hips against him.

Ryker refused to be rushed. He left her lips to trail blazing kisses along her jaw. His tongue stroked the now healed bite mark. Kyana braced herself for the pleasurable pain that would accompany his possession. Instead of fangs, he closed his mouth over the pounding pulse in her neck, pulling lightly.

She moaned, arching into him. The act of being fed upon without mal intent was the most erotic sensation she'd ever experienced. Her body warmed. Heat built between her legs. Her moan of pleasure, her whispered plea for more, were all that lay between them.

She turned her head, found the pounding pulse point

at the base of his jaw with her lips and followed it to his throat, then closed her mouth over it. He tasted like the ocean. Salty, sweaty, sunny.

In him, she tasted daylight for the first time in two hundred years.

He pushed away from her, and Kyana bit her lip to keep from whimpering in protest.

"You taste sweeter than you act," he whispered. "I always suspected you had a soft, gooey center."

She swallowed. "If you don't take off those damned pants, how will you know if you're right?"

He brushed his lips lightly over hers before leveling himself away again to stare at her. Kyana lay naked and vulnerable beneath him, but she fed off the power of her sexuality. The look of longing, of need, filling his eyes held her still. She reveled in the thrill of him drinking in the sight of her.

Ryker straddled her waist. Slowly, never letting his gaze stray from hers, his hands lightly gripped her ribs, his thumbs caressed the undersides of her breasts.

The need in his eyes reflected her own desires. It took a minute for her to realize he was waiting for her permission. Awed by the respect of his actions, she bowed her back in silent invitation. He dipped his head, flicked his tongue over the nipple, then pulled it into his mouth.

Kyana wrapped her legs around his waist and rocked against him as Ryker shifted his attention to her other breast. His hands trailed lightly down her side to her hip, his fingers biting painfully into her skin. She couldn't determine if he was trying to stop her movements or encouraging her to continue. The choice had been taken from her. She was already addicted to his touch. Her need to feel all of him ruled her thoughts.

Reaching between them, she tugged at the button on his pants and pushed them lower.

"Not yet," he groaned against her throat. He wanted to take his time, wanted to make the moment last, wanted to taste every inch of her before giving in.

Shifting, he eased down her body to trail hot, moist kisses over her belly. He circled her belly button, then continued lower to nip lightly at her hip.

Kyana's purring turned to panted pleading. She pushed his pants off his hips. Lifting her legs, she caught the waist of his khakis between her toes, gently straightening her legs to slide the garment to his ankles.

He growled. She chuckled and held her arms out to him. He kicked the jeans completely off, then covered her again, skin to skin. The heat of his body warmed the chill from hers that the faux sunlight of Below wasn't able to erase.

Ryker's hands trembled as he gripped her hips. He wanted to bury himself inside her, but the need to continue his exploration of her body burned hotter with each shiver and sigh she released.

"Now," she said, taking him lightly in her hand and guiding him inside her. She lifted her hips, completing the connection.

Ryker remained still, enjoying the feel of her hands lightly caressing him from hip to shoulder. "Now," he repeated when the desire pulsing through her eased and her whimpers for more pushed his own need out of control.

To Kyana, his movements were criminally slow.

Nothing like she wanted. She needed hot and hard and explosive. She needed to know his desire for her was as wild as her need for him. She'd never felt like this before. Never allowed herself to take more from sex than the act of release. She'd never thought about her partner's needs and wants. Never worried if his pleasure burned as intense. With Ryker, she worried about this and so much more.

When she attempted to take control, to rush them toward their reward, his fingers tightened on her hips until she followed his lead.

Kyana gave herself to him. Let him slowly stroke the fires until they threatened to burn them both alive. His movements matched the slow crests of the waves lapping at the shore. Their panted breaths mingled. Their moans of pleasure mirrored their building needs.

The first waves of her orgasm stole her breath. She cried out his name. He answered with hers as he too claimed his prize.

The weight of him crushed her, but he wasn't half as heavy as the awkward silence that followed their climax. The moment wasn't altogether unpleasant. She liked the feel of the coarse hair on his thighs rubbing her legs, liked the heat of his smooth, hard chest pressing against her bare breasts. She just wished she knew what the hell to say to him now.

Never had she experienced sex so tender. Not even when she was human. Prince Mehmet had raped her of her virginity at the ripe age of fifteen, and every time he'd called upon her afterward, he had been just as brutal. He was the only human she'd ever mated with, and so those violent experiences had traveled with her into her life as a Vamp.

Before joining the Order, she'd allowed only other Vamps to share her bed, and since giving her oath to the Ancients, that side of her bed had remained cold with the exception of the nomadic Witch Silas, who'd been her "booty call" for a couple of years off and on. Silas still managed to end up in her bed whenever he rolled back into town, but she hadn't seen him in over six months.

Waiting for Ryker to roll off her, she frowned as she realized she wasn't as sated as she'd thought she'd be. She wanted more of Ryker. Wanted him to hold her and show her that what they'd just shared wasn't alive only in her imagination.

"No thinking," Ryker whispered, claiming her lips in a gentle possession that stole her breath. But just as her body melted against his and her thoughts became a drunken, incoherent mess, he ended the kiss and rested his forehead against hers. "You have to get dressed."

A soft sigh escaped her, fanning his face. When she opened her eyes, she saw the same need in the depths of his eyes as she felt in her soul. This time, there was no sting of rejection. Just a mutual understanding and a shared need that couldn't be explored now.

She eased out of his arms and pulled on her clothes, feeling his gaze sear her naked back as she dressed in silence. When she was done, she sat back down and stared out over the ocean.

"So what were you thinking about when I woke up?" she asked when she got her breathing under control. She needed to know what had changed in him.

Why he'd gone from pushing her away to giving her something he'd been denying her for ten years.

"That you're not as coldhearted as people think you are."

She tensed and opened her mouth to deny the horrible accusation. Instead, she said, "Is that a bad thing?"

"No. But I don't understand why you let people see only one side of you."

"Not all people. Haven sees me for what I am."

"So do I, Ky. Whether you like it or not."

Though she didn't like it, she believed him. Ryker never looked at her like she was nothing more than a vile Dark Breed. He made her feel almost normal, and lying here with him today, she hadn't allowed herself to get caught up in the fear of rejection. Instead, she'd allowed herself to enjoy him. It wasn't like her. Hell, except for Geoffrey, she couldn't remember a single time in almost two hundred years of existence when she'd just enjoyed a man's friendship. It always turned to sex. Fuck 'em and forget 'em, though it had been months since she'd gotten even *that* from anyone.

And, as much as she hated to admit it, that wasn't what she'd gotten from Ryker today. When she finally found her voice again, she managed to say, "Back to friends?"

"I'm always your friend, Ky."

"I think I like the way you see me," she said, letting the honesty of her words fill her soul. "Sometimes. Other times, it's irritating as hell."

Ryker smiled. "I can fake it if you like. Pretend I think you're just a raving bitch."

"I *am* a raving bitch. It's called Lychen, remember?"

She stood and stretched, then scooped up Ryker's discarded shirt and tossed it in his face. "Your turn to dress. We have to meet Hank."

Ryker stood and quickly redressed before following Kyana back toward Spirits. His smile reminded her much of a contented kitten with an endless supply of fresh cream.

"What's that grin all about?"

He pointed to her feet. "Forget something?"

Kyana stared down at her bare toes and cursed. Her boots! She ran back to their spot on the beach, but her boots were nowhere to be found.

"Where'd they go?"

Ryker pointed to the ocean, his grin growing wider by the second. "I think the tide is a thief."

"Sonofabitch."

Ryker's laughter followed Kyana as she dove head-first and fully dressed into the waves in search of her precious shoes.

Chapter Twenty-one

Still barefoot, Kyana stomped into Hank's new office/living quarters twenty minutes later. She was tender in delicious places and knew she smelled like Ryker and sex, which only made her more self-conscious of the eyes following her as she entered the small room.

A trail of water followed her as she slumped against the wall and silently dared Geoffrey or Hank to mention her distressed, saturated state. Hank wisely held his tongue. Geoffrey wasn't so smart. He opened his mouth to say something when Marcus stomped into the room, following her path with a string of curses and a mop.

"I'm going to ban you from this place," Marcus said, wringing out the mop in a bucket he'd deposited in the hall. "I just had these floors redone."

He looked past Kyana into the room and nodded at Hank's equipment. "Got everything you need for your search? Need more of my enormous skills to push things along?"

Geoffrey smiled. "Nice that you're so eager to help, mate."

Marcus scowled. "Just want my damned café back, so get on with whatever you're doing and get out." He grumbled his way out the door, his flanneled back disappearing down the stairs.

When he was gone, Geoffrey's smile only broadened as he turned it on Kyana. "Have a good tup, you two?"

Kyana felt Ryker stiffen. "Watch yourself or we're going to learn how far Peter Pan can fly."

"Hey, no name calling." Geoffrey grinned. "Until the wee tot's in bed at least. His mum won't appreciate us teaching him new habits."

Kyana turned to find Hank and his wife smiling at them and the "wee tot" watching her with a little less fear in his eyes. When Hank's gaze met hers, she put an end to Geoff and Ryker's bickering with a smooth change of topic.

"Were you able to get all your stuff running?"

Hank pointed at the monitor and pushed a couple of buttons. Pain flashed in Kyana's skull and she moved farther away from the electronics. "Had a few issues at first, but then some really big guy came in and said a bunch of really weird words and everything started working the way it's supposed to."

Marcus must have had to power the equipment with magic to make it work Below. "So the search for the owner is on?"

"Been running about an hour." He turned the monitor so she could see the flashing images. "So far nothing, but they mentioned a list. Figured we could start running them and comparing those in the systems with the print. It's a lot quicker to find a match if you have a suspect to work with.".

She held out her hand. Ryker passed Geoffrey's list to her, his fingers brushing the backs of hers as he did so. She swallowed.

She looked to Geoffrey. "Where did you leave Haven? I don't want her here until we've cleared Drake or caught him."

"She went to meet him, I think. He phoned her again before I came back here."

"Good, because I'm not exactly sure how to tell her that her boyfriend could be a Cronos supporter." Slimy weasel that he was, it wouldn't surprise Kyana one bit if Drake turned up with a record. "And if word gets back to her that we're investigating him, I'll—"

"I know, I know," Hank grumbled. "No need for threats in front of my boy."

Kyana leaned as close to Hank's equipment as she dared and whispered, "I don't make threats. I make promises. And I've never broken a promise in my life."

"Got it." He forced a smile, most likely for his son's benefit. "Unless you show her that list, she'll never know he's on it. Right, honey?"

Hank's wife gripped her boy's shoulders and bobbed her head. "It's just like before. You don't discuss police business at home."

Not wasting any more time, Hank quickly typed in Drake's name. After a few short minutes, his system beeped and he nodded. "He has a record. Theft, forgery, and fraud mostly. Never prosecuted. Always paid restitution. Did a little probation."

"Proof enough." Kyana turned for the door only to be stopped short by Ryker's grasp.

"Now compare it to the print you got from the scroll."

Hank spun back around and hit several more keys. Both Drake's print and the one from the scroll were side by side. It took a while, but this time when the computer beeped, Kyana's heart stopped. It wasn't a match. "Are you sure? Can that thing make a mistake?"

Hank shook his head. "See the loop here? And the scar there? They aren't on your known print. It's not a match."

Kyana didn't know how this revelation made her feel. She hated Drake, and the thought of catching him red-handed and throwing his ass in prison made her have a small orgasm. But at the same time, she was relieved the print wasn't his. It would have killed Haven if Drake had been guilty, and Kyana didn't want to be the messenger for that death.

"What do you want me to do?"

Kyana sighed.

Ryker pointed at the list. "Start running the names with the golden marks next to them. We could still get lucky."

Hours later, Kyana decided luck wasn't in the cards. Hank was halfway through their list of names and still they hadn't found a match, and Marcus had poked his head in a dozen times, hopefully inquiring whether they were finally finished. Each time they'd told him no, his face had fallen and he invented another curse word.

Oh, there were plenty of Cronos supporters with records, but none of them matched the fingerprint Hank had lifted from the scroll. Hank stood, his bones creaking loudly in the now quiet room. He plucked his son from his wife's arms and laid the boy on the bed, then helped his wife settle beside their child. He pulled the covers up to their chins, then kissed both on the forehead. "Shh, Daddy's right across the room. You're safe here. Nothing bad's going to happen."

Kyana felt like such a voyeur that she had to turn away, but she couldn't block out the whispered conversation.

"Daddy, don't go. The bad people could come back."

"See those two over there. They don't let bad guys down here. Nothing's going to hurt you."

Kyana glanced at Hank. Just twenty-four hours ago, he'd considered her one of those bad guys. As much as she tried, she couldn't pull her gaze away from the little boy. He clung to his dad, tears streaming down his face as he quietly cried. But it was the panic, the fear in the child's eyes that ripped at Kyana's heart.

She had been little more than a child herself when she'd learned monsters were real, but she'd cried herself to sleep every night—when she was able to sleep at all. Fear of the bad guys had dominated her every waking moment and terrorized her dreams. She would have given anything for a father like Hank to soothe her dreams and offer a loving kiss. She'd suffered through that nightmare alone, until Henry finally came into her life.

"You okay?"

Kyana jerked, horrified that Ryker had caught her so lost in thought. "I'm fine."

Ryker watched Kyana quickly compose her face, but she wasn't so quick to compose her body. "You're shaking."

She shrugged. "It's cold in here, and I'm soaking wet."

"Tell you what," Hank was saying to his son. "You sit here and help me work. Would you like that?"

Kyana stepped around Ryker and knelt a good distance away from the computers. As Hank's son settled himself on his father's lap, he turned to grin at Kyana.

Ryker watched, fascinated.

Kyana offered the little boy a small smile. "What's your name?"

"Avid."

"David," Hank corrected.

Ryker had never seen her interact with a child—human or non. Hell, for that matter, he'd never seen her interact this kindly with anyone but Haven and Geoff.

"Do you have bad dreams, David?"

David nodded, and whispered, "Bad guys with big teeth and long fingers like this." He curled his hands into tiny claws. "They make people go away and they never get to come back again."

"That is scary." Kyana rested her hands on her knees. "You know what might help you not be so scared?"

David shook his head.

"Knowing that you have people like me and Ryker over there who will protect you and keep you safe." She leaned a little closer. "We have big teeth too, so we can stop the bad guys."

"Really?"

Kyana nodded. "Yeah. You wanna see?"

David nodded.

"Okay, but remember, my teeth can't hurt little people." When he nodded again, she revealed her fangs. She even sat still while David ran his fingertip lightly over her canines.

Satisfied, David sat back against his dad's chest and stuck his thumb in his mouth.

Kyana dug something out of her pocket and pressed it in the child's hand. She folded his fingers around it, then held his little hand in both of hers. "You hold this when you go to sleep. It will help keep the bad guys away."

David's eyes were drooping. Hank kissed his son's head. "Thank you."

Kyana nodded and quickly pushed to her feet. Her discomfort hung in the air. Ryker simply watched her, offering silent strength and encouragement.

"Your kid's seen more than he was ever meant to see. He just needed to know how to put it all into perspective to stop fearing those things he can't understand. That he'll never be able to understand."

"You're a kind woman," Cynthia said, her smile soft and lovely.

When it looked like the woman might hug Kyana, she backed up, running into Ryker's chest. He closed his arm around her waist. She looked up at him with such pleading he knew she wanted out of the uncomfortable situation. He nodded at Hank. "Why don't you take the rest of the night off. Curl up with your wife and son and enjoy his peaceful sleep while the computers keep looking for the owner on their own. We can pick this back up with specific names from the list tomorrow."

"I'll keep working."

"No, really. I'm beat too," Kyana rushed out, moving to the door. "I live Above, in your world, so I'll be here about sunrise."

"Sunrise it is."

"Can you eat?"

"Cynthia!" Hank growled.

"What? If they're going to be here that early I was going to offer to find them some breakfast. It's called being nice. Our world might be upside down, but we should still remember our manners."

"Trust me," Kyana said. "You don't want to make me and Geoff breakfast. David may never touch anything liquid again."

"I might join you though," Ryker added, nudging Kyana for her rudeness. "My diet is a bit more normal."

Cynthia smiled. "Then we'll see you in the morning."

Ryker bid them good night and had to sprint down the stairs to catch up with Kyana. She'd almost made it to the portal alcove by the time he reached her. "Wait," he said, grabbing her arm. "What are you doing?"

She jerked her arm out of her grasp. "Going home. Alone."

He reached for her again, but the deadly look she sent him changed his mind. "How 'bout dinner first?"

Instead of answering, she turned back to the portal. This time he did grab for her. "Come on, Ky. Can we talk about what you did in there?"

Why was she so angry all of a sudden? The softness

that had overtaken her while she'd spoken with David had turned to dark stoniness, and Ryker didn't understand it at all.

She jerked her arm free. "What I did was lie to a little boy. I made him think monsters couldn't hurt him. That he could actually win against them."

"And why can't he? It's not lies, Ky. It's hope."

"*False* hope, and that's worse than no hope at all."

"Then why did you do it?"

Kyana clamped her teeth so tightly that the muscle in her jaw pulsed.

"Talk to me. Tell me who was there to keep *your* monsters at bay." Though Ryker was pretty sure he already knew. From what he'd seen, *no one* had been there for her. But he wanted her to open up to him on her own terms, and not just be the unwanted voyeur to her tragic past.

"The monsters don't go away. They *never* go away. They simply change form and come at you from different directions. They keep changing and coming at you until the day you can't fight fast enough or long enough and then they win. That's what I should've told David."

"Ky—"

She stabbed him in the chest. "Don't. Whatever you're going to say, just don't."

This time when she turned away, Ryker let her go. "What did you give him? The talisman to keep the monsters at bay. What was it?"

"There is no such talisman." Kyana turned; her cold stare cut through him. "Like I said, it was all a lie."

Chapter Twenty-two

Hoping to make it to her room uninterrupted, Kyana eased into the dark house and closed the door behind her. Thoughts of her afternoon with Ryker kept muddling her brain, making it hard to remember why she was in such a bad mood. She didn't really know how to act around him after what they'd done. Nothing had changed really. Just a fuck.

But it felt like nothing was the same.

"Mm, lass. You look good wet."

Kyana jumped, bashing her elbow into the doorjamb as she kicked it closed.

She glanced down at her still-damp pants, vest, and bare feet. Not exactly her most badass ensemble. "What are you doing here, Geoffrey?"

He lay stretched out on the wide, black leather Mikonos sofa with only a light blanket tossed carelessly over his lap. "Haven loaned me your shower."

"What was wrong with your shower?"

He shrugged. "Yours is bigger." His gaze traveled

slowly over her. By the time his eyes returned to hers, they were almost black. "So why the new look?"

"Long story," she mumbled, still pissed about her missing boots. In search of something filling, she headed for the kitchen. "Where's Haven?"

He nodded toward the first-story bedroom that belonged to Haven. "Might not be a good idea to go in there."

Kyana grabbed a pitcher of lukewarm blood that must have been leftovers from Geoff's dinner, and poured herself a glass. "And why not?"

"Drake showed up about ten minutes ago."

Groaning, she put down her glass and stomped upstairs to her room. Drake might be off her most-wanted list, but he was still on her most-hated. She was going to have to soothe her foul mood before seeing him or risk pissing Haven off when she literally bit off Drake's head.

After a quick shower, she pulled on a faded pair of jeans and a white tank top. "Where are Farrel and Crag?" she called out, heading back down to check on Haven.

"I told them to stay Below in case Hank gets hungry or something."

"You couldn't have sent your own to do that? Since when do you order my minions around?"

Geoff shrugged. "Mine have important stuff to do. Yours . . . are about worthless."

A protective jolt brought her hands to her hips. Her minions served their purpose and they were loyal to her. She could overlook their flaws. She moved to the end of the couch and tapped his feet. "Lay off the minions. And why are you still naked?"

He leveled himself up on the pillows and grinned. "Drake kicked me out of Haven's bed before I could grab my pants."

"What were you doing in Haven's room naked?"

Geoff's grin disappeared. A mischievous glint sparkled in his dark eyes. "You know, Drake asked me the same thing."

Kyana looked at the closed bedroom door, then back to Geoffrey. "You and Haven aren't . . ."

"I wouldn't answer that question when Drake asked it, and I'm not going to answer it for you either." His smile looked strained. "Unless you want to tell me if you're finally tuppin' Ryker."

"Not worth it." She stalked to Haven's bedroom and pounded on the door.

"Go away!"

Even Drake's voice had the ability to grate on Kyana's nerves. "I'm coming in, so I suggest you cover your tiny bits."

The door wasn't locked, and Kyana nudged her way inside, desperately trying to avert her gaze lest she catch a glimpse of something she truly didn't want to see. From the corner of her eye, she saw Haven standing by the window, Drake's frame blocking most of Haven from sight. They were fully clothed, thank Zeus, but Haven's nose was red, her skin was blotchy.

Kyana glared at Drake. "What did you do?"

Damn, but she couldn't stand him. Oh sure, he was cute enough, with his longish, dark hair, bright eyes, and strong chin. But his charming, almost nerdy, Matt Damon qualities that instantly won everyone over turned Kyana's stomach. Anyone who tried as hard as

Drake did to make people like him couldn't be trusted.

"He didn't do anything, Kyana. Give—"

"You should leave now," Drake said.

Kyana narrowed her eyes. "I've got a better idea." She moved slowly to stand in front of him, separating him from Haven. "You leave. Before I decide that the laws keeping you safe aren't worth abiding anymore."

He copied her posture, crossing his arms and narrowing his eyes. His show of defiance made her want to laugh. "You wouldn't dare."

"After the night I've had, you shouldn't test me."

He seemed to debate it for a moment before grabbing his jacket off the bed and storming out of the room, slamming the door behind him.

Kyana heard him say something muffled to Geoff, heard Geoff growl, then heard the front door close. She relaxed her fighting stance and reached out her hand to Haven. "What happened?"

Haven shook her head and covered her face with her hands. Inadequacy flooded Kyana. She didn't know how to ease Haven's pain or how to make things better. Somehow, telling her she was better off without the jerk didn't fit the bill, even if it was the truth.

Kyana took Haven's elbow and led her to the bed. "Why were you crying?"

"Drake overreacted, that's all. I understand why he's so angry but . . ."

Kyana sat next to Haven. "But what?"

"He wouldn't let me explain." Haven glanced at the door. Her eyes filled with tears. "He said some horrible things. Things that weren't true," she rushed, as if she thought Kyana would believe anything Drake said as truth.

"He thinks you're sleeping with Geoffrey."

Haven nodded. "I tried to explain."

Kyana sighed. Only Haven, bless her honest heart, would think she could explain away a naked man in her bed.

"I was only loaning him body heat," Haven continued. "And I wasn't even naked. Okay, so Geoff was, but he was asleep so nothing could have been happening in the first place."

Kyana sighed again. She was way out of her element here with the girl-talk stuff. She rubbed her temple, hoping to ease the steady ache before it began pounding. If she told Haven what she really thought of Drake, it would cause a tension in their friendship when Haven kissed and made up with the prick.

"I'm only guessing here, but if you give Drake time to cool off and get over his shock at finding a sexy, naked Vamp in your bed, he'll call. But until that hickey fades"—she pointed to the right side of Haven's neck—"I'd suggest you wear your hair down."

"Hickey?" Haven chuckled and tossed a pillow at Kyana. "There's no hickey!"

Kyana laughed and resisted the urge to tease her friend more. The sorrow had left her eyes, and to Kyana, that was all that mattered. "No, there's no hickey. But be careful next time. Geoff tends to nibble while he's sleeping."

Haven grinned. "I thought you said you'd never slept with him."

Kyana stretched out and pulled the covers up to her chin. "I thought you said the same thing."

She lay there for a long quiet moment, pondering whether to confess to Haven what had happened this afternoon with Ryker. She could use some advice on how she was supposed to behave now, given that this situation was completely foreign to her. She wasn't used to having to see her lovers day in and day out. But she and Ryker were partners right now. Avoiding him wasn't an option.

But telling Haven about sleeping with Ryker would lead to too many questions that Kyana didn't have answers to yet. Possibly never would.

As her eyes drifted closed, Haven's voice chirped up again. "So, any progress with finding the key?"

"Not really." *Unless you consider eliminating Drake from the suspect list progress.* "There are still a lot of names to sort through."

"What I don't understand is how the gates were unlocked in the first place. I mean, even if someone got their hands on the key, no one can enter Tartarus except Hermes and Hades. It would take more magic than I've ever heard of for anyone—especially someone human-born—to breach that realm."

Kyana shrugged and rolled onto her side. "Someone managed to slip past the Fates too. Maybe they used the same Illusion Charm to get into Tartarus."

Haven shook her head adamantly. "Not possible. How many times have your illusions run out before you could get back to your real clothes? They wouldn't last that long."

"But they lasted long enough for someone to get into the Fates' cave. We know that much already."

"The trip to the Fates' cave isn't too bad if you can time the ferry right. But I've heard enough about the Underworld to know there's no Illusion Charm in the world that would last long enough to travel down the miles required to reach the depths of Tartarus."

"Several charms, then? One wears off, you put another on—"

"Then Hades would have been alerted of the trespasser before the second charm could be used. Doesn't make sense."

No, it didn't. And Kyana didn't know enough about spells or charms to work through it on her own. She didn't like relying on others to figure things out, but Ryker might have been right. Maybe paying a visit to a Seer was the answer. Maybe then they could at least find out the hows and whys that would lead them to the right whos.

Chapter Twenty-three

Kyana wrapped her robe around her still wet body and returned to her room. She peeked out her shuttered windows. Judging by the sky, she still had several hours of night left before meeting Ryker back at Hank's. Hopefully, by then, she'd have a few answers.

Kyana quickly dressed and slid on a worn pair of boots. She traded her water-logged flare gun for a fresh one and fastened her drying weapon belt around her waist before going downstairs to search for the others.

"Hello?" she called out to the empty living room.

She inhaled deeply, catching a whiff of the fading aroma of Haven's supper and the soap Geoff had used, but their bodies weren't there any longer.

Slightly peeved that they'd gone ahead without her, Kyana left the house. She didn't bother to lock the door. There was no need. Haven had a bazillion protective charms guarding their house. Better security than any lock or guard dog could offer.

As she made her way silently down darkened streets,

she stuck to the shadows. The Dark Breeds in St. Augustine had been contained a good deal—far less prevalent than they'd been a few days ago. Still, she wasn't foolish enough to let down her guard.

On St. George Street, muted lights filtering through blanket-covered windows caught her attention. There were still humans in the city. Humans who should have learned by now that light attracted those that went bump in the night.

She made a mental note to let Ryker know some still hid within the combat zone. Maybe he could convince them to leave or join the others on the beach Below. It was the best she could do for them. They'd never willingly take help from her or her kind without someone they trusted to vouch for her.

When she finally made it back to the Castillo, she fired the untested flare and watched her name light up the night sky. Eagerness to find a Seer and learn how their traitor had gotten into Hades's realm quickened her steps. She needed to find Ryker or he'd be pissed to all hell that she was back on the case without him. But she really didn't want to waste time looking for him. Finding a Seer would cause her enough delays. They were a rare breed. Only one in every thousand Witches was born a Seer, but at least one lived in this part of Below. She'd made a reputation for herself. But having heard of the woman wouldn't help Kyana find her.

She pressed through the fort to the portal that would take her Below, and after stepping through the magic, she took in the chaos around her. The streets were alive with night dwellers. Most, unlike Kyana, still kept the same hours Below as they did Above. Kyana didn't understand it. Even if the sun was fake here, why miss a chance to see it?

She turned toward Spirits to check on Hank's progress, but caught sight of Haven exiting the herb shop next door and stopped. She smiled at her friend. Dark circles ringed Haven's bloodshot eyes. She apparently hadn't slept enough to forget about the hurt Drake's lack of trust had caused her.

"Where are you off to?"

"To try out a new charm." Haven reached into her sweater and pulled out something resembling a tea ball hanging from a long silver chain.

"Attractive."

Haven rolled her eyes. "It's a charm, not a fashion statement. It will help with that"—she looked around and lowered her voice—"that *thing* I've been practicing."

A smile bounced around Kyana's belly before finally smacking her in the face. She knew exactly what Haven was talking about. Astral projection. Haven had been trying to master that skill for years, but since very few could do it, even fewer were willing to teach it. The talent was looked down upon by the Ancients— proclaimed too dangerous and too close to the boundaries separating white magic from black. Haven wasn't a rule breaker, but this was the closest she'd ever come to being in contempt with the gods.

"I thought you gave that up," Kyana snickered.

The last time Haven had attempted to project herself into the spirit world, she hadn't been able to find her way back home and her body had lain coma-like for three full days. Kyana had been forced to get help

from another Witch friend, Silas, to pull Haven back
into their realm.

"I gave up the casting bit," Haven muttered, holding
out the charm. "But this is the Charm of Nine Gods. It
does the casting for me." She let go of the giant tea ball
and it bounced against her breasts, spilling bits of herbs
onto her sweater. "Cost me my half of this month's
mortgage, but since our bank is probably shut down or
demolished, I'm pretty sure it will be okay."

"Kyana!"

Kyana spun around to find Geoffrey grinning at her
from across the street.

"Hey. Where'd you disappear to?"

Haven waved good-bye as Geoffrey made his way
over. Her eagerness to test out her new charm had
Kyana uneasy. Someone should be there with her when
she experimented with the damned thing.

"Here and there," Geoffrey said.

"Have you seen Ryker? I need to get back to work,"
she added, hoping desperation didn't tint her voice.

"Nope, but you're not supposed to meet up again for
a couple hours."

"How do you know when we're supposed to meet if
you haven't seen him?"

"There are much better ways of getting information
besides talking to someone. More accurate too."

Kyana rolled her eyes and resumed her path down
the street.

Geoffrey fell into step beside her. "Where we off to,
then?"

"The Seer Nettles. Ever heard of her?"

"Lass, you should know by now that I've heard of

everyone. But you're going the wrong way if that's who you're looking for."

He took her arm and led her down a back street, did a U-turn, and directed her down streets made up like a miniature neighborhood. Town houses lined the sidewalks, each with neat little porches and manicured lawns. Kyana had never had reason to be on the dwelling side of Below, and was taken aback by the normality of it.

"Quaint."

"Too much like San Francisco for my tastes." He pointed down another street. "That way. So why are we finding Nettles?"

"Just have some questions I want answered."

"You make an appointment?"

Kyana frowned. "Why should I?"

Geoffrey laughed, the sound carrying over the whispers of conversations drifting from inside the homes. "Lass, you'd have an easier time of it trying to see the pope without permission. Nettles has a line a mile long out of her house every day."

Well then, maybe she *was* legit and would actually be of help. "I can be persuasive." She studied him for a moment. "Did we miss anything exciting today?"

"Apparently, four major cities in the U.S., along with London, Paris, and some city in Africa—Johannesburg, I think—are starting to rebuild. They're ushering as many living as they can find to those areas."

"So what cities does the U.S. believe are clean?"

"D.C., Miami, Seattle, and San Diego. Four corners, looks like. I think they're trying to clean up Nashville now, to give a central U.S. safe point."

"So what, they expect to keep Lychen, Leeches, Shyfters, all of the Underworld's pesky critters, out of these cities by sheer will?"

Geoffrey laughed. "They think their military guns are powerful enough to kill what's already dead. But hey, whatever gives them hope of living through another day. And truthfully, a wee bit of progress *is* being made. To think we might get rid of every loosed demon would be stupid, but we can clean up enough of them to make this world inhabitable by humans again."

"Optimist."

A sad longing crept up Kyana's chest. She was a tracer. She should be out there killing and imprisoning the bastards responsible for all this chaos. That she wasn't in the thick of battle was disheartening, though she knew all the tracers' captures wouldn't mean a thing if *she* didn't do her job.

"Shouldn't we let them know the relief is only temporary?" she said, stepping onto the sidewalk. "Those Dark Breeds we've thrown back are just going to climb out again if I can't find that damned key."

They passed another row of small houses where an old Mystic was beating a dusty rug from her balcony, sending bits of debris into Kyana's hair. She shot the woman a nasty look and scooted under the awning for protection.

"Hopefully we can find that key before they get back out. According to Hades, the climb out of Tartarus is tedious. It would take days for one to get loose again."

"But the ones we caught a week ago have probably already— Wait, Hades? Since when do you talk to Hades?"

"We're here." Geoffrey said, pointing to a pink two-story structure that looked like a gingerbread house. True to his word, a line stretched from the bright yellow door, down the street, in rows of three. At least a hundred people waited beneath the faux moon for the Seer's door to open, even though the sign on the neon green porch railing proclaimed she would only assist souls between seven and seven, and there were more winding around the back of the houses.

"What is she, a miracle worker?"

Geoffrey shrugged. "Some say."

Kyana shouldered her way through the throng of Witches, Mystics, and whatever other sorts were in her way. People tossed curses at her like rotten fruit, but she ignored them and pushed her way through the front door.

Chaos erupted. Three enormous Witches pounced on Kyana. Her warrior instincts kicked in; however, before she could throw so much as a single punch, Geoffrey had her arms pinned over her head and her back pressed to his chest.

"What the hell are you doing?" she asked, struggling against his hold.

"Saving you from being turned into a nasty little pond critter." To the goon squad, he said, "Could you let the Seer know Kyana is here for a reading?"

"She must wait outside until called upon. Like everyone else," the Witch in the middle replied, pointing to the door.

"It's all right. This is the one I told you would be coming. Let her through."

The voice carrying into the foyer sounded like it belonged to a very small bird. Kyana craned her neck to see around the Three Stooges and found a very small, scrawny older woman blinking up at her.

Geoff released Kyana and led the way into Nettles's small living room. The Seer sat at a table surrounded by crystals and candles of every shape and size. Four incense burners, each with a bowl of brightly colored, finely ground powder next to it, formed a half moon around the centerpiece—an antique, golden-framed mirror.

"What, no crystal ball?"

The insult didn't cause Nettles's smile to waver. "I can retrieve the one I use to entertain the children at Halloween if it will make you more comfortable."

Geoff chuckled. Kyana shot her elbow into his ribs. "I'm guessing if someone had questions about charms and spells, you'd be the one to ask."

Nettles pointed to the chairs opposite her and waited for them to sit. "I've been expecting you." She looked at the door, then back at Kyana. "One is missing, though. Should we wait for him?"

Feeling uncomfortable under the Seer's intense stare, Kyana got down to business. "What can you tell us about Illusion Charms and cloaking spells?"

"Since I am a Witch, most likely a lot. What particular information are you looking for?"

Kyana shot a glance at the Three Stooges, still standing in the foyer glaring at her. All it took was a nod from Nettles and the trio slid a door closed giving them the privacy Kyana wanted. "Is there a spell or charm that would allow someone to travel through Tartarus undetected by Hades?"

Nettles shook her head. "Hades allows only one other to roam freely through his realm, but not even Hermes can enter undetected. If someone entered Tartarus, even with a charm, he would know it immediately."

If Hades had such tight control over his domain, how did this chaos happen in the first place? Unless . . . "If his powers are fading and a Chosen hasn't been found and trained, would it be possible for someone to break in, then?"

Nettles shook her head. "Maintaining the souls in Tartarus is too important of a task. Hades would've begun training his replacement long before his powers began to fade."

Kyana rubbed the back of her neck. "Okay, so there's no long-lasting spell to get someone into the hottest parts of Hell. There's no way someone could just ramble around undetected. Yet someone did make it into Hell and was able to use a key even Hades himself hadn't known existed and get out again undetected. How is that possible?"

The Seer lit the burners and sprinkled dust from her colorful bowls into the flames. The tiny bursts of reds and greens and yellows danced eerily in the mirror, mesmerizing Kyana. She didn't know how long she stared into the glass before Nettles's voice claimed her attention.

"One not of this realm, but firmly rooted within it, walks through time. This one rules, but has no power. The key lies in the heart of the loyal. To uncover the hidden, you must find the one to which the blood flows."

Nettles sat back and closed her eyes. "You have what you seek."

"No, still just as lost as I was when I got here, but have a pounding headache thanks to the incense. Appreciate the help." When she tried to stand, Geoff grabbed her arm. "What? That twitch behind your left eye says you got the same thing from her mumblings that I did."

"It is my duty to tell you what I see. It is up to you to determine what it means."

Kyana freed herself from Geoff's grip and studied the Seer. "I know your kind talks in riddles, but do you think you could cut to the chase just this once and tell us what the hell that's supposed to mean?"

Nettles simply shook her head. "In order to find the truth you must look outside the circle to see the world."

"Think outside the box," Geoff whispered.

Kyana glared. "Yeah, that one I got." But it still didn't offer a single answer. All she'd done since taking this mission was think outside the bloody box. She was beginning to think the box was surrounded by nothing but a huge black void.

"Okay, let's break it down," she muttered. "*One not of this realm.* A ghost? A ghost wouldn't be from this realm, but rooted to it before death."

Geoff shook his head. "Wouldn't work. A spirit could get into Tartarus, but it couldn't use the key."

Kyana drummed her fingers on the table, replaying the first part of the Seer's prediction. *One not of this realm, but firmly rooted within it, walks through time.* An image of Haven's charm came to mind. "What about astral projection? That's here, but not here, and the soul's on a time limit when it's out walking about on its own."

"Very few are left alive with the ability to perform such magic. It's not taught or encouraged."

"Yeah, I know, the gods frown upon it, but is this why? Because the spiritual body can go undetected where other souls can't?"

"If that were the case, it would be law, not a recommendation."

"Bloody hell," Geoff hissed. "Thought you were on to something there, lass."

"Yeah, me too." But a part of her was relieved. The last thing she needed was for every Witch who had tried to cast the spell or owned a Charm of Nine Gods to be under suspicion. Hauling Haven's ass before the courts wouldn't make any of them happy.

Kyana paced the small room, running all the possibilities over in her mind. A row of framed photos lining a low table caught her attention. The family resemblance was too strong not to recognize Nettles's family through the generations. A cross-stitch plaque was positioned above the photos. Kyana recognized the language as Romanian and had to search her memory to translate. *Alive in memory until we're together again.*

Something Icky had shown Kyana burned through her brain. Cronos's promise to return to his children. To live again. Dread settled in her belly like a boulder. Cronos was dead. There was no one alive powerful enough to resurrect him. So how could he make such a bold promise to the ones he'd created?

She returned to the table. "Could a restless spirit cause this much havoc?"

Nettles gave a small shrug. "Havoc, absolutely. But one could not perform the feats you've brought before me today. A spirit cannot grasp on to anything tangible. It is much like astral projection in that sense. Interacting with the physical world would be almost impossible."

Kyana scowled. "Almost?"

"Well, certainly. But only gods are capable of such magic. It is how Zeus and others sired so many children with human women."

Dawning slithered over Kyana's skin. "They possessed the bodies of men to seduce their chosen women."

Nettles nodded. "Yes. And to do so, they had to release their physical forms for a short time and enter the spirit realm before entering their host."

Geoffrey frowned, his blue eyes darkening. "What are you playing at, lass?"

Kyana couldn't contain her grin. "It fits. *Not of this realm, but once was, now leaving them to walk through time*. If this spirit is taking over another's body, then they'd rule but have no real power."

"But only gods—"

Geoffrey cut Nettles off. "I think you're grasping at straws now."

Nettles shivered. All color drained from her face. "I sense very dark, very powerful black magic at work here."

"Dark indeed." Glaring at Geoff, she silently willed him to catch on more quickly. "Only a god, Geoff. What god do we know who'd be willing to create so much devastation by unlocking Hell?"

"If you're talking about Cronos . . ."

Nettles gasped at the mention of the fallen god.

"That's exactly who I'm talking about. He promised he'd come back. Maybe he did."

Nettles's sputtering caught Kyana and Geoff's attention. "But . . . but he's *Cronos*. It takes a willing host to become possessed. Who would willingly allow Cronos access to his body?"

Kyana stood and motioned for Geoff to follow. "Right-o, Nettles. Whoever Cronos possessed would have to be a follower of his. Someone who already worshipped him, dead or not."

Geoff's grin spread from ear to ear. "Someone who can obviously leave fingerprints behind."

Kyana nodded. "If Hank finds a match to that print, we're going to find the person who was willingly possessed by Cronos."

"Yeah, not going to do us a lot of good since half the names Hank ran last night had records. It's going to take forever to figure out who's responsible."

Geoff wiggled his eyebrows and smiled at Nettles. "Not necessarily."

Slowly, Kyana turned to look at the Seer. "You'd be able to connect the dead Chosen to the person who killed them."

"Presumably, yes." Nettles reached out her small hand. "Give me your list and I'll try."

Kyana stood and held out her own hand. "For that, you'll have to come with me."

"You don't have the list?" Geoffrey and Nettles asked together.

"Well it would be damned difficult for Hank to work

from it if I took it with me every time I left the room."
Kyana motioned for the Seer to stand. "It's just as easy
for you to come with us. Spirits isn't that far. You can
have a look, point out any names that give you the hee-
bie-jeebies, and then we'll bring you home."

"Perhaps if you had waited for the other as you were
meant to, the list would be in your possession now."

Kyana grinned. "Nice to know I can throw a Seer a
curve. I never do what's expected of me." She motioned
for Nettles to stand. "Let's go get that list."

Nettles shook her head. "You'll have to bring it here.
I'll need tools to seek the link you're searching for,
and a Seer's magic is always strongest in her dwelling.
Come back to me with that list, and I'll see if I can take
you closer to the truth."

Chapter Twenty-four

This list is incomplete," Nettles said, running her long fingers over the crumpled pages.

Kyana elbowed Ryker out of her way, trying desperately not to sniff him too obviously as she pushed past him, and sat down beside Geoffrey on the other side of Nettles's table.

"We know. This is only a list of people whose ancestors were Cronos supporters. We realize there have been new recruits since then, but it was a launching point."

Ryker was still glaring at her, angry that their first trip to the Seer's had excluded him, but he was here now, so he needed to deal and stop boring holes in the back of Kyana's head.

"This," Nettles said, pushing a bowl of blue powder to the right of the list, "I've charged to link the deaths of the Chosen to your list. I feel it working, so you do indeed have a murderer here."

Excitement spread through Kyana like a tidal wave. She felt Ryker squeeze her shoulder and knew he was feeling the same thing.

"But this . . ." Nettles moved a yellow powder bowl to the left of the list. "I've attuned it with your key. It has no energy at all."

"So whoever has the key is not on the list," Ryker muttered.

"I think not."

Kyana leaned in, getting a whiff of overpowering floral fragrance that made her sneeze. "But someone who's been killing Chosen, we do have *him*, right? Who?"

"He doesn't work alone, and I don't know his name yet. It will take a few moments for the powder to find the source of its power."

Nettles closed her eyes and placed the fingers of her right hand inside the blue powder. She brushed off the excess, then smeared her fingertips along the pages. "There. Now we wait."

"For what?" Kyana asked.

"You'll see."

Kyana fidgeted and stared at the paper, finally giving up when she saw nothing happen, and she looked up at Nettles again. "So, can we talk during this or is that a no-no?"

"You may speak, though I've already seen your question." Nettles cocked her head to the side and smiled, though she didn't look up from the list. "You wish to know why, if I'm as good as people say, I didn't foresee the breakout."

Damn. She *was* good. It was a question that had been bothering Kyana since meeting the Seer. "Well?"

"I am not an Oracle, Kyana. I am a Seer. I see what has been and what is, but only Oracles can see what will be. Why they didn't predict the breakout is beyond me. Perhaps they were blocked by someone more powerful than they."

"Someone like Cronos," she muttered. Every single minute that passed, Kyana grew more certain that Cronos was responsible for everything happening. From the breakout, to the possession of a body that turned the key to Hell. She was beginning to fear that his promise to Icky's people hadn't been an empty one. Maybe he really was trying to rise again.

When she voiced that fear aloud, however, she received three incredulous stares in response.

"You really buyin' that, lass?" Geoffrey smirked. "And who's going to raise him? I certainly don't know anyone powerful enough, and I know *everyone*."

Kyana snapped her glare toward Ryker. "And you? You think I'm gullible too?"

He shrugged, towering over Kyana as he twisted his mouth in contemplation. "I think it's far-fetched, but I'm beginning to think Cronos is the only one powerful enough to do any of this. Zeus, Poseidon, and Hades alone aren't powerful enough, even, but together as brothers, they could manage the feat if their powers weren't fading."

"So you agree? Cronos could be trying to rise again? It makes sense, you know. Who else would want to possess someone and open Hell? The only person who knew such a feat was possible. Cronos. Think about it. He would have to possess a body to actually hold the key, true, but only Cronos wouldn't alert Hades to his presence. It might have been someone else walking down the halls of the Underworld, but it would have been Cronos's soul. Undetectable since technically, he *was* Hades and Zeus and Poseidon before they ever reigned. He'd have permission to enter because no one would have thought to prevent it."

"All right," Geoffrey offered. "Suppose the two of you haven't completely gone mad. Why would Cronos bother with any of this, then?"

"Who *wouldn't* want to come back from the dead?" Kyana pushed herself from the table and paced behind Nettles, who seemed just as intrigued by the topic as everyone else. Her gaze kept returning to the pages, checking to see if anything magical was happening, and since it wasn't, she pressed on. "Killing the Chosen means there's no one left to replace the gods. Gods Cronos would feel cheated him out of his own power. He tried to kill his sons once. It would be a lot easier to try again if they were weak."

She knew better than anyone the lengths a person might go in order to obtain power. Hell, if she was Cronos, she'd certainly do everything she could to come back and reclaim what was rightfully hers.

"One problem," Ryker said. "To raise Cronos, one would need all four Eyes of Power. Zeus's staff, Hades's amulet, Poseidon's trident, and Cronos's own ring. All of which are still safe and sound. No immediate danger of having him pop up."

Good point. But Kyana wasn't convinced. Who was to stop Cronos from getting his hands on the Eyes of Power? He'd already proven he could possess bodies and sneak around.

"What did you do with that ring, anyway?" she asked.

He glanced at Geoffrey. "The less people who know, the better."

Did he not want to say in front of Geoffrey? Or did he mean he wasn't planning on telling Kyana either? She opened her mouth to ask but Ryker cut her off.

"And why unlock Tartarus? Just to create chaos?"

"Maybe. Chaos that had us all running around like mad, saving anyone and everyone when the real focus was on the Chosen. Besides, I'd think it would drain the gods even faster if they had to use their powers to clean up the mess of the breakout. Two birds plus one stone equals—"

"Hush now." Nettles's interruption would have pissed Kyana off if the Seer hadn't looked absolutely delighted with herself. She pointed a shaking finger at the papers. "The magic is working."

When her hand touched the pages again, her body gave a small tremble. "The blood of the Chosen pools at his feet. It circles and surrounds, but doesn't touch him in any way."

"So he's ordering their deaths, but his hands remain clean." And *he* had to be Cronos. Kyana was sure of it now.

"Correct." Nettles pushed the list across the table and tapped her nail on a name that was lit up with blue glitter. "This is one you seek. The other, he is not listed here."

"I'll be damned," Ryker said, a whoosh of escaping breath making the candles on the table flicker. "You found him, Ky."

Chapter Twenty-five

She knew it! Drake Mallone, the slimy, weaselly little bastard. No matter that his fingerprint hadn't matched the one on the scroll. Okay, so he wasn't the one Cronos had possessed, but he was guilty of murdering Chosen! It might not have been his scent on the scroll, but he'd know who it belonged to.

Kyana nodded her thanks to Nettles, grabbed the list, and bolted from the room, Geoff hot on her heels.

"That clatty clackled bastard of a cunt," Geoffrey seethed, looking ready to gnaw through Nettles's table. "I knew there was a reason I wanted to kill him."

"Other than for being Haven's boyfriend, you mean?"

He sneered at her, and Kyana quickly navigated the streets of Below, desperately trying to rein in her own anger.

Ryker caught up with them just outside the portal alcove and jerked Kyana around to face him. "You have that kamikaze look in your eyes, Ky. Don't go off half-cocked and do something stupid. This is where you let me do *my* job."

She hated that he was mastering the skill of reading her so well. "I should have known it was him. Who lets the woman he loves return home alone to unknown circumstance when the world is so dangerous? Where was he when Haven returned? And since he's been back, I've seen him once, maybe twice. What the hell is keeping him so busy?"

Ryker nodded. "We'll find out as soon as we get our hands on him."

"And if we're scary enough, we'll find out whose smell is on the scroll." The lock, she was beginning to suspect, smelled of Cronos. Just as the island had.

"You sure you don't want to step out of this now that we have his name? You're not dealing with a stranger here, Ky. You're dealing with your best friend's boyfriend. This is personal. It could get ugly."

It would kill Haven if Kyana took Drake in. Goodbye friendship.

But if Kyana wasn't the one to bring him to justice, good-bye pride.

"I'm sure," she muttered. "For her sake, I'll try not to rip his head off, but I'm not making any promises."

She would do her damnedest to stay calm until she was sure Haven was safe, though. The last thing she needed was for Haven to confront Drake and put herself in danger. Better to keep Haven out of it altogether.

"Yes you are making promises. To me. I've let you do your job and now you're going to promise to let me do mine. I'll question him, Ky. The right way."

"Whatever." She started for the door. "Let's go.

We'll see if he's with Haven at my place. I want that bastard's balls in my hand before sunrise."

Ryker grabbed Kyana's hand before she could open the door to her house. "You have to play it cool. If he's in there with Haven, we don't want her to get hurt."

Kyana glared. She didn't need to be told that. Haven was her best friend. She deserved to be told what was going on and shouldn't have to watch her boyfriend get torn to pieces.

Geoffrey stepped around them both and opened the door. Darkness shuttered the house, but it didn't hamper their movements as they made their way through the living room. Haven had been here recently, but her scent was fading. She wasn't here anymore.

Hoping to figure out where her friend might have gone, Kyana pushed open Haven's bedroom door.

"Give me a mo," Geoffrey said. "Maybe I can find out where they are before we go traipsing about." He pulled a cell phone from his back pocket. Kyana boggled, watching him flip it open. "Where did you get that?"

"I've had it."

The rapid succession of button pushing fascinated Kyana as she watched from over his shoulder—a safe distance away. A Vampyre with a cell phone just felt . . . wrong. She'd only attempted to use one once, and the radio waves had nearly made her head explode. Apparently, since Geoff didn't have a problem with the device, it was her Lychen makeup causing the havoc.

He pressed the contraption to his ear. Kyana could hear the ringing from where she stood.

"She's not answering." He snapped the phone closed and shoved it back in his pocket. The frustration on his face aged him a hundred years. "Stay put. I'll be back in ten."

Before she could demand to know where he was going, he was gone.

"We'll find Drake," Ryker said, his smooth tone grating on Kyana's nerves.

"Yeah, we will. I just want to find Haven before he knows we're after him."

"He can't possibly know anything, so she should be safe."

"The last thing I want to hear is *should be* when you're talking about one of the only human types worth saving in this entire world."

Leaving him standing in the middle of the bedroom, Kyana attempted to reach out with her Vamp senses. She searched the entire house, not bothering to turn on lights, hoping to gain some idea where Haven had run off to. She could trace Haven and Drake, but concrete answers would be faster.

"Where the hell are they?"

Returning to the bedroom, Kyana brushed past Ryker, who was bent over, looking under the bed as though Haven might have been stuffed under it. She needlessly flipped on a light and waited for him to look up at her. She held up her hand, her fingers three inches apart. "You do know we're not looking for little people."

The puzzled look on his face was adorable and did nothing to hide the faint brush of pink on his cheeks. "I thought maybe a note could have fallen off the night-stand when we opened the door," he mumbled.

She turned away to check the room again. Drake's scent was strong here, but it trailed away with Haven's. They were definitely together.

She had opened the closet to check the rows of Haven's clothes when she heard the sound of leather and chains. She spun around to find Geoff standing at the door.

"That was fast," Ryker said, pulling himself back to his feet and brushing off his knees.

"No sign of them Below," Geoff said, rubbing his eyes with his thumbs. His heaving chest told her he'd touched his Vampyric power long enough to break into a sixty-mile-per-hour run at some point. Still, how had he found out anything so quickly? Where had he gone?

"Okay, so we look Above," Kyana said. "You stay here. If she comes back, let me know. If I find her, I'll do the same."

"I'm coming with you."

"Not this time." She pulled open the front door. "If you go, I'll have no one to let me know if Haven comes home."

She waited only long enough for Geoff to nod in agreement before turning to find Ryker blocking the exit.

"You need someone to go with you."

"No, I don't. You go back to the fort. Start whatever needs to be done to have Drake questioned the minute I return with him." Kyana tried to shove him out of her way but he didn't budge.

"And leave you to bring Drake in alone?" He shook his head. The knowing gleam in his eyes didn't ease that he's-getting-too-familiar feeling itching beneath her skin. He didn't trust her not to rip Drake's throat out.

"You're not going without me, Ky. Drake is mine."

Like hell.

Knowing she didn't have time to fight over this, she conceded. Sprinting to her room, she pulled off her boots, then tossed them and a change of clothes into a backpack. She returned to the living room and shoved the bag against Ryker's chest. "You better be able to keep up and don't you dare lose that bag. I won't take it easy, and I won't wait on you."

He stepped away from the door. "Do your thing."

Kyana knelt, placed her hands on the ground, and lowered her head. She closed her eyes and blocked out everything but the Lychen trying to claw its way free.

Ryker watched Kyana's muscles stretch, pull, and rearrange around her frame. The fine hairs all over her body oozed from her pores, thickening into a svelte coat of ebony, fascinating him. It was all he could do to tear his gaze away and open the door so she could follow whatever scent she'd picked up.

He barely opened it a crack before she slid between his legs and leaped down the steps onto the sidewalk, lifting her head to the breeze. The wind kicked up, ushering leaves onto the street, ruffling Kyana's silky coat like tiny ripples of water. Ryker followed her outside, shut the door, and slipped her bag over his shoulder.

Fifteen minutes later, Kyana had come to a dead stop in front of the lighthouse, her tail thumping wildly as she whimpered in victory. Ryker craned his neck and found himself peering up at a hundred and sixty-five feet of black and white spirals.

Keeping close on her heels, they circled the base until they came to the entrance. It was cracked open. Either squatters had broken in, or someone, hopefully Drake, had come for the view. As soon as they stepped inside the stark white entrance, Kyana faced Ryker, nipping at her bag.

With a sigh, he dropped the duffel and turned his back to her.

A moment later, she tapped his shoulder. "Let's go."

"You sure he's here?"

Kyana nodded. "Yeah, but Haven's not with him."

"Good. Then we don't have to worry about her getting hurt when we take the bastard down."

Chapter Twenty-six

The poor prick was drunk and barely coherent when Ryker and Kyana finally reached the top of the lighthouse. Drake had been waiting for Haven to show up, and, apparently when she'd stood him up, he'd lost his misery in a case of Sam Adams. As they'd dragged him down the spiral staircase, he'd tried to fight back, but his rubbery arms and legs hadn't done him much good. The fact that he hadn't even asked why they were taking him in for questioning was enough for Ryker to suspect the ass was a hundred percent guilty of the charges that were about to fall on his head. Still, Drake needed to be questioned, and Ryker doubted he'd spill anything useful with his brain as muddled with booze as it was.

As they passed through the Castillo de San Marcos and into Below, they were greeted by several groups of gawkers, shocked, no doubt, to see a Mystic—ex or not—being dragged like a common criminal by Ares's general. But Ryker kept a firm grip on the back of Drake's neck, shoving him through the crowds

Below toward the street of town house–looking dwell-
ings where Jordan Faye was residing while she trained.
Geoff was waiting on the doorstep of Jordan's place.

"'Bout damned time," he grumbled, snatching
Drake's arm as though he thought he might take over
the capture. Ryker yanked Drake back, receiving a
howl of pain from Drake.

"How did you know we were coming here?" Kyana
asked.

Geoffrey shrugged, the tick in his jaw as tense as
the grip Ryker was using to keep Drake pinned to his
side. He knew, if given half a chance, Kyana and Geoff
would tear into his catch without worrying whether they
got any of their questions answered. It was up to Ryker
to make sure they didn't fuck this up. He narrowed his
eyes, silently warning Geoff to cool his temper.

"We get him to Jordan with all his fingers and toes,"
he said, pushing past Geoff and Kyana to shove open
Jordan's door. "We question him, and if he isn't helpful,
we see if she can read him. Until I have my answers,
he's off-limits. Got it?"

He wanted the bastard beat down as much as they
did, but he was too well trained to let his emotions get
the better of him, and he knew from experience that
any punishment Kyana or Geoffrey could deliver to
Drake would pale in comparison to what the Order
could do. He wanted justice for all the murders Drake
had committed. Death was just too easy. If either of
them stepped over the lines of the law, he was going
to have to take them down. While knocking the hell
out of Geoffrey might brighten his day, Ryker didn't
want to delve into round two with Kyana. Not after

he'd worked so hard to find a peaceful existence between them.

"If he gets away—"

"He won't." Ryker cut Kyana off before she could deliver yet another empty threat. "Everybody inside. Now."

Shoving Drake through the doorway first, Ryker slipped inside Jordan's temporary quarters. The Chosen Fate gasped at the intrusion, and stumbled onto the worn sofa behind her. She wasn't alone. A round Latina woman sat in the chair opposite, her dark brown eyes wide with fear, and standing behind the sofa were Lachesis and Clotho. Neither Fate looked the least bit taken aback by the sudden intrusion.

Drake shoved his weight backward, slamming into Ryker's chest. Ryker didn't so much as rock against the weight. Drake's frantic gaze bounced between the Fates. "Tell him to let me go. I'm still protected by the laws of the Order."

Fear seemed to have sobered him. His slur was gone and the glazed look coating his eyes had cleared.

"Answer their questions and no one will hurt you."

Drake jutted his chin toward the Fates. "I don't want them touching me!"

"Then talk. If we get what we need from your lips, they won't have to dig through your skull."

Drake's eyes bulged and his face turned tomato red. He seemed to consider his options for a second. "I'm not answering shit."

Lachesis stepped forward. "What has this man done? Is he the one?"

Ryker nodded. "One of them, yes. You can read him and get us the answers he's refusing to give?"

Lachesis gestured toward Jordan, who had gone as pale as the moon. The Latina woman had eased into the corner of the room.

"Jordan has my powers now, but with my help, she might be ready to do as you ask."

"No way. I want to hear him say it. I want his admission." Kyana leaned into Drake and growled. "We know your hands are bloody. We know you're responsible for killing off some of the Chosen. What we don't know is who you're working with, Drake. Who has the key to Tartarus?"

"Jesus, you have no idea who you're messing with, do you?"

Kyana smiled. "Do you mean you? Or maybe Cronos?"

When Drake's eyes widened in surprise, satisfaction filled Ryker's gut. "That's right. We know all about Cronos's attempt to come back. He waited. He knew, just as all the gods knew, of the prophecy about the gods losing their powers. It's no coincidence that the gates of Tartarus opened just when the gods are their weakest, is it? It was planned this way. But you've murdered people for no reason, Drake, because we're going to stop whatever scheme Cronos has cooked up. If you want any leniency at all, you'll give us the name of the one Cronos has been contacting."

A glimmer of insanity flickered in Drake's eyes. "Let's say you're right and I'm working for Cronos. You expect me to be so afraid of what *you* might do to me that I'd double-cross *him*? How stupid are you people?"

"You're a damned coward," Kyana hissed. "What the hell did Haven ever see in you?"

"You shut the hell up about me and Haven." Drake's face reddened but just as quickly paled again. A smirk replaced his scowl. "Is that what this is really about? Trying to eliminate the competition? I always suspected Geoff had a thing for Haven, but you, Kyana? Are you a dyk—"

Ryker watched as Geoffrey's fist slammed into Drake's nose, but was too angered by Drake's smugness to stop it. Drake fell against Ryker, his hands covering his face as he let out a scream.

This was getting them nowhere. Ryker adjusted his grip on Drake and shoved him toward Jordan. "Let's get this over with."

"Wait. Who's she?" Kyana asked, thrusting her chin toward the chubby, cute Latina. "Whatever he tells us should probably be heard only by a few."

"She is Carmen," Clotho said, her tone bitter. "My Chosen. And she can hear whatever is said here."

Kyana watched Ryker drag Drake toward Jordan and force him to his knees. When she stepped farther into the room, she noticed that each of the Fates and the Chosen had tearstains on their cheeks.

"Is something going on? Something that might prohibit Jordan from performing? She looks upset."

Clotho moved to the corner of the room and pulled Carmen into her arms. "We've just found out another Chosen was murdered."

"Whose?"

"Artemis's." Clotho sniffed. "We've had several more deaths recently, but Artemis is in need of a replacement soon. I'm not certain we'll find one in time, but we're working on it."

Artemis? Her powers must be fading more rapidly than Kyana had realized for the Fates to be so worried. No wonder the goddess had been less than useful on the hunt for the key.

"The sooner you get answers from him," Kyana said, thrusting her thumb toward Drake, "the sooner we can stop these deaths."

"What should I ask him?" Jordan asked. Her body had taken on the aura of the Fates since Kyana had last seen her. She was all shimmery and glowy. A far cry from the filth-covered body Kyana had recovered from the trash.

Unwilling to stand by as a silent spectator, Kyana stepped forward. "We need to know who he's working with."

"He can lead us to the next Chosen marked for death," Ryker added. "If we know who else is out there killing the Chosen and who their next target is, we can finally stop the killings and get back your key."

Jordan stood and rested her hand on Ryker's arm. She smiled up at him, a lovesick puppy. "I'll try."

"Whatever you think you can do, it's too late." Panic or fear caused Drake's voice to quiver.

With a furtive glance at her mentor, Jordan clenched her fists and closed her eyes. Then, reaching out, she placed her palms on either side of Drake's head. He jerked, attempted to scramble out of her reach, but Ryker simply kicked him back into obedience.

"You'll regret this," Drake seethed. "Whatever you find out will put you in danger. He'll kill you all faster than you can fucking blink!"

Jordan opened her eyes, wiggled her fingers. "Nothing. I was, however, able to sense the truth of his words. He is not working alone, and he most certainly fears this person more than he fears any of us."

"That's it? That's all you got?" Kyana demanded.

Jordan looked pleadingly to Lachesis. "I don't understand. He's somehow able to block me from reaching deeper to uncover the answers you seek."

A self-satisfied smirk crossed Drake's face. His crooked, bent-out-of-shape nose had finally stopped bleeding, but the crusty red liquid still covered it. Kyana couldn't tell if the sight made her hungry or nauseated.

"I told you. He's beyond your reach. And he's not alone. There are dozens more like me. Hundreds. Thousands even. If you kill me, someone else will take my place."

Kyana hated the smugness of his challenge and wished, more than anything, that she could take him up on it and break his pale neck.

"I told you, she is not ready. She'll need my help." Lachesis stepped forward and placed her hands on her Chosen's shoulders. With light force, she pushed Jordan to her knees so that the woman knelt eye to eye with Drake. "Keep your hands upon him, Jordan. When he speaks, I want you to find the truth or lies in his words."

As Jordan nervously nodded, her tongue flicked over her dry lips. With stiff legs, Lachesis circled Jordan and came to stand at Drake's back. She placed her fingertips to the back of his skull and closed her eyes.

Drake looked ready to jump out of his skin, his gaze darting frantically about the room, no doubt looking for escape. *Good luck, Chuck.* Kyana stood between him and the door, and the chances of him reaching a window before she or Ryker caught him, well, Drake wasn't quick or spry enough for that.

"You are taking orders from someone else?" Lachesis asked, her airy voice filling the small house like a ghostly moan. Kyana leaned against the wall near the door, her body alert for any sudden movement from Drake.

"Drake rubbed his palms down his dirty jeans. "I don't have to answer your questions. You hold no power here. None of you do."

The smile livening up Lachesis's face was far more sincere than Drake's. She was loving this, being able to use her powers, even if it was through Jordan, who looked ready to vomit or faint.

"Remain silent if you wish," the Fate cooed. "We have no need for words to know your truth."

A bead of sweat rolled from his hairline down his broken nose. "Liar."

"Shall we test it?" Lachesis nodded at Jordan, who once again closed her eyes. "Is the person you work for a member of the Order?"

"He is not," Jordan answered on behalf of Drake. "Though he once was."

Leaning over Drake the slightest bit, Lachesis whispered, "See? Remain silent. We will speak for you."

"Does he mean Cronos?" Kyana's question earned

her a startled glance from Lachesis. She obviously wanted to question Kyana's mention of the feared god, but didn't want to risk losing her link to Drake.

"No, not Cronos," Jordan answered. "Another, the most loyal of worshippers."

"Damn it, give me a name!"

Ryker's fingers bit into Kyana's arm in response to her outburst. He leaned into her back and whispered in her ear, "Give them a chance, Ky."

A gentle smile covered Lachesis's face.

"No." Drake struggled to get away. "I won't tell you. I won't."

Jordan wiggled her fingers and set them to either side of Drake's head once again. This time, his head slumped forward, the fight in him gone as Jordan's magic penetrated his blood.

The door burst open. Jordan gave a squeak of alarm and jumped away from Drake, her connection to him broken. Drake collapsed onto his side, unconscious and barely breathing from the sudden sap of magic draining his mind.

Kyana turned to shout at their intruder, only to find Atropos standing in the entryway. She held a steady glare on Kyana as she drifted across the room to stand behind Clotho and rested her hands on her sister's shoulders.

"You brought it?" Clotho asked, reaching up to clasp her sister's hand.

Atropos nodded. "What is going on here?"

"We were *about* to find out who has the key," Kyana snapped, her gaze falling on Drake. "Can we finish now? Or is he going to be out like that for a while?"

"A moment please," Clotho said, her voice steady and calm even while Atropos's gaze was wild and scolding. She took a scroll from Atropos and scanned it. "Have we located a tracer for these?"

"Not yet," Atropos said. "Geoffrey, maybe."

Lachesis snapped her head up. "Not Geoffrey. He has other tasks to see to."

"What do you need a tracer for?" Kyana asked.

Lachesis's gaze fell upon Drake, who appeared almost paralyzed. "Best not to be spoken of in detail before unwanted company."

Clotho passed the scroll to Ryker. "New Chosen for those murdered yesterday and today. Among them, Artemis's. They'll need to be brought in quickly."

"Later," Kyana said, pressing her boot to Drake's back. She gave him a little kick. He didn't move but she still didn't feel comfortable speaking freely with him in the room. "Don't let him so much as breathe in that scroll's direction."

"We're not so irresponsible, you insolent—"

"Atropos, please." Clotho turned her attention away from her sister and focused on Ryker. "Artemis is weak. She cannot assign her tracers to their duties. As Ares's second, I trust you can do it for her?"

Ryker nodded. "Of course."

Her gaze held Ryker's. "Instruct them to be swift, Ryker. We're running out of souls."

"I don't mean to interrupt this party, but isn't it more important to finish dealing with Drake so we can solve your problem of dwindling souls?"

Clotho leaned in toward Ryker, pressing her face close to his, and whispered. "We've had to start pulling from the Order. The humans holding the souls are dying too quickly. We need stronger bodies now."

Kyana watched Ryker scan the list. He paled, and his gaze flickered to Kyana.

"What?"

He shook his head and started to roll the scroll closed, but Kyana snatched it from him, determined to see what had him so panicked.

"Kyana, don't—"

She swung around, putting her back to him, and read. Nearly fifty names glittered in golden ink and she scanned them quickly looking for anything that might stand out as odd. When she reached the end of the list, her gaze locked on two names. One goddess. One Chosen.

Her heart stopped beating, her cold hands warmed.

"The new Artemis . . . is Haven."

Chapter Twenty-seven

Panic gripped Kyana's heart. Haven, the new Artemis? Any other time, this would have evoked an insane amount of envy, but right now, it only evoked terror. She stood, wiping her damp palms on her jeans. "We need to get to Haven. Now. If it gets out that she's a Chosen . . ."

Drake rolled onto his side, his brown eyes heavy with magical residue, but his lips were curved in a sinister sneer. "The moment her name was written on that scroll, she was as good as dead. Look for her if you want, but the ones who want her already know."

Kyana lifted her foot to kick the bastard in the ribs, but Ryker seized her arm and dragged her to the door. "There's no time for that, Ky. Let's go."

She sprinted beside him, her brain reeling as they flew down the steps and onto the streets Below. There was no time to request that a god locate Haven via beacon. All she could do was pray the scent of Haven was fresh and that she wasn't following a week-old trail. They spent so much time here, it was difficult to tell if the weak scent was simply residual effects. She could shift, and maybe the smell would be stronger, but if she did so and found Haven in trouble, she'd be too weak to be of much help when she shifted back.

"Which way?"

Kyana sniffed the air. Haven's pheromones were strongest to the east and so she headed that way without bothering to make sure Ryker still followed.

"He was bluffing, right?" she asked, shoving her way through a crowd spilling out of an emporium. "How could Cronos's followers already know? The Fates just created that damned list."

"No idea. But we're dealing with Cronos and I'm not sure any of us know what he is capable of."

The steady beat of her boots against the cobblestone blocked out the thoughts screaming through her mind. Haven was okay. She *had* to be okay.

They swung around the corner and Haven's scent hit Kyana like a sledgehammer to the nose. This was fresh. Minutes fresh. Kyana looked up to find herself staring at the door to Spirits.

"Here." She shoved open the door and the air-conditioned bar instantly dried her damp skin. The oak-based scent of Haven's perfume lingered strongly among the smell of hookah and overcooked meat. So did that flippin' foul sulfuric stench that she'd picked up on the lock and on the island. Haven's fear was as pungent as the hookah smoke. "She's not okay."

The room swayed and Ryker's hand slipped to the small of Kyana's back as the knowledge that they were too late struck her numb.

"We'll get to her, Ky. Go, follow her scent. There's

a back exit. I'll guard it until you come out. Make sure no one slips out."

Kyana nodded and scanned the tables and booths looking for any sign of Haven. She traced Haven's scent through the kitchen, ignoring the stares of the cook and servers who'd stopped to watch her.

"Has anyone come through here?"

The employees shook their heads, but Kyana wasn't swayed. The perfume was too strong.

She pointed toward a closed door at the back of the kitchen. "Where does that lead?"

The squat cook wiped his hands on his apron. "The cellar. But no one passed through here."

These employees were mostly Mystics who enjoyed the extra cash that came with working at Spirits, but judging by the looks of the sorry lot, not a one of them was very good at his chosen path in the Order. These morons would be unaware if an Illusion Charm had passed right under their noses. Ignoring the cook's protest, she squeezed between the counters and let herself into the cellar. It was faintly lit, and as Kyana crept downstairs, she followed the soft sound of sobbing ahead. When she reached the bottom, the scent of Haven and something stronger stopped her.

Kyana took a deep breath and held it. Oak, lavender, and . . . blood?

She sniffed the air. Definitely blood. The scent made her dizzy, but the sight before her constricted her chest. Haven lay on the floor in the middle of the cellar. A pool of blood beneath her. Kyana roared and flew across the room, skidding to a halt over Haven's body and collapsing beside her.

Being as gentle as possible, she cradled Haven in her arms. Blood pooled beneath Haven's back, caulking the wooden planks and soaking her shirt. Kyana brushed the hair from her friend's face, stared in horror at the three stab wounds gushing and pulsing around Haven's ribs. "Somebody help me," she roared, rocking Haven slowly. "It's okay. You're going to be all right."

Even as she said the words, she knew they were a lie. Too much blood. Haven wouldn't survive it. Panic broke down the stone wall between Kyana's fear and the outside world, making them bleed together until she couldn't see from the tears and agony tearing at her insides. A tear escaped, followed by a rush of emotion that held her frozen and scared out of her mind.

"Haven, please. Open your eyes." She rocked faster. *Don't die don't die don't die don't die.*

Haven gripped Kyana's hand. "Kyana."

"Oh, Haven," Kyana whispered, wiping blood from Haven's mouth. The sound of running footsteps reached her ears. "Help's coming. Just hang on."

"It's okay, Kyana. I'm going to see Hope again."

Kyana squeezed her eyes shut and bit back the urge to scream. Haven wanted to see her twin sister who died years ago? What about Kyana? Hadn't they become sisters?

"Don't you dare die for her, damn you. Live for *me*!"

A faint smile cracked Haven's lips. Her breath released in a long, slow sigh. Her heartbeat slowed. The swoosh of blood quieted. Haven's head fell limp in Kyana's hands. Kyana bit back a cry of agony and instead screamed for Ryker.

"No! Damn you!" Kyana slumped over Haven's

body, trembling, crying, dying right alongside the only being in the world she'd trusted implicitly. Just like everyone else, Haven had left her alone, and for a brief moment, Kyana hated her with every fiber of her being.

Chaos erupted behind her, but Kyana couldn't bring herself to care. Geoff appeared out of nowhere and bellowed for a Healer, but she couldn't lift herself from her hold on Haven's body. Geoff knelt beside them. He took Haven's hand. Kyana slapped him away, unwilling to share this moment with anyone, but when she forced herself to look at him, the anguish coloring his face tore at her already shredded heart.

Please no, please no, please no.

Kyana and Geoffrey huddled together with Haven between them. They tried to draw strength from each other. Tried to give Haven the will to open her eyes though it was impossible.

Or was it?

She twisted, wanting to fly at Ryker and pound his chest but unwilling to release her friend. "You're a fucking god. Do something!"

"A demigod, Ky. I can't— We have to wait. Maybe—"

Anger and hatred exploded inside her. "I don't give a shit about your beloved rules and fucking laws. You saved me! You can save her too."

"I can't," he repeated.

Geoff's howl of anguish mirrored the cold chill covering Kyana. She didn't know how long they sat there, cradling Haven between them. His body shook. His breath hitched. He pressed a tender kiss to Haven's forehead. Leaning forward, Kyana mimicked the kiss, her tears squishing between her lips and Haven's cold cheek.

Haven's hiccupped breath caressed Kyana's face.

She's alive!

Kyana fought back a scream. Haven was still alive. However, the glassy look in her eyes told Kyana it was only a matter of seconds. Ryker had told her to wait and she'd listened, nearly losing Haven once. He couldn't do anything. He'd just said as much.

It was up to Kyana. Not giving herself time to think of consequences, or even if this was something Haven would want, she raked her wrist across her fang.

Keeping her hand steady, she allowed the thin ribbon of blood to pool. Taking Haven's wrist in her free hand, Kyana raised it to her lips. As gently as possible, she sank her fangs into the weak pulse. She kept her gaze locked on Haven, understanding now the sorrow and regret she'd once seen in her Sire's eyes.

"Kyana . . . no." Haven's whisper was a deafening scream. Her blue eyes fluttered open, capturing Kyana's gaze with the power of a lightning bolt. "Let me . . . go. Don't want . . . that . . . in me."

Kyana's heart tripped over itself as she watched Haven. Watched her blood ooze over her wrist, ready to be given. "I'm sorry, Haven. I'm so sorry but I can't let you go."

She waited for that last second between life and death. Sweat trickled down her back as she concentrated on remaining still and waiting for the perfect moment. When Kyana felt death reach down its hand, she held her wrist to Haven's mouth, letting the blood spill over her lips.

Haven tried to turn her head away, but Kyana gripped her tightly, forcing her to take the life she offered even as she prayed for forgiveness. As the blood trickled into Haven's mouth, Kyana's heart raced and at the same time, broke. The transformation from friends to Sire and Childe was complete.

Haven would live.

But she would never be the same.

Chapter Twenty-eight

The roar of outrage could have come from any of them. Ryker. Geoffrey. Even Kyana.

All Kyana knew was that she was being thrown away from Haven like a rag doll. Haven's chest heaving, her back arching, her body shaking like an epileptic's, it all turned Kyana cold. She lay where she was thrown, half in shock, half horrified by what she'd done.

Selfish bitch!

The tirade of name calling inside her brain was an incoherent brutal assault. She shouldn't have done it. Should have stopped to honor Haven's wishes. Haven had accepted death. Had looked forward to the afterlife. Kyana had taken all that away. Haven had fed on the blood of a half Vamp/half Lychen, and while life was finding its way back to her, so was darkness.

What have I done, what have I done, what have I done?

Witch, Lychen, Vamp. There was no telling what that concoction might breed in Haven. No telling what sort of monster Kyana had created.

Haven stretched her mouth and her canines elongated into piercing daggers. Finally able to move, Kyana scrambled into the corner and retched, dry heaving until her abdomen seized up and she thought she might die.

Death would have been kinder for Haven than the fate Kyana had just bestowed upon her. Why hadn't she listened? Why hadn't she let Haven go? Why had she condemned her only family to a life she'd pleaded against?

"What did you do, Kyana?" Geoffrey screamed, kneeling to the left of Haven while Ryker knelt to her right. "Why?"

Geoffrey knew all too well the hell Kyana had just condemned Haven to.

"I'm sorry. My god, I'm so sorry." Kyana retched again, raking her nails into the dirty floor.

"I told you to wait." Ryker's anger shook the walls. "Why didn't you trust me?"

"You said you couldn't do anything!"

"No, but others might have. You're surrounded by—"

"We're surrounded by weak, almost powerless, useless gods. What could they have done?"

Haven let loose a cry of agony that shattered several bottles of wine on the shelves across the cellar. Her hands flung out, her long nails raking Ryker's face, cleaving a racetrack of red from ear to nose. Violence was breeding in her. As was hunger. It wouldn't be long before the thirst made her a raving lunatic.

"Restrain her." Ryker let go of Haven's arm and let Geoffrey take hold of it. He cupped his cheek, the cracks of his fingers filling with blood. His slate gray eyes locked briefly on Kyana. He looked away. "She needs to feed soon or she'll go mad."

The stale blood from the butcher wouldn't stanch Haven's craving, but he darted from the room before Kyana could draw moisture into her mouth to tell him so.

"I'm fucking blind!" Haven thrashed, bucking Geoffrey away as she twisted beneath him.

Kyana winced at the obscenity. Personality was shifting, and that was the proof.

She's not your friend anymore. She's an animal, just like you.

Pushing herself to her knees, Kyana crawled to Haven's side. "It's okay, Haven. Your eyes are changing. You'll be able to see better than ever in just a moment."

Geoffrey's head jerked toward Kyana. "Don't."

"Don't what?"

"Try to make this better. Keen sight isn't worth what you've made her."

Haven screeched again, her hips throwing Geoffrey to the floor. Her wrists slipped from his grip, and in the next instant, she was fisting his hair and struggling to force his neck back. The insane look in her eyes spurred Kyana into action.

"No!" Kyana shoved Haven hard enough to send her onto her back once again.

The wild newborn in her would be hard to restrain. The only way to keep Haven from hurting herself, or one of them, was to take her out of commission. Kyana grabbed Haven's hair, exposing her neck. Kyana drove her fangs into Haven's jugular.

It took all Kyana's strength to keep Haven's thrashing under control. But if she could feed long enough, and take enough blood, Haven would be left weak and helpless until she could feed.

The warm blood coating Kyana's throat nearly drove her out of her mind. She felt a slight tingle as her nails began to grow and the itch of her gums as her fangs elongated. There was nothing like living blood, and it fed the Dark Breed inside Kyana, tempting the beast she'd kept caged for eighty years. She might have fed forever, reveling in the glory of fresh blood if not for Geoffrey grabbing her and throwing her off Haven's now unconscious body.

"Drink anymore and you'll kill her."

Shame flowed through her as she realized that was exactly what she would have done. The starving Dark Breed in her wanted to drink until that glorious moment when the heart stopped and there was nothing left to steal.

Geoffrey knelt beside Haven's body. "She's alive, but if you don't run, you won't be."

"What? I'm not leaving—"

"You turned her! Without consent. Do you realize what that means?"

Once again, coldness iced Kyana's blood. "I've just signed my death warrant."

Something shimmered in Geoffrey's eyes. They softened, pleaded to her. "Go, Kyana. I'll take care of Haven, then I'll find you. Please. Go."

Kyana didn't move. She'd take her punishment. She wouldn't run.

The door behind them burst open. Certain she'd

turn and find those ready to take her to prison, Kyana kept her back straight, her gaze locked on Geoffrey. When no harsh hands grabbed her, she inched her body around. Instead of sentinels, she found Marcus standing in the doorway.

His hands were coated in blood and from his fingertips dangled a silver dagger. Drip. Drip. Blood plopped from the edge of the blade and onto the floor as Kyana lifted her stunned gaze to find Marcus's face. His dark eyes were wide with surprise, and as his frightened expression met Kyana's stare, he dropped the weapon and shot off down the hallway.

Kyana was on her feet before her brain could process what had just happened. The blanks filled themselves in like booms of thunder in her head. Marcus, like Drake, was an ex-Mystic. As she flew up the stairs after Marcus, she couldn't grab on to a single coherent thought. A Cronos worshipper, right smack in the middle of everything going on as the owner of Spirits. Liar. Asshole. *Murderer!*

She bounded over the kitchen counter, her knee slamming into a gawking cook as she twisted to land on her feet, her gaze trained on the back of Marcus's flannel shirt. He was too big and cumbersome to get very far. Kyana was on him before he could reach the dining area. Her instinct to snap his neck was muted by the weight of her duty. If she killed Marcus, then all the other Cronos supporters out there would remain safe.

She wiggled on top of him, flipped him under her, and wrapped her fingers around his throat, forcing him to look into her eyes. "Why, Marcus?" The sad, timid quiver in her voice filled Kyana with shame, but she needed to know. "You know Haven. You *like* her. Why would you hurt her?"

He bucked, and though he was strong, he wasn't stronger than Kyana. All his efforts gave him was slight mobility of his arm. He smiled, inched his fingers to his chest, and gripped a pink crystal in his fist. Then, he was gone. Air. Kyana found herself on her ass, her cupped hands empty.

"No!" she roared, thrusting herself to her feet and sprinting into the dining room even while knowing it was pointless. "Come back, you bastard!"

Cold arms wrapped around Kyana's waist, dragging her back into the kitchen and away from the open-mouthed patrons. "Come, lass. You won't be finding him until that charm's worn off. Haven needs you now. Justice will come later."

Kyana thrust her elbow into Geoffrey's gut, but before she could wriggle out of his grasp, he pulled her back into his chest, his breaths now tiny, pain-filled pants. "Not *now*, lass."

Spinning in his arms to face him, Kyana wanted to claw his eyes out. Wanted to hurt someone, *anyone*, since she couldn't hurt Marcus. "I'm going to be tried and sentenced very soon, Geoff. How can I die peacefully knowing that sonofabitch is still out there?"

"We need to get Haven to safety." Geoffrey struggled with his hold on Kyana. "Get your damned priorities straight."

Kyana's knees buckled. Geoff caught her before she could go down under the weight of her grief. He was right. In her heart, she knew he was right. That made it no easier to just let Marcus go. No easier to accept that she wouldn't be the one to deliver justice to the slimy bastard.

Defeated, Kyana looked pleadingly at Geoff. "We need to take Haven somewhere safe and then I'll turn myself in. If you don't catch Marcus before my trial, Geoffrey, I'll haunt you forever. I swear to Zeus."

"I know, lass." Sadness crept over Geoff's face. He reached out, took Kyana's hand, and pressed it to his lips. She felt like a child afraid of the monster in her closet. Of course, this monster was one she'd created herself.

"Let's go find her a Healer," she whispered. "Maybe if we can purge my blood out of her before she turns . . ."

Ryker stepped through the door holding a Styrofoam cup. "This was all I could get. I don't think it's eno— What happened? Where's Haven?"

"Out cold."As calmly as she could, Kyana told him about Marcus, watched the disbelief turn to anger in his silver eyes.

"You let him get away?" He was searching the kitchen as though he expected to find Marcus stashed in a cabinet.

"Let him?" Kyana roared. "I didn't *let him*. He used an Illusion Charm. One minute I had my hands around his neck, and the next, I was holding air."

Muttering, Ryker turned and stomped back down the steps of the cellar. Kyana chased after him, stopping him halfway down. Something brushed her arm and she shrugged it off, yanking Ryker around to face her.

"You can see through my Illusion Charms, why can't you see through his?"

His eyes narrowed. "Your charm makes people see things that don't exist, like your clothes. I can see through that," he snapped. "Marcus is making us *not* see something that is very real—himself and Haven." His shoulders sagged and he seemed to realize he was taking out his anger on the wrong person. Kyana could understand. She was in the same mindset, only intensified by about two trillion.

"Okay, what about a full god? Maybe Artemis? Have her track Marcus down so I can rip out his heart."

"Can't, lass." Geoffrey approached from behind, making the rickety stairs creak beneath their combined weight. "She can't leave Beyond. She's too vulnerable. Even stepping through a portal to get here could drain what little power she has left, and even if she came, I'm pretty sure her powers are too weak to do us much good."

"Someone tell me again why we're working so hard to save gods who are so damned worthless?" Both Ryker and Geoff glared at Kyana's outburst. "Just get Haven so we can get her purged and you two can hunt down Marcus and do what I can't."

Geoffrey slid his arm around her waist and pulled her to him, forcing her to bury her face in his neck. "You can still run, lass."

She sagged against him, drank in the spicy smell of him. It comforted her. It no longer mattered that she would die without having saved the world. She'd saved Haven. It was enough.

"Geoffrey, I'm sorry. But you can't run from the gods. This is my home, it's all I know. If I run, I spend years if I'm lucky hopping from place to place. And eventually, they'll catch me. I'd rather die with my friends by my side than alone in some dark alley."

She felt Geoffrey's head move above hers, looked up to find him staring with pleading eyes at Ryker. Pushing away, she took a moment to gather herself.

"She's not going to listen to me either," Ryker said, his voice cold, emotionless, contradicting the softness she found in his eyes. He already counted her dead.

"Let's go." Tired of being the focus topic, Kyana stiffened her spine and lifted her chin. "I want Marcus and Drake locked up before my sentencing. I want them to pay before I do, and I want Haven safe."

But as Kyana peered over Geoffrey's shoulder into the kitchen, she knew she wasn't likely to get what she wanted after all. At the top of the stairs, blocking any plans of escape she might have had, stood an army of sentinels. And in their center, Ares. The God of War pulled a broadsword from its sheath on his hip. A slow smile curved his pale lips.

"Seize her."

Chapter Twenty-nine

As the sentinels inched forward, Geoffrey and Ryker moved to stand in front of Kyana. She wanted to push around them and face her punishment with her head held high, but her feet were rooted to the wooden planks of the cellar floor. Geoffrey gripped her elbow, pinning her in place behind him.

The guards who'd stepped forward halted when Ryker held up his hand. "You didn't need to do this. She won't run."

Ares's cold stare settled briefly on Kyana before returning to his son. "Because you would prevent it or because she wouldn't do as you told her?"

The God of War smirked. He knew the answer. There was no father-son love here. Ryker's defense of Kyana would likely do her more harm than good. She didn't even want to consider what it would do to him. Kyana straightened her back and glared at Ares. "He was bringing me in when you interrupted."

"Do not speak again." Ares never looked at her, his attention locked on his son. "Step aside, Ryker."

She wouldn't fight. She wouldn't run. She didn't want Ryker or Geoff to suffer for what she had done. She tried to step toward the two guards who moved to restrain her, but they flew backward against the wall before she could reach them.

Ryker grabbed her arm. His body shook with barely suppressed rage. He was prepared to fight Ares and his entire guard to protect her. She rested her hand on his arm. "It's okay, I'll go with him." To Ares, she added, "But you should know, bringing me in right now shouldn't be your priority. We know who snuck into the Underworld. He was here. I had him and he—"

"A Half-Breed telling me of my duties?" A silver brow shot upward into Ares's hairline. "Will you never learn your place, Kyana?"

"She's right," Ryker said. "The one who tried to murder Haven—"

"Ah, but she wasn't murdered, was she? The Half-Breed made sure of that. It is *that* crime that I'm eager to see punished today. Artemis will send her tracers after the others."

Kyana opened her mouth to demand he let her go hunt Marcus, but snapped her jaw shut before she could make a sound. What good would her release do now? With his Illusion Charm, Marcus would be impossible for any but Artie to find. His scent, his pheromones. All of it would be concealed as completely as his body. And since he was retired from the Order, the gods wouldn't be able to use his beacon to locate him either. Marcus was the perfect puppet for Cronos to play with.

"If you insist on taking her in now, I'll escort her," Ryker said.

"You can't—" Ares shook his head, disgust clearly visible in his chiseled features. He looked toward one of his guards. "You accompany them."

"Don't worry, Kyana. I'll get Haven to safety. She'll be fine . . ." Geoffrey fell silent as he descended the last few stairs into the cellar. "Fuck me, she's gone."

Kyana pivoted and stared in horror at the sight of the empty corner where Haven had lain unconscious. There was no sign of her. No broken window, no sign of struggle. She'd vanished, and the only thing she'd left behind was the smell of her fear.

Or not. Ignoring Ares's demand that she stop moving, Kyana rushed to the corner. Panic ripped through her as she bent and scooped up the glimmering bauble that had caught her eye. Haven's beacon, interlaced with a charm.

"Where the hell did she go?" Geoff stared up at the ceiling as though he expected to see Haven dangling from the rafters.

Kyana shot her gaze across the cellar, searching the shadows and corners for any sign of Haven or anyone else. There was nothing. No one.

"Marcus," she whispered, recalling the faint brush of her arm on the stairs. "He's cloaked them both."

Even though she didn't breathe, Kyana was very close to hyperventilating. Her eyes burned as she struggled to keep her fear in check. She was going to have to run, going to have to accept a death sentence without fight when they finally captured her again, but no way in hell was she letting Ares take her in while Haven was in danger. Save Haven, then face her own fate.

Pushing off on the balls of her feet, she shot straight

up and wrapped her fingers around the rafters. Curses exploded beneath her as she monkey-barred her way across the cellar and over the heads of her pursuers. When she reached the stairs, she kicked out, catching a sentinel in the head, then landed on his body, cushioning her fall. She took the steps three at a time and made it to the door before a hand grabbed the back of her head and slammed it into the jamb.

"Take her," Ares said. And when Kyana struggled against the five sets of hands trying to rip her away from the steps, something hard struck her in the back of her skull. Everything went black.

In the corner of her cell, Kyana slid to the floor and rested her tender head on her bent knees. Since waking ten minutes ago, she'd screamed herself hoarse; demanding to see Ryker or Geoffrey, or anyone for that matter, but no one had answered her calls. Her head pounded from where Ares had knocked her unconscious with the hilt of his sword to bring her in, and her frustration and panic only intensified the pain.

Marcus had Haven, and Haven was going to die if they weren't found soon. Kyana was the best tracer they had, but even she wasn't sure she'd be able to find her friend in time. Without Artemis to see through the illusion, there was really no way to discover where Marcus might have taken Haven.

Kyana had never felt more hopeless or helpless in her life, and it was her own damned fault.

The reality of what she'd done hit her like a fist in the gut, bringing with it another wave of nausea. She pulled Haven's beacon from her pocket and ran her fingers over the smooth cold stone. If Haven had just held on to the beacon, they might have been able to use it to find her. But she hadn't. She'd dropped it, and now Kyana had it, locked inside a prison where it would do no one any good. If Kyana had listened to Ryker, Haven would be lost to them completely. Turning her without consent might have been against the law, but at least Haven lived. Now it might have been for nothing. Haven might die anyway.

But why? Surely Marcus had sensed that Haven had been changed when he'd seen her. Why bother killing her now, when there was no way the Fates would allow Haven to remain Artemis's Chosen? Taking her, killing her, would be useless.

So many questions swirled in Kyana's head, making her dizzy, and none of them mattered anymore. She might be executed before ever discovering Haven's fate. She'd die alone, afraid for Haven, and pissed off to all hell. And what about the key? Without it, the world Above would never be safe, never be restored.

A sound pulled Kyana from her thoughts. Standing, she moved as close to the barrier as possible and peered toward the opening, hoping to see Geoff or Ryker returning with news of Haven.

Kyana's blood simmered as Ares glared at her from the darkness.

A shock zinged from Kyana's fingertips to her throat, making her feel as though her veins were going to explode. It took her a moment to realize she'd pressed her hand against the invisible barrier. She jerked back to see blisters coating her palm and wrist.

"Careful, Kyana," Ares cooed, pacing the small path

in front of Kyana's cell. "Wouldn't want you to die even sooner than expected, would we?"

There was a pantherlike quality about the god. A white panther perhaps. White, wavy hair reaching his shoulders. He looked ancient, yet fit; confident, yet ready to pounce.

"Fine, kill me," she said, cupping her injured hand to her chest. "But please, find Marcus. Now. Find him and get Haven. She's still a Chosen until the Fates appoint a new one. If you stand by and let her die—"

"You dare to tell me of my duties *again*?" Ares's face reddened, the vein above his brow bulging, giving Kyana her first glimpse of the father-son similarity with Ryker.

"What have I done to make you hate me so much that you would risk a Chosen's life to see me punished?"

He watched her, silently pacing, stalking, preying. "Foolish Half-Breed. You needed only to have been reborn with the tainted blood you possess."

"Your son is a Half-Breed. Is that why you loathe him as well?"

Venomous eyes pierced her flesh, making her suddenly grateful for the magically charged barrier between them. "You know nothing of me or my son."

Well, maybe there was love lost there after all.

"So it's just Vampyre you despise. Or Lychen, maybe?" She cocked her head, studying him. "Is that why you won't go after Haven? Because she has my blood now? Maybe she's not worth saving any longer, Chosen or not?"

He looked like he'd enjoy nothing more than ripping

off her head and shoving his massive sword down her throat.

"You pretend you're not ready to piss yourself at my presence, Kyana. We both know the truth, though, don't we?" He stopped his stalking and pressed a large, bronzed hand to the invisible panel. Nothing happened. His nostrils flared. "You stink of my son. You tainted a demigod with your filthy body. You should burn."

Kyana flinched, completely caught off-guard that he knew that she and Ryker had slept together. She had no intention of discussing her personal business with Ares, however, and forced herself to return his glare. If he intended to kill her before her sentencing was handed down, she wouldn't go cowering at his feet.

"Why are you here, Ares? Is this to be my execution . . . you taunting me to death?"

His dark gaze roamed over her body, leaving Kyana feeling naked and exposed. "What you are should not have been. Your Sire was the only one of his kind. We let him live because of his vow to never create another. The hunt began the instant you were turned."

At the mention of her Sire, Kyana's heart twisted. "Henry wasn't with the Order. How—"

"The Order was created to maintain a balance between the human world and ours. Dark Breeds were allowed to walk freely as long as they obeyed our laws, despite their lack of loyalty to the Ancients. The instant he stole your human existence, he signed his death warrant."

Henry hadn't stolen anything. He'd *rescued* her from her human existence.

"You're wrong. Henry was killed by a wannabe Vampyre hunter. I was there."

She'd held his body as he lay dying, promised him retribution as he'd died for the second time in his life.

"And who do you think hired him? I made certain Henry was sent to Tartarus where he belonged."

"Why?" she seethed. "Because he was a Half-Breed? If that's the case, then why was I allowed to join the Order?"

"Because Artemis saw something in you. An unwise decision on her part, as you've proven today." His teeth flashed white beneath the fine hairs of his silver beard. "I will watch you die today, Kyana, as you should have died that day with your Sire."

She made the mistake of reaching out for him and crashing smack into the pulsating barrier. Electrical charges slashed through her body, dropping her to her knees as they paralyzed her. Ares reached through and shoved her backward before the electricity could kill her. Kyana curled into a ball, cradling her singed hands to her belly as she fought against the blackness and to control the tremors racing through her body as she heard Ares's footsteps fade away.

A hand touched her shoulder. Kyana nearly jumped out of her skin. The need to fight, to protect herself, kicked in, and she swung blindly.

"It's me, Ky." Ryker sat beside her, gently eased her to his side and wrapped his arm around her shoulder.

Kyana threw her arms around his neck, grateful he'd finally come. She took his silent offer of strength and rested her head on his chest, breathing in his sweet scent. "Where have you been? Did you find Marcus? Haven? What's going on?"

"I would have come sooner but Ares forbade anyone to see you." He cupped her chin and sighed. "I tried, Ky. I tried to find Marcus and Haven but they've disappeared. Geoff is still looking, but I—I had to come make sure you were okay."

She stood, pointing at the exit. "You have to go back out there and look—"

"I'm not a tracer. Trust Geoffrey and the others. He'll find her."

"She could be dead." Kyana fought back the panic that was making her brain feel muddled again.

He sank his hand into Kyana's hair, holding her tightly to his chest as if to absorb her pain. "It's not been that long."

"How long does it take to kill someone? How do we know she's—"

"She has your blood now. Killing her won't be that easy. Especially for a Mystic. She could easily overpower him."

She wanted to imagine Haven happily cutting her way through Marcus, but the only image that floated through her mind was that of Haven being slaughtered. Even if she did overpower Marcus, Haven could flee, let the Dark Breed inside her feast. Either way, Haven was lost to them all. Maybe forever.

Tears clogged Kyana's throat and she struggled to hold them back. She failed miserably and sank to her knees. Ryker followed her to the ground, refusing to give up his hold on her.

When she finally calmed long enough to speak, she leaned her head against his chest and whispered, "Do you think—"

"Stop thinking. Just for a little while."

He was right. There was nothing she could do. At least not this minute. All she could do was try to calm herself so she could manage the array of thoughts racing through her brain and make sense of them. Clear her head. Calm down.

She sat quietly, borrowing Ryker's warmth, his strength. This could be the last time she saw him. There was so much she wanted to ask him. So many things she wanted to say. However, the words refused to transmute from her brain to her lips and instead, they sat in silence.

She didn't know how long they sat there, but Ares's visit played through her mind. She wasn't worthless or an abomination or inhuman. For eighty years she'd devoted her life to the Order. Kyana had followed their rules and laws, done what she'd been told, though not willingly or without argument at times, but, until recently, she'd never failed to complete the missions assigned to her. Even as a feeding Vamp, she'd never killed without provocation. She'd protected the innocent.

She'd never taken a life or created one . . . until today.

She might not understand things like love and compassion and what it truly meant to have a family, but it didn't mean she wasn't deserving of those things. That she didn't want them, need them as much as the next person . . .

"Still thinking?"

A sigh fluttered past her lips as she buried her face deeper in his neck. "Can't help it."

His shirt was bunched in her hand. Slowly, she shifted to stare up at him. His blond head was inches from hers. His silver eyes watched her as though they knew what she wanted. He wrapped his arms around her, holding her tightly to him, and watched her, waiting. She wanted to lose herself in him again. Wanted to go numb. Wanted to forget just for a little while.

"How do I make you crazy?" she whispered.

Ryker tried to control his response to Kyana's question. He didn't want her thinking about this. Not now. The answer would do nothing to alleviate her fears . . . and it wouldn't make what they were about to go through any easier.

Though he knew what she was talking about, he said, "What?"

She traced his jaw with her thumb. "You said from the minute you met me that I've made you crazy. How?"

"Not now, Ky. Can't we just sit here—"

"Now is the only time I have. Just once, can't you answer a bloody question?"

He leaned his head against the rough stone wall and studied her. He didn't want to do this, but he couldn't deny the pleading in her eyes either. He held her gaze so there'd be no doubt in her mind that he spoke the truth. "I want you. I've *always* wanted you."

"No. Not always. Not ten years ago when I offered myself to you. It took you ten years to screw me, Ryker. That's not a whole lot of *want*."

"I know, and I didn't *screw* you."

"Whatever you want to call it, I don't care." Her eyes

clouded as she tried to read the unspoken meaning behind his words. "If you wanted me all that time . . . why'd you reject me all these years? Why did it take so damned long?"

"I never rejected you."

"Don't patronize me."

"I'm not. I'm trying, for the first time since I met you, to be completely honest here."

"Okay, then. Be honest. What is about me that kept you away from my bed until recently when I offered it to you so blatantly?"

"Simple. You embrace the Vampyre half of yourself. I embrace the Lychen."

She had that look in her eyes again, like she wanted to call him a liar. Instead, she said, "No one embraces Lychen. It's feral. Inhuman."

Ryker shook his head. "It's fiercely loyal. Protective. I refuse to be a conquest. I want more than you're capable of giving me."

"So it's not *what* I am that turns you off, it's *who* I am."

"Damn it, Kyana, it's not you that turns me off, it's your tendency to be blind. You've never seen what I wanted to give you ten years ago. You still don't see in the mirror the woman I see every time I look at you. Never seen me as more than a man who is willing to take what you had to offer and walk away. That you're worth more than a quick lay. That you're worth *something* to *someone*. That I wanted that someone to be me."

Her bitter laugh fanned his face. "But you ended up fucking me anyway. I guess that means you quit seeing those things in me? Finally saw that a good screw was my best asset?"

Ryker wanted to punch the wall. He would have if he'd thought it might have done any good. "I made love to you because I finally realized I'd rather have the smallest piece of you than nothing at all."

Her laughter died and her expression turned solemn. "You're saying things you think I want to hear. I just want the truth from you. Even if it's ugly and makes me call you a bastard for having the balls to say it."

She jerked out of his arms and paced the tiny cell. "I'll tell you what you're too afraid to say. You loathe everything I value, value everything I loathe. You think I'm a bitch. That I'm heartless because I can't find compassion for a race that—"

Ryker held his breath, watched her, waited . . . hoped. This was as close as she'd ever come to mentioning her past. He knew what had happened to her, he'd seen it, lived it in her nightmares. It would be so simple for him to say the words she couldn't bring herself to say, but he wanted her to trust him enough to share that part of her with him.

"A race that what, Ky? Tell me."

"Nothing. Nothing but Haven matters to me now and I'm stuck here, helpless to do anything to save her."

Disappointed that she still didn't trust him with the truth of her past, he gently tugged her chin his way, forcing her to meet his gaze. "You don't have to be in Lychen form to be a bitch. But I can see beneath the hard-ass shell you wear. You act like you don't give a damn, that all you're after is what you can gain, but I've never believed it."

Kyana pulled out of his grasp, but didn't move away. She studied him intently. "Then you're a fool."

"I saw you tend that dying tracer ten years ago, watched you mother him as he died, watched you mourn him. I see the way you protect your friends, feel how the mere mention of a past you won't talk about hurts you now. You're not as heartless as you'd like everyone to believe."

Kyana looked away.

He brushed his mouth lightly across hers. "You have a right to feel. Not just for Haven but for whoever you decide is worth letting in. Until you accept that, believe that, you're going to be alone."

"I am alone. Pity from you won't change that."

Ryker raked his fingers through his hair in frustration. What was it going to take to make her stubborn ass *hear* him? "Even facing what might be handed to you tonight, you can't let someone care about you."

Dawning swept over Kyana, forcing her to push away from him completely. This wasn't about her and him. This was about Ryker wanting to make her last night memorable. Hell, if she asked for it, he'd probably screw her brains out just to offer her a way to stop worrying for a while.

"I don't need you," she whispered. "You're right about me. I'm only interested in an orgasm. Go away, Ryker. Stop making me feel like a victim."

He winced, and momentary grief struck Kyana in the chest. She shoved it aside. Better to die never knowing what could have been than leave him living with the regret of what shouldn't have been.

It was her turn to take care of him for a change.

Chapter Thirty

The coquina walls of Kyana's cell were closing in on her. She felt much like the lions she'd once seen in the Jacksonville zoo. Caged. Trapped. On display. Ryker had stopped glaring at her, but his anger was choking all the life out of the room. Yet he'd refused to leave.

Geoff strolled into view behind the electrified archway, breaking the glare-down between her and Ryker. Kyana anxiously greeted him from her side of the cell, desperately searching his face for some sign that he'd found Haven. His smile didn't reach his eyes. Dread seized her chest.

"You didn't find her," she whispered.

He shook his head. "I haven't given up, lass. Just wanted to see you. To say . . . to just make sure you were all right."

To say good-bye. He'd come in case Kyana's sentencing ended badly. Kyana swallowed. "I'm fine. Go to Haven. Find her, please. I have to know she's okay before they come for me."

"I've still got tracers searching but it's difficult without Marcus's scent. We gave up trying to trail Haven's. Whatever she's becoming, the change in her essence would throw us off anyway."

Kyana stilled. *Whatever she's becoming.* Because of Kyana's mixed heritage, there was no way to know . . .

She hated the pitying gaze Geoffrey was giving her now.

Ryker rubbed his nape and sighed. Whatever anger and animosity had lain between them was unimportant now.

"I'm not sure what good it will do, but I'll help. But Kyana, don't forget. There's also the possibility that she finished turning before he could get her to wherever he was taking her. She could have killed—"

Kyana held up her hand, stopping him from offering more false hope. What just happened between them no longer mattered. The anger had left his eyes, and compassion and understanding now filled them. She rested her hand on his chest.

"Just go. She needs you both more than I do."

"We'll find her," he whispered, pressing a kiss to Kyana's forehead. He stepped to the barrier. The shimmery buzz of magical energy flashed as he stepped through the invisible bars holding her captive.

When they reached the arched exit, both men looked back. Unspoken good-byes etched lines into their beautiful faces, and Kyana bit back tears, terrified that this image of them was the one she'd take to her final grave.

"Go," she said, shooing him away. "I'll be fine."

And just like that, they were gone.

* * *

How long had it been since Geoff and Ryker had left in search of Haven? Thirty minutes? An hour? Eternity? Kyana couldn't tell. The tiny window in her cell gave no hint of time's passing. There was only the sound of her breath to fill the never-ending panic tightening her chest more with each fraction of a second that passed.

It was hard to trust others to fix what she'd broken. She trusted Geoffrey and was learning to trust Ryker, but it came with great difficulty. Being trapped like a bloody animal made her feel helpless and out of control.

"Damn it!" She was going to have to beg for freedom long enough to look for Haven. Then the gods could deal out whatever punishment Kyana had coming. But she couldn't die not knowing.

Kyana buried her face in her hands and let out a half laugh, half scream. Whom could she beg? There was no member of the Ancients left that she hadn't thoroughly pissed off. She sat on the cold, dirt-covered floor. Something dug into her hip. Shifting, she reached into her pocket and felt Haven's beacon. It was tangled and wouldn't come loose. Straightening her legs, she rolled onto her back and dug deeper, feeling another small sphere brush her fingertips.

Haven's beacon fell from her fingers and rolled toward her boots, and the other object tumbled after it.

Kyana picked up the necklace and let the tea ball–like charm spin slowly. The Charm of Nine Gods. She'd forgotten about it. Haven had spent a small fortune on the charm, and as excitement pounded in Kyana's veins, she knew the money was going to be well spent.

Her enthusiasm over her find gave way to sinking fear. She didn't know anything about the charm or how it worked. Haven said it would do the casting, allowing her to astral project, but Kyana still remembered the last time Haven had tried such a spell. Their friend Silas had warned that such attempts were extremely dangerous. Leaving her body, going on a blind search for Haven, could force her to spend eternity wandering the shores of the River Styx hunting for a body forever lost to her.

She wanted to do something productive, but could she really help anyone if she used the charm?

Kyana sighed and studied both necklaces. There had to be a way to use them to locate Haven. If she could get the beacon to Ryker or Geoff, they could use it. When she rushed to the opening, energy passed through her body and she jerked, unable to control the spasms racking her body. Blessedly, the spasms forced her back. She collapsed to the floor, curled into a ball, and prayed to every god she could think of that the pain wouldn't kill her before she had the chance to give the beacon to someone who could use it.

After several minutes, the burning pain eased. She crawled to the opening, careful to keep her body from the invisible barrier still pulsing with magic energy. Her first three attempts to call out to her guards were nothing more than garbled grunts. The fourth produced a whisper. Kyana forced air into her lungs, hoping the needless oxygen would give her the strength she needed.

"Guards!"

One of the sentinels marched into the hall, his massive hand on his sword.

Kyana rose to her knees. "I need to talk to the tracer Geoffrey."

The guard shook his head. Kyana hated the blank stare that confessed he didn't know who she was asking for. "Ryker. Can you find Ryker?"

Again, the guard simply shook his head.

"You have to know Ryker. *Everyone* knows Ryker." She stood. "Just give him a message. Tell him I know how to find Haven."

Seeming to take pity on her, the guard took a step closer. Not questioning her good fortune, she asked again, "Just get a message to him."

"Those you seek are no longer here."

Kyana gritted her teeth. "I know they're not here, but they're Below. Someone has to know where they are."

"I cannot leave my post, Dark Breed. Especially not on the request of a prisoner."

Kyana attempted a hiss that came out sounding more like a deflating balloon. Damn, why couldn't she use a cell phone? She fingered the Charm of Nine Gods, and unease settled in her gut as she realized what she was going to have to do.

The guard turned to leave. "Wait," Kyana called out. "The Seer Nettles. Can you get her for me?"

His gaze traveled over her. "You're in need of a Seer?"

"I want to see if she can tell me if my friend will be okay before I die. That's all."

He studied her in silence, and after a long moment, nodded, then left the room.

"I'm not helping you commit suicide." Nettles watched

Kyana from outside the cell, her brown gaze wide in disbelief. "I'm not going to invoke that charm for you. Astral projection is frowned upon by the Order because it's dangerous. That charm you hold there is ten times more powerful and a hundred times more unstable than a simple casting. You'd have an hour at most, maybe less. That's what makes it so dangerous."

"Then teach me how to use it," Kyana pleaded.

"That charm is meant for a Witch. I don't know what it will do to you. It probably wouldn't even work. Or it could send you into another realm where you'd spend eternity looking for a body forever lost to you." Nettles's little body shook with her adamant refusal.

Her tight face softened as her gaze swung to Kyana's black and red hands. "I've asked the guards to obtain permission to let me in there to tend that, but then I'm leaving. I'm not helping you use that charm, do you hear me? Give me the beacon. If I can't find Geoff or Ryker to give it to them, I'll use it myself to find your friend."

Right. That wasn't happening. If Nettles didn't find Geoff or Ryker, she'd go after Marcus herself? No way was Kyana putting another person in danger. Enough of that was going around already. And if she gave Nettles the beacon and Haven wasn't found, Kyana's chance to use the Charm of Nine Gods and the beacon would be gone. No. There was only one shot here, and it was going to have to be Kyana who finished this mess.

"Nettles, you're afraid it will go wrong and I won't make it back. I get it." Seeing the skepticism in the Seer's face, Kyana forced all sincerity into her voice. "I'm going to die anyway. They're not going to let me walk after what I've done. I have to be the one to do this. If something goes wrong, better it happen to someone whose fate is already sealed. Right?"

"It goes against my oaths to the Order to help you die."

"I won't die. Trust me. I'd rather get my ass back in time to face my execution so I don't become one of those invisible creepy things along the River."

Seeing the walls of Nettles's resolve begin to crumble, Kyana pressed on. "I know you have no reason to help me, but you're my only hope. Please."

Nettles said nothing, her teeth worrying her bottom lip, her hands raking her short, spiky locks over and over as though she was having a furious, silent conversation with herself.

Kyana kept talking, afraid to give the Healer time to think it over. "What I did to Haven . . . she deserves a chance to live despite it. Worry about her, Nettles. Not me!"

What were normally kind, soft eyes now turned hard as Nettles ceased worrying and fidgeting. She glared at Kyana, her small hands falling to rest on her hips. "If you make me the cause of your restless eternity . . ."

Relief filled Kyana from toes to hairline. "I won't."

Nettles threw back her head and shouted in a voice unfitting her mousy stature, "Guards!"

In silence, they waited for the young sentinel to appear, then Nettles addressed him in a tone that let him know she wasn't about to be refused. "Let me in there. I need to tend her wounds and give her something to help her sleep."

The guard pulled a golden disk from beneath his

tunic. The gold chain reached his belly, the disk a golden, sparkling replica of a Chinese Throwing Star. Its five spiky points looked deadly, but fit easily into a thin groove to the right of Kyana's cell. Even as he slipped it into the lock, his free hand was unsheathing the sword at his hip.

The static sound that had become white noise to Kyana faded, and the sentinel nodded to Nettles, his wary gaze never leaving Kyana. "You may enter."

"You'll have to leave us," Nettles said, stepping into the tiny cell.

"I'm not leaving."

Nettles poked him in the chest, her easygoing manner forgotten. "You *will*. She is wounded beneath her clothes, and prisoner or not, she has the right to her privacy while I tend her."

"Madam, I cannot—"

"Lock the cell and go! I'll call for you when I'm done. She won't be able to escape."

The guard's eyes narrowed, his face paling. "You'd willingly put yourself behind the gods' magic?"

"I would. Now go."

Looking as though he was in awe of Nettles's courage, the sentinel did as he was asked and sealed the small entrance once again with the invisible, static-laced barrier.

"Is that such a big deal? You letting yourself behind the gate?" Kyana asked, suddenly worried.

Nettles shrugged. "In order for the magic to be released and let me out again, the god who provided the spell, likely Ares, must still be strong and powerful. There's a chance the god will fade before that key is used again to set me free, but I doubt that will happen in the next ten minutes."

Kyana shuddered at the thought of being trapped in this tiny room for all eternity.

Nettles finished pulling items from her purse and motioned Kyana forward. Kyana held out her hands and allowed Nettles to apply a cool, pleasant-smelling balm. It wasn't unusual for a nonhealing Witch to carry such things. Most liked to play with herbal remedies whether they specialized in them or not.

"That guard's going to come back any minute. What do we need to do?"

Nettles mixed some dark powder into a bottle of water. "Drink this."

It was a good thing Kyana didn't need to breathe because the smell would have strangled her. She downed the foul liquid. Her stomach rebelled, nearly forcing the horrible brew back up and onto her boots. Her eyes watered. Her throat burned. "What was that for?"

"To help you relax and be more susceptible to the magic we're about to perform. This charm is meant for Witches. I'm not sure I have everything we might need to make it work for one like you."

"It'll work." It had to. Kyana took a needless breath. "Will others be able to see me in my new state or will I be free to move around?"

"Some will see you and dismiss the event without thought. Others will feel you but not know what's caused the hair on their arms to stand on end. Most will have no idea you're there." Nettles laced the charm and Haven's beacon together, then placed them in Kyana's hands. "By lacing the beacon, you should be able to take it with you in spirit form. Listen to your heart and follow its glow. It should lead you to Haven. The closer you get to her, the brighter the light should become."

There were far too many *should*s muttered with Nettles's instructions. All the moisture evaporated from Kyana's mouth. "And what happens if it doesn't?"

"No more peaceful nights of rest for you. Ever," Nettles warned. "Now think of Haven."

Kyana swallowed her nerves and closed her eyes. In her mind, she pulled up images of her best friend. Memories of happier times with herself, Geoff, and Haven before the world fell apart.

Nettles's voice droned on. Kyana couldn't make out the words as the world faded and the images in her mind took hold. She prayed that this would work, that she'd be able to save Haven, that Haven would still possess a piece of herself that wanted to be saved.

"Oh my gods, what have we done?"

The panic in Nettles's voice caused Kyana's eyes to snap open. "Is it done?"

She clutched her throat with one hand, her breast with the other. "May the gods forgive me, it is."

Kyana followed Nettles's gaze to the floor where her own body lay crumpled and lifeless. "Whoa."

She reached out, attempted to touch her own fleshy cheek, but her hand disappeared like smoke against the pale skin on her sleeping self.

"Go, Kyana!"

Kyana jumped, snapping out of the near-trance state caused by seeing herself so vulnerable. Right. This wasn't the time to ponder the incredible magic allowing her to do this. She had to get to Haven.

It took a moment to acclimate herself to the weight-lessness, but she managed to make her way less than gracefully to the exit.

"The guard will think you're sleeping," Nettles said, her voice a loud whisper. "I'm going to go find Ryker, but meanwhile, watch for the color to fade from the charm. When it's pewter again, your time is up."

Kyana tried to speak, but the echo in her head nearly deafened her. She turned and, with a prayer that the barrier wouldn't work on her spirit form, Kyana stepped through the gate.

Chapter Thirty-one

Kyana gripped the charm-laced beacon in her fist and followed its faint pink glow through the twilight of Below. As Nettles predicted, some passersby glanced at Kyana but quickly looked away. Most of those winding their way through the cobblestone streets seemed not to sense her at all. Frustration fogged her mind. Below was as massive as the world Above. She didn't have time to search every inch, but Haven couldn't be far. There hadn't been time for her and Marcus to leave the patch of Below that fell beneath St. Augustine. But where to begin?

Listen to your heart and follow the glow.

Nettles's instructions fought through the haze of Kyana's brain. She concentrated on Haven, filling her mind's eye with images of her friend's smiling face. Not questioning the odd sensations prickling her skin, Kyana moved through the streets, past the bathhouse, beyond the portal gate, through alleyways and packed side streets.

She stopped in an older section of the city where

open fields and scattered buildings had once made up an old market.

Holding the beacon out before her, Kyana turned in a slow circle, feeling useless and helpless without her working senses. When she faced the largest of the old greenhouses, Haven's beacon turned a rich blood red. Moving with a speed that rivaled her Vampyric powers, she entered the dilapidated building, her body sifting through the stone walls as easily as mist through hair. The harsh glare of the naked bulb hanging from a beam in the center of the building revealed pieces of furniture covered in dusty sheets. Potting soil and terra-cotta planters littered the floor. Whoever had worked here had long ago vacated the premises.

The beacon's pulsating glow suggested Haven should be near but Kyana had to be reading it wrong. The greenhouse was silent and void of any hint of people. She turned to leave when a low, pain-filled groan pulled her toward a darkened corner. A figure lay curled in a fetal position, but there was no mistaking the clothing, the hair.

Haven! She was alive.

As she moved closer to Haven, the sight of thick chains wrapped around her wrists and ankles froze Kyana in place. She hadn't thought this through. Why hadn't she considered that she might find Haven alive and be useless in helping her escape? How was she going to free Haven when she couldn't even touch her?

Haven opened her eyes. Yellow, cold, lifeless eyes. Evil lurked in their depths. If Haven wasn't tamed soon, that side of her would consume all the light, all the good that made her who she'd been in life.

Kyana couldn't let that happen. She reached for the bonds, but her fingers refused to close around the chains. Haven snarled and lunged, obviously able to see through the charm's magic. The wildness in her eyes and garbling in her voice told Kyana that she was no longer considered a friend. The minute her blood had slipped over Haven's lips, that friendship had died. Kyana stiffened her shoulders. She still had a job to do, then she could return to her fate and hope the others were able to help Haven straighten out the mess Kyana had made of her life.

Anger simmered in her belly. She focused on that emotion, the anger, the frustration.

The naked light bulb above her head shattered. Haven snapped her head away, safeguarding it from the bits of glass spraying in their direction. The shards drifted through Kyana, landing noisily on the wooden floor around them.

Excited over the prospect of being able to *do* something, Kyana focused harder on her anger. The air around her turned frigid; a layer of ice slowly coated the glass along the windows near Haven's head.

Yes! I am here! I exist!

Footsteps. Then a shadow formed, large and filling the doorway. In the darkness, Kyana couldn't make out any features. Apparently her keen sight had been left behind with her body, just like everything else. A noise, somewhere between a pop and a whoosh, came from the intruder, then a burst of light illuminated his form. Marcus's robust form filled the entrance from the hall, his beard dirty and bloody. Good. Haven had given him a fight.

He placed the lit match to a candle, carefully set the candle on a table by the door.

"Break all the lights you like, Haven. I'll still see you just fine."

Something shiny flashed in his hand, and Kyana followed it, sucking in her breath at the sight of the dagger he fisted. Zeus, she wished she could rip his throat out. She'd trusted him. Set up Hank and his computer right under his nose. What blind idiots they'd all been.

I'm going to kill you. I'm going to gut you, and rip off your head, and smash your skull with my bare hands.

Her silent threats meant nothing. She'd be dead before she could carry them out. Still she imagined ripping him apart and dancing in his blood, allowing the images to feed her, fill her, until slowly, she began to feel more real.

She was going to feed his dick to his ass.

As Marcus turned away from his third and final candle, Kyana lunged at him. The moment her form hit him, a wave of nausea passed through her just before she came out the other side. Marcus jerked. Shivered. He looked around the room, his eyes wild.

"Who's there?"

He held his dagger in front of him now, his lips a pale shade of blue.

The sheets covering the tables flew in every direction. Behind her, icy veins cracked the window above the door. A layer of frost bled across the floor at her feet, circling Marcus's boots. Her anger had become tangible. Real. She could use it if she focused.

Marcus took a step forward, his boot slipping on

the thin sheet of ice. "What the—" He caught himself. His glare, filled with hatred and fear, turned toward the corner. "Who's here, Haven?"

Haven stared at Kyana. For half a second, Kyana saw her friend within the depths. Then Marcus took a step toward Haven and she gave a throaty warning, struggling against her bonds.

Leave her alone! The shout resonated within Kyana's head. Kyana fisted her hands and swung. Several terra-cotta pots crashed to the floor at Marcus's feet.

He froze, his nostrils flaring. He closed his eyes and inhaled, then smiled. "Ah, Kyana. I smell yo-o-u," he taunted. "They executed you a bit sooner than I expected."

Another planter crashed to the floor, missing Marcus by inches.

"Is that the best you got?" Marcus laughed and took another step toward Haven. "The only ones around to hear the noise work for me, so make all the racket you want."

She had to buy Haven a little more time. Had to keep Marcus occupied until Nettles could find Geoffrey and Ryker, until they could find the greenhouse. Her fury caused icy crystals to form around Marcus's boots and spider outward.

He laughed at her weak attempt to stop him. His breath clouded. "You're wasting your energy. If you had time to perfect being an apparition, and someone to train you, you could really do me harm. You should join our side. Cronos would love having the mighty Kyana working for him, just as he's going to love Haven. You've given him the perfect gift, you know. The perfect weapon. She's going to be a beauty."

The perfect weapon? How was Haven a weapon? Energy drained from her as defeat threatened to take hold. Her questions would have to wait. She needed the last bit of her energy to hold Marcus off.

Kyana drifted to the candles. She tried to pinch out the fire, but no heat touched her skin. *Damn it!*

The flame flickered.

Narrowing her gaze, she concentrated on the flickering light and screamed out her fury over being duped by the likes of an ex-Mystic. The flame danced, then puffed out. She quickly extinguished the remaining two candles, plunging the large room into total darkness.

"Are you worried about your friend, Kyana?" Marcus asked, rotating in a small circle. "No need. I suppose I should thank you. If you hadn't turned her, she never would've been powerful enough for our purpose. Now she's far more useful alive than dead."

Kyana strained to see. She'd existed with her supernatural strengths for so long that she felt disoriented in the dark without them. However, the sound of Marcus stumbling into tables as he too tried to gain his bearings gave her a bit of satisfaction.

He tripped over a chair. His curses rang in her ears. Kyana smiled. She followed beside him, using what little bit of solidity she possessed to shove tables and planters into his path. Pots of long-forgotten soil crashed into his face and chest. Worktables knocked him to his knees. Each time he tripped and fumbled in the darkness, adrenaline gave her more energy. She threw everything she could in his path, hoping to keep him disoriented and away from Haven.

By the time she realized Marcus was doing nothing more than moving in a tiny circle, it was too late. He'd known her abilities would fade. That she'd exhaust herself trying to stop him. Her remaining strength was quickly waning. She held the Charm of Nine Gods to her face; the brightly polished gold had faded to a dull brass. She didn't have much time left. He'd played her for a fool. Again.

With a roar, she dove for him. Marcus shuddered, his knife-wielding fist swung at her form, passing through her. With the last of her strength, she grabbed his hand as she passed through his body. As she fell to the floor, the clang of the weapon bouncing off a clay pot and skidding into the darkness brought her a moment's peace.

Marcus shoved rotting tables out of his way, searching for his dagger. Kyana lay on her side, watching the distance close between Marcus and Haven.

Run! Damn it, Haven. Get your ass up and run! I can't help you anymore. Fight the hunger and run!

As if hearing her, Haven looked at Kyana. The lifelessness in Haven's eyes dissolved into fear, then anger. She thrashed against her bonds.

That's it. Fight.

Marcus closed in on Haven. She swung out with her feet, tripping him. He dropped to his knees, his head banging off the stone sill. "Bitch!" He fumbled in the darkness for Haven. He straddled her waist, his hands closing around her throat. "Just because I don't want to kill you doesn't mean I won't!"

Haven gurgled. Bucked against him. Fought to break her bonds. Then she stilled. Her crazed laughter made

Kyana's skin crawl. Her eyes glowed yellow-green in the faint light filtering through the melting ice covering the windows. Her body went rigid. The bones and muscles stretched and re-formed. Haven had found her dark side and it wasn't Vampyric. The Lychen dominated.

No! Don't do it, Haven. Please. *You'll never fight the darkness if you give in.*

Kyana's scream was a silent gush of frigid breath. She tried to struggle to her feet, but she could no longer move, could no longer prevent what was about to happen. She could do nothing more than watch as her best friend made her final transition to becoming a Dark Breed.

Chapter Thirty-two

Kyana lay on the hard, dirt-strewn floor among broken glass, shards of pottery, and crushed work benches. Drained. Lost in the darkness. She could hear Haven's claws skittering across the floor as she struggled with Marcus. Hear him pleading for his life. Gripping the Charm of Nine Gods in her fist, Kyana waited for the time on her spiritual state to lapse.

Would she simply open her eyes and find herself on the banks of the River Styx, or would she spend eternity in the old greenhouse lying among the rotting tables and shattered pottery?

It didn't matter. Nothing did. Time was up.

The floor beneath her cheek vibrated. Not sure what she'd see, and not brave enough to find out, she squeezed her eyes tightly shut. Her transportation to the Underworld had arrived. Kyana always believed she'd face her final death with dignity . . . not curled on a dirty floor, too weak and powerless and afraid to face her destiny.

"Kyana!"

Ryker? Warmth filled her belly, giving her enough energy to lift her head and look toward the closed door. But he was too late. Haven had fed, and Kyana was too weak to make her way back to her body. Concentrating on the door, she tried to shove it open. It moved just enough to let a little light in. Enough to reveal Ryker and Geoffrey. Enough to distract Haven. She lifted her head and growled.

Desperation unfogged Kyana's tired mind. She focused on the door again. It flew open, then banged closed with such force it flopped on broken hinges.

Instinct had Haven crouching, her gaze locked on the door. Her golden fur coat quivered as she bared her teeth. Kyana could do nothing more than watch and pray Ryker's and Geoff's senses were on high alert.

Geoff entered first. The minute he stepped out of the small patch of light, Haven attacked. He caught her mid-air. Spun her around. Pinned her to his chest, making her whimper.

"I've got her," he shouted, moving Haven into the shadows and letting her struggle until she was too worn out to hold on to her newly found body and she slid back into her normal, albeit naked and still struggling, form.

Kyana listened as he promised Haven she'd be okay. They had her. No one would hurt her again. Kyana wished the words had been meant for her too.

She closed her eyes and waited for death to claim her.

An army of footsteps made the floor quiver beneath her cheek. Kyana stilled her mind, pushed aside all fear and doubt, and waited.

"Kyana?" Ryker called out to her.

She opened her eyes, turned her head in the direction of his voice. She tried to speak, but again, nothing but faint breath passed her lips. Ryker entered the greenhouse, his arms burdened, but she couldn't see what he held.

"You have to show me where you are." He turned, searching the large room for her. It was then she realized what he held cradled in his arms. Her body. He'd brought her body.

Kyana fought against the lethargy. Tried to stand. Tried to let him know where she was. She had depleted her energies trying to stop Marcus. There was nothing left.

"Damn you, Ky!" His shout hurt her ears and warmed her heart. "I swear on Zeus I'll stalk you through every level of Hell if you die on me."

A faint fog settled around her. Icy fingers crept outward. Haven's gaze locked on Kyana. Haven stilled. She released her grip on Geoff's arm. Slowly, she raised her hand and pointed in Kyana's direction.

Geoff followed the direction of Haven's trembling hand. "Is it her? Is it Kyana?"

The part of Haven that Kyana had always called friend whimpered.

"To your right," he yelled at Ryker.

Carefully, he moved in the direction they indicated and lowered Kyana's limp body to the floor. A sound pulled his gaze to the door, then back to Geoffrey. "We have company."

"Keep them off us," Geoff yelled, his back to the

door, his attention on Haven. "I can't fight and keep control on her."

Ryker's gaze shifted to Kyana's body, just three feet from her form. "Time to prove how kick-ass you are, Ky," he whispered. He turned back to Geoffrey and pointed at Marcus. "Keep your eye on that bastard. If he so much as moves, kill him."

Ryker stood, his feet braced, his head held high . . . His hands, as usual, were void of any weapons.

Anger boiled in Kyana's belly and spread outward. Ryker might be able to hold his own in a fight but he couldn't guard his own back. If Marcus woke, Geoffrey had his hands full with Haven. It would be up to Kyana to subdue the barkeep again. She had to make one more effort to finish what she'd started.

As though she could guard his back by sheer will, her gaze stayed locked on Ryker as she inched toward her body. With a howl of pure outrage, Ryker defended their sanctuary. Shrieks of pain and the splinter of bone and tendon filled the air. Marcus's minions were strong and their numbers surprised her. Ryker wouldn't be able to hold them off on his own for long. How could so many be working against the Order and the gods and goddesses remain unaware?

Gripping her anger like a shield, she closed the distance until her fingers passed through her own hand. She could no longer distinguish the screams of pain from Ryker's cries of fury.

Fear chilled her form. She'd been so worried about finding her friend, about saving her, that she hadn't asked how to return to her body.

A movement caught her gaze. Marcus had awakened, and was now pushing to his feet. The glint of steel in his hand claimed her attention. He'd found his dagger and was moving toward Geoff and Haven.

No! Kyana's scream did nothing more than cloud the air in front of her face. She watched horrified and helpless as Marcus slowly raised his arm, as the dagger plunged deeply into the side of Geoff's neck, as her friend slumped forward, his body protecting Haven.

Kyana gripped the Charm of Nine Gods in her fist. Hoping it would be enough, she pushed to her knees, crawled the remaining distance to position herself next to her body. With a deep breath, she closed her eyes and fell.

The world faded to black. Silent. Cold. Empty.

As quickly as it began, the sensation of nothingness disappeared and Kyana continued her fall back to the greenhouse. The sounds of bones snapping, painful howls, and death gurgles filled the void. The smell of blood hung heavy in the air. The numbness that had been her existence for the last hour was replaced with gut-wrenching pain.

Kyana rolled onto her side. Shards of broken pottery cut into her cheek, and nausea churned her stomach. Struggling to her knees, she tried to latch on to reality again. It took only a heartbeat to focus on the chaos around her. Ryker stood in the doorway, singlehandedly protecting them all. Bodies lay broken and beaten at his feet, but still the minions came.

She shifted her gaze to Geoff and Haven. Haven was struggling from under Geoff, who lay slumped on the floor, a pool of blood spreading out from beneath him.

Marcus stood over Haven, ready to attack again. Ryker was too distracted by the waves of minions rushing through the doors to see what was happening behind him. It was up to Kyana. Woozy, she stumbled in their direction. Marcus wouldn't win. Not like this. Not while she had even a tenuous hold on life.

He raised his arm. Pure evil twisted his face.

With a roar, Kyana launched herself at him, striking him in the chest. With a grunt, he fell to his knees. He shoved her aside as though she weighed nothing at all. She gripped his shirt with all the strength she had left, keeping him from escaping. Knowing she had no other means to fight him, she used the one weapon she had available.

She sank her fangs into his neck.

The taste of his blood was pure heaven, and with every swallow, strength surged its way back into her veins. Her heart sped, her adrenaline rushed. Still, she drank, no longer just hoping to stop Marcus, but hoping to drain every last bit of life from his traitorous body.

"Stop!" Marcus's feet thrashed, his legs kicking out as he tried to twist out of her hold, but she was too strong now. Too eager to finish what she'd started. "Make her stop!" His words gurgled in his throat.

"Kyana, no!" Ryker thrust his elbow into his last opponent's windpipe and rushed to her side. He reached for her, freezing when he saw Geoff crumpled over Haven in a pool of his own blood.

It took all of Kyana's willpower to tear her fangs out of Marcus's flesh. She swallowed, the thick, warm blood coating her throat as it made its way down into the fire of her belly.

"He has to pay," she whispered, afraid to speak more clearly for fear of sounding like the animal she could feel rising within.

Even as Marcus jerked in her arms, Kyana's own body spazzed a bit, in shock at the taste of living blood.

"And he will. But not like this."

The heady scent of so much spilled blood in the room was likely driving Haven as mad as it was Kyana. Forcing her thoughts away from the call to feed, Kyana jutted her chin toward Haven and yanked Marcus's head farther back so that her next bite would be unobstructed. "Get her out of here, Ryker." Her tone, deep and guttural, left no doubt of her intentions.

"Let go of him, Kyana. He's not worth the price that comes with killing him."

Kyana wrapped a handful of Marcus's hair in her fist and yanked viciously. "What price? Death? I've already got that comin', babe. Remember?"

Ryker's eyes slowly melted back to their normal pewter state. "You don't know that. We still have a chance."

She flicked her tongue across the punctures on Marcus's neck. "I don't care. He has to pay for what he's done to the Chosen, to Haven, to Geoffrey."

Ryker's eyes darkened, but he still tried to talk her down. "You're not strong enough to feed and remain the same, Ky. You'll be Dark Breed again and I won't be able to let you leave here. I'll have to kill you."

Kyana swallowed, her chest heaving. The punctures on Marcus's neck called out to her the way Sirens called to lusty sailors. She wanted to finish this, wanted to fill her belly with his blood until her stomach was bloated and her desire sated.

The monster clawed at her insides, begging her to give it a home again. She focused on Ryker. His silver eyes were glazed with emotion as he silently begged her not to force him to take her life. His duty and honor to the Order, to the man he was, would demand it. She couldn't do that to him.

"Fuck you," she whispered to the beast trying to dominate. The monster inside her growled back. "I'm stronger than you."

With a primal roar, she twisted Marcus's neck until it snapped and dumped his body on the floor.

Chapter Thirty-three

Kyana pulled her gaze away from Marcus's still form to look at Ryker. The anguish had left his eyes. Oh, he wasn't pleased that she'd killed the ex-Mystic, but his relief that she hadn't fed the starving beast inside her was written all over his face.

"Satisfied?"

His fingers trailed lightly over her lips and jaw, his eyes approving even if he couldn't condone what she'd done out loud.

She gave in and rested her cheek briefly against his hand before pushing away. "We need to . . . help Geoff."

She looked at her friend, still slumped over and unconscious, the knife wound in his neck beating with rivulets of dark blood. Beneath him, Haven lay panting for breath, obviously weakened by her first Lychen shifting. She struggled to free herself from the weight of Geoffrey's body and failed. She collapsed beneath him, her face pale and covered with perspiration.

Ryker moved away from Kyana and knelt to check on Geoff. "He's alive, Ky. Just unconscious."

Kyana sagged with relief, leaning her weight against the unbalanced table behind her, her knees weak, her body exhausted. He helped Haven stand before facing Kyana again. "Will you run now? Get as far away from the Order as possible? With your skill, you can hide among the humans. The Ancients may not find you."

She read the pleading in his eyes, but running wasn't an option before and it wasn't one now.

"No," she said, her tone flat, her tongue thick.

The vein in Ryker's temple bulged, and she watched in fascination as his jaw ticked. "Fine."

He hoisted Geoffrey onto his shoulder, and without so much as a grunt, did the same to Haven and stood. "Then get back to your cell before an army of pissed-off gods arrive and decide to carry out your execution without letting you plead your case."

Without sparing Kyana another glance, Ryker stalked out of the greenhouse, leaving Kyana to follow without assistance. She'd fed. Her Vamp strengths were on overload. The controlled side of her that had ruled for the last eighty years fought for dominance. Her gaze fell on Marcus's body, and she could barely restrain the urge to spit on his corpse. The punishment for killing him was one she'd gladly pay.

As she stepped over him, her foot snagged his torn shirt. She managed to pivot to keep from landing directly on top of him and went down on all fours, her nose inches from his chest. She shoved herself backward with enough force to jar her teeth. She didn't know how long she sat there looking at his cooling body, the puckered scar running down the middle of his chest and curving just beneath his last rib holding her complete attention.

She reached for her dagger at her hip before remembering Ares had taken her weapon belt. She settled for a large, lethal-looking shard of pottery. Ripping Marcus's shirt, she wrapped the fabric around her hand, then gripped the weapon. Carefully, she cut along the scar. Blood seeped from the wound, making her woozy with hunger. Kyana fought the need to feed and concentrated on laying the flesh of his chest open.

"What the hell are you doing?" Ryker's low rumble caused the broken pottery to quake in a morbid dance. "You snapped his neck, Ky, he's dead."

She looked over her shoulder at him. She didn't want to consider what she must look like sitting on a corpse, her hand in its chest. Instead of trying to explain, she said, "The key lies in the heart of the loyal."

"What?"

"Nettles's riddle. I thought she meant the one who was most loyal would tell us where the key was."

"Are you fucking crazy?"

Kyana shrugged. She knew she was slipping to the edge of insanity, ripping into a human body like it was nothing, trying to find literal meaning in Nettles's riddle. But her gut pushed her on. Using her makeshift knife, she lifted the edges of his skin, trying to work her way through the bone. Giving up on the hope she could complete her task without getting his blood on her hands, she dropped her scalpel to the dirt floor. Leveling herself on her knees, she straddled Marcus's waist, then reached into his chest with both hands, and with a low growl, ripped the bone and muscle out of her way.

Slowly, she removed his heart, and beneath it, she found what she'd spent the last week looking for. She dug into Marcus's chest and removed the star-shaped disk the color of slate, holding it out in her bloodied hand for Ryker to see.

"The key was literally in the heart of the loyal."

"Holy hell." His stance relaxed. The swirling in his eyes calmed and sparkled with hope. "You did it, Ky. You found the key to Tartarus."

Even as she smiled, sadness filled her. Ryker wanted to believe this act would undo all the wrong she'd done. She couldn't bring herself to dash his hopes. She slipped the disgusting key into her pocket, then struggled to her feet. "Let's get out of here."

Ryker pulled off his shirt and used it to bandage her bloody hands. As he helped her to her feet, his whispered words of hope and belief fell silent beneath the roar in her ears. She didn't make it two steps out the door before the world turned topsy-turvy and everything went black.

Despite the whirlwind of chaos and worry surrounding her, Kyana welcomed the darkness. Thoughts of Haven and Geoffrey and Ryker—her little family—led to dreams of her Turning. The pain of her husband's brutal attack, Henry's loving hands, and, most vividly, the curious bond that had formed between them. Visions of times she'd felt him watching her though he hadn't been present rolled through her brain like grainy black-and-white film until finally, Henry's face became Kyana's, and Kyana's became Haven's.

Kyana had forgotten about the link. Forgotten that

she'd sometimes be able to see, feel, hear Haven. She was Haven's Sire, would become aware of things both private and sacred, and as Kyana gave herself over to the vision, she reached out to her best friend, hoping for a glimpse of Haven to take her swiftly through her dreams.

Had Henry's head hurt this badly when he'd reached out to her? Had he nearly stopped when his skull threatened to implode? Kyana's temples pounded and her muscles burned. If she could just get a handle on this skill, maybe she could face her sentencing knowing Haven would be okay.

One glimpse. Just one glimpse.

But it wasn't Kyana's curiosity that pushed past the pain and made her hold more tightly to the threads of sleep. It was the weeping echoing in her brain, weeping that was not hers and could only belong to one person. Haven. It drew Kyana like a magnet, yanking her vision through blackness toward an unknown destination. Flashes of white whooshed past her, sending daggerlike pain behind her eyes. Her brain shrank and grew, shrank and grew, until finally swelling like a sponge that had soaked up every ounce of moisture in her skull.

The blackness cleared and the flashes of white dulled to reveal a foggy room filled with a lone bed and nothing else. In the center of the mattress, Haven knelt, her long golden hair filthy and clumped. Her body, naked and scratched, was covered in dark splotches. She seemed to feel something shift in the sparse room, her head lolling to one side as though straining to hear whoever had invaded her privacy.

Her yellow, glowing eyes were pocketed with purple moons, and her fangs were not the same pearly white as her other teeth. Instead, they were painted red. As were her lips and chin. But the wildness in her eyes contrasted harshly with the low moan of agony emitting from her open mouth and the tear tracks running through her dirt-smudged cheeks.

Kyana tried to speak. Much as when she'd been under the influence of the Charm of Nine Gods, she found herself unable to voice the sounds her throat and tongue struggled to make. But *unlike* the Charm of Nine Gods, this state obviously didn't allow Haven the ability to see Kyana.

Through the fog, Kyana followed Haven's anxious gaze. What Kyana saw on the floor in a semicircle around the bed legs nearly sapped her ability to hold on to the link. Three bodies, gutted, throats ripped out, spread out before her covered in blood and bodily fluid. The trail of red oozed from their bodies, spidering outward, disappearing under the bed. Shock pumped through Kyana, paralyzing her from removing herself from this horror she didn't want to witness.

No. Haven had not *done this!*

But the truth was brutally painted right in front of her. She tried to back out of the room, but her legs didn't work here either. She was nothing more than disembodied eyes and ears and, Zeus save her, she wanted to be blind and deaf forever if it meant striking this image from her memory.

No no no no no no.

The blood splatter on the wall stole her breath as she followed its design. Bloodied handprints smeared on the wall, and in their center, someone . . . *Haven* . . . had written three words in blood.

Cronos will live.

Pain racked through Kyana. The steady banging in her ears was unbearable. The sight before her unthinkable. The taste of fear and guilt and horror coating a tongue she couldn't feel—unimaginable. She was vacuumed back into darkness, the scream in her head so loud she couldn't hear the whoosh of lights. And the next thing she knew, she was thrashing against the cold hard floor of her cell.

"Bloody hell, Ryker. Hold her down damn it."

Geoffrey's voice burst through the bubble of muffled noises in Kyana's head. She focused, desperate to hold on to something familiar as she fought to control her body. Each time she convulsed, strong fingers bit into her shoulders, shoving her back against the cold stone. Her skull cracked against rock, making her ears ring.

"Jesus, I'm trying. What's wrong with her?" Ryker's smell covered her like a blanket, warming her as she pressed her back to the floor in desperation to find calm.

"I'm calling for a Healer."

She had to find her way out of whatever this was, this link with Haven. Had to get out of this cell and get to her friend. How did this link work? Had she seen what was about to be or what had already been? Henry had never spoken much about his link to Kyana and now she hated him for not preparing her properly.

As though emerging from the ocean, Kyana's next

shriek opened up her lungs, and though she didn't need the air, she drank it in, heaving as her lungs filled and the cloudy bubble around her slowly cleared.

"Haven! Get me to Haven now!"

She threw Ryker off her, sending him onto his backside as she lumbered to her feet. Her head spinning, she gripped Geoffrey's shoulders for balance, blinked in an attempt to see more clearly. "The link, Geoffrey. She's going rogue. Get to her, or get me the fuck out of here so I can."

There was no doubt in his expression. He obviously knew too well about the effects of turning another. She couldn't contemplate what that meant right now. Her heart was close to thudding right out of her rib cage and she couldn't tell if it was real or a lingering effect of her link with Haven.

"What did you see, Ky?" Ryker circled her, stepping between Kyana and Geoffrey.

Geoffrey's blue eyes had darkened to almost black. "It doesn't matter. Whatever you saw, it's already happened. I'll go, but I can't stop it." His words were thick with emotion.

As he moved to step through the gate, Kyana caught his arm. Weapons clanging in migraine-inducing harmony had pointed in the direction of the cave entrance. "Ares is coming. When he opens the barrier, I'm going too."

"You can't—"

Kyana shot Ryker a glare that dared him to stop her. "I'll be damned if I'm sentenced before I see for myself the damage I've done."

While her voice was cold and steady, the fear in her

throat choked her. The last thing she wanted was to see what she'd seen . . . again.

Ryker's gaze softened. He looked at Geoff. "Stay with her. I'll see what I can do." His gaze lingered on her for another moment before he stepped away, slid through the barrier, and strode down the dark hall toward his father.

Knowing this wasn't going to go well at all, Ryker moved to the entryway, blocking the entrance. Ares strode around the bend in the long hallway, his head held high, a small, pleased smile turning the corners of his mouth. It sickened Ryker to know he shared blood with someone cruel and heartless enough to find pleasure in another's death.

"Step aside," Ares said, his hand resting on the hilt of his sword.

Ryker refused to budge. No way in hell would Ares use that thing, and if he tried, Ryker would give him a taste of the powers he'd honed over the years. Powers even his almighty father didn't share.

"You will not disgrace yourself, your title, or the Order by blocking my entrance." Ares's voice carried no farther than the two of them. "Step aside, now, and let me do what must be done."

Holding his ground, Ryker shook his head. "She's made a connection with Haven. We believe she's going rogue. Ky needs to see her, try to reach her before it's too late. Then she will come with you peacefully."

"A Sire's link?"

Ryker nodded.

"Then what she saw has already come to pass. Going to her now will change nothing." However, he did point to several of his guards. "Go to the Healing Circle. If the Witch has completed her Turning before they've purged her of Marcus's blood, kill her."

Ryker growled. "Haven is a Chosen. Not even you can kill a Chosen."

"The Witch is an abomination that never should have happened. What made her worthy of being a Chosen died when tainted blood flew over her lips."

"Kyana is prepared to die. She just has to know that her friend, her only family, isn't going to suffer for the things she's done."

"Do you plead for the life of the Dark Breed?"

Yes, he did, and he had, all the way up the ranks of the gods to Zeus. It hadn't made a difference. Despite what he'd told Kyana about her having a chance of surviving this, it wasn't probable. When her trial ended, she would most likely be sentenced to die—at the hand of Ares if his request was granted.

"No, I plead for you to let her die with a little peace."

Ares smiled. Ryker wanted to use his fist to knock it off his face. "As my Elite General, you've stood witness to many barters. What you're asking will come with a heavy price. Are you willing to pay it for her peace of mind?"

Ryker knew when he'd made the request the price would be high. There were only two things Ares had ever demanded of Ryker as his son. Ryker had never been willing to concede to either of them.

Straightening his shoulders, Ryker nodded. "I am."

"Very well, then. The price for your request is to be a Chosen."

Ryker nearly roared with outrage. The power of

his mind caused his skin to tingle. His vision sharpened, became more focused on his target as his eyes changed from silver to blood red. He battled beyond the outrage. By demanding Ryker as his Chosen, Ares got everything he wanted. He got his son on Olympus and would get Ryker to acknowledge before the gods that Ares was his father—two things he'd avoided since learning who his father was. Because of free will, the gods would not accept Ares's claim unless Ryker acknowledged it first. An acknowledgment he swore on his mother's grave he'd never make.

With a glance over his shoulder at Kyana, the sight of fear in her eyes made his choice for him. With a barely discernible nod that sealed his fate, Ryker stepped back and allowed Ares to enter. They made their way back to Kyana together.

"He's going to escort you to Haven, Ky, and take you to your sentencing from there."

"Thank Zeus." As her gaze found Ryker's, she mouthed a silent thank-you.

He tried to smile, to let her know she was welcome, but fell short. Worry flickered in her eyes. She glanced at Ares, then back to Ryker. With a slow shake of his head, he stopped the question he could all but see forming in her mind. If she knew what her brief freedom had cost him, she wouldn't get the peace she craved, the peace she deserved.

Without even looking in Kyana's direction, the God of War slipped the disk key from his belt and shut down the pulsing barrier. He snatched her arm, jerked her from the cell, then pivoted to glare at his son.

"When this is done, when she's sentenced and gone,

I will expect you to fulfill your end of our bargain immediately."

The carnage extended far beyond the bloodied room Haven had been kept in. From the front entrance of the Healing Circle, up the stairs and down the hall, unconscious bodies lay strewn about like rag dolls. These, thank Zeus, were still alive, but each one they'd wakened confessed that their naked charge had plowed through them all and escaped the boardinghouse.

By the time Ares dragged Kyana to Haven's door, her throat was so full of bile that she had to stop and release it. All over Ares's sandaled feet. He grabbed her hair, yanking her upright, which brought Ryker forward.

He seized his father's wrist. "Touch her like that again and the deal is off. In fact, look at her cross-eyed and we'll finally test the limits of the powers I inherited from you."

Ares's steely gaze narrowed but he said nothing. Instead, he pushed open the door, releasing the stench of blood into the pure white corridor. A sense of unholiness filled the air, as did a familiar scent, even more foul. The sulfuric stench burned Kyana's nose. It was the same odor she'd smelled on the obsidian lock. Whoever had touched that lock had been here. Had been in that room with Haven.

"Someone provoked her," she whispered. "It wasn't just the Turning . . . something evil touched her in here." She looked to Ryker and whispered. "Cronos. I smell him."

Had he possessed Haven as he had Marcus? It was

a definite possibility. Haven hadn't had time to fully turn yet. She was weak and the perfect choice for possession.

"You cannot assuage your guilt by placing it elsewhere," Ares said, motioning her forward. "You did this. Have a good look, Kyana. Your lack of restraint created a beast never before bred within the Order. Witch, Vampyre, Lychen, all in one very angry body. Your fault. Look!"

Kyana wanted to scream at him to shut the hell up, but he was right. This was her fault and she wouldn't be a coward. She would look, would drink in the aftermath of her hasty actions. She stepped into the room and fell to her knees. There it was. Just as she'd seen except Haven was gone. Long gone. Blood stained the walls. Bodies on the floor. *Cronos will live* screamed out from the white walls in garish finger paint made of a Healer's blood.

"I just wanted to save her," she whispered, dragging herself back to her feet and charging for Ares. "Let me go. The blood is still fresh, I can track her. I can bring her back and save her before she's lost forever."

The laugh that escaped Ares's throat brought a chill over Kyana's body. "Save her? She is *rogue*! She has murdered the innocent and broken the most severe laws of the Order. There is no *saving* her."

Kyana hugged her arms around her body, suddenly so cold she couldn't stop her teeth from chattering. "Please, let me go after her."

"There is no time, Kyana," Ares said, his face smug. "We must return for your hearing."

She turned to face Ryker fully, pressing her body to

his. She slid the bloody key from her pants and slipped it discreetly into his hand. "You helped me get this back, Ryker. Finish what we started."

"That's your glory to claim. We still don't know that you won't be okay—"

Kyana swallowed. Fear for Haven, for herself, for the world as a whole, clogged the vessels that made her heart beat, constricting her chest like a vise.

"Who gives a shit about glory? Close Tartarus." This was no longer about power or glory or infamy. For the first time since Tartarus had broken open, Kyana had a personal stake in this war. She stepped toward the hall and cast one last look back. "If I don't come back—if I can't—promise me you'll find my sister and fix what I've done."

Chapter Thirty-four

Kyana had expected to find herself sprawled out in the Fates' cave when Ares ported them to their destination. Instead, when the queasiness subsided, she found herself standing in a room made of alabaster, marble, and every other white stone ever created. It was blinding. Golden light slashed through the uncovered stained-glass windows, striping the floor, forcing her to squint and cup a hand over her eyes to gain her bearings.

"What is this place?" The only furniture in the room was a long table lined with ten tall, gilded chairs. She stood, spinning in a slow circle, trying to take in everything. It was a difficult task, given how heavy her heart and mind were. Whatever Ryker had promised Ares in exchange for Kyana's freedom had been for nothing. Kyana was still going to die uncertain about Haven's fate.

"My home." The sultry voice spun Kyana around to find Artemis leaning in the arched doorway. "My room of trials, to be precise."

"Beyond—I mean, Olympus?" No one lacking god blood was allowed here. Except maybe those about to be sentenced to die. Having never been in this particular predicament before, Kyana couldn't be sure.

Artemis gave a slight nod and stepped into the enormous, echoey room. "This court is prepared to hear your plea today, Kyana. Please be seated."

Kyana obeyed Artemis, rested a warm hand on Kyana's shoulder, and turned her attention to Ares. "You should have let her go with Ryker to close the gates of Tartarus."

"She deserves no glory. She was meant to save the world but was too late. Now she'll be the reason it's destroyed."

Kyana felt as though she had been sucker punched. It was true. She'd done her duty and found the key, but not before she'd unleashed the tool that could raise Cronos.

Ares and Artemis's angry whispers echoed through Kyana's soul. She forced herself to block everything else but the thoughts in her head. She'd failed them all, but before she could worry about how to save the world, she had to find a way to save herself.

As six robed figures followed Artemis in a line to the table, Kyana took a deep breath and held it. Their golden cloaks hid most of their features, but Kyana recognized the Moerae and their Chosen without seeing their faces.

"I know you're anxious to have this ordeal over and done with," Artemis said. "But we've another matter to tend before we continue with you. I trust you can be patient?"

Patient? To have her head handed to her? *You bet your ass.*

"Take your time," Kyana muttered, her gaze skimming the vast room, unwilling to settle upon any one face. Forcing her rubbery legs to take her forward, Kyana sat rigidly in the cold chair and watched as the Moerae and their Chosen took their seats. Ares took a robe from a guard who'd quietly stepped into the room, donned it, and sat beside Atropos.

Great. She hadn't thought *he* would be one of the judge and jury. Between Ares and Atropos, Kyana was toast.

One last hooded figure entered from an archway to Kyana's right. This one was draped in black, his face completely concealed by the large hood shadowing his face. But his colors named him, regardless. Hades.

Cold chills broke out over Kyana's arms and neck. Her body itched to bolt, to make a run for it. Unable to watch as Artemis took the center seat at the table, Kyana fought to control her breathing and dropped her gaze to the floor. It didn't rest there long before she forced herself to raise it again. She was a fighter, damn it. She barely recognized the frightened little monkey she was becoming. If they were going to sentence her to death, she was going to take it with her head held high. In the heat of the moment, she still thought saving Haven had been the right choice. It wasn't *her* fault that Below was so poorly guarded that Haven hadn't been given proper care or protection and had gone rogue.

Kyana swallowed and listened to the dull sounds of her judges whispering to one another. Who was she kidding? Yes, it was her fault. Those dead Healers, the fear in Haven's eyes, the possibility of Haven's power bringing Cronos back to fuck them all. All Kyana's fault. She'd take responsibility, but she wouldn't give up. She could find Haven and hold her to some sort of humanity as Haven had done for her all these years. If they would just let her go . . . she'd beg for mercy, her pride be damned, if it meant a shot at doing right by her friend this time.

Behind her, heavy doors banged open and sandaled feet slapped against marble. Kyana twisted in her seat to peer over her shoulder at the interruption and found herself staring into Drake's face.

Was he the reason her trial was being delayed? Two guards held Drake upright, his feet sliding under him as his body just sort of hung limply between them. He didn't look beaten or battered, much to Kyana's disappointment, but he'd definitely been through *something*. The glazed, dazed look in his eyes made him appear drugged.

Another chair appeared about four feet from Kyana, and the guards shoved Drake into it, but didn't budge from his side. Too bad. Kyana wouldn't have minded reaching over and ripping out his throat. If she was going to go down anyway, why not go down with a little of Drake's blood on her hands?

"I thought you might wish to witness his trial," Artemis said.

Kyana looked up to find the goddess watching her with dark amber eyes. "What?"

"You have many marks against you, Kyana, but I, for one, have not forgotten what you have done for the

Order. The least we can do is allow you to have your questions answered before you're sentenced."

Well. What was she supposed to say to that? Not that she didn't want to see Drake punished. She did. Big time. She shot Artemis a smile, noting with a bit of satisfaction that neither Ares nor Atropos seemed to share Artie's benevolence.

"Thank you."

Artemis nodded, then gestured for Ares to stand before taking her chair at the table of judges. Artemis would likely lead Kyana's trial, as she was Kyana's boss, but Drake was no tracer. The God of War himself would question the bastard. Kyana couldn't summon any pity for the prick.

"You are Drake Ivan Mallone, correct?" Ares started, placing his large body in front of Drake's chair.

Huh. His initials were D.I.M. No big shocker there.

Drake didn't look up. Hell, he didn't look capable of lifting his head. "I am."

"Joined the Order of Ancients in 1995, retired in 2004?"

"Yes."

"Why did you leave the Order, Drake?"

"Didn't believe in it anymore." Drake's voice was smooth as butter. No slurring, no hesitation. He was drugged all right, but completely coherent. What had they given him?

"Because the god you worshipped was the enemy of the Order?" Ares presented his back to Kyana and paced the small space between her and Drake's chairs.

"Yes. The true god. The most powerful. I would do his bidding."

"You agreed to give us the facts about the deceased, Marcus Talstoy, in exchange for your life, did you not?"

"I did."

"What?" Kyana bolted from her chair, outraged by this tidbit. Ares had his hand on her shoulder and her ass back in her seat before she could move another inch. "You're going to let him live? He killed Chosen, for Zeus's sake!"

"Control your bitch, Artemis," Ares sneered. "Or I shall."

"Kyana." Artemis stood behind the table and glared daggers in Ares's back before giving Kyana her attention again. "The ability to see the truth of his words is still ours, but the Fates' powers have weakened a good deal, far more quickly than their Chosen can pick them up again. Finding the truth is simple. Forcing secrets is much more difficult. Without Drake's cooperation, we may never discover Marcus's connection to Cronos. Now, let us continue in peace, or I'll be forced to escort you from the hall myself."

Kyana opened her mouth to protest, but something twinkled in Artemis's eyes that held Kyana's tongue silent. There was more to this promise than Kyana had been told. There was no way they'd let Drake off scot-free after murdering Chosen. Kyana would have to be happy with that small comfort.

"Go on," she muttered.

Ares sneered at her again, then turned back to his captive. "Who unlocked Tartarus?"

Drake's head bobbed against his chest. "Cronos."

"And how did he manage this?"

"Possession. Marcus was willing. It was Marcus's

body in Tartarus that night, but because it was Cronos who resided within it, Hades's security enchantments were never set off. Cronos had leave to come and go from the Underworld when he reigned. That privilege was never stripped of him when he was exiled."

Kyana glanced up at the table to find Hades shifting in his seat. She narrowed her gaze, trying to catch a glimpse of his face, but the shadows were too thick.

"And is this also how Marcus caught sight of the scroll that listed the Chosen?"

In an attempt to shake his head, Drake limply thrust his head from side to side. "Illusion Charm. Cronos had no part in that."

"But he only saw it once!" Clotho pushed to her feet and leaned over the table. "We added new names to that list, and yet he still found them. Cronos must have—"

"Marcus performed a spell in your chambers," Drake interrupted. "He ingested some of the coating used on the parchment and linked himself to that scroll. Each time a new name was added, he knew the minute ink was put to paper."

That explained how Marcus had known about Haven. He must have been far more skilled in magic than anyone had given him credit for. Kyana had to bite her tongue to keep from tossing out her own questions—questions about his relationship with Haven and his betrayal of that trust, but if she followed that instinct, she'd be thrown out until her own hearing. She slid her hands under her butt to keep them from reaching out and strangling him.

"Cronos had the key in his possession all this time?" Ares asked.

Drake nodded. "He had it enchanted before his death. A Witch on the isle performed the ceremony, and when Cronos died, the key died with him in a sense. He kept it tied to his spirit form. When he took over Marcus's body, it became as tangible as Cronos himself.

"He'd expected it to return to the spirit world with him when he left Marcus's body, though. Hadn't counted on that hiccup." A slow smile spread across the visible part of Drake's face and an eerie bubble of laughter spewed out of his mouth. "When Marcus woke up again, he was in so much pain, covered in so much blood, I almost left him to die. Should have. Bastard went after my girl."

So, Drake wasn't so loyal to Marcus? Maybe didn't like him all that much? But he *hadn't* left Marcus to die. Maybe he'd been too afraid of Cronos to do so, but either way, his actions had put Haven in danger.

"How did the key end up in Marcus's chest? Cronos wouldn't have been able to touch anything outside of Marcus's body."

"He sewed it inside while in Marcus's skin. I didn't like seeing my lord in so much pain. He felt everything he was doing to Marcus's body, but I didn't interfere. I knew that as soon as Cronos fled the body, only Marcus would feel the pain. And it was about time too. I was tired of being Marcus's lackey. Getting my hands bloody for the cause while he reaped all the rewards with our lord."

Whatever drug they'd given Drake was handy. He was spewing forth everything, no protesting, no holding back.

"And that is everything you have to tell us?" Ares

asked, pulling Drake's hair to force his neck back and his eyes up. "What of Cronos's plans?"

"His plans? To come back, of course. To reclaim the throne stolen from him by his sons." Again, the smile crept onto Drake's face. "He'll kill them all. Take what is rightfully his. All of you . . . all of you will be reduced to nothing under his reign. He knew of the prophecy, waited for your weakness. Now he has the one with the power to make him whole once more, and when he is, there will be but one god, and it will be Cronos." His brown eyes darkened and narrowed at Ares. "I've told you everything. Release me as you swore you would."

"Oh, I will." Ares turned and nodded to the sentinels who'd backed away from Drake's chair with Ares's approach. "Take him into the holding cell until my work here is over."

"But you said—"

Ares glared at Drake. "I know what I said. I said you would not be our prisoner and we would not kill you. I hold true to my word. There is an island I think you might enjoy spending the rest of your days exploring." He leaned over Drake, his smile far more sinister than anything Drake had managed so far. "I will port you there, personally, and Ryker will port us out . . . without you. I advise you to find shelter quickly. I hear it's not a pleasant place to be once the sun sets."

Chapter Thirty-five

Once Drake was subdued behind closed doors, his wailings quieted, the hall grew tense all over again. Kyana squirmed as all eyes rested upon her. It was her turn, and she wasn't ready.

"Hearing Drake's testimony reminds me of how severe the charges against you are, Kyana," Artemis said, her amber eyes damp and wide as she studied Kyana. "You've been a prize to me. A valued huntress that has fulfilled more tasks for our cause than any other. Your rare breed makes you priceless. But your judgment, it seems, has made you a liability. We've heard Drake's testimony, seen what a destructive weapon you created in your friend. If Drake Mallone is correct, than you've just given Cronos the means to return and destroy us all. How am I to defend you now, child?"

Atropos pushed off her hood, her black eyes narrow little slits of distaste. "She's always been a liability. Disrespectful. Insolent. She's never done her duties for any reason other than her own glory."

"Yes," Ares said, looking far too pleased. "She thrives on having the other tracers know her by name. They envy the combination of breeds inside her that allows her to do what they cannot. But it is luck that has made her so different. Not skill."

Kyana seethed beneath her carefully calm demeanor. How *dare* they accuse her of being lucky? She was good. *Damned* good.

"I made a mistake," Kyana blurted out, uncertain when her turn to talk would come. "But I didn't do it for glory. I did it to save Haven and I won't plead for forgiveness for something I would do again."

When Ares tried to interrupt her, Artemis silenced him and motioned for Kyana to continue.

"She was dying. She asked me not to turn her and I did it anyway. Murdering an Order member is against the laws, but letting one die isn't? You purged me when I came to you. Taught me how to tame the monster in me and become a valuable asset to this cause. It's what I believed would happen to Hav—"

"Enough!" Atropos stood and leaned across her table, spit accumulating in the corners of her mouth. "You've always thought yourself to be above our laws. Do not lie now and pretend to have cared about the specifics of them when you broke them."

"She was trying to save a friend. I believe that," Jordan said, leaning closer to Carmen. "Like she saved me."

Beside Carmen, Atropos's Chosen remained silent. Kyana had never met her, but she kept her head bowed, her hands wringing nervously on the table. She would be of no use to Kyana, but Jordan might be. Artemis would be. Carmen, Lachesis, Clotho, their stance was unclear. That put two judges on Kyana's side; Ares, Atropos, and probably Hades against her. The odds were not in Kyana's favor. She'd need at least five of them on her side to be saved.

Sweat beaded on the back of her neck and dripped down her shirt.

She felt as though a wildfire was blazing in her throat. "I can find Haven. I can bring her back and get her help before—"

"Before she raises Cronos?" Lachesis peered out from beneath her hood. "We know what you found in that room, know what caused it. I may not have all my powers, but with Jordan, we were able to see what happened there. What *you* caused."

"She's powerful enough to succeed, Kyana," Clotho said. "The Witch that mingles with the monster you created is skillful enough to perform the ritual, and the beast is strong enough—or will be soon—to keep us from getting our hands on her in time."

Kyana shut her mind to the image those words provoked. "No. I felt her. I *know* her. Whatever Cronos is doing to control her, he won't find it easy. She didn't want to do what she did at the Healing Circle. He *made* her."

"Exactly. He controlled her. Each day, his hold on her will grow stronger."

"But I'm like her! I'm the only one who can match what she is and go head-to-head with her. I've been this genetic mutation for longer, and I'm her Sire. I can link to her, be one step ahead of her and bring her back here. Damn it, she's been loyal to this Order for years. You owe her a chance to redeem herself for something that wasn't her fault!"

To Kyana's surprise, it was shy Carmen who removed her hood and, albeit nervously, spoke up. "But that's not right, is it?" She looked to Clotho. "She's not as powerful as the thing she created. Hannah is a Witch too. She has an extra breed in her, right?"

Clotho smiled. "Her name is Haven, and yes. You're quite right." The goddess turned her gaze to Kyana. "You have my vote, Kyana. My choice is to set you free so that you may find Haven. Other tracers would be forced to keep their hunts at night, while your Lychen form can save hours by prowling the days. And the link you have to her . . ." She looked to her sisters. "Can we afford to lose that link to someone so potentially dangerous?"

Hope nearly sprang Kyana from her chair. "If I don't succeed, I will return here and cut my own damned life thread." And she would, because if she failed, it meant Haven was a lost cause, and Kyana wasn't sure she could live with that.

"Let her go," Jordan said. While her tone was a tad shaky, she held her back rigid. Gone was the timid mouse Kyana had pulled from the rubbish bin. "She saved my life. I cannot vote to take hers now."

"She scares me. I—don't know her, but how can letting a monster free be a benefit to what you've been telling me is our cause?" This from Atropos's Chosen, who received a pleased smile from Atropos in response.

"Frances is correct," Atropos said. "Setting one lawbreaking beast free to catch another is a moronic way of thinking and I will not have a hand in it. My vote is no."

Artemis sighed, her gaze never wavering from Kyana's. She wasn't certain, but she could have sworn she saw nearly as much fear in the goddess's eyes as was in Kyana's heart. "Two for letting Kyana go with conditions. Two for carrying out the sentence of death. You know where my thoughts fall on this matter, so make that three for letting her resume her duties and stop Cronos from carrying through on his threat. Ares? Do I even need to ask or shall we just call it three for and three against now and save you your breath?"

Two more. I just need two more. Kyana's gaze swung to Lachesis and Carmen, and rested on Hades. Two of them would have to choose to save her. Hades's silence wasn't comforting. She'd never met the god, but she wished she could see his face so she might gain some glimpse into his thoughts.

Ares watched Kyana closely, his gray eyes looking so much like Ryker's at that moment, she was strangely comforted despite the dislike aimed in her direction. His gaze swung behind her. Kyana turned to find Ryker himself standing in the south doorway, his arms folded across his chest, his stare steadily focused on his father.

"Ryker," Artemis snapped. "Tell me it's done."

He gave a brisk nod. "Tartarus has been sealed."

"You've done us proud." Artemis's tone softened and she smiled. "You have our thanks."

"It was Kyana who found the key. Thank her."

Ares narrowed his gaze. "Yes, Artemis." His tone dripped with sarcasm. "Let us thank the one who has delivered doom to our doorstep."

"Tread carefully," Ryker hissed through clenched teeth.

Obviously displeased by Ryker's defense of Kyana, Ares folded his arms across his chest and glared. "You should not be here, Ryker. This is a sentencing."

A cold smile curved Ryker's mouth. "You've been trying to get me to Olympus for years, Ares. My first venture here, and you want me to leave?"

"He may stay," Artemis said. "If this does not go in Kyana's favor, she should be allowed a friend. But Ryker, if you cannot remain silent, you will be asked to leave."

Unable to bear the thought of Ryker watching her fate unravel, Kyana almost asked that they make him leave. But instead, she turned away and allowed herself to realize that his presence made this all a bit more bearable. If only Haven and Geoff were here, she'd go out with family around her. That would have been a gift.

"Very well. Stay. Your presence will not sway my vote." Ares nodded at Artemis. "I vote no. She is too unpredictable to believe she'd abide by any conditions."

"Carmen?"

The Chosen seemed to shrink to the size of a Milk Dud. "I trust Clotho. If she believes in saving Kyana, then I do too."

Artemis smiled. "Four to three."

Don't count your chickens. There were still Lachesis and Hades. Lachesis wasn't Kyana's biggest fan, and yet she didn't loathe Kyana the way Atropos seemed to. But judging by the pitying stare she delivered to Kyana now, this wasn't looking good.

"I'm sorry, Kyana. I cannot risk putting any more faith in hopes that you'll change. When I read you eighty years ago, I saw your desire to do something good, and also read your desire for power. Your greedy tendencies. If eighty years wasn't enough to tame that side of you, I can't believe a little more time will do it. Though my vote really doesn't matter at this point, I must side with Atropos on this."

Kyana's heart sank. A hand touched her shoulder and she jumped at the light squeeze. Ryker wrapped his hand around her nape and gave a tender massage. He knew she was doomed too, but his eyes didn't say his final, silent good-bye.

Confused, she turned back to the table. Why did Lachesis think her vote didn't count? She'd just evened up the score, leaving only Hades to deliver the final nail to Kyana's coffin. Her vote had mattered a lot. Yet as she scanned the faces peering down at her, the expressions all seemed to read that the matter had been resolved. Artemis and Jordan looked pleased, Atropos and Ares looked ready to spit. It was as though they'd all assumed Hades would set Kyana free, which was a ridiculous notion. Hades wasn't known for his forgiving nature. He wasn't even particularly nice.

"Then it's settled. Kyana is free to go after Haven." Artemis clapped her hands together, her face positively beaming.

Ryker leaned over Kyana's shoulder. "I told you not to give up hope."

She looked up at him, completely confused. "But Hades hasn't voted. Not that I'm looking a gift horse in the mouth or anything, but—"

"But they know I would never vote against you, lass."

Kyana's neck twisted painfully as she snapped her attention back to the table and toward that sexy, familiar Irish accent. Geoffrey stood among her judges, his black hood falling around his shoulders as he smiled smugly down at her.

"Wha—"

"I couldn't say anything until the final blood ceremony was complete," he said. "It was too dangerous to let anyone know Hades had found his Chosen."

"You . . . you're *Hades*?"

Her world tipped on its head. Understanding righted it again as she remembered his quick healing, his speed, his tap on information he shouldn't have been able to gain all this time, his disappearance in his tracking duties. She'd never been given the full, original list of Chosen. Geoffrey must have been picked early . . .

Holy shit. Geoffrey was becoming a god.

She'd never had a particularly fond view of any of the gods except for Artemis, and now both of the men in her life were godly. She wanted to ask a million questions of Geoffrey, but only one tumbled out of her mouth. "I'm free?"

Geoffrey grinned. "Find our girl, lass. Prove to these window lickers that they're wrong about you."

"Better leave now too, before one of your votes has time to change." She could hear Ryker's smile in his voice. He didn't seem at all surprised by the revelation that had Kyana reeling.

"You knew?"

He nodded. "Geoffrey and I came to an understanding and he confided in me. A way to show I could trust him. I would have found out anyway, but it was nice to see him try to offer something of himself—"

"You ass. You kept this from me. I wouldn't have been so . . ."

"Scared?" Ryker brushed her hair from her face. "It's okay to be scared, Ky. It means you still have a bit of humanity in you."

She wanted to kick him in the shin and kiss him at the same time, but neither action seemed appropriate. She also wanted to get the hell out of here before Atropos decided to clip the life thread despite the outcome here today.

As she allowed Ryker to help her to her feet and toward the door, Artemis moved from the table to join them. Her gaze was no longer filled with satisfaction, but worry.

In the privacy of their small corner of the room, the goddess touched Kyana's arm. "You must perfect your link to Haven. It's the only thing that's going to give you an advantage. If Cronos truly has uncovered the secret to resurrecting himself and is able to communicate and persuade her, she only lacks four things to help him. If she gets them, the fight is over. We can't win."

Kyana smiled, feeling for the first time that she might have a chance to save Haven. "What things? If I find them first, she'll have to come to me to get them. That's how we find her."

"The Eyes of Power."

Kyana swallowed. Of course it would be something so ominous. Zeus's staff. Poseidon's trident. Hades's amulet. And Cronos's ring.

Artemis clasped her hands in front of her, her glowy face pale. "The only way to raise a god of Cronos's power is to obtain those things that gave him the power in the first place. He'll need all four before he can regain the power to finish what he started all those years ago. Then he'll be after his sons. Their lives are in your hands, because if their powers keep waning so drastically, they're practically defenseless without fully trained Chosen. There's no need to look for the Eyes of Power. Their owners still retain possession of them, save for one—Cronos's ring—which Ryker has made certain was given a safe home. Find her, Kyana, and know that she'll kill you if you stand in the way of her claiming those conduits. If Cronos's hold on her is strong, she won't see you as a friend any longer."

"She can try. I won't let her, and I won't let her harm the gods or herself. Believe in me, Artemis. I can do this. I can bring Haven back. She can be your Chosen, and everything can be okay again."

Kyana could hear the desperation creeping into her voice.

"I've always believed in you. But I pray you can be swift in this. You won't be the only one hunting her. You must be better than the other tracers already sent after her."

"We don't need other tracers," Ryker said. "Call them off."

"I can't." Sadness replaced worry. "I no longer control them all. Until I have my Chosen, I'm not strong enough to lead so many."

"I will bring your Chosen back."

Artemis shook her head. "I have no Chosen, Kyana."

"Yes, you do." Kyana threw up her hands. "You have Haven."

"Even if Haven was strong enough in her new body to take my powers, the murder of those Healers are too fresh . . . it will take months to purge and purify her. That is time I don't have."

"So I'm supposed to bring her back so she can be put to death?"

"A trial is her only hope of survival. You must find her before she can raise Cronos. If the other tracers find her, they will carry out her execution to prevent her from completing her task."

Geoffrey appeared behind Artemis and slipped to Kyana's side. "She's right, lass. Those tracers won't offer Haven a chance to live. They've been ordered to kill on sight."

Determination built like fire in Kyana's belly. She was ready. She'd work on the link until she could summon it at will. "I'll find her first."

"And what will you do then?"Artemis asked.

"I'll save her."

"And if you can't?" A tear slid down Artemis's cheek and she lightly cupped Kyana's. "Are you prepared to do what's necessary?"

Kyana swallowed. "If I can't save her?"

Artemis nodded. Kyana felt Ryker's fingers run through her hair. She sank against him, drinking in his support. "Yes. What will you do if you can't safely bring her down?"

Kyana jerked her face away from Artemis and pulled away from Ryker's hold. Standing on her own, she said, "Then I'll kill her."

"I have one last gift that will help you in this, Kyana."
Artemis nodded solemnly, then turned to speak to those
remaining at the table—the Moerae. "Clotho, prepare
your ceremony. My choice has been made." Artemis
turned, and with a smile held out her hand. "Come,
Kyana, and become the new Goddess of the Hunt."